LITTLE
BOY
LOST

BOOKS BY RUHI CHOUDHARY

Our Daughter's Bones
Their Frozen Graves

LITTLE BOY LOST

Ruhi Choudhary

bookouture

Published by Bookouture in 2021

An imprint of Storyfire Ltd.
Carmelite House
50 Victoria Embankment
London EC4Y 0DZ

www.bookouture.com

ISBN: 978-1-80019-410-6
eBook ISBN: 978-1-80019-409-0

To my grandfather, Justice B.P. Singh,
who lived a distinguished life.

PROLOGUE

Thump.

Thump.

Thump.

The only thing Mackenzie could hear in the cacophony of sounds was the thumping of her heart.

Rain splattered against the glass. Thunder grumbled. Wiper blades squeaked, sweeping the windshield. Tires crunched the gravel underneath.

A fork of lightning sliced open the sky, briefly illuminating the path ahead. The dark, winding road, on a moonless, rainy night. Tall, thick trees lined both sides of the empty road. Not a car in sight, not a person.

Mackenzie looked to her side. Nick's grip on the steering wheel was unforgiving. His knee bobbed in place. She remembered his words to her merely a few minutes ago.

Your father was murdered.

She looked away and closed her eyes. Her stomach swooped in fear. A little whisper hissed at her to tell him the truth about everything. He was her only friend, her partner at work, the only person left in her life who she trusted.

But every time she blinked, her father's face would cloud her mind. His receding hairline, beady eyes, and wrinkled face. She swallowed her tears. She would not cry for a man who spent years beating her mother in his drunken stupor. She would not cry for a man who waltzed into her life years later and lied to her face about what had transpired that night twenty years ago.

"Mack?" Nick's voice punctured the fragile silence. "Maybe this is a bad idea."

"No. I have to see for myself."

She turned to look out the window and caught her reflection. She'd always looked like her mother, but right now their resemblance was uncanny. It was as if Melody's face was staring back at her, and she was transported back twenty years.

A mangled body on the floor. Blood seeping around the head. A large dent in the skull. Eye swollen to the size of a golf ball. A frying pan with dried blood. A horrified Melody covered in bruises.

I'm so sorry, Mackenzie.

She had snapped. It was self-defense.

You have to help me bury him.

And so they did.

For twenty years, Mackenzie had believed that she had buried her father that night. Until a month ago, when he had shown up at her doorstep very much alive.

The car came to a halt. Mackenzie moved on autopilot. She didn't even register the rain beating down on her as she walked up the dirt road toward the motel. Rivulets of rain chased down her face. Miller Lodge was directly ahead of her, where her father had been staying. The medical examiner's van was parked out the front, along with a squad car.

She entered the building, with Nick tailing her. Mackenzie didn't quite register her surroundings. She knew there were people around her—motel guests and workers, disturbed and curious. She knew some uniformed officers were with them taking statements.

Nick placed a hand on the small of her back and guided her upstairs.

She stumbled and swayed, but managed to climb the stairs. The hallway was bathed in yellow, flickering light. The door to a room was open—a small crowd gathered around it.

Someone walked toward her. The shape was blurry, but as he got closer, his outline gained clarity.

It was Sergeant Jeff Sully.

"What the hell are you doing here, Mack?"

She didn't respond. Her eyes were glued to the end of the hallway—the room where someone had murdered her father, where she imagined his body lay.

"C'mon, Sully. Just let her have a look," Nick said.

Sully's unibrow dipped low, but he grunted his approval. "Just for a minute. Don't touch anything."

Mackenzie faintly nodded and followed him. She felt eyes on her. Her coworkers watching her warily, like she was a vase about to crack any time. All other sounds fell away—the gurgling thunderstorm, hushed whispers, footsteps, and clicking cameras. All she heard was her breathing.

The room was small—it was the only thing her brain registered.

Her father was slumped against the foot of the bed, his body tilted at an angle, hands splayed carelessly. There was a red and black wound on his forehead and ropes of blood ran down his neck to the collar of his shirt. His eyes were closed, lips slightly parted.

Someone had shot him in the head.

Bile rose in Mackenzie's throat. Clutching her mouth, she sprinted out of the room, into the hallway, shouldering past the throng of people.

"Mack!" Nick was right behind her.

She heaved and calmed her erratic pulse. She had seen many, many dead bodies over the course of her eight years with the Lakemore PD. But those hadn't been her father.

"Go home." Nick held her shoulders and looked her in the eye. "I'll ask Peterson to drive you. We'll find out what happened to your father. I promise."

Mackenzie found herself nodding—the truth sat on the tip of her tongue.

"I…" She wanted to confess everything to him.

But she couldn't bring herself to, not when she felt like she was going to explode and her nerve endings were frayed.

"I'm sorry." Nick crushed her into a hug. "I'll come over when I'm done here."

He released her and called over Officer Peterson to drop her home.

As Mackenzie walked away, her eyes darted to the authorities around her, as if they would turn against her anytime or someone would jump at her from the shadows.

Charles has been murdered. And she knew in her bones that it was something to do with Melody and that night. The truth was going to come out soon, potentially bringing her down in the process.

A thought made her insides clench in terror as she recalled Charles's dead body.

Was she going to be next?

CHAPTER ONE

March 2, 2019

Lakemore, WA

"Lakemore PD is asking for assistance in finding three young boys who went missing on a field trip." Debbie, Lakemore's most watched reporter, spoke earnestly, absent of her usual judgmental manner. *"Lucas Williams, Theo Reynolds, and Noah Kinsey are nine years old and disappeared during a field trip to the annual spring festival. If anyone has any information on the whereabouts of these boys, please contact the special hotline Lakemore PD has set up."*

Mackenzie stood, her feet wide apart, and held the dumbbell in front of her chest. Sitting into a deep squat, she stood back up and repeated the motion again. Her skin was matted with sweat, pools of it cooling her scalp. Her quads burned just the right amount. She felt like her body was unwinding slowly after being stiff for a long time. She wasn't the one to slack off on working out—or anything really. That's why her coworkers called her "Mad Mack": she was madly and obsessively dedicated to her work and responsibilities. At least, normally she was. It had been over two months since Charles was found murdered in a motel room. The following weeks had taken a toll on her, and she had been too mentally exhausted to push herself as much as usual.

The morning light burst through the thin film of clouds into the spacious living room overlooking the front yard. It was a tasteful house—an open concept kitchen, sweeping staircase, box-beam ceilings and solid hardwood flooring. It was a house she had decorated with all her heart to spend her life in with her husband, Sterling Brooks. But after ending her marriage with him three months ago, following his infidelity, she was left alone in the big house, still carrying the echoes of the past.

Living alone had been harder than she'd imagined. It wasn't new to her—her childhood had been hauntingly lonely—but she had grown used to living with her husband, having company and sharing chores. Now she was returning to her old life, and it felt odd. Like picking at an old wound that was only half-healed.

The bell rang. She jolted.

Mackenzie checked the clock. She wasn't expecting any visitors early in the morning. Wiping her face with a towel to look presentable, she opened the door. A middle-aged woman with light brown hair and bronze-kissed skin stood in jeans and a sweater, holding a tote bag. She was shorter than Mackenzie, stout and sturdy with thick wrists.

"Hello, I'm Irene Nemr."

"Hi…" Mackenzie tried placing her to no avail.

"Sorry to bother you!" She chuckled. "I just moved in next door and thought I should pop in and introduce myself."

"Oh, right. Welcome to the neighborhood. I'm Mackenzie Price." She shook her hand. "Would you like to come in?"

"If you don't mind!" She came inside, looking around the living room and foyer. "Nice chandelier. You have good taste."

"Thank you. Can I get you something?"

"No, thank you. I'll keep this short. I have other neighbors I want to say hello to."

Mackenzie smiled. When she and Sterling had moved in, they hadn't gone out of their way to mingle with the neighbors; her job's unpredictable hours didn't allow her to commit to a lot of social gatherings. But Irene looked like someone who intended to bring some unity to the neighborhood. "Where are you from?"

"Philadelphia. I just moved here a month ago."

"What brings you to Lakemore?"

"The company I work for has headquarters in Olympia. But the real estate is expensive there, so I thought why not spend less money and buy a bigger place here."

"Smart decision. Lakemore is a nice town."

This wasn't entirely true. Lakemore was a town plagued by poverty, known for bad weather and an even worse crime rate, but Mackenzie didn't want to put Irene off.

Irene glanced at the television behind Mackenzie with a skeptical look. The news of the missing boys was playing on loud volume. "Mrs. McNeill told me you and your husband have been living here for over three years now."

She swallowed down a lump in her throat. "My ex-husband. I live alone now."

"I'm also divorced."

Mackenzie squirmed. The paperwork was filed, even though the judge was yet to grant them one. But nevertheless she was a divorced woman now. "I'm afraid I have to get to work. I'm with the police. As you can tell, it's a busy time for us."

Irene raised her hands. "Of course, of course. Mrs. McNeill told me you're a detective. Very impressive. We can chat later."

Once Mackenzie ushered her out of the house, she got ready. Her eyes were glued to the television screen showing pictures of Lucas, Theo and Noah, three boys who seemingly disappeared without a trace twenty-four hours ago.

Mackenzie was twelve years old when her mother had sent her to New York to live with her grandmother. But eight years ago, Lakemore had called her back. She returned, joining the Detectives Unit in Lakemore PD, handling homicide, missing persons, felony assaults and cold cases; they were plenty in the small Washington town. While the rest of the world was getting with the times and opening itself to possibilities, Lakemore was staunchly planted in the past.

Even the residents of Lakemore now joked about how they were stuck here. But Mackenzie felt a loyalty to the dwindling town. Under the film of destitution, she saw potential. She wasn't alone. Slowly some people were rebuilding Lakemore—and Mackenzie was one of them; locking away one criminal at a time.

"Anything new?" she asked her partner, Nick Blackwood, as she entered the office. Nick was tall, with broad shoulders and a chiseled jawline. His black hair was cropped short with some speckles of gray.

He raised a finger, gesturing her to wait, picking up the phone. "Yeah. Okay. Sure. Thanks for cooperating." He put back the handset. "There are over a hundred volunteers combing through the woods."

Mackenzie still had Lakemore's map open on her desk. There was a barren strip of land near the edge of the woods around Fresco River. There had been a petition to build a casino there but it was denied. Now that land was used for the annual spring festival when food trucks and vendors set up shop there, marking the start of spring in Lakemore.

The three boys had wandered off during the festival. The teacher had realized when she was rounding up the kids and doing a head count.

"It's easy to get lost in those woods. No hiking trails or cabins or any signs," Mackenzie said, looking at the mark where the three boys were last seen and the edge of the acres of unregulated, dense woods.

"There are animals in there. No bears, but coyotes and cougars." Nick came up behind her.

"Let's try to stay positive." She shuddered.

Nick nodded. "Hopefully one of them dropped something. Would make it easier to track them."

Detectives Finn and Ned of the Detectives Unit were still gathering statements from the people present at the festival. There were over a hundred people, including the twenty kids belonging to the fourth-grade class.

"Do you think they ran away?" Mackenzie proposed. "Things were rough at home? Gangs are known to recruit children as young as seven years old to sell drugs on the streets."

"I don't think so. They're all middle-class kids with stable home lives. Not the type who get involved in that kind of mess." Nick looked past her.

Mackenzie followed his gaze. Lucas Williams's parents were in the lounge hysterically talking to Detective Troy Clayton.

Handling missing children cases was without a doubt the hardest part of their job.

"Where are Theo's parents?" she asked.

"Out with the volunteers scouring the woods."

"And no security cameras in place?"

He shook his head. "There's nothing there."

The three innocent faces flashing on every screen in Lakemore had captured the attention of the residents. Mackenzie's chest tightened as she stared at their faces—so young and innocent, their grins wide with missing teeth. They were lost in an unfriendly terrain without food and water, surrounded by wild animals cloaked by foliage and trees.

Mackenzie saw a man coming out of Lieutenant Atlee Rivera's office. He was young, tall and muscular, with golden hair in curls around his head. He fiddled with his tie as Rivera talked to him.

"That's the new guy, right?" Mackenzie asked Nick. "Austin?"

"Austin Kennedy from Port Angeles."

"I saw him yesterday but didn't get a chance to talk to him really."

He crossed his arms, a tick in his jaw. "Did you hear?"

"Hear what?"

"He's taking over your dad's case."

CHAPTER TWO

"Over ten officers have taken our statements!" Lucas's father gritted his teeth.

"I'm sorry, Mr. Williams. But the more you repeat yourself, the more likely it is you might remember a detail you forgot, which might be relevant," Mackenzie explained gently to the parents huddled across from her.

Lucas Williams's parents were older than most in Lakemore. His father was bald with bushy gray eyebrows. His mother had curly hair to her shoulders, dusted with gray strands. She clutched her husband's sleeve in a fist, and her lips moved constantly in a silent prayer, as her husband did all the talking.

"Like we said before. Lucas wasn't acting strange at all. He's a happy kid."

"Nothing out of the blue happened in the last few days? Anyone following him or trouble at school?"

He closed his eyes and shook his head. "*No.*"

Mackenzie tapped her pen to her notepad. Children often kept things from their parents, often dragged into illegal activities. But Nick had a point. The more she spoke with the parents, the more she realized that they didn't just seem the type.

"Was Lucas good friends with Theo and Noah?"

"They were in the same class, so they were friends."

"They never came over, or Lucas never went over to theirs?"

"They only hang out at school. We've never even had a real conversation with the parents until now…" His eyes drifted to the man sitting in the other corner of the lounge. Mackenzie followed his gaze to Noah's father, a single parent—his worn-out eyes lined with black circles as he stared into empty space.

While the station was plunged into chaos with moving bodies, trilling phones and frantic conversations, underneath it was a thick layer of gloom. The profound and quiet sadness of the parents as the worst scenarios ran through their minds.

"We conceived after great difficulty, Detective Price." Mrs. Williams spoke for the first time. Her eyes were filled with tears, her blinks slow and heavy, like she was close to passing out. "I underwent years of hormone treatment. I was forty when we were blessed with our little angel. He's a sweet boy. Shy. Artistic. Gentle. If anything happens to him…"

Mr. Williams held her hand. "Don't go there. We can't think like that."

"Finding them is our priority," Mackenzie assured.

"Can we go now? We'd like to help the volunteers and look for Lucas ourselves," Mr. Williams asked sharply. "You have no idea how painful it is to *sit* here and not do anything."

"Of course. We'll stay in touch."

Mackenzie rubbed her forehead and watched Nick as he concluded his interview with Noah's father. His shoulders and neck were stiff, a pulse in his neck throbbed visibly. Nick was a parent too. He understood their fear and helplessness far more than she did.

"Are you okay?" she asked him after he returned from seeing off Mr. Kinsey and Mr. and Mrs. Williams.

"Rest assured Luna's not going on any field trips," he muttered, taking out a cigarette pack and fiddling with it. He had been a smoker for years before Mackenzie wrenched the habit out of him. But whenever he was stressed or thoughtful, he'd play with a cigarette.

"So from what I gather, the boys were friendly but not the best of friends. Seems like they didn't have much in common besides from being in the same class. It sounds like they got lost," Mackenzie said.

"It was a chaotic festival. And boys that age can be hyperactive, running around. Justin is talking to their classmates," he informed her. Justin Armstrong was the junior detective on their team. He often assisted them in cases, bringing his razor-sharp focus and discipline to the table. "Maybe the kids saw something."

"Detective Price?" Austin approached them, carrying a file. "I never got a chance to introduce myself to you. I'm Austin Kennedy. I know it's crazy today, but can I get a few minutes with you?"

"Regarding?"

He held up the file and waved it, like she'd recognize it. "Your father."

Her face fell. When the case had been declared closed a few weeks ago due to no new lines of inquiry, she had been relieved. Her fear that it was connected to the past, and that she was next, had ebbed. Not that she didn't want to know who killed Charles, but the desire to keep her past a secret was far greater. But now a new detective, potentially hungry to prove himself, could scrape out something new—or old.

"Sure." She kept her expression impassive and followed him into one of the small interrogation rooms.

The room had blue walls with an exhaust fan and a crooked table with plastic chairs around it. Mackenzie had interrogated several suspects in this fusty space. For the first time, she knew what it was like to be on the other side.

Austin opened the file in front of him. Mackenzie tried to sneak a peek. He cleverly pulled the file closer to his chest, obscuring her view.

"I thought it was a robbery gone wrong," Mackenzie started, trying to fish for information. "At least that's what Ned said."

"It was a fair assessment to begin with, given a string of robberies in Riverview, only a few miles away."

"But you found something new? That's why you're interested in this case?" Mackenzie knew her attempts were transparent at best. She interlinked her fingers on the table and leaned forward. Austin flipped the pages but kept a curious eye on her.

Taking a shivering breath, she leaned back. Even if her face was blank, her body was giving away her jumpiness. The interrogation room she had often used to her advantage worked against her now. The claustrophobic space, flickering lights, and subdued voices from outside all made her feel trapped.

"I just thought we could go over the key details."

"Is that why you brought me to this interrogation room?"

"The conference room is occupied. This was the only place where we could get some privacy." A smile played on his lips. "Is there a particular reason why you feel so uncomfortable here?"

An icy rush slithered up her spine. "Well, you are looking into my father's murder. So excuse me for being a little *uncomfortable*."

"Hmm." He frowned. "Let's start from the beginning. Your father's name is Charles Laurent. But you only found that out a few months ago?"

"Yes. Days before he was killed. Up until then, I always thought his name was Robert Price."

"And Robert Price was the name of the man your mother, Melody, was married to?"

"Yes."

"According to your previous statement, you were born to Melody and Robert Price—whose name is on your birth certificate. But Melody had been having an extra-marital affair with Charles, who also happens to be your biological father. She left her husband, Robert, and came to Lakemore to live with you and Charles. Except she told *you* and everyone in town that Charles was Robert Price."

Mackenzie felt her face warm. Her mother and Charles had woven a complex web of lies and manipulation that was slowly being unraveled, not just for her but also for her coworkers. She didn't miss how some of the cops whispered behind her back or watched her curiously. All of a sudden, Mackenzie was a reality show. "That is correct."

There was no point in denying or hiding it. Senator Alan Blackwood, Nick's father and an old family friend of the Prices, had recognized that Charles was not, in fact, Robert Price when he'd met him at the Lakemore PD Christmas party last year. He had been the one to inform Mackenzie of Charles's identity. If she hadn't come clean to the police, then they would have found out from Alan that she knew. Withholding critical information about a murder victim would have made her look guilty.

And she was guilty—not of killing Charles, but of burying Robert Price.

"How old were you when Melody brought you to Lakemore?"

"Four years old."

"Do you have any memory of Robert Price—the *real* Robert Price?"

She shook her head. "Not exactly. I have some very faint memories. They were never clear—and I thought they were of Charles. But when I found out about his lies, I realized they were of Robert. Though I don't know what he looks like."

"Did you ever meet Robert Price or have any contact with him?"

"No." Her tone was clipped. "My mother didn't even keep a picture of him."

"So, the last time you saw him you were four years old?"

"Yes." Mackenzie lied. The last time she had seen Robert Price was when she was twelve years old, lying dead on the kitchen floor—a battered and bruised corpse beyond recognition. "Why do you think that Charles's murder is related to Robert Price?"

Austin's mouth flattened. "Well, Detective Price, twenty years ago, a Robert Price went missing in Lakemore. Who now we know was actually Charles. And around that same time, a Robert Price was reported missing in Nashville. Now, Charles—the *fake* Robert

Price—showed up alive before he was killed. But the real Robert Price—your *legal* father according to your birth certificate—was never found. Isn't that a strange coincidence?"

It wasn't a strange coincidence at all.

It was a mess.

She swallowed repeatedly—a lump sitting firmly in the back of her throat. Austin's predatory eyes were fixed on her. And for the first time, Mackenzie couldn't get a read on someone.

After Mackenzie and Melody had buried the real Robert Price's body in the woods, Melody had reported him missing. But Robert's family in Nashville must have reported him missing as well. Meanwhile, Charles, who knew what had happened that night, left the state only to return twenty years later.

"It is a strange coincidence."

"Did you know that Robert Price was searching for you and Melody after your mother ran away?" Austin asked, reading from a file. "His family said that Robert was furious that he had no idea where his child was."

And Robert had tracked them down. He'd confronted Melody and Charles, who had panicked and beaten him to death. The man Melody had helped bury was not the father she remembered—an alcoholic abuser who her mother claimed she killed in self-defense—but a stranger. An innocent man.

"I… I didn't know that."

"I'll tell you what. I think whatever happened to Charles has something to do with Robert Price."

"Maybe it has something to do with the fact that Charles had massive gambling debts from Vegas," she countered.

"That was almost twenty years ago."

"Loan sharks can hold grudges, Detective Kennedy."

"Good point. Except we can't find any large sums of money that Charles borrowed," he said smugly. "We have to keep our options open. Something about this smells personal to me. Is there anything else you know?"

The little fan in the room whirred slowly, creaking. The sound scratched Mackenzie's eardrums, grounding her. "No."

His eyes narrowed. After a beat, he nodded.

There was a knock on the door. Nick poked his head in, his face ashen. "Sorry to interrupt."

"No problem. We're done." Austin closed the file. "For now."

Nick walked in, with his hands in his pocket. "They found Lucas."

Mackenzie shot up from her chair. "What about the others? Is he okay?"

He shook his head, solemnly.

Her heart sank. "Oh, no."

CHAPTER THREE

Lucas Williams's body was found next to a creek, under a bridge. Some of the volunteers had made the heartbreaking discovery. Mack and Nick sat in silence on the ride over, only broken when Mackenzie's phone pinged. It was Sergeant Sully.

"Mack? How far are you?"

"Less than ten minutes."

"Just a heads up—I have dispatched some cops there to contain the crime scene so that it's not trampled over by the rest of the volunteers. Rivera and I just left the scene to inform the parents."

Mackenzie couldn't imagine how that conversation would play out. "Yeah, okay."

Sully stayed on the line for a few seconds, quiet, before hanging up.

Mackenzie rested her head against the leather and closed her eyes. The disappearance of the three boys had even sent Sully out into the field. Her shrewd sergeant wasn't lazy—just more effective delegating, having to balance administrative work on top of supervising the Detectives Unit of seven senior and three junior detectives.

Nick parked the car close to the bridge, along with squad cars and the Medical Examiner's van. They climbed out to be met with gray sky and drizzle, though some green was beginning to pop back up in the woods. It was a welcome sight after an unrelenting winter, which had arrived strong and early and left just as quickly in February. The freezing weather had coincided with a recession and protests, not to mention a disturbing murder case that had exposed a spate of kidnappings. But spring had arrived after much anticipation—maybe now Lakemore would get a breather.

Alas.

Mackenzie spotted a crowd. A small group of volunteers stood a few feet away, behind the yellow crime scene tape. Some patrol officers stood in front of them, making sure no one got by. Under the old bridge built of stone, technicians from the Medical Examiner's office stood wearing their protective gear.

Mackenzie and Nick navigated their way down around the moss-covered rocks and wild shrubbery. She felt Nick tense next to her and squeezed his shoulder. He relaxed and nodded.

Justin turned to greet them in a gruff voice, his thick eyebrows visible above the mask. He handed them coveralls, gloves and skull masks.

Everyone was prickly, on edge, and grim. The volunteers had tears in their eyes as they tried getting a view. There were five technicians blocking the view of the body, three patrol officers and two from the Sheriff's Office. As law enforcement officers, they were trained not to let emotions get the best of them. Over the years, all of them were somewhat desensitized to violence. But when the victim was a child, there was no amount of training or experience to keep those emotions at bay. Mackenzie could see the cracks in their demeanor. She took a deep breath. Someone had to stay unaffected—and it might as well be Mad Mack.

"What do we have here?" she asked in a firm voice—no wobble or hesitance.

The technicians moved.

Mackenzie's breath got stuck.

Lucas Williams was draped over a giant rock. His legs were stiff; one straight as an arrow, the other bent at an angle. His hands crossed over his chest, the tips of his fingers touching his collarbone. His eyes were open. Flies buzzed over him, feasting on his mouth and ears. He looked smaller than Mackenzie had imagined.

She cleared her throat and kneeled next to Becky Sullivan, the Chief Medical Examiner. "He was moved after he was killed, I'm guessing?"

Becky nodded, her eyebrows furrowed. "Yes. Before rigor mortis set in. We're in livor mortis now." She lifted his Batman T-shirt and pointed at the purplish red discoloration of his skin. "He died only a few hours ago."

"Cause of death?"

"There are strangulation marks on his neck and a blow to the head."

Mackenzie stood up and turned to the officers. "The victim was moved here very recently. I want to expand the perimeter and get forensics to sift through the soil for evidence."

They nodded and dispersed.

She noticed something on the ground, by the rock. It was a white handkerchief stained with blood. "Looks like this fell out of the victim's pocket or his grip," she judged, based on the position of the cloth compared to the body. "It has dried blood on it. But the victim isn't bleeding anywhere else."

"Just where he was hit on the head," Becky agreed.

"Assuming that's the victim's blood, how did it get there? Was the blow to the head not fatal? Was he trying to keep pressure on his wound?"

"I can't tell you that now. But that blow would have knocked him out at least."

Had Lucas regained consciousness before he was strangled? Mackenzie felt this was unlikely. But then how did the blood get on the handkerchief? Perhaps it belonged to the killer.

"Make this one a priority. Lift prints and DNA," she instructed and turned to Justin. "Who are the volunteers who found him? Justin?"

"Sorry, ma'am. What?" He licked his lips.

She wanted to comfort him but instead she steeled herself, clenching her jaw. "We have to focus, Justin. Who found him?"

He gestured at a middle-aged couple standing with the group, drinking water and shaking their heads.

Mackenzie turned to Nick, who had been unusually quiet, and froze. He stared at the body with a haunted look on his face. "Nick?"

He didn't respond. He jerked out of his trance and looked at Becky, his eyes ablaze. "Becky?"

She took a shuddering breath. "His tongue has been removed."

"What's going on?" Mackenzie asked, her eyes darting between them.

"You weren't here, Mack. But this…" Becky looked at Lucas. "This is Jeremiah's M.O. Little boys strangled to death, their tongues cut out, and bodies arranged with arms crossed over the chest."

Jeremiah Wozniak—the infamous serial killer that Nick had captured eight years ago when he led his first case.

A child killer who was in prison for life with no chance of parole.

CHAPTER FOUR

Nick turned on the faucet and water gushed out. He placed his hands on the edge of the sink and hung his head low. Mackenzie stood behind him, looking at his reflection in the mirror. She couldn't see his face. His broad shoulders moved as he took measured breaths.

The door opened, and Troy walked in, whistling. "Mack? This is the men's restroom!"

"Use the other one, Troy." She pushed him out gently and bolted the door shut.

Nick appeared oblivious to the short exchange. He splashed water on his face repeatedly.

"It can't be Jeremiah," she said.

He turned off the faucet and dried his face with a paper towel, ignoring her.

"He's in prison. It's some copycat killer."

Nick sighed and trashed the towel.

"He murdered *eleven* children." Nick faced her and crossed his arms. His eyes were burning—arresting Jeremiah had clearly not diminished his rage. "Parents were scared to send their kids to school. The media was having a field day. All of *us* were under protection because the town was turning on us, for being unable to protect those kids. There was a wave of collective hysteria that had consumed the town. And not to mention, dealing with that piece of shit, Jeremiah, always playing mind games."

She stepped forward again. "Nick, Jeremiah is behind bars."

"You weren't here to witness any of that." He ground his jaw. "You were in New York. It's going to happen again."

She wasn't the kind to give anyone false hope. "C'mon. We have to talk to the teacher. She's waiting for us in the conference room."

Ruth Norman was the missing boys' teacher who had accompanied the fourth-graders to the festival. A middle-aged woman, bony and tall, she had red hair like Mackenzie in a bob cut that covered her forehead.

"Can I get you some water?" Mackenzie offered.

Ruth winced. "I... I was responsible for them."

Nick glanced at Mackenzie helplessly. Ruth's slightly bug-like eyes were red. No tears leaked out, as if she'd run out of them, but she still dabbed a handkerchief to her cheeks. She peered around the station, paranoid and scared.

"What exactly happened yesterday?" Nick asked. "And please don't leave anything out."

"We arrived at the spring festival a little before nine thirty in the morning. Before we got off the bus, Sarah and I instructed the kids to follow me and behave and not to wander off. We got off the bus and walked around together in a group."

"Sorry, who's Sarah?"

"The other teacher. She was assisting me. School policy requires two teachers to accompany students on field trips. Every two minutes, I did a quick head count..." She closed her eyes and scrunched her nose. "Goddammit."

"What?" Mackenzie leaned forward. "Do you remember something?"

Ruth pinched the bridge of her nose. "They hate me. Everyone hates me. The school is thinking of firing me. Do you know that? My negligence is the reason that *three* of my students went missing. The parents..." She gulped, struggling to breathe. "They look at me like I'm the devil. I... I can't believe I did this. I never thought that... Oh my God. Oh my God. And now Lucas..."

It didn't take long for the reporters to sniff out the news that Lucas was murdered.

"At what time did you lose sight of the boys?" Mackenzie asked.

"I was doing a head count every two minutes. Then twenty minutes later, one of the kids, she fell down and scraped her knee. She was bleeding quite a bit. I asked Sarah to get the first-aid box from the bus. While I was waiting for her to get back, I did another head count and realized that Lucas, Theo, and Noah were m-missing." Her voice trembled around the edges. "I started panicking. I looked around and couldn't see them. I hadn't expected the place to be so crowded that early in the morning. It was a Friday! When Sarah got back with the kit, I decided it was time to put the kids in the bus and then look for the boys. I asked Sarah to stay behind in the bus with the class, while I walked around the festival, looking for them. B-but I couldn't find them. Then… I called 911."

"You didn't hear anything?"

"I heard loud music and people shouting conversations," Ruth snapped. "It was so *loud*. Like a fish market."

The annual spring festival tended to become chaotic. On the weekends, patrol would be dispatched to do rounds and maintain order. Mackenzie imagined how easy it would be for someone to slip into the mayhem and never be seen again.

"I understand it was chaotic. But was anyone acting strange?" Mackenzie pressed.

She shook her head. "I'm sorry."

They asked her more questions and urged her to remember more, but Ruth didn't have anything to add.

"If you remember anything, then please let us know." Nick handed her a card. "And could you give us Sarah's information?"

After Ruth had narrated Sarah's number and address, she stood up to leave, clutching the card handed to her tightly. She looked out the glass walls of the conference room to the frantic bodies and the news playing on a loop.

"I did this." Ruth blinked. "This town will kill me."

"Ms. Norman, if it would make you feel safer, we can have a squad car outside your house at all times," Mackenzie offered.

"No," she whispered. "I deserve this."

When Ruth left, Mackenzie dropped back on the chair with a sigh. "We should talk to Sarah. Maybe she saw something."

Nick was staring at where Ruth had been sitting with a frown. "I've talked to her before."

"Who?"

"Ruth Norman." He rubbed the back of his neck. "She taught two of Jeremiah's victims. Ravi and Johnny. She looked familiar, but I couldn't place her."

"You talked to her eight years ago. You interview a lot of people."

"Yeah, but how many times has *she* been interviewed by the police? She didn't say anything if she recognized me."

"She's going through a tough time."

"Yeah." He raised his eyebrows and dropped the topic.

Mackenzie immersed herself back in work, going through the recorded witness statements. Her eyes kept flitting to Nick. He was holding it together, brooding as he called Sarah to confirm an interview. But his foot tapped relentlessly, and his idle hands roamed his pockets trying to find cigarettes in vain. Mackenzie knew her partner—he never overreacted. But Lucas's body had thrown him off, like it was an omen of things to come.

CHAPTER FIVE

March 3

Mackenzie inched her car into her driveway. It was past midnight by the time she returned home. A part of her was glad that she didn't have a husband to come home to anymore. She always felt guilty the nights she worked late and Sterling would be up waiting for her.

She swung the car door closed, the sound slicing through the silence of the neighborhood. She noticed her new neighbor's living-room lights were still on. Another night owl.

Mackenzie made a mental note to take something to Irene's soon. Maybe cookies. It was nice of her to come over and introduce herself. The least Mackenzie could do was welcome her in the neighborhood—even though she herself wasn't really a part of the whole community culture.

Opening the front door, her hands fumbled to turn on the switch in the dark and eerily quiet house. Light flooded the room. It looked impersonal and staged, like the house was being shown to prospective buyers. Mackenzie had gotten rid of all the pictures she had with Sterling. They were boxed, sitting in the attic. No evidence of anyone *living* here—no clothes lying around, no dishes in the sink, no impressions in the couch, no remote lying haphazardly somewhere.

There were small tokens of their time together scattered around, but the house still didn't feel personal enough with Mackenzie spending most of her time at work.

She hated coming home. It was becoming like a place to just crash for the night like a motel. The air itself felt accusatory, as if blaming Mackenzie for ripping apart the one thing that had made it a *home*.

But that had been Sterling's doing, not hers; the moment he'd chosen to throw it all away for a meaningless affair.

She opened the fridge, looking for something to eat after surviving the entire day on granola bars and Sour Patch Kids. Her fridge was empty; she was still not quite used to cooking on a regular basis and keeping leftovers. Her ex-husband had spoiled her.

Just when she decided to settle for mac-n-cheese, her phone rang. It was Becky.

"Becky? Is everything alright?"

"Not really. Do you mind meeting me at the morgue?"

"At the morgue? It's half past midnight."

"I know. Just come. And please bring Nick."

"Okay," Mackenzie answered, puzzled.

Tossing the package back in the cupboard, she called Nick and left immediately for his house. What had Becky discovered? She had been performing the autopsy on Lucas. What could be so urgent?

By the time she reached Nick's, it was raining cats and dogs. Waiting for him, she quickly applied her makeup again to distract her mind from going into dark places.

Nick jogged out of his house and climbed inside the car; his dark hair stuck to his forehead, water dripping from the tip of his nose. The short distance from his front door to Mackenzie's car had left him drenched. "Did Becky tell you anything?"

"No, she was cryptic." She eyed his tie. "It's midnight. I think it's okay if you don't show up with a tie."

"Is that why you applied your makeup again?" He gave her a cheeky grin, despite the sleep in his eyes.

As Mackenzie took the highway to Olympia, Nick kept tapping his knee.

"What do you think she found?" she asked.

"I don't want to say it out loud."

"Because of Jeremiah?" She tested the words. He didn't answer. But the question hung in the air. The same M.O. suggested a copycat.

Mackenzie honked and squinted to look through the windshield to make sense of the swirling shapes of cars ahead of her. The wiper blades struggled to keep up with the beating rain.

"Should have let me drive," Nick said, knowing Mackenzie hated driving in the rain.

"O ye, of little faith."

The drive to Olympia was slow—all lethargy from working long hours evaporated. Nick kept loosening his tie and brushing his raincoat. His mind was obviously flooded with dire possibilities; they filled Mackenzie's head too.

They reached the morgue, which was located in an industrial-looking concrete block that had been renovated recently on the outside. But as Mackenzie and Nick walked along the dingy hallway, there was nothing new about the yellow tiled walls, stained gray floorboards, and swinging bulbs overhead casting menacing shadows. Their soaked shoes made an incongruous squirting noise in the silence and water dripped from the hem of their clothes. A cold draft made the back of Mackenzie's neck break out in goosebumps.

Becky appeared at the door to one of the labs and ushered them over. Her long dark hair was tied messily, wisps of baby hair sticking out. Dark circles underlined her tired eyes.

"What happened?" Mackenzie asked.

Lucas's tiny body was covered entirely with a white cloth.

"I found something inside Lucas's esophagus. I give my official report tomorrow to Rivera and Sully, but I thought Nick would want to see this before." A look of deep concern never left her face.

Dread unfurled in Mackenzie's gut.

"What is it?" Nick's voice broke, bracing himself.

Becky wheeled over a cart with a steel tray atop. "This was found folded and shoved down his throat."

Covered in blood was a crinkled piece of paper with a smudged postage stamp in one corner. Becky used forceps to spread it open to show words typed in cursive. The black ink was partially smeared but clear enough to make out the text.

A cold fist wrapped around Mackenzie's heart.

Find Johnny's killer, or they all die.

CHAPTER SIX

"Arabella" by Arctic Monkeys blasted through the speakers of the car, but the music did little to alleviate the tension in the compact space. They were still in the parking lot after their grim and baffling meeting with Becky. Other than the concrete building in front of them, they were surrounded by trees. But the storm had knocked out the street lights, making it appear like they were in the belly of complete darkness.

Mackenzie switched on the light and offered Nick a small flask of whiskey that Becky had handed to her. "I'm driving so…"

Nick's sharp Adam's apple bobbed as he stared off into emptiness. "No, thanks."

"It will help you sleep." She waved it in his face.

He turned to face her. "What are you on?"

"What do you mean?"

"Encouraging bad habits. The Mackenzie I know would have offered me a vegetable."

She deflated and took out a container from the glove box. "I packed celery sticks."

Nick stared at it, mildly horrified, and snatched the whiskey from her, gulping, and making faces. "Dammit."

Mackenzie grimaced as he gagged and popped a celery stick in her mouth. For a moment, the scene felt oddly perfect. She sat stiff like a board, eating her vegetables. Nick was relaxed in his seat, drinking whiskey. Just like how it was supposed to be.

Except it wasn't.

"So what do you think?"

"About?"

She threw him a flat look. "The message, Nick. Johnny was a victim of Jeremiah, right? You mentioned him after we talked to Ruth. She was his teacher."

"Yeah." He wiped his mouth with the back of his hand. "We're dealing with a psychopath who wants to create chaos. Nothing more. Because Jeremiah did kill Johnny."

"Sounds fair."

"I've had enough." He closed the lid, resigning. "Not as young as I used to be."

"You got that part right," she quipped, looking pointedly at the gray appearing in his hair.

"Yeah, join the club." He pointed a finger at her head.

She gasped, dropping the celery and looking at her hair in the rearview mirror. It was blazing red. When Nick chuckled next to her, she threw one of the sticks at him. But despite their teasing, Mackenzie sensed the troubled undertones. The corners of Nick's eyes were tight, and his hand was absentmindedly looking for his pack of cigarettes.

The sun bloomed above the horizon as the clear sky burst into flames of peach and gold, not even a wisp of cloud floating. Mackenzie jogged past the row of quaint houses by one of the many lakes in town. She crossed the street to run on the other side, too far to smell or hear anything. These were homes with families, with mindless chatter and harmless fights. It was so quiet in Mackenzie's house.

Mackenzie halted, catching her breath, and faced the lake. The ripples of water glinted like diamonds under the blazing sun. She looked at her hands and saw them smaller and younger. A pair of calloused and older hands of a man clutched them tight.

Her pulse galloped at the faint memory. It was only months ago that Charles revealed to her his true identity and she had cursed herself every day for forgetting about Robert Price—the father who had looked for her for years, only to be buried by the same daughter when he finally found her. She didn't remember him really, but some memories were coming back to her and she latched onto them, the possibility of remembering a father who was good to her too sweet to ignore.

Something caught Mackenzie's eye. A figure behind a tree. Someone in a jacket? She couldn't tell. It was most likely one of the morning strollers. She ignored them and did her stretches. But their shadow lingered. Were they just standing by the lake behind a tree or trying to spy on her?

A shiver ran down her spine. Ever since Charles was murdered, she was on edge. When it had been declared a robbery gone wrong, she had relaxed a little, but with the case now reopened and Detective Kennedy not convinced…

She squared her shoulders and marched closer to the tree. Better to confront in broad daylight. But when she reached the tree, there was no one there.

CHAPTER SEVEN

Captain Murphy, the chief of police, was a stubborn man. Refusing to retire, he was like superglue stuck to the department. A man well liked by the mayor, he wasn't going anywhere anytime soon. Despite Mackenzie's eight years with the Lakemore PD, she hadn't established a strong relationship with him. He was old-school, enjoyed cracking mildly inappropriate jokes with men and only getting involved when the case was high profile. Which is why he was gracing the Lakemore PD with his presence this morning.

Justin and Jenna, another junior detective, were going over the reports, while Rivera and Sully engaged in a serious conversation. There was no hint of her quirky sergeant's usual humor.

"Twenty bucks says that Sully will pick up a new hobby by noon," Troy muttered in Mackenzie's ear.

"Give him some credit. By five in the evening."

"You're on." He winked and went to his office.

Mackenzie entered the conference room.

"Get any sleep last night?" Becky asked, munching on a cookie.

"Not really."

"Sorry I called you over so late."

"It's okay. You were right. I wouldn't have wanted Nick finding out in front of everyone." She looked around at their bosses. She might not have been around for the case involving Jeremiah, but it was personal for Nick. And Becky had made the right choice to allow him some time and privacy to absorb the information.

Nick breezed into the room, looking fresh and clean-shaven. He headed straight for the espresso machine and poured himself a black coffee. His face gave nothing away, but his sharp jaw was slightly clenched.

"Becky, take it away," Sully said when everyone was ready.

"Lucas Williams, age nine, was found with two injuries," Becky began. Mackenzie looked at the picture. Lucas's small body draped over a giant rock, his small hands crossed over his chest, his eyes open and empty. "His tongue was cut off."

"He looks like one of Jeremiah's boys." Murphy peered at Nick through his glasses. "That's the guy you caught, Nick."

"Let's not jump to any conclusions," Rivera said.

Murphy waved a dismissive hand at her, not sparing her a glance, making her raise a stiff brow. "Nick, this is too much of a coincidence. It's got to be a copycat."

"Captain Murphy, why don't we let Dr. Sullivan finish with her findings?" Rivera raised her voice and gestured Becky to continue.

"There are strangulation marks around the neck and two blows to the head. The victim was strangled post-mortem, and the act resulted in minimal damage to the hyoid bone. The cause of death was a single blow to the *mastoid process*, a portion of the temporal bone of the skull, puncturing the sternocleidomastoid. Instant death. Zero pain."

Mackenzie looked at the close-up picture of the injuries to the head. The blood had been cleaned but the scarring and dent from the blow were still evident. "*Two* blows you said? They look very close together."

"Yes. It seems like the killer was targeting the mastoid on purpose. The first time, he missed, but the second time he got it right."

"So he went out of his way to kill him in a painless way?" Sully said. "Sure as hell doesn't sound like Jeremiah. That asshole would strangle those kids while they were still alive."

Nick's hands were jittery on his lap under the table. "Becky?"

"Yeah." She licked her lips and took a staggering breath. "On the next page, you'll see a piece of paper that was left folded inside his esophagus."

"Jesus Christ," Murphy gasped.

A series of expressions crossed everyone's faces—shock, confusion, and fear. The silence that followed was piercing.

"Who is Johnny?" Rivera asked.

"Johnny Cooper was one of Jeremiah's victims," Sully said, his eyebrows drawn together.

Nick gulped down the scalding coffee. "He was found in a shallow grave a month after we arrested Jeremiah. His body had decomposed, but Becky was able to confirm that his tongue had been removed. The method of killing was also the same. Strangulation." He repeated the facts like he was trying to convince himself.

"Which is why the killer strangled Lucas after killing him. They knew we'd figure out that's not the cause of death," Mackenzie said. "It was for the ritual. To make sure everything's the same as how Jeremiah used to do it. Were the details of Jeremiah's M.O. made public at the time?"

"Not during the investigation, but after his arrest, the details became well-known. Though the entire town was so fixated, I wouldn't be surprised if there were some leaks while he was still at large."

"Dr. Sullivan," Justin said. "There are no signs of a physical assault on Lucas. And the killer was able to strike the right spot on the skull a second time?"

"That's right. Seems like they were targeting the specific area on the skull. I'm running a tox screen," Becky confirmed. "The lack of signs of struggle indicates that the victim was likely unconscious."

"Any signs of sexual assault?"

"None. No ligature marks around the wrists either. No signs of Lucas being held captive."

"He was probably drugged then," Mackenzie said. "We'll have to wait for the tox screen."

"Just one more thing." Becky placed a picture of the plain white handkerchief in an evidence bag. "Lucas's parents confirmed that this wasn't his. And the red stain on it isn't blood. It's ketchup."

"Ketchup?" Nick regarded the blot of red in the center.

"I've sent it to the Latent Print Unit to look for prints."

"Let's hope that yields something. With any luck it came from the killer. We are still searching the woods?" Rivera asked.

"Yes, ma'am," Jenna answered. "We have patrol, Sheriff's Office, and volunteers pitching in."

"Good. And the Amber Alert?"

"With no suspect description or information about any vehicle, we don't have enough to issue an Amber Alert yet. But we have entered the information on NCIC and flagged it as Child Abduction," Jenna said, referring to the National Crime Information Center.

"Why does this person think that Jeremiah didn't kill Johnny?" Mackenzie asked. "Why not just share their doubts with us instead of killing a boy and holding the other two captive?"

"Because they're messed up, like Jeremiah." Nick grinded his teeth behind closed lips. "This isn't about them having genuine doubts, they're looking for a reaction. Taking and killing a child isn't enough excitement for them."

Murphy pulled a face. "I'm due to give an interview to Debbie tomorrow. You better not embarrass me, Nick. Jeremiah was one of the biggest cases we ever solved. If we arrested the wrong guy for Johnny's murder then—"

"We never arrested Jeremiah for Johnny's murder. The charge was added *after* he was already in prison before his trial began," Nick said in a hard voice. "And we had solid evidence. This person is mistaken."

Rivera placed her hands on the table, smothering the simmering tension in the room. "We can't trust this killer to keep his word. We have to find them on our own before we end up with two more dead boys."

"There are *no* witnesses?" Sully asked. "Three boys go missing from a festival and no one saw anything?"

"There were a lot of kids at the festival, outside of this class," Justin said. "It was a crowded place."

"Nick and I spoke with Sarah, the other teacher, she corroborated Ruth's story." Mackenzie updated them on their conversation with Ruth.

Sully clicked his tongue and shook his head. "Nick… you gotta talk to Jeremiah. Are you ready for that?"

Nick flashed him a bitter smile. "I don't have a choice."

This case was digging up old wounds. The Jeremiah case had made Nick's career—his first victory, capturing the serial killer hunting little boys in Lakemore—had catapulted him to fame in local authorities around Washington. When Mackenzie had joined the department and had Nick assigned to her as her partner, he was just coming off the heels of all the attention. Mackenzie was the only one who had seen up close the damage the case had done to him; how disturbing and grueling it had been, and now they were opening back up again.

She caught a glimpse of Detective Austin Kennedy, talking on the phone. Had he discovered something?

Mackenzie shook off that thought and focused on Theo and Noah—two more young lives hanging in the balance.

CHAPTER EIGHT

"Lucas Williams, a fourth grader at Lakemore Secondary School, was found murdered in the woods surrounding Fresco River," Debbie said to the camera with a solemn face. *"The heartbreaking discovery was made by volunteers yesterday morning. The parents of the boy were informed immediately. Despite our repeated efforts to get a statement from Lakemore PD, we've been unsuccessful. According to various sources, the location of the other two boys is still unknown, which is why the police are being so tight-lipped about any progress made. If anyone has any information on Theodore Reynolds and Noah Kinsey, please contact this hotline."*

Mackenzie sat back in her chair, pretending to go over the witness statements that she had read at least a dozen times already and could recite verbatim. But her ears strained to listen to Nick over the phone, as he scheduled a meeting with Jeremiah. His voice was curt. His sentences brief. His grunts abrupt.

"Thanks," he muttered and slammed the headset.

She wheeled into his cubicle. "Who was that?"

"Jeremiah's lawyer, Holly. Still has that enthusiasm of someone fresh out of law school. Got on my nerves." He dragged his hands down his face.

"And why did she sound happy to hear from you?"

"She keeps filing appeals for parole. They keep getting rejected. As they should, but—"

"If there's renewed interest in him, she might use it to her advantage?"

"Can't see how, but lawyers have a way of twisting things around."

Sully emerged from his office, shuffling a pack of cards mindlessly as he strolled over to the water cooler.

Troy put his arm out in front of Mackenzie's face, palm facing up and fingers wiggling. "Pay up."

She checked the clock and sighed. It was quarter to noon. Sighing, she slapped a twenty-dollar bill in his palm.

"When can we meet him?" Mackenzie asked.

"Tomorrow morning." He pulled out a cigarette from his drawer and twirled it.

She plucked it out of his grasp and tossed it in the garbage. "I've downloaded Johnny's case files from both our local database and HITS."

"Not here." He looked around the stuffy office—a rare occasion when most of the people were at their desks, slogging away at forensic reports and witness statements. Debbie's voice played in the background. "I need air."

"Sure." She stood up and grabbed her jacket.

Mackenzie and Nick sat on the hood of her car, facing a quarry. A giant pit carved into the earth right in front of them. There was a pond in the bottom. Tall trees surrounded the edge. The place looked abandoned and felt detached from the rest of the world.

A good spot to get rid of a body: Johnny's remains had been discovered here.

"Do you come here a lot?" Mackenzie asked.

"First time since we found him. It's a quiet place but feels haunted."

Mackenzie opened the file in her lap and started reading out loud. "Johnny Cooper was reported missing on September twenty-fourth, 2010." His picture was clipped on top of the page. Johnny had a gentle face, with lush hair that covered half of his forehead. He looked like an intelligent boy—dark eyes, thick eyelashes, and a shy smile. "He was found on October first in 2011." She flipped the page to the pictures of his decomposing remains—almost skeletonized with some rotting tissue. "That was one month *after* you arrested Jeremiah."

Nick sucked on an unlit cigarette, his eyes sweeping across the quarry. "Yeah, when he went missing, we immediately assumed he was taken by Jeremiah. He fit the profile of his other victims."

"He never reached school. According to his stepmother, Heather, she received a call from the school that Johnny never showed up. How did you discover his body?"

"The Grayson Football Coaching Center was supposed to be built here. But when they started construction, they discovered Johnny's remains. Construction was obviously halted, and eventually they decided to build someplace else because it was too… disturbing."

Mackenzie looked at her secluded surroundings. The closest residential area was at least three miles away. It was not anywhere near Johnny's school or his house.

"According to the autopsy, he had injuries to the hyoid bone and the left lateral thyroid and the cricoid cartilages… so his throat basically. He was strangled to death. And peri-mortem fractures on ribs bil—"

"Bilaterally. The killer mounted Johnny, pressed his knees into his chest, crushing his ribs, and strangled him." Nick winced, without even sparing a glance at the report in Mackenzie's hands.

"You remember him."

"I remember all eleven of those kids."

A warm breeze blew, ruffling their hair. The sound of rustling leaves echoed in the quarry. Mackenzie's legs dangled, kicking the license plate. She closed the file for a moment after seeing Nick's faraway look.

"Johnny was the only victim we found after the arrest was made. The only body found that wasn't fresh. Jeremiah would send us riddles, giving us clues as to where the bodies were—left in places they'd be found easily. That's how he played the game. He wasn't just enjoying killing them; he was also enjoying the attention and the 24/7 news cycle. But I never got the message for Johnny. It must have got lost somewhere," he said. "There was one more boy who went missing around the time Jeremiah was at large. We never found him and probably never will, assuming Jeremiah won't divulge that information in the hopes of using it as leverage somewhere down the road."

"What evidence did you find that implicated Jeremiah?"

He scratched his stubble. "Johnny fit the profile, and forensics proved his tongue had been cut out. Jeremiah's M.O.; that confirmed it. That detail was not public when Johnny went missing."

"Jeremiah's DNA was found in the ears of his victims." She remembered reading about it.

"He left it there to taunt us. We always had a way to catch him. In Johnny's case, since the body was found a year after his disappearance, Becky ruled that the DNA could have deteriorated since it wasn't preserved properly amid environmental fluctuations over time."

"I know I wasn't here, but he wasn't as well known as the other victims, was he?" Mackenzie had transferred when the case was wrapped up, but it had left scars on everyone it touched. It felt like the town was recovering from whiplash. Law enforcement officials and reporters had been working tirelessly and then suddenly it was over. The adrenaline wore off and left everyone bone-tired.

"No. Because he was found after it was over. The kids we were discovering while hunting him down became famous. Johnny was just… forgotten." His eyes zeroed on Johnny's picture peeking from the file.

"Did you suspect anyone else?"

He shook his head. "When Johnny was reported missing, I assumed it was Jeremiah."

"Do you think it could be someone else? That this killer isn't mistaken or lying?"

Nick was taken aback. "It *was* Jeremiah, Mack. Who else would cut out his tongue?"

"I know. But I'm just playing devil's advocate. You said yourself there was a small chance that the details of the M.O. could have been leaked when Jeremiah was still active. And now we have a dead kid on our hands with instructions to find Johnny's real killer."

"What are you implying?" A look of betrayal crossed Nick's face, like she was questioning his work.

Mackenzie's stomach lurched. "I didn't mean it like that. Anyway, Johnny had family, right? We should talk to them again, just to be thorough."

"A stepmother. And a brother. He was eleven at the time. Do you mind if I smoke?" He looked like he was in pain.

"I do. Very much. Especially after spending a year to get off that habit."

Nick took out a cigarette and began picking it apart. "You should have told me that your father was lying about his identity," he said after a minute, changing the subject.

"I thought it didn't matter. I thought it was over."

"So did I," he whispered.

CHAPTER NINE

It had been a long day. Mackenzie had barely slept in the last twenty-four hours, spending the night before tossing and turning after returning home from the morgue. Her thoughts had swung frantically from Lucas and the other boys to the renewed investigation into Charles's murder. The entire night she had felt like she was standing on a precipice, waiting for someone to push her.

As the car came to a halt, she jolted out of her thoughts. The air was full of dust and sand. Construction was underway right ahead of her on an empty plot surrounded by barbed wire. Backhoes and trenchers dug into the earth. A crane stood idle. Flatbed trucks were parked with logs of wood, steel girders, timber, and pipes. A cluster of constructions workers wearing hard hats moved around, wrapping up as their shift came to an end.

"Would you recognize Tim?" Mackenzie asked Nick out of the car.

"It's been too long." He stopped one of the men. "We're looking for Tim Cooper? We called the company and they said he's out here on the job."

The man with a scruffy face nodded and turned around. "Tim! Get over here!"

A young, well-built man approached them. He looked like all the younger guys, his face smudged with dirt, making his blue eyes pop. A tool belt hung loose around his waist. "What's up?"

Mackenzie flashed her credentials. "Got a minute?"

Tim's jaw clenched and his grip on a roll of paper tightened before he handed it to the man. "Give these plans to Dave."

The man nodded and walked away, throwing curious looks over his shoulder.

"Tim, I don't know if you remember me…" Nick shifted uncomfortably, his eyes squinting against the setting sun.

"I do." Tim swallowed hard, but his eyes were hard. "You're the detective who came to tell us that Johnny was finally… found."

Tension simmered between them in those few seconds of silence. Tim had only been a young boy, eleven years old, when his baby brother went missing, only to turn up dead. Now he was a grown man, hardened by the trauma of losing his only sibling.

"We had some questions about Johnny," Mackenzie said.

"Why?"

"Just revisiting some details to make sure we didn't miss anything."

Tim snorted. "Eight years after putting his killer behind bars? Think you got the wrong guy?"

"No!" Mackenzie stated quickly. "Jeremiah Wozniak deserves to rot in prison for the rest of his life. But his lawyer is trying to get him out, and there are rumors floating around that she might have found her smoking gun. We're going over all of his victims again to make sure the cases are airtight."

This was the party line they'd decided on when re-interviewing witnesses and suspects from the original case. It wasn't a complete lie either; whether he had killed Johnny or not, Jeremiah was exactly where he belonged.

Tim seemed to buy it. "I see."

"Did you ever see anyone suspicious talk to Johnny or follow him?" Nick asked.

He shook his head. "Can't remember."

"Did Johnny ever say anything to you?"

Tim's eyes misted with tears. He wiped his mouth and looked around, fidgeting. "You know what. This is a bad idea. Why don't you get out of here?"

"I know this isn't easy, but—"

"No, you *don't* know!" He pushed a finger into Nick's chest. Mackenzie's instinct was to jump forward, but Nick raised a hand behind him, telling her to back off. Tim's jaw trembled and spit sprayed out from in between his lips. "You don't know what it was like. You have no clue. Johnny would have been seventeen today. You don't know what it was like to be eleven years old and find out that your brother's bones were recovered at some quarry. I bet it doesn't matter to you anyway. You're so used to seeing dead bodies, telling people someone they loved died and moving on. That's what I was to you. Just another victim's family. Tell me. How much do you think about people like us?"

Construction workers walked around them, carrying their hard hats tucked under their arms. But Nick and Tim seemed to be in their own bubble, one even Mackenzie couldn't penetrate. In that moment, she saw the enormity of what they were a part of; the scars that were left behind. Tim wasn't exactly wrong; it was part of their job to solve a case and move on. If they sat around thinking too much about it, they would never be able to function. They didn't lack empathy, but they were trained to squash it in exchange for efficiency.

But now Mackenzie couldn't escape it. She had never reopened a case. Now she would know what it felt like to return to the carnage of emotions left behind.

"You're right," Mackenzie said in a clipped tone. "We don't. But I don't see why that should stop you from cooperating with us. We care about the truth. Help us."

Tim glared at Mackenzie before turning his gaze back to Nick. "I'll repeat what I said all those years ago and you didn't take me seriously. Johnny was depressed. He wasn't acting right weeks before his disappearance."

"How?"

"Not talking as much, not eating. He loved to play capture the flag, no matter what. Always cheered him up. But a few days before he went missing was the first time he said 'no'." Tim narrowed his eyes at Nick. "But you know this. You ignored me, dismissed my statement. After all I was an eleven-year-old kid. What would I know, right?"

"That's not what—" Nick interrupted, but Tim spoke over him.

"And now you're back, wondering if you made a mistake?" Tim snorted. The wind picked up, blowing up gusts of earth around them. Mackenzie rubbed her eyes, dirt prickling her eyes. "You look haunted, Detective Blackwood. You deserve this."

"Tim, where were you on Friday morning?" Mackenzie asked.

"Why?"

She hitched a shoulder. "Just tell us."

"Probably at work. Look, I told you everything I know. Now let me move on." He shouldered past Nick toward his jeep.

Nick was frozen in place, not even turning around to watch Tim drive away.

The lot had emptied out. Light began to peel off Lakemore as the sun dipped into the horizon, brushing the sky with fiery colors of orange and gold.

Nick's hair moved gently in the wind as he stared off into the horizon. "He's not wrong."

"He's emotional, understandably so. Don't take it to heart."

"We talk to Jeremiah tomorrow. Hell knows what *he's* going to throw in my face." He stuck his hands in his pockets.

Mackenzie's mind was reeling. "Tim is nineteen years old. Strong. Loved Johnny."

"What are you getting at?"

"You know."

"Oh come on, Mack!" He scowled. "Seriously?"

She gripped his elbow. "He's not the eleven-year-old kid you met anymore, Nick. He's a grown up with demons and motive."

"Jeremiah killed Johnny, Mack," he said sternly. "I'm all for confirming what we have to, but that doesn't change the facts. And Tim has nothing to do with this."

Nick didn't wait for her reply and walked back toward the car. Mackenzie stared after him with a sinking stomach.

CHAPTER TEN

March 4

The file on Jeremiah Wozniak sat open on the kitchen island. It was a thick one, with papers almost falling out. Mackenzie had spent part of the night and early morning poring over the disturbing details of Jeremiah's life. When she had eventually tried to sleep, she kept hearing the soft whimpers of a child, or seeing the smoky, gray eyes belonging to Jeremiah.

Jeremiah had been born in Lakemore and brought up by a drug addict living in a trailer park. By the time he was seven years old, he was rolling joints, and heating heroin in spoons for his mother. When he turned eight, he watched his mother's pimp almost strangle her to death and when he tried consoling her, she beat him up. Up until the age of twelve, Jeremiah got into fights at school. Then, suddenly, his personality changed. He retreated into a shell, barely speaking, barely smiling, and barely interacting with his classmates. Later, he'd tell the forensic psychologist that his mother's boyfriend had been sexually abusing him. Jeremiah turned his attention to killing animals—squirrels, rabbits, and one time his neighbor's dog.

Jeremiah scored over thirty-five out of forty in the PCL—a psychological assessment tool to diagnose psychopathy. His traumatic childhood aggravated the dangerous tendencies he was born with that otherwise could have remained dormant.

He didn't have run-ins with the law—opting to live an isolated and lonely life, in the shadows of the society. A face that was easily forgotten. A name that didn't amount to anything. No one could imagine that a warehouse worker fostered blood-curdling fantasies.

The innocent-looking file was filled with horrors. Its existence in her home was bothering her; Mackenzie wanted to shred it and burn the remains. She turned on the blender and irrationally hoped that the noise would clean the air.

Her eyes darted to her front yard. The weeping willow was coming back to life—a good omen, she felt, like she might start to heal too.

The faint sound of her landline trilled over the sound of the blender. Switching the appliance off, she went over to the coffee table. She never wanted a landline—it was an outdated mode of communication—but Sterling had insisted on having one. They rarely received any calls on it, so Mackenzie was surprised to hear it ring now.

"Hello?"

Silence.

"Hello?"

Silence.

She was about to hang up when she heard someone breathe on the line. She shivered, the hair on the back of her neck standing up straight. Still pressing the phone to her ear, she glanced around the house.

"Who's this?"

No answer. Just even breathing.

"Don't call again." She gritted her teeth and slammed the phone back. Too bad the landline didn't have caller ID. Maybe she was overreacting. Maybe it was a prank or some problem in the connection. But an inkling told her it wasn't.

She was jumpy as she packed her bag and grabbed her jacket. On her way out, she gave the knob an extra twist, making sure it was locked.

*

Mackenzie stood in the poorly lit hallway, waiting for Nick to return from the restroom. Bulbs flickered overhead, casting circles of light on the gray floor. Prison guards moved around them with stoic faces. A stale stench hung in the soupy air. Her heart contracted faintly in her chest, still shaken up from the strange incident in the morning. Since Charles had been found murdered, she had been on edge. There was never any evidence, but sometimes the air around her felt different. And now this.

"Here you go." Nick returned, waving a Milky Way bar in her face. "Saw a vending machine."

"I didn't want it," she replied, puzzled.

"Your stomach was making sounds the entire ride, Mack. You didn't eat breakfast today, did you?"

She huffed and grabbed the bar from him. "Thanks."

"I'm sorry about yesterday."

She tore the wrapper and took a big bite. "Don't worry about it."

A tall, broad woman with thick brown hair appeared at the end of the hallway. Mackenzie discarded the wrapper and swallowed the candy bar. The woman wobbled toward them in pencil heels, files almost spilling out of her arms. She wore a colorful shawl over her cardigan and her eyes were framed with thick spectacles, reminding Mackenzie of her drama teacher back in school. "Detectives, I'm Holly Martin. Mr. Wozniak's lawyer. We spoke on the phone."

"I'm Detective Blackwood. This is my partner, Detective Price," Nick introduced them, his energy the polar opposite to Holly's.

Holly grinned wide, her white teeth a string of pearls. "So glad to meet you both. Jeremiah talks a lot about you, Detective Blackwood. Said you're the only one who appreciated his notes."

Mackenzie squirmed. Despite being easily in her fifties, Holly had the sparkle of a newly minted lawyer, with almost a skip in her step. Juxtaposed against the grimness of the gravity of the situation, her eagerness felt distasteful.

"You weren't his lawyer when he went to trial," Nick noted, as they began walking.

"No. That was another firm. When Jeremiah was convicted, he fired them. We took his case a little over a year ago, actually. This is good progress that you're interested in talking to him again. Though I am surprised. I saw the news. Everyone's talking about those missing boys." She eyed them.

"We're on top of that," Mackenzie assured. "Why did you take Jeremiah as a client?"

She paused in front of a closed door and waggled her eyebrows at them. "It's *Jeremiah Wozniak*. One of the most infamous serial killers to come out of Washington. There's a crew in town filming a true crime series on this guy. That's when Jeremiah contacted us, wanting better representation. This is good publicity for our firm, and for me. Who's to say no to that?"

"For someone defending a child killer, you look very excited." Mackenzie didn't bother to hide the bite in her tone.

Holly, one of the few women taller than Mack, looked down at her with an exasperated look. "That holier-than-thou attitude won't work with me, sweetie. I've spent the last two decades defending scum like Jeremiah. Being nice or likable isn't part of the job description. Deal with it."

Before Mackenzie could fathom a response, Holly opened the door. Yellow light bathed the compact, windowless room, with a desk in the middle. The first thing Mackenzie registered was the claustrophobia. Walls had never looked so solid and unyielding. The next thing she saw was a man sitting behind the desk in an orange jumpsuit, his hands in cuffs.

He was big and bulky. Long, gray hair fell to his shoulders in strings, some of it tied in a thin ponytail. Tattoos covered his strong arms; of snakes, the cross, scriptures written in Latin, and bible quotes. His face was aged—he was in his fifties but looked older, except for his eyes, which shone like beacons in the dimly lit room. And Mackenzie felt icy cold. All warmth was sapped from the room and death itself sat in front of them—with gleaming eyes and a wicked smile.

"Why is it so dark in here?" Holly moaned at the guard standing behind Jeremiah as they all took a seat. He flipped a switch and a white tube light turned on above the table with a hum. "Ugh. Is that going to be noisy?"

The guard shrugged and ignored her.

Mackenzie felt Nick tense next to her briefly.

"Detective Blackwood," Jeremiah coaxed in his throaty voice. "I told you you'd see me again."

Nick's discomfort melted. And Mackenzie saw the side to him that didn't come out often. His eyes turned completely black, his face clouded with fury. He pulled a chair back and sat on it—looking bigger. "You know why I'm here?"

Jeremiah chuckled under his breath and then pinned his glare on Mackenzie. "You weren't there before."

"I'm his partner."

"Partner," he said, like he was tasting the word on the tip of his tongue. "Does that mean you'll die for him?"

"It means I'll kill for him," she deadpanned.

Jeremiah's lips turned into a sneer. He leaned forward, ready to retort, when Holly interrupted. "You were a little vague on the phone."

Mackenzie and Nick weren't at liberty to share that a potential copycat was at large, certainly not with the likes of Holly Martin. They had to tread carefully.

"Have you made any new friends recently?" Nick asked Jeremiah, his jaw tight. "Someone you're talking to a lot. Sharing secrets with?"

Jeremiah made a show of thinking. "No."

"Why are you asking this?" Holly's eyes narrowed.

"Johnny Cooper," Nick said, changing tack. "Remember him?"

Jeremiah chewed on his fat lip, his eyes bouncing between Mackenzie and Nick. "Who?"

Nick took out a picture of him and slid it forward on the table. "This kid. Remember?"

Holly tilted her head curiously, while Jeremiah didn't even sneak a peek.

"Tell me, Blackwood. Did you keep my notes?"

"Answer the question, Jeremiah," Mackenzie ordered.

"I wasn't talking to you."

"Don't make me send you to the infirmary," Nick warned.

"Now, now. There's no need to threaten my client. Let's be professional."

"It's alright, Holly," Jeremiah sniped. "Blackwood and I are old friends." Jeremiah spoke in a cruel voice, his brutality evident in his cold eyes and the harsh twist of his lips. Combined with his large size and unkempt hair, he looked like a monster—the kind that made children hide under their beds.

"One of the charges my client was convicted on was the murder of Johnny Cooper," Holly said, her eyes calculating. "Are you saying that that conviction was *wrong*?"

"No," Nick asserted.

"Then why are you asking these questions? I'm his lawyer. I have the right to know what's going on."

"Take it up with the DA," Mackenzie replied. "Mr. Wozniak, do you remember what happened with this boy?"

"The unicorn." Jeremiah hissed at the picture. He bared his teeth, like the mere sight of Johnny gave rise to violence inside him. Mackenzie snatched the picture away. "He's in my mind. I kill him over and over, every day. How are you going to stop that?"

"Shut up, Jeremiah," Holly scolded.

"He roams in my soul." Jeremiah looked up at Nick, his face still hovering close to the surface.

"What the hell is he talking about?" Mackenzie turned to Nick.

Nick sighed and drummed his fingers on the table, eyes skimming over his nemesis.

"I told you this all those years ago too. But you didn't believe me. You thought I was playing a game with you, manipulating you. How does it feel to know that poor little Johnny has been rotting away all these years while his murderer walks free?"

"You're lying," Nick bit out.

Jeremiah let out a growl. "If I'm lying, then why are you here asking questions?"

The air in the room thickened and Mackenzie suppressed a wince. They couldn't reveal why they were here; it was a delicate situation.

"My client pled not guilty to all charges in his original trial, including the count of Johnny's murder." Holly tried to defuse the tension and signaled the guard. "I think it's best to discuss the case with the prosecutor first, as I'm sensing there might be grounds for appeal. I'm going to advise my client not to answer any more questions."

"I'll see you again, Blackwood." Jeremiah was dragged away by the guard through the other door.

"Your client is in here for killing eleven kids," Mackenzie retorted once they were alone. "He's not getting out of prison."

"It takes one little tear to rip the whole thing apart." Holly scoffed, standing up. "I assume the prosecutor on this case will be in touch soon?"

Nick nodded. "Elliot Garcia. He'll be in town tomorrow."

"The white knight of Thurston County. I've sparred with him many times in court. This will be fun." She walked out the door haughtily.

Mackenzie huffed. "Jeremiah didn't give us much. Should we try again? Try to get him to crack?"

Nick placed his hands on the table. "He won't. I know him. He thinks he has power over us so he'll only give us something when he feels like it."

Mackenzie felt a prickle of annoyance. She didn't know Jeremiah as well as Nick, but she had enough experience to know that such people found pleasure in two things: killing and playing mind games. Unfortunately, they were running out of time to play by Jeremiah's rules. "What the hell was he talking about before? Unicorns?"

Nick sighed and ran a hand through his hair. "That's Atticus's poem. 'Our unicorns'. Jeremiah's always been a bit of a wordsmith. He's saying that Johnny is the one that got away."

There was no reason to trust a man like Jeremiah. But could there be any truth to the message left in Lucas's throat?

CHAPTER ELEVEN

It had been three days and there were no reported sightings of Theo or Noah. A task force of uniformed cops was checking the scarce tips, but so far, they were all bogus. Unfortunately, they hadn't secured enough information to issue Amber Alerts. The departments in the neighboring cities of Olympia, Riverview and Tacoma had received all the necessary information and were on the lookout. Border patrols had been in place, checking every vehicle that was going in and out of town. But this was a storm for Lakemore to weather.

The residents had started being careful about sending their children out. School was still open, but playgrounds were mostly empty.

Back at the station, Mackenzie fidgeted in her seat, staring at the pictures of Theo and Noah pinned to her desk. Every time she blinked, the image of Lucas splayed on the rock flashed in her mind.

The sharp ringtone of her phone brought her attention back.

"Detective Price."

"I have an update, ma'am." Justin's gruff voice filtered through the phone.

Mackenzie rolled her eyes at him addressing her as ma'am. "What is it?"

"I just met with Tim Cooper's supervisor. According to the schedule, Tim was supposed to report on site on March first at ten in the morning but failed to do so."

She froze. "Where was he?"

"He called in sick and stayed home. Went to work the next day in the afternoon."

"Does he live with anyone? Roommate? Partner?"

"His coworkers confirmed that he lives alone."

"Alright, thanks Justin." Mackenzie hung up and clutched the phone in her hand.

She spun on her chair to face Nick's cubicle. The drive to the station after their chilling confrontation with Jeremiah had been silent. It felt foreign. Typically, after such a visit, the car ride was spent discussing the details. Or just talking for the sake of talking.

"Justin spoke to Tim's supervisor," Mackenzie said, determined to keep things normal. "Tim doesn't have an alibi for Friday."

Nick's shoulders fell. He turned around. "Why are you after Tim?"

She felt eyes on them. Troy and Ned were in the office, slogging away at their desks. "I'm not after anyone. I'm just doing my job."

Nick's face pinched in annoyance. He picked up his coffee mug and left the office.

Troy chewed the end of his pencil—an annoying habit of his—and watched her with raised eyebrows. "Trouble in paradise?"

Mackenzie was taken aback but casually shrugged it off. "It's not his fault. The visit with Jeremiah rattled him. Rattled me too. I wanted to smack the smirk off his face."

"He also probably saw Murphy's interview with Debbie. God, it's embarrassing to work for a self-serving idiot like him."

The interview had been playing on a loop in the lounge. Mackenzie hadn't watched it in its entirety, but she had caught enough bits and pieces to know what a disaster it had been. Murphy had lied through his teeth about the extent of his personal involvement in the case and had blown a fuse when Debbie questioned the competency of Lakemore PD.

"*Only weeks ago, the FBI was investigating your office for corruption. The people don't have a lot of faith in Lakemore PD and now we have a child killer in our town.*"

The two had spent the rest of the interview arguing and poking holes in each other's credibility.

Rivera appeared, placing an elbow on the cubicle wall. Her blue pantsuit had a coffee stain and her thick dark hair was pulled back in a hasty bun. It was the least put together the lieutenant had ever looked since joining the Lakemore PD a few months ago. "Any updates, Detective Price?"

"Jeremiah claims that he didn't kill Johnny, but as we know, his word isn't reliable. There's no doubt he was responsible for those other murders he pled not guilty to. And Johnny's brother, Tim, doesn't have an alibi for the time of the abduction."

Rivera rubbed her fingertips together. "That won't be enough to get a warrant for his phone records. Get uniform to watch him."

Mackenzie made a note of it. "I've asked Justin to check for sex offenders living in the area."

"Good call." She gestured Mackenzie to follow her into a corner.

Mackenzie looked over her shoulder at Troy, whose usual laid-back demeanor dropped as he stared keenly at something on his computer.

Rivera spoke in hushed tone. "I want *you* to go over the case files for Johnny."

"Me?" she almost squeaked.

"Yes." Rivera glared. "People are hesitant to even consider that a mistake was made in Johnny's investigation, which I understand. I'm not accusing anyone, but I want to make sure that nobody cut corners. It was an intense time for the department and sometimes mistakes happen. The FBI investigation into us is just wrapping up, so this time I want to keep tabs on everything. You weren't part of the original investigation. A fresh pair of eyes might help."

"Yeah…" Mackenzie trailed off, thinking about Nick. They were a team. Since she'd joined Lakemore PD, they had done everything together. He had been her constant companion, her rock, and her anchor. Checking his work felt like she was going behind his back.

"Detective Price, I know you're worried about your partner." Rivera read her face. "But your first duty is to justice and those boys."

Mackenzie nodded reluctantly and squared her shoulders. "Yes, Lieutenant."

Rivera turned to leave before pausing. She spoke with a note of gentleness. "He'll understand."

"I know."

Mackenzie went back to her cubicle, her head throbbing. She massaged her temples while trying to contain her spinning thoughts.

As she guzzled down a bottle of water, Austin Kennedy stood up from his chair, reading something on his phone. She froze, her heart stopping. Even with the case taking up her time, Austin's presence was looming, strangely omnipotent. He had a frown marring his face, pausing briefly next to Dennis's unoccupied desk. He peeled his eyes off the phone and read an open file on Dennis's desk.

To her knowledge, Austin and Dennis weren't working together on any case. Why was he snooping?

It wasn't even fleeting. Several seconds later, he lifted his head to find Mackenzie watching him. He gave her a nervous smile and left the office.

Mackenzie leaned back on her chair, cracked her knuckles. She looked back at Dennis's desk, wondering what Austin was up to.

CHAPTER TWELVE

The comforting smell of chocolate chip cookies fresh out of the oven was just what Mackenzie needed after a long, grueling day at work. She had started baking more often since her divorce, in a vain attempt to fill the void Sterling had left and make her house feel like a home again. She placed the cookies on a plate on the counter, waiting for them to cool a little.

She looked around her empty house. Sterling had taken his belongings over a month ago. The small things that belonged to both of them remained: a ship in a bottle they bought from their honeymoon in the Bahamas, an ugly fruit bowl Sterling's aunt and uncle had sent as a delayed wedding gift, a salt shaker set—one dog shaped and the other cat shaped—that Sterling gave her on their first anniversary because she wanted a "weird and cheap" present. Her husband was gone, living in an apartment, but the remnants of their marriage were scattered all around her house.

She leaned against the counter and crossed her arms, her heart feeling heavy in her chest. Maybe she was meant to be alone. Growing up, she had witnessed an abusive marriage; her alcoholic father's smacks and punches and verbal poison. The years with her grandmother were more peaceful, but lonely. They had their moments, but she was too old and sick. Then Sterling had arrived—handsome, good, and charming—just what she needed in her life at the time.

Since he had left, her home had become a reflection of how she had felt all her life. Lonely and empty.

She checked the time. It wasn't too late. She placed the cookies on a plate and went out. The lights in Irene's house were bright, casting a soft glow.

Mackenzie paused in front of it and looked at the cookies again. It was such a simple gesture—making a neighbor feel invited. But Mackenzie felt almost silly for standing with cookies in her hands. A gun would feel more natural.

Shaking her head, she marched to the door and knocked. The hum of the television seeping outside hushed and footsteps grew louder.

Irene opened the door. "Oh, Mackenzie. What a pleasant surprise!"

"Sorry to show up unannounced. I don't have your number." Mackenzie awkwardly raised the plate. "I thought I should drop by some cookies. To welcome you."

"That's wonderful. Thank you." She took them. "Why don't you come inside?"

"It's okay. I don't want to intrude…"

"Please. I insist. We'll have some together. I was craving dessert today."

Irene's house had the same layout as Mackenzie's. All houses in the row did. She had expected Irene's house to be more homely, but the furniture and décor was lifted straight from a catalogue, with a steel blue sofa, white tripod floor lamp, charcoal ottoman, chrome tables, and abstract paintings. The only personal touch was a wall full of framed pictures of a younger Irene with family and friends.

"Your place is so clean," Mackenzie approved, noticing not even a speck of dust on the coffee table.

"I'm anal when it comes to cleaning." Irene pointed at the dusting cloth tucked into the waistband of her jeans and took a bite of the cookie. "They're delicious!"

"Thank you. It's my grandmother's recipe."

"I never knew my grandmother." Irene sighed and sat across from her. "What a shame."

Mackenzie's eyes drifted to the television playing Murphy's interview on a loop and a panel discussing Jeremiah.

Irene closed the television with an apologetic smile. "I imagine you get enough of that at work."

"Yeah. You live alone?"

"Yes. My ex-husband and I didn't have any children. So it's just me." There was lingering sadness in her voice as she looked around her pristine home. Like it was a gilded cage.

"How long were you married for?"

"Twelve years."

"That's a long time." Mackenzie looked down at her hand. Her ring finger no longer had the impression of the wedding band that she had worn religiously every day for the last three years. It had quickly faded into oblivion, like it was never there.

Irene's gaze glided over Mackenzie. "Do you want wine? I feel it's a wine night."

"Maybe just one glass. Thanks."

Irene smiled and went to her kitchen to pour two glasses.

"Do you work?" Mackenzie asked.

"I'm a product manager at a tech company."

Irene didn't look like someone who spent a lot of time behind a screen. She had a fairly strong build for her age; her posture and movements were precise and pronounced. Mackenzie guessed she was athletic. "Are you liking Lakemore?"

She handed Mackenzie a glass with a small smile. "I don't know. It's a bit depressing."

"Tell me about it. I moved from New York."

"New York? How come?" Irene frowned.

"My mother sent me to live with my grandmother for a couple of years. Better schools."

"Hmm." Irene drummed her fingers on the table and took a hesitant sip. "It must have been a good experience for you though. Getting a taste of life outside Lakemore. This town feels like a bubble."

"It grows on you." Mackenzie caught a glimpse of a dreamcatcher by the window. It was the only intimate object—other than the pictures—something so out of place in a house that was meticulously decorated for symmetry and sterility. Melody had had one for a while before Charles trashed it. "Where did you get that? It's pretty."

"It's my ex-husband's." Irene waved her hand dismissively. "It's the only thing I have of his, well, that and a few pictures. It wasn't a bad break-up, which I think makes it harder, doesn't it?"

Mackenzie spoke through the lump in her throat. "It's hard to move on when you don't actively hate them."

"Sounds like your separation was recent. I'm sure you have family to depend on?"

Mackenzie's heart clenched. She pretended to check her phone to hide how much the question had hurt. She had no family, not anymore. "Uh-oh. I have a meeting."

"Meeting?"

She gulped down the wine in one go and wiped her lips with the back of her hand. "Yeah. Police force. Odd timings. Thank you for tonight. Let's do this again."

"Oh, okay…" Irene stood, puzzled, as Mackenzie ushered herself out quickly, closing the door behind her.

Once outside, the fresh air loosened the seams that held Mackenzie so tightly together. She walked back to her house with tears burning in her eyes. Charles, her last remaining family, was dead. And he'd never been a proper father to her anyway. Her mind went to Robert Price, the man who never gave up looking for her, who had taken care of her as a parent should. She remembered so little of him, but since she had learned the truth about Melody and Charles's deception, fragments had been returning to her.

"*That's how you do a crab, Mackenzie.*"

"*Show me how to do a bunny again, Daddy!*"

She remembered shadow puppets on the wall. Big strong hands making signs next to her tiny ones.

The memories would come out of nowhere, filling her with both joy and despair. Joy because she had known happiness with a parent—even if he wasn't her biological father—and despair because she had lost it too soon.

Mackenzie wondered what it would have been like if Melody hadn't separated them, if Robert had raised her instead of Charles. Would she have been different if she had grown up in a caring family? If she'd had a parent who didn't frighten her, but made her feel safe?

She had been avoiding knowing more about Robert since Charles's death. It had seemed necessary to distance herself completely from the past—a self-preservation tactic.

But Mackenzie knew she couldn't stay away forever. She had to find out about Robert Price: the father she had loved, and had buried.

CHAPTER THIRTEEN

March 5

The next morning, Mackenzie walked into the conference room, holding a cup of coffee for Nick. Theo's parents were inside, and as soon as she entered, the charged atmosphere hit her.

"How's the search in those woods going?" Theo's father demanded. "Did you find anything?"

"Not yet, Mr. Reynolds," Nick explained patiently.

"How many men do you have looking?" He crossed his arms as Nick delved into the details with him. Mackenzie placed the coffee in front of Nick covertly.

Mr. Reynolds was a beefy, bald man with a temper. His voice boomed whenever he demanded answers from the Lakemore PD and he didn't hold back. He had also been the most involved parent, wanting to know every detail of the case and making his own suggestions.

"Mr. Reynolds, we have posters everywhere in town," Mackenzie reassured him again. "The news is flashing Theo's and Noah's pictures 24/7, we have a special hotline set up, and—"

"Do you have patrol at the border checking cars?"

"Yes. We have covered all exit points," Nick explained. "The Sheriff's Office is also helping. We have alerted all the police departments in surrounding cities all the way to Seattle. They have Theo and Noah's information and are on the lookout. We can't get into the details, but we *are* following up on every possible lead and will let you know as soon as we find anything."

"I don't think you're doing enough!" he barked. "Are you guys offering any reward?"

Mr. Reynolds kept shouting accusations at Nick, demanding more resources and questioning the progress of the investigation. Nick maintained his composure, patiently handling a fuming parent whose child was missing. But Mackenzie could see the exhaustion in his face—the bags under his eyes, a worn-out expression, the sighs and constant running of his hand through his disheveled hair.

Nick hadn't stopped working. He was never one to shirk his responsibility, but Mackenzie could tell that it was fear eating him from the inside—fear that it was going to be like last time; that there was a child killer in Lakemore and he might not be able to save the boys in time.

She turned to the meek woman sitting behind Mr. Reynolds, who was wiping her nose with her sleeve. Mrs. Reynolds hadn't uttered a word. She was a frail woman, her bloodshot eyes bulging out of her thin face as she stared blankly at the floor.

"Here you go." Mackenzie handed her a Kleenex and took a seat next to her. She didn't know what to say. They had already made their promises that they were doing their best.

They sat in silence while Mr. Reynolds continued to rage, loudly enough to draw curious gazes from those walking past the conference room.

"He's hot-headed," Mrs. Reynolds whispered to Mackenzie. "But he's a good father and a good husband."

Mackenzie couldn't help but slide her gaze over her skin, looking for any bruises or blemishes.

"He doesn't hit me, Detective." Mrs. Reynolds gave her a watery smile.

"I'm sorry," Mackenzie said, embarrassed. "It's just instinct."

"I get it." She looked down at her lap. "Ever since… Lucas… Does that mean Theo could be d-dead too?" Her shoulders shook and fresh tears streamed down her cheeks, joining those that had already dried.

"Please don't think that way. We're doing everything—"

"I just can't stop thinking of Lucas's parents." She blew her nose into the Kleenex. "I-I can't go through that. I w-won't survive." She suddenly clutched Mackenzie's hands, her grip surprisingly firm. Her eyes were unfocused, her breaths sharp and irregular, like she was on the verge of a panic attack. "If anything happens to my child, I'll kill myself. I'm serious. I… I'm not s-strong. I *n-need* my son to breathe. And I haven't been able to breathe easily since he…" Her eyes rolled to the back of her head, and she slumped into Mackenzie's arms, unconscious.

"Oh my God!" Mr. Reynolds rushed to his wife, lightly slapping her face. "Honey, can you hear me?"

Nick immediately called an ambulance and brought some water to splash over Mrs. Reynolds's face.

Mackenzie checked her pulse—it was there but faint. The entire episode was a blur to Mackenzie as people around her moved efficiently, but all she could do was stare at Mrs. Reynolds, praying that this fragile woman wouldn't have to face the sorrow of losing her son and promising she was going to do everything in her power to make sure that didn't happen.

CHAPTER FOURTEEN

Mackenzie stopped by her desk on the way to Sully's office and quickly addressed her appearance. Satisfied with her poker-straight red hair pinned in a high ponytail and ironed black pantsuit, she braced herself for a meeting with Elliot Garcia and Spencer Irving—the prosecutors on Jeremiah's case.

The DA's office had caught wind of the note in Lucas's throat and had set up the meeting.

"Why are they here?" Mackenzie whispered to Nick.

He clenched his jaw. "I don't know. I'll be back in a sec."

She opened her mouth to voice a thought but sealed her lips closed. What if the DA had sent Jeremiah's old prosecution team here because they thought there was some truth to the killer's message?

When she entered the office, her eyes immediately found Elliot Garcia, sitting on a chair with his ankle over his knee and thumbing his phone. He was shorter than Mackenzie, a slim man with salt-and-pepper hair. His pebble-shaped eyes were sharp and piercing, like he could see into your soul.

A prosecutor for over two decades, Garcia had had a prolific career. He had prosecuted some of the county's most high-profile cases and had the highest success rate. He had put serial killers, murderers, rapists, and even members of the mob behind bars. Four years ago, during a trial, he had been shot in the arm when he had gone out on a job. A security detail was dispatched to protect Elliot and his boss instructed someone else to take over the case. But Elliot had shown up in court the next day, without a thread of fear in his eyes. It was this kind of unfaltering bravery that had earned him the nickname "the white knight of Thurston County".

Mackenzie had met him a couple of times, through Sterling and work, but they had never worked closely. She found him sharp but slightly aloof and absorbed. An oddity one comes to expect from someone brilliant.

Next to him sat Spencer Irving—younger and cleaner cut. He reminded Mackenzie of a preppy kid at an Ivy League school; jet-black hair styled perfectly, a clean-shaven face, thick glasses, and a crisp, ironed suit. He wasn't as legendary as Elliot but he was definitely on the rise. Spencer was Elliot's protégé; the Robin to his Batman. The only edgy thing about Spencer was a tattoo snaking up his neck—just visible above his collar.

"Where is Nick?" Spencer asked.

"He just stepped out for some fresh air," Mackenzie informed. "We spent the last hour with one of the missing kids' parents. It was rough."

"I see."

Elliot had no response, his eyebrows furrowed as he concentrated on his phone.

"How's the FBI investigation going?" Spencer asked Sully. "We hear all kinds of rumors in Olympia."

The fallout from the Erica Perez homicide case a few months ago had exposed a massive conspiracy in Lakemore. The FBI had come to town to investigate several offices, including the Lakemore PD, for corruption.

Sully groaned and put aside his pen. "Our department is going to get a clean chit anytime. That's all I care about."

Nick entered the office, his cheeks slightly pink and eyes dazed.

Elliot jumped to his feet and shook his hand. "Nice to see you again, Nick."

Mackenzie rolled her eyes. Everyone was eager to be Nick's friend since his father was a senator.

"Yeah." He nodded absentmindedly. "Are we waiting for the lieutenant?"

"No. I'll update her later. She's with Murphy right now," Sully said, putting away his calligraphy worksheet—his latest hobby.

Elliot snorted and pocketed his phone, his foot twirling in the air. "Saw that disaster of an interview yesterday. Is he off his meds?"

"I deal with him only when I don't have a choice." Sully set his pen aside. "So why are you here?"

Elliot shot Spencer an affirming look. "We're strictly here on an advisory capacity. This is a high-profile case and the DA thinks it's best if the offices are in communication from the start."

Mackenzie and Nick exchanged a skeptical glance and even Sully's eyes narrowed. "There have been high-profile cases before."

Spencer sucked air through his teeth. "The DA is concerned about Jeremiah's possible involvement. His name still causes a stir. We all remember what happened when he was at large. Eleven children murdered and the town in utter chaos."

"The fact that this may be a copycat is strictly under wraps," Sully assured, twirling his pen in his fingers. "We are keeping uniform officers away from the details as they leak to the media most of the time."

"We won't be hovering, Sergeant." Spencer gave him an easy smile. "We would just appreciate being kept in the loop so that we can control the narrative. These things have a way of spinning out of control."

Mackenzie recognized lawyer talk when she heard it. Even though the Lakemore PD was in the clear, pending FBI investigation, it seemed like the town's other official bodies still wanted to keep a close eye on them.

Sully stroked his bushy mustache, conceding. "Yeah, yeah."

Elliot made an impatient sound. "You two visited Jeremiah? What did he say? We know about that message the killer left."

"He denied killing Johnny," Mackenzie said.

"Well, he denied killing those ten other boys too," Elliot snapped. "We can't take him on his word alone."

"He's a psychopath," Nick spoke up. "He likes to play mind games."

Elliot folded his lips behind his teeth and drummed his fingers on the armrest, glancing at Spencer. "This renewed attention is because of the documentary series. The timing is suspicious. He's been looking for a way out of prison for a while now, filing all kinds of appeals and motions. Maybe this documentary gave him an idea."

"The documentary sheds light on his life and crimes and the trial." Spencer fixed his glasses. "If an investigation opens into one of his previous crimes, it puts a whole new spin on the story. Is he guilty *at all*? Jeremiah is going to act innocent in front of the cameras, sure enough."

"And if this thing catches on fire, we have the worst possible scenario on our hands," Elliot added with a grave expression. "Trial by media and public. We lose complete control. Facts will take a back seat to opinions. Instead of following the law, we'll follow the path that leads to least chaos. Our actions will be less about justice and more about giving the public what it wants."

"But Jeremiah's DNA was found on multiple boys. How do you deny something like that?" Mackenzie asked.

"No offense, but Lakemore PD's reputation is tarnished. The FBI might be giving you a clean chit, but people and the media could suggest conspiracy and corruption."

The atmosphere tightened in the room. Mackenzie pressed her back against the wall, her pulse skyrocketing. She didn't like anything other than the facts to dictate the course of a case but she knew that truth could be about perspective. She liked to be left to her own devices, but this case was already on the verge of becoming a circus show.

She looked at Nick. A look of resignation clouded his face.

"*Could* there be some mistake in Johnny's case?" Mackenzie asked slowly, uneasy with the question but knowing it had to be asked.

"You better hope not!" Sully smirked dryly. "That would be a blow this department won't be able to withstand. People might even lose their jobs." He looked pointedly at Nick.

Elliot flashed her a tight smile, mildly offended. "It was the same M.O. And there was video footage of Jeremiah approaching him the day he disappeared."

"That tape isn't with us in the evidence locker." Mackenzie recalled going over the evidence they had catalogued last night.

Nick's head jerked in her direction, his eyes narrowed. She avoided his eyes. She still hadn't told him that Rivera had asked her to confirm Johnny's case details.

"We didn't obtain the video, that's why," Sully said, oblivious to Mackenzie's slip. "It was the prosecutor office's investigator who did."

"We'd like to get a copy of it," Mackenzie said. "Just to be sure."

Elliot rolled his eyes. "Waste of time but of course."

"We've been thinking more on the possibility that Jeremiah is orchestrating this thing from prison." Nick crossed his arms. "He planted that message, and he's looking for a way to shorten his sentence or even get out."

"Who the hell would do something like this for him?" Elliot asked.

"He has a sister," Nick confirmed. "She supported him throughout the trial. Didn't shed a tear when she saw the grieving parents of those kids. She's been visiting him at least once a week all these years."

Mackenzie frowned. He never told her he had checked Jeremiah's visitor logs.

"Maybe his sister is a psychopath too. Runs in the family," Sully mumbled, his hands twitching.

"I think we should be open to the possibility that Jeremiah isn't behind this?" Mackenzie suggested, much to the annoyance of Elliot and Nick. "I'm not accusing anyone, but it's possible that someone actually believes something went wrong. If Jeremiah *were* behind this, why would he specifically choose Johnny's case to screw with us?"

"Because in Johnny's case, there was no DNA found on him. His remains were discovered a year after his disappearance, it had deteriorated. Jeremiah knows which case to dig up to cause a commotion," Elliot said. "But we won't be falling for it. His manipulation won't work this time."

"I agree," Sully added. "Even if this isn't Jeremiah's doing, it's the work of a madman who wants to send us on a wild-goose chase. But we won't drop the ball on this one."

"The Sheriff's Office has covered half the woods," Nick said with purpose. "Nothing yet. They're being more thorough, looking for any clue left behind."

"Think they're holding the boys somewhere in the woods?" Spencer asked.

"I doubt they'd be close to where Lucas was left."

Everyone fell silent as the horror of Lucas's murder filled the room. Elliot interlaced his fingers on his mouth. Spencer fiddled unnecessarily with his cufflinks.

"Do we have any suspects?" Spencer cleared his throat.

"Johnny's older brother, Tim, doesn't have an alibi for the morning of the kidnappings," Mackenzie said, ignoring Nick's blazing gaze on her.

"Do you remember him from the trial?" Sully asked Elliot.

He shrugged. "Not really. Jeremiah had so many victims; the courtroom was always packed with family members. Though, I do remember it was strange that Johnny's stepmother never came. At the time, I thought it was too hard for her."

"Heather," Nick mumbled. "She was… an odd one, I remember."

They spent the next few minutes going over the case details and the status of the search party. Patrol was stationed at the borders;

uniform was interviewing everyone present at the festival again and also looking at family members and anyone with a criminal record. They were also checking for any active sex offenders in the area.

Mackenzie's training kicked in when she discussed their plan and findings and she almost managed to detach herself from the horror of the case. But every time her eyes drifted to the pictures of Theo and Noah, her throat closed. The few moments of silences dispersed in conversation were brimming in anxiety.

"Alright." Sully stood up, adjusting his belt buckle and dabbing a handkerchief to his face. "We'll see you around?"

"You bet." Elliot shook his hand. "You have our office's full cooperation."

"You'll find them," Spencer reassured Mackenzie and Nick, his lips twitching in a nervous smile.

Mackenzie's shoulders felt heavy, but she tried to stand tall. There was no way to move but forward; they had to find those boys before it was too late.

The men filtered out of the room before her. She was following them out when Sully called her back. "Mack?"

She turned around to find the sergeant taking off his glasses and assessing her. For a moment, she wondered if it had to do with Charles's murder. What if Austin had discovered something? What if they knew what she'd done?

"Drop this," he warned instead.

"Drop what?" Breath hissed out of her lungs in relief.

"Trying to figure out if the killer is right about Johnny."

"I'm just playing devil's advocate. Someone has to."

Sully sighed. "I oversaw that case, Mack. We're positive that the charge added was accurate. I know you're more paranoid than usual after the Perez case, but this has to stop."

Mackenzie quashed her urge to argue and gave him a curt nod. It wouldn't be the first time that the higher powers were trying to cover their own asses.

CHAPTER FIFTEEN

The drive was stifling, like the air in the car was saturated with something heavy. Mackenzie fumbled to turn on the air conditioning and pointed it at her. The cool air fanned her face, and she took a steadying breath. But it did little.

It was the silence between her and Nick that was bothering her. He drove with his body tense and eyes glued to the road ahead. Ignoring her.

She licked her lips, wrestling with what to say. He was the one who always knew what to say. "Nick?"

"Hmm?" He didn't spare her a look.

"Are you okay?"

He contemplated before answering. "Yeah."

A part of her wanted to stomp her feet. Instead, she said, "You didn't tell me that you were looking into the sister and her visits to Jeremiah."

They always discussed their theories usually.

"You didn't tell me you've been reviewing evidence in Johnny's case." He responded so quickly it was as if the words had been sitting on the tip of his tongue.

"Rivera told me to. I couldn't say no."

He exhaled and took another turn. "I'll never discourage you from doing your job, Mack. Even if I feel like there's nothing there."

"I know. Did you get any sleep last night?"

He shook his head. "Not really."

She left it at that. "We're here."

The trailer park came into view. The faded, scratched trailers had seen better days and were scattered about at random. It was a sprawling area, right on the border that Lakemore shared with Riverview—a breeding ground for criminals.

"This part doesn't even look like Lakemore." Mackenzie scrunched her nose as Nick found a parking spot.

He scoffed. "That's because you see Lakemore with rose-tinted glasses."

"No, something is different."

"What? Poverty, check. Rainy and unpredictable weather, check. Woods, check."

Her eyes scanned the faces, determined to find a concrete reason. Residents of the trailer park stood outside smoking cigarettes and chatting up with each other. Men dressed in wifebeaters and women in stringy hair and loose T-shirts. The lines on their faces were too deep for their age. "They look dull. Like they don't care."

"Rose-tinted glasses." Nick clicked his tongue.

After parking the car, they made their way to one of the homes that belonged to Jeremiah's sister, Patricia. Her trailer looked just like the others, except for a small crowd gathered around it.

Mackenzie removed her sunglasses. "What's going on?"

"Let's find out."

They navigated their way around the people to the front of the house. A woman wearing a crew T-shirt and a Bluetooth headset stood in front of the stairs, holding a notepad. When they flashed her their credentials, she pressed a button on the headset. "How may I help you?"

"What's happening inside?"

"Oh, right. My boss is in there. We're filming for the documentary so he's going over the scenes and interview questions with her. It's probably best you wait."

"Yeah, don't think so." Mackenzie raised an eyebrow and pushed past her.

The door was ajar. They knocked and entered after a woman told them to "come in". It was a poorly maintained, compact space with broken furniture and strong stench of alcohol and cigarettes. A cross hung on the wall—and next to it a picture of Jeremiah with his sister.

Patricia was a big woman with black hair falling down to her shoulders. She was the spitting image of Jeremiah.

There were also two men in the room. An older, thickset man, wearing a robe and cross around his neck, and the other wiry, his gray hair gelled in spikes. A video camera was placed on a tripod, facing Patricia and the old man.

"Our mother's boyfriend did unspeakable things to Jeremiah when he was only a little boy." Patricia's eyes glinted with tears. "He wanted to hurt me, but Jeremiah would always find a way to hide me or distract him. And then he would... he would do everything to him that he wanted to do to me." She sniffled into her handkerchief.

The filmmaker, Mackenzie assumed, watched, engrossed.

Patricia continued, speaking to the camera, rage slowly spilling out of her with every word. "Monsters aren't born. They're made. The system made him like this by making sure that he never left poverty, that no one ever listened to him, that no one protected him. And then that same system punished him. You can't have people grow up in hell and then expect them not to do hellish things. It's—"

"No, no, no." The filmmaker turned off the camera. "Don't go down that route. Don't blame the system. You do that and it will alienate the viewers."

"But this is how I feel. I'm trying to be honest."

"Your honesty isn't acceptable, Patricia, with all due respect. You can't justify your brother's actions. At all." He spotted Mackenzie and Nick standing at the entry. "This is a private meeting! Who let you in?"

When they introduced themselves, he became friendlier.

"I'm Michael Trelawney."

"Didn't you direct that documentary about the hunger crisis in Yemen?" Nick asked.

"Yes, yes, that was me. Won a few awards for that. No big deal." He puffed out his scrawny chest. "Trying to venture into true crime now. A hot topic. Viewers just eat it up."

Mackenzie looked over at Patricia, who shot daggers at them. She didn't hide the fact that she despised the police and clenched the hand holding the handkerchief into a fist.

"Get out of my house!" she hissed. "I remember you, Detective Blackwood. You sent my brother to jail. I don't want to talk to you."

"Patricia, please. Take a deep breath," the priest tried pacifying her.

"Listen to me, love," Michael said. "This is good for your brother. Let them talk to you. Maybe they'll even agree to feature in the documentary."

"Absolutely not." Mackenzie was horrified.

"Can't blame a bloke for trying. We're all trying to make our living, aren't we? I sent a request to your office, and it was rejected. Do reconsider it. It would really give the whole thing another dimension. Pack a bit of a punch."

She blinked. Only this morning she'd had a mother faint in her arms, worried sick about her missing son. And now, here she was, talking to a man who profited off these brutal crimes. "Don't you have any shame? Jeremiah murdered young boys. It's not... *entertainment*."

Michael bit his lower lip and took off his glasses, the smile wiped off his face. He leaned forward. "You don't get to judge me, Detective. While you go around judging me for merely *reporting* on something someone else did, it's people like *you* who watch these things for entertainment. You discuss it with your friends, tweet, and stay up into the wee hours of the night being utterly fascinated, and then when it's over, you forget all about it. Meanwhile, the families of the victims never sleep a wink ever again. It doesn't make us bad people. This is just the reality we live in."

"Okay. Cool it." Nick raised a hand. "Look, Michael, we need to talk to Patricia, so could you please leave us alone, just for a short time?"

"Sure." Michael put on his glasses and checked his watch. "I'll be back again tomorrow. And, Pastor Giles, we'll record you first. Patricia, *practice*! Don't look *too* sympathetic. Audience will hate you playing the victim." With that he left.

Pastor Giles also stood up to leave when Nick clicked his fingers. "Pastor Giles? I remember you. You were at the trial."

"Yes, yes, I was." He smiled and shook his and Mackenzie's hand. He was in his early seventies with a gentle but forgettable face. "Jeremiah and Patricia have been part of my church since they were kids. I'll give you some privacy."

"No, please stay. I don't trust the cops around here. God knows what they'll say about me," Patricia insisted. "What the hell do you want, Blackwood?"

"How often do you visit Jeremiah?" Mackenzie asked.

"Why?"

"Because we're asking you."

Patricia looked between them, her eyes narrowed. "His lawyer contacted me this morning. Told me that something's up. Are you reopening the investigation into one of the cases he was convicted for?"

"No," Nick retorted. "So? How often?"

"Once a week. He's the only family I have. And you put him in jail."

"Now, now, Patricia," Giles placated her. "Just answer. Don't get angry."

"Does anyone else visit him?" Mackenzie asked.

"Just me and Pastor Giles."

"And has Jeremiah talked to you about anything different recently? Mentioned a name or a place or a person? Anything at all out of the blue?"

Patricia sat back with a sneer. A throaty laugh trickled out of her as she fumbled for a cigarette. She took her time lighting it and inhaled the smoke, enjoying the fact that they were waiting for an answer; capitalizing on the little surge of power she had in that moment. "Look at that. You want me to cooperate with you when we both know how much you hate my brother."

"This is important," Mackenzie emphasized. "Did Jeremiah mention Johnny Cooper by any chance?"

"Who the hell is Johnny Cooper?"

"One of your brother's victims."

"Who cares about him?"

"Patricia!" Pastor Giles shot her an indignant look. "Kindness, Patricia. We've talked about this."

"Where were you on Friday morning?" Nick asked.

"I'm not saying a word without Holly present." She jerked her head. "I know my rights. I won't be bullied. Get out."

Nick stormed out of there, fury written all over his face. Mackenzie lingered behind, despite wanting to chase after him. She turned to Patricia and tried a more diplomatic approach. "Patricia, it would make your life easier if you just tell me where you were on Friday morning. You could call Holly, but do you really want to bother her with small things when you'd rather she focus on your brother?"

Patricia huffed. "I was working."

"What do you do?" Mackenzie noted that, with Nick out of sight, Patricia seemed more receptive.

"I do online administrative work for a travel agency."

"So you work from home?"

"Yes."

"Can anyone confirm your alibi, Patricia?"

"No," she replied tersely.

"Has Jeremiah's behavior changed recently?" Mackenzie addressed both Patricia and Giles this time. "He mention anything new or different?"

"He seems to be in a better mood since the documentary was announced, but that's about it," Giles said. "I hope it has a positive impact by giving him an opportunity to reflect on his actions again."

Patricia rubbed her temples. "That's all we can tell you, Detective. Now, do you mind leaving?"

Mackenzie could see she wouldn't get any more out of her. She thanked them both and left.

Nick was waiting for her outside. "She saw me and just shut down. Did she tell you anything?"

"Not much. She doesn't have an alibi for Friday." Mackenzie tried to keep up with his fast pace back to the car.

"That director—Trelawney. He's a big name. I bet Jeremiah's happy about this. Even if it doesn't end up helping his case, he'll love the attention." Nick grimaced.

"Trelawney too. Can you imagine how much traction it will get if the news gets out that Jeremiah is linked to an ongoing investigation of the missing boys? Add to that the possibility of a faulty conviction and Trelawney is going to be selling this to a streaming giant for millions." The thought of anyone unwittingly benefitting from something like this made her feel sick. Her phone rang. It was Justin. "Hey, you have something?"

"I do, ma'am," he said in his buff voice. "The Latent Print Unit was analyzing the handkerchief found on Lucas and just got back."

"Any hits?" Usually there was a backlog, just like with every lab in the state, but the nature of the case had expedited analysis of their evidence.

"Lucas's prints were on it. And they found a match in IAFIS." He referred to the national fingerprint identification system. "Ian Rowe."

Mackenzie racked her brain for that name. "What's his history?"

"He's a registered sex offender and had a stall selling door pulls at the festival."

She stopped dead. "He was there when the boys disappeared?"

"Yes, ma'am."

CHAPTER SIXTEEN

Mackenzie read the information Justin had forwarded her on Ian Rowe as the car went over another speed bump. Reading in the car always made her feel queasy but she had trouble sitting idle while Nick drove. Fighting the nausea, she read aloud: "Ten years ago, he was written up for indecent exposure in a park. Some parents reported he would hover a lot, just watching kids. His defense was urinating in public. So he got off after paying a fine. But eight years ago, he was caught sexting with a minor. He possessed some explicit pictures on his phone."

"Jesus." Nick's hands clamped around the wheel. "How old was the minor?"

"A fifteen-year-old boy. They met on some shady website." She fought to keep the disgust out of her voice. "So that's a felony. He went to prison, but got out six months ago on parole. And he had to register."

"I'm never letting Luna use the internet," Nick muttered. "There was no evidence of sexual assault in Lucas's case."

Mackenzie's insides twisted. "Not all kinds of sexual assault leave evidence that can be picked up during an autopsy."

Nick killed the engine in front of a dingy-looking halfway house situated next to an alley lined with dumpsters.

Climbing out of the car, Mackenzie's ears were attacked with all sorts of sounds. Animals rattling around in dumpsters. A car backfiring. The vibrating hum of railway tracks beckoning a train that whistled from afar.

"Smells like piss." Nick wrinkled his nose.

The downtrodden halfway house was located in a poor area of Lakemore—not too far from the trailer park at the border of Riverview. Across the street were a small convenience store and a modest apartment building housing people living on welfare. On one side, there were railway tracks spreading wide.

There was a bony man sitting on the steps leading to the front door of the halfway house. Wearing an oversized T-shirt, he read a newspaper. His dark hair grew in curls around a bald patch.

"Looks like him." Mackenzie zoomed in on the picture Justin had extracted from the Washington State Identification System. "He's lost a lot of weight."

"Ian Rowe?" Nick flashed his badge.

Ian eyed them suspiciously from above the newspaper. "I didn't do anything."

Nick sized him up. Usually, he played the good cop—the friendly face and easygoing charm—but this time there was nothing amicable about him. "Why do you think we're here?"

Ian put away the newspaper with a sigh. "I don't know, man. The cops are always after me. Even look at me like I'm some pervert."

"I don't know what reputation you expect to gain after sexting and exchanging pictures with a fifteen-year-old kid," Mackenzie bit out, placing an elbow on the railing.

Ian leaned back, resting the small of his back against the steps— straining to appear nonchalant as the two detectives crowded him. "Everyone knows how corrupt you are. I spent over seven years in prison. Met a lot of guys who shouldn't have even been there in the first place. And a lot of them are serving harsher punishments."

"Like you?" Nick scoffed, unimpressed by Ian's brash confidence.

He scowled. "Whatever, man. What do you want from me?"

"You were at the spring festival on Friday?" Mackenzie asked.

"That's right."

"What were you selling?"

"Random things. Ring holders, door pulls, stuff like that."

"How do you have access to those things?" She took out her diary and began taking notes.

Ian hitched a shoulder. "Work part-time at a furniture shop. One of the guys in the house got me the gig. Some of us help each other out like family."

"Are you aware of the boys who went missing at the festival?"

The train barreled past them, its sound reverberating in the air. Ian's eyes turned shifty and unfocused. "Yes."

"Well, did you see anything?" Nick prodded.

When Ian realized what they were implying, he bared his teeth. "No. It was *packed*. I didn't notice anything wrong."

"Did you talk to any of them?"

He shrugged. "Why would I?"

"Then why don't you tell us how your handkerchief ended up next to the body of the boy who was found dead?" Mackenzie asked.

Ian looked like a deer in headlights, his cocksure behavior replaced by terror. "I didn't do anything!"

"Your fingerprints were on it."

He tried moving away, like it was instinct. But when Mackenzie and Nick threatened to lunge at him, he stilled and raised his hands in defeat, gasping. "Look, I swear I didn't know it was *that* kid."

"What do you mean?" She was running out of patience.

"There was a hotdog stand next to my stall. I saw one kid standing close. He had ketchup smeared all over his chin, so I just offered him my handkerchief," he explained. "But then I got busy with customers and that hotdog stand was very popular. It was almost a stampede! I don't know where the kid went, but I didn't care. It was just a handkerchief." When Mackenzie and Nick continued glaring at him, he persisted. "Our interaction was so fleeting, I didn't even really register his face. I *swear* I had nothing to do with this."

"And how long were you there for?" Nick asked.

"Why? You want to pin the whole thing on me? I know I'm an easy target!"

Mackenzie gritted her teeth. "Listen to me, you piece of shit. You are out on parole. Choose your words carefully."

His nostrils flared, and his neck turned red. "I left before ten."

"That early?" Nick lifted an eyebrow.

"I had to drop off the items I was selling at the store and then go see my parole officer."

"Did anyone see you leave?"

"I don't know." He shrugged. "It was stuffed with people, man. Everything was a blur."

Mackenzie gave him her diary and pen. "Write down the information of your parole officer."

He handed Mackenzie back her diary, after writing down the details. "I'm a victim of the system."

"Yeah, yeah. We've heard that before."

The front door opened, and a tall man with a brawny build poked his head out. "Ian! It's starting!"

Ian stood up unsteadily, suddenly nervous. "Is that all? We're watching the game."

"For now," Mackenzie cautioned, before walking away.

The man at the door must have noticed the holster around Mackenzie's waist. His face changed. With a sneer, he spat on the ground.

"Let's confirm with the parole officer." Nick took the details.

Another train was approaching—this time from the other side. And Mackenzie squinted at the chaos in this little pocket of the town. It was always loud—the ground almost vibrating under their feet and whistles and wheels scratching the air. It smelled foul, with the alleyway populated with overflowing garbage. The constant stream of unpleasantness was grating.

As she got inside the car, Mackenzie wondered if Ian's momentary interaction with Lucas had given rise to a temptation to inflict more harm. And whether he had decided to give in to that temptation.

CHAPTER SEVENTEEN

The clock struck eleven at night when everyone filtered out of the office. Mackenzie and Nick's other cases had been siphoned to other detectives so that they could solely focus on finding Theo and Noah before it was too late.

Mackenzie had headphones on. She drummed her fingers on her desk, waiting for the motion-detecting lights in the hallway to switch off. Once they did, she took off the headphones and stood from her chair. Glancing around the office and making sure she was undoubtedly alone, she sauntered over to Austin's desk.

Her pulse was surprisingly calm. She moved on autopilot—agile and confident.

First, she checked the webcam on Austin's computer. No light. *Off.*

There was a lot of paperwork on Austin's desk. Before she touched anything, she took out her phone and snapped a picture. Then she got to work. Carefully, she sifted through the papers, looking for any details on the investigation.

Mackenzie couldn't afford to get blindsided.

She wanted to avoid looking up the database for the case details, as that would leave a record. Not that she was a suspect or even a person of interest, but for ethical reasons she had to stay away.

But as she flicked through the pages, she felt torn. She wanted to know what happened to Charles, but at the same time she was afraid of what she might find. Then there was this sudden onslaught of paranoia. That strange phone call and someone watching her when she had gone for a run. Were they coincidences? Or was something coming for her? Something to do with Charles?

It seemed like Austin hadn't printed out anything related to Charles's murder. Were there no updates? Or did he take work home? Did he avoid leaving hard copies on his desk because she worked with him in close quarters?

She was about to give up, when she saw a page. It was from the Washington State Patrol Crime Laboratory Division—a forensic ballistics report. It listed the items obtained at the scene, the place and date of sample collection and the conclusions. The ballistics expert concluded the firearm used was a 9mm beretta pistol.

Mackenzie paused. That gun was easy on the recoil. And it wasn't the gun used in the robberies. She knew that because Ned had mentioned in passing that a 0.357 Magnum had been used.

Then there was another page. Charles's wallet and watch were found in the dumpster behind the motel. There was cash inside the wallet. Three hundred dollars. And the watch was worth at least five hundred bucks. He had won it gambling in Vegas, he had told her.

So, this is what had led Austin to believe that Charles wasn't a victim of a robbery. Not only did ballistics not match the other victims, but also his money and watch weren't stolen. Whoever killed him took his belongings to throw them off but had made the rookie mistake of discarding them close to the crime scene. Not the work of a seasoned criminal.

Mackenzie put everything back on his desk the same way as before, pulled up the picture and confirmed that everything was in place.

By the time she had gathered up her things to head home, her stomach was filled with knots.

CHAPTER EIGHTEEN

March 6

Mackenzie laid out the pictures of Tim Cooper, Patricia Wozniak, and Ian Rowe on the table in the conference room. She picked up a cookie and took a bite. It was like biting into a rock. "Yuck." She wanted to spit it out instantly, but remembered she was at work.

Above their pictures was Johnny's picture. She had spent an hour reading Nick's notes and witness statements from the time Johnny had disappeared. As of yet, she hadn't come across anything out of the ordinary. But there was still lots to get through.

Meanwhile, she had gotten to know Johnny a lot.

His favorite superhero was Wonder Woman. When his friends had teased him saying, "she's a girl", he'd replied "so?".

He wanted to set up a lemonade stand to earn money to buy a video game.

He had a knack for languages, especially Spanish.

While his friends preferred to go out and play football, he preferred staying indoors and playing with GI Joes.

He wanted to grow up to be a chef.

Mackenzie's chest felt tight as she stared at the picture. Johnny Cooper never got to grow up, never got to buy the video game he had his eye on, never got to even celebrate his tenth birthday. His life had been snuffed out, while the world continued to spin.

Nick walked into the conference room, looking fresh. For the first time in days, his hair was combed and his chiseled jaw freshly shaven.

Mackenzie caught a whiff of spice and leather. "Why are you wearing so much aftershave? You even look like you showered."

"Jeez, thanks, Mack."

He placed another picture next to Patricia's: Pastor Giles. He was the character witness for Jeremiah at his trial—Mackenzie recalled from the notes she'd read.

They displayed the crime scene pictures of Lucas's homicide. There were faint drag marks in the brown soil. Another picture had measurements printed over the marks. Little flags and identification markers were buried around it. There were some shoe prints, but volunteers had trampled the crime scene before it was secured.

"The unit concluded that the dimensions of the dragging marks matched Lucas's size. They didn't find any blood at the scene from Lucas's head injury, and the drag marks look very clean, not consistent with anyone struggling while being dragged," Nick said. "All this suggests that Lucas was likely already dead when he was placed on that rock. Is Becky still running the tox screen?"

"Yeah, she'll have the results anytime now." Mackenzie checked the clock. "The unit has taken samples from his clothes to see if they can catch something that can give us a clue as to where he was being kept."

Nick rubbed the back of his neck. "Yeah, our killer must have known that those woods would be searched first, since the festival happened at the edge. The body wasn't left too far into the woods."

"They wanted us to find him obviously. The question is: if we don't get to them on time, where are they going to leave the next kid?"

Nick's lips quivered. "And who is the next kid?"

Mackenzie tried to keep her emotions out of it. Even if Nick looked put together on the outside today, she knew the case was slowly eating at him on the inside. At a time when he was on edge, she had to be strong for the both of them. Her phone rang. "Hello?"

"Mack, it's Becky."

"Hey, do you have anything?" She put her on speakerphone for Nick to listen to as well.

"I'm sending you the report now, but thought I should discuss the main findings on the phone. The toxicology results came back this morning. Lucas's plasma sample had significant levels of 7-aminoflunitrazepam, which is a degradation product of flunitrazepam."

"English, please," Nick groaned.

"Rohypnol," Mackenzie answered instead. "The date-rape drug."

"In post-mortem specimens, it starts to degrade, so we look for its degradation products as markers," Becky said. "Rohypnol concentration in his blood is estimated to be around eighty micrograms per liter. Which puts us just under the fatal dosage for adults."

"It was enough to knock him out?" Nick inquired.

"Definitely. The effects are felt within thirty minutes of being roofied and last up to hours. I also detected ketamine in his urine. An anesthetic drug."

"And both are odorless and tasteless?" Mackenzie placed her hands on her waist.

"That's right. The kid probably had no idea he was drugged."

When they hung up, Mackenzie flipped through the pages of the forensic report again.

"Why drug him with Rohypnol *and* ketamine?" Nick wondered at her side.

Idly, she registered how he hadn't turned to playing with cigarettes or a lighter since yesterday. "Ketamine reduces pain and just generally dulls all feeling; it would probably make him less scared. And remember how Lucas was hit on the head? Right on the bone. Instant death."

"So our killer gives Lucas the date rape drug to knock him out and ketamine as an extra insurance that he doesn't feel any pain?"

There was a knock on the door and Jenna breezed in holding a USB stick. She regarded Nick, pointedly ignoring Mackenzie, like she always did. "Elliot and Spencer sent a copy of that video. The one with Jeremiah approaching his victim."

"Thanks, Jenna."

Jenna nodded and hightailed out of there just as quickly.

"Didn't realize I was invisible. That's a useful superpower." Mackenzie took the flash drive from Nick. Even though she had been the one to ask for it, Jenna had handed it to him. The junior detective had always preferred Nick to Mackenzie.

"Jenna has been busy coordinating the search efforts." Nick's expression was somber. He was staring at the stick like it contained a recap of every nightmare he'd ever had.

"I should watch this." Mackenzie started awkwardly, plugging it into her laptop. "Rivera asked me—"

"Yeah, you told me. Mind if I sit in?"

"Oh?"

"I can give you context." He shrugged.

Was this wise? Rivera had told her to verify all the evidence—a fresh pair of eyes. Mackenzie could review everything having Nick by her side. Not only would he appreciate being involved, but also she'd feel more comfortable not doing anything "behind his back".

"Of course."

The date and timestamp were on the bottom right. It was the view of a dirt road surrounded by scarce trees and utility poles. There was a main street visible around the corner, with the dirt road veering off it. Her finger trembled over the touchpad. She knew there was nothing violent in the video; it only showed Jeremiah approaching Johnny. But it was the last sighting of the boy. Perhaps just hours before he was strangled to death.

She swallowed hard and hit play.

The video blinked several times, showing an empty road and some cars zipping by in the corner. The trees swayed in the gentle September wind. The time was seven thirty in the morning. Five minutes later, Johnny appeared at the end of the dirt road, almost skipping while walking. He wore blue jeans and a yellow T-shirt, a black backpack and a red fanny pack. He paused, closer to the camera, like he saw someone.

Jeremiah came into the frame thirty seconds later, his hair shorter and appearance far less haggard than what Mackenzie had seen. He was also much larger—his giant frame engulfed Johnny's little frame.

Johnny walked past him, but Jeremiah said something and he turned around. At twenty minutes to eight, Johnny went east, disappearing from the frame. Never to be seen or heard from again.

Jeremiah watched Johnny and then slipped out of frame by walking in the opposite direction.

The video ended, and Mackenzie and Nick sat in charged silence. There was no audio, and the quality was too poor for lip-reading. The last captured moments of Johnny were translucent and foggy.

"The prosecution authenticated the tape I assume?" Mackenzie's voice broke the silence.

Nick nodded. "They established that Jeremiah made contact with Johnny the day he disappeared. He was later found strangled, with his tongue removed."

"So he must have seen Johnny again, perhaps followed him."

"He denied it. But he denied everything." He pressed the heel of his hands into his eyelids. "We argued that he must have followed Johnny. Ironically, the footage is from his surveillance. Jeremiah had a shed there with one camera by the door. That's why he didn't approach him right away. It all fit. Jeremiah sent me messages with clues for where the next body would be found.

There was no message for Johnny. But I assumed that maybe I just didn't get it."

Mackenzie's synapses fired in all directions. "Jeremiah said that that's the first and last time he saw Johnny?"

"Yep."

"What was his alibi?" She rubbed her head mindlessly. Realizing wisps of baby hair were sticking out, she hitched a breath and pulled her hair back tighter.

"That he was with his sister. But she would obviously lie for him. It wasn't airtight."

"Why was Johnny taking this route to school? It's kind of dangerous."

"Tim told me that usually Johnny walked with his friends on his usual route, but around a week before he vanished, he had become withdrawn from his friends and everyone. He liked being alone. So he changed his route too. To avoid interaction."

"I see…" She remembered Tim saying Johnny was down in the days leading to his disappearance. "So, let's say someone *suspects* that Jeremiah didn't kill Johnny. I wonder why though? *If* it's not Jeremiah behind this, then why would anyone think that?"

"They're just messing with us, Mack."

"I don't like this," Mackenzie said in a tight voice. "Being held at gunpoint by this lunatic. And, even if someone else did kill Johnny, what are the chances he'll stick to his word and let the kids go if we keep our end of the bargain?"

"It's literally a hostage situation." Nick let out a mirthless laugh. "We can't rely on negotiating with him."

"We need to at least explore the possibility that Jeremiah didn't do it though," Mack said gently. "I'm *not* saying he didn't—" Mack added hastily as Nick's expression turned fierce—"but if that's what our killer believes, we need to at least show willing. And it can't hurt to interrogate the people who knew Johnny again—there must be a connection. I say we start with Johnny's stepmother. But before that, I want to go and see Ian's parole officer."

"Oh, I already did."

She froze. "What? When?"

"Just this morning. She confirmed that Ian showed up at eleven thirty for his appointment and appeared normal."

Mackenzie didn't know what to do with her hands. "Okay… okay."

"Mack, it was on my way. Just an impulse decision." He shrugged casually. "I was about to tell you, but then Becky called and the video arrived."

"Right. Of course."

It wasn't a big deal. They didn't always check all the leads together. It wasn't the most efficient use of their time. But then why couldn't she brush it off easily?

Mackenzie's eyes glided to the television mounted on the wall in the lounge area outside the conference room. Usually it played either news or football matches 24/7, but since the abduction of the boys, primetime broadcasts showed continuous coverage of the case. The news had filtered onto the radio as well. The entire town was playing detective.

The screen showed fourth-graders standing in a row in front of their school. Each held a square-shaped white canvas with the same words scribbled in their squiggly handwriting in vivid colors.

Bring our friends home.

Ruth Norman stood behind them, slender and tall. Her chin tilted up as she faced the camera with a resolute expression. Her lips trembled, and the tip of her nose was red. She took shivering breaths like she was on the cusp of bursting into tears.

The children looked forlorn; their lower lips jutting out and their eyes dim. They were too young to fathom the violence of the situation. The innocence in their grieving was palpable. While they stood in solidarity, their teacher stood like a martyr.

CHAPTER NINETEEN

Mackenzie and Nick stood in front of the modest, single-story house where Johnny's stepmother lived. There was no porch, just a house on green pasture, and no fence around the property. The sky was a rich blue with blazing sunlight. It wasn't the rich part of town, but spring could paint beauty on any patch of ugliness. With colors blossoming and nature waking up after a freezing-cold winter, it was *supposed* to be happier times for Lakemore.

"The last time I was here, it was to tell Heather and Tim that we had finally found Johnny." Nick winced at the memory.

Mackenzie eyed him suspiciously. He stood still like a statue; his hands weren't twitching for a smoke. "I'll take the lead on this one. That okay?"

"Fair. Let's go," he said, trudging toward the door.

Three knocks later, a woman pushed open the dingy door. She had curly dark hair and large pores on her skin. "You?" She recognized Nick.

"Mrs. Cooper, we need to talk. This is my partner, Detective Price."

"What's happened now?"

"Can we come inside?"

She made a show of being inconvenienced, but gestured them inside.

Mackenzie casually glanced around the simple living room with its old and worn-out furniture. There was only one picture, perched on a table. It was of Heather with a man around her age. Not a single one of Johnny or Tim.

Heather threw herself on a couch by the window and crossed her legs. She opened a little container and pinched a small amount of tobacco, placing it between her cheek and gum. "Well, get on with it."

"We need to talk about Johnny," Mackenzie said, as Nick lowered himself into an armchair.

"Why?" Heather chewed, giving them a lazy look. "We buried him. It's over."

Mackenzie's eyebrows shot up. Heather's callousness didn't sit well with her. She took out her pocket notebook and began taking notes as she asked the questions. "Did Johnny ever say anything to you that felt out of the blue? Anyone you saw around a little too often in the weeks leading up to his disappearance?"

"You asked the same questions all those years ago, and I'll say the same thing. I don't know. Plus, why do you care? Isn't his killer in prison?"

"We're… looking into his death again," Mackenzie admitted carefully. Heather was Johnny's legal guardian; it was their obligation to keep her in the loop.

She cracked her neck and scoffed. "Don't you have more important things to do? Like finding those missing kids? Johnny's dead. Nothing is going to change that."

Mackenzie stifled a gasp and looked at Nick, who shook his head.

"He was your son," she reminded her.

"*Step*son. I married my husband. Too bad he came with two kids, but I thought what the hell?" She shrugged, sprawling on the couch. "We'll manage. They have their dad. I'll just help out. Then in two years, my husband died in a car accident and left me solely responsible for those two brats who were never mine. I didn't sign up to be a *parent*." She spat the word like it was an offense.

There was bitterness stuck on Heather's face. Like it had become a part of her, seeped into her skin and coiled the muscles of her face into a perpetual frown.

"When was the last time you spoke with Tim?" Mackenzie asked.

"When he turned eighteen. He moved out, and I haven't seen him since. Fortunately."

Heather was shameless in her lack of any affection toward her stepchildren. She almost wore it as a badge of honor.

Mackenzie glared at her, but Heather was unfazed. She continued the line of inquiry, trying to disguise her disgust. "Other than Tim, was Johnny close to anyone else? Some aunt or uncle, perhaps?"

"There was no family he was close to, I can tell you that. My husband's sister died a long time ago. There's nobody else."

"Whenever a victim of Jeremiah was found, their families sometimes received letters and care packages from people," Nick said. "Did anyone send anything to you after Johnny was found? Something extravagant? Or did anyone ever ask you too many questions?"

Mackenzie knew where Nick was going with this. There were instances of people's curiosity about a murder victim spiraling into a dangerous obsession.

Heather rolled her eyes. "Nothing like that. There were some nosy neighbors and a lot of casseroles that lasted me weeks. Look, my friends are coming over. Can you leave now?"

"If you think of anything, will you let us know?" Mackenzie asked.

"Yeah. I'll get right on it," she muttered and waved her hand to dismiss them.

Mackenzie looked around the house one last time and ached for the childhood Tim and Johnny must have endured.

She stomped her feet on the way back to the car.

"Mack, slow down," Nick called.

"I want to throttle her!" Mackenzie growled. Her rage was white-hot. "What's wrong with her? He was just a kid. A *child*. Who talks like that?"

"Yeah, I was pretty taken aback when I met her for the first time too." He put on his sunglasses.

She took her keys to unlock the door, but her shaking hands dropped them on the ground.

"Maybe I should drive? You know what they say about road rage." He raised his hand, and Mackenzie tossed him the keys. She climbed inside the car and yanked at the seat belt with extra force, locking it in the buckle.

Nick started the engine and glided the car away from the neighborhood. Mackenzie watched as the Cooper household's reflection in the side mirror got smaller, rage still coursing through her. Real mother or not, Heather's cruelty was despicable.

"I told you Johnny is a dead end. There's nothing there to find." Nick sighed.

Mackenzie pulled out her phone and opened Maps. "You said that Ian's parole officer confirmed he showed up at eleven thirty?"

"Yeah."

She put a pin on the parole and probations office in Lakemore and the location of the spring festival. "It would have taken him forty minutes to get there from the festival. But he left an hour and a half before… didn't he say he had to stop by the store first?"

"Yeah, to drop off the door pulls and whatever he was selling." Nick gave her the address of the store.

Mackenzie did the calculation in her head. "It takes ten minutes to get to the store and assuming he spent fifteen minutes putting everything back… still it would take him an hour to get to his meeting."

"With traffic it can take an extra thirty," Nick added. "But we don't know how bad traffic was that day on that route."

"His story of just handing out his handkerchief to a kid is credible, I guess. We did confirm it was ketchup, and it had both their prints." Mackenzie's grip on the phone went limp. "Besides, the note, the lack of evidence… it doesn't feel like a crime of opportunity. This was premeditated; meticulously planned."

"Someone is using Johnny to make this into a game and throw us off." Nick's face was hard, like he had decided. But Mackenzie saw a flicker of doubt in his eyes briefly.

"Unless this is Jeremiah's doing from behind bars to somehow help his case."

"Or this is Jeremiah's revenge." His smile was bitter. "All these years he got bored and found someone to mess with us on his behalf."

Mackenzie didn't voice the possibility that it could genuinely be a case of vigilante justice, someone who believed Johnny still needed justice. There was someone with motive, and he didn't have a solid alibi. But she didn't want to mention Tim again until she had his records—and to access them they needed something concrete.

"Let's ask Jenna to confirm Ian was telling the truth and that he did swing by the furniture store," Mackenzie said, feeling a sense of control return to the situation. She liked making lists and plans and moving forward, not being sitting ducks for their killer. "A sex offender with a history with underage boys was in the vicinity of this abduction. I want to be one hundred percent sure."

"Agreed." Nick hesitated. "So, how're you doing with everything?"

"What do you mean?" The question caught her by surprise.

"Your dad? The investigation?"

"Oh." Her chest deflated.

"I know we haven't really had a chance to talk since Lucas. I wanted to check in with you."

"I don't like it," Mackenzie confessed.

"What do you mean?"

Her unstable family life and what had transpired in her childhood had been Mackenzie's closely guarded secret for the last twenty years. Nick knew that her father had been an alcoholic and that her home life was disturbed and ugly as a result. But he didn't know that Charles used to hit Melody. He didn't know that Mackenzie had buried a body.

Mackenzie also hadn't revealed the secret to her ex-husband in the six years that they were together. That was a box she had decided to keep locked forever. Now a detective was on a mission to find out the truth, which could mean Mackenzie's hypocrisy and lies would finally be exposed for the world to see. She almost felt violated, like someone had the authority to sift through the dark pieces of her life. Like her life wasn't just *hers* anymore.

"I mean I don't like people poking their nose into my business." She licked her lips.

"Did Austin tell you why they ruled out their previous theory?"

"Nope. I asked about it when we talked first, but he didn't give me an answer."

"You know you can talk to me about it right?" He glanced at her. "I know I've been a little out of it. But I'll be there if you need me."

"I know." She looked out the window; only a strip of blurry green was constant, like they were in a tunnel. It wasn't that Mackenzie didn't trust Nick; she knew he would take her secret to his grave. But she didn't want to burden him. He might have been fidgeting less and looking sharper, but the pain of the case never left his eyes. It was all too personal for him.

And just like with Sterling, she didn't want him to look at her differently. Everything was at stake. Not only her relationships but also her career—the one she had worked hard and tirelessly to cement. The revelation could unravel her entire life, and she could lose everything.

Too much honesty could be just as harmful as deception. She had to find the right balance.

CHAPTER TWENTY

By the time Mackenzie and Nick reached the station, Lakemore's weather had plummeted along with Mackenzie's mood. The bright and airy afternoon had dissolved into gloomy skies, the colors dulled as though a large shadow had curtained the town. When Mackenzie got out of the car, she felt her hair immediately gain volume and spring into curls. Uneasiness clawed at her skin, coaxing her to fix herself.

"I got to take this." Nick frowned at his phone and wandered away.

"Sure." She spotted Austin weaving his way around the cars in the parking lot, heading toward her.

Her heart rose to her throat. Had he found out that she was snooping around his desk?

Taking a deep breath, she looked at her reflection in the window and rearranged her bobby pins with shaking hands. Salvaging some of her armor, she turned to Austin right in time.

"Detective Price—"

"You can call me Mack," she said with a forced smile.

"Right. Mack." He tested the word.

Austin wore a black raincoat and played with his keys. His blonde hair was in perfect curls around his head. When he smiled, a dimple dented his cheek.

"Where are you going?" She tried sounding casual.

"Salem."

"Oh, Oregon? That's a long drive. Almost three hours."

"Yep." He tossed the keys in his hands, giving Mackenzie a smile that said he knew what she was up to. He always looked at her with a calculating gleam in his eyes. She knew he was expecting her to prod, and she wanted to—which is exactly why she gave him a curt nod and shouldered past him.

"Detective Price!" Austin called out, already forgetting Mackenzie's suggestion to call her Mack.

"Yeah?"

"Since you're here, I might as well ask now. Did your mother ever mention anyone by the name of Damien Price?"

Damien Price. She scoured through her memory, drawing a blank. "Doesn't ring a bell. Who is he?"

"Robert's brother."

Her heart hammered against her ribs. Robert had a brother. Was he still waiting for answers all these years later? Did he still harbor a hope that his brother would return?

"Are you okay?" Austin narrowed his eyes.

Mackenzie nodded, her joints feeling heavy. "I... I just never knew he had a brother."

"Okay. Well, see you later."

He got inside his car and pulled out of the parking lot, leaving Mackenzie standing ashen-faced. She had often wondered if Robert had any family. But now she had a name. She had confirmation. Damien Price. A man whose brother she had buried in the woods behind Hidden Lake.

An onslaught of rain fell around her. Water collected in her boots, soaked her clothes, and seeped into her hair. She had frozen, unable to move a muscle as the sight of Robert's bloodied body on the kitchen floor swarmed her mind.

"Mack!" Nick cried, pulling her arm. "Get inside!"

She let him drag her back to the station.

You have to help me bury him. Melody's voice was stronger than the pitter-patter of the rain.

Once inside, warm air slammed into her and a blanket was put around her shoulders. The scenery possessing her mind fragmented and she registered Nick panting in front of her, soaking wet. "What happened to you outside?"

"I was thinking." She avoided his eyes and headed to their office on the second floor. "Who were you talking to?"

"Dad called." He rolled his eyes. "The case is picking up steam on news channels in Seattle. And there was one more thing. Austin contacted him."

"Why?" She paused in her tracks.

"He was the one who told you that your father was lying about his name. Austin just wants to interview him again."

Mackenzie pled. "I'm so sorry. I hate your family being dragged into this mess."

"Not your fault."

Back at her desk, she fired open her computer. She had set up a Google alert for any news relating to Theo, Noah, Lucas, and Jeremiah. There was one notification and a link to a video.

A swanky man for some entertainment network sat across from Michael Trelawney.

"*Mr. Trelawney, a little bird told us that you're working on something new and that not a lot of people know about this secret project.*" The journalist waggled his eyebrows.

Trelawney threw his head back and chuckled, flattered by the attention. "*I'll tell you what. It is going to be raw, gritty, and uncomfortable.*"

"*You won't reveal any details to us at all?*"

"*It's going to be a surprise. But I promise to take you on an unforgettable journey.*"

"It just keeps getting worse and worse." Mackenzie felt sick to her stomach. Jeremiah's reign of terror on innocent children was being packaged into an intriguing tale for mass consumption. Mackenzie wrapped the blanket closer to her body, the back of her teeth chattering from the cold. "Did you ever suspect Heather of killing Johnny?"

It was a heavy question. Heather might be cold-hearted, but to imagine she'd be capable of murdering her stepson was blood-curdling. Unfortunately, it wasn't unheard of.

Nick hesitated, and Mackenzie wondered if she'd made a mistake by going down that road again.

"I did," he replied after a beat. "Heather's alibi for that morning was that she slept in late—"

"Oh, so that's not an alibi really—"

"With her boyfriend."

"Oh." She frowned.

"And when it was confirmed that Johnny's tongue was cut out, I crossed her off the list. She was never made aware of that detail. Anyway, I'm taking Luna out for dinner. Probably will go home and shower first though. Do you want to join?"

"*Excuse me?*" Mackenzie almost shrieked.

Nick sighed. "Join for *dinner*, Mack."

"Oh, next time. I have some work to catch up on." She grimaced, cheeks burning, and turned to her desk, randomly opening files. Nick chuckled behind her as she yelled. "Get out!"

Finn was working on his desk, too engrossed by a report and the DMV database open on his computer. There was a fresh cup of coffee on Dennis's desk, the steam gushing out in swirls. She could hear the faint sounds of him in a meeting in Sully's office. The rest of the team was out on field or gone home early.

The uniform was following up on all the tips they were receiving from the special hotline. The Sheriff's Office and volunteers were combing through the woods thoroughly, looking to spot any evidence. A small team had been set up to coordinate with departments in Tacoma, Riverview, and Seattle to chase up on any leads or sightings.

But it felt like Theo and Noah had vanished into thin air.

Mackenzie opened a tab incognito and looked up *Damien Price*. There were way too many people by that name. Remembering that Austin was headed to Salem, Oregon, she narrowed down her search. She had no idea what Damien looked like, but twenty minutes after throwing in Robert's name, she found him and his address.

Damien was a software engineer at a company.

Legally, Robert Price had been her father, which made Damien kind of her uncle. Mackenzie's heart sank. How could she ever face him after what she had done?

She opened Johnny's case file, trying to push her spiraling thoughts about Robert to the back of her brain. Even though she had involved Nick earlier, it was easier to review all the previous evidence and statements without him, since she was expressly looking for mistakes. It still felt wrong though.

Striving to keep an impartial eye, she studied everything in detail. Jeremiah had already been arrested for killing other boys by the time Johnny's remains were discovered. Even though everyone was almost certain that Jeremiah was the killer, Nick had still conducted a thorough investigation.

"Johnny never reached school," she whispered to herself. "And on the video he was alive at twenty minutes to eight. Which means something happened in those twenty minutes."

Jeremiah's alibi was that he had gone to see his sister after his chance meeting with Johnny. But there was no proof except for Patricia's word, which was unreliable.

Mackenzie leaned back on her chair and looked at the ceiling above. A crack ran through it. She stared at the sliver of black, concentrating hard on the facts. Patricia lived in a trailer park. Why didn't anyone else see Jeremiah?

She straightened with a snap and flipped the pages. Nick had asked uniform to ask Patricia's neighbors if they saw anything. She read through the statements—they all denied it. But then something caught her attention. Three of the neighbors mentioned that there was a commotion in one of the trailers.

A robbery followed by some domestic disturbance.

Many reported that they were too distracted by that to pay attention to who was going in and out of Patricia's trailer. They also said the cops were called and someone was arrested.

Not unusual for a place like that, but still something about it niggled at Mackenzie.

She accessed their local database to see if a case was registered on that date from that area. There was one—charges of theft and trespassing were filed with the Special Investigations Unit—not the Detectives Unit, which she was a part of. To access the details, she needed Rivera's permission.

Mackenzie made a mental note to get on it tomorrow. She couldn't put a finger on it, but it bothered her. As she left—more than an hour later—she couldn't shake off the hunch that there was something there for her discover.

CHAPTER TWENTY-ONE

Mackenzie parked her car in the driveway just as the stars began appearing in the sky. She was about to shut the door behind her when she heard a grunt and a thud.

Her next-door neighbor, Irene, had fallen off a hammock in her front yard.

"Irene?" Mackenzie sprinted to her. "Are you okay?"

Irene was on the ground, moaning. "Ouch. I fell the wrong way and hurt my wrist."

Mackenzie helped her get up and looked at the hammock untied on one end. "You didn't set it up properly."

"That's mildly embarrassing." She stood up and touched her wrist. "I thought it'd be nice to take a nap under the stars."

Mackenzie inspected her wrist, and Irene winced. "It's a bit tender. Do you have any ointment?"

"No. I'll just put ice on it."

"I have an ointment that will help more. Come with me."

"Are you sure? You just got back from work," Irene protested meekly. "I don't want to bother you."

"Don't worry about it."

Mackenzie led Irene to her house and pushed the door open, ushering her inside to the kitchen area. Once again, she missed coming home to the smell of cooked food. Sterling would usually have whipped something up for dinner. Now her house smelled like nothing.

"Have a seat. It's somewhere in the medicine cabinet." Mackenzie opened a cabinet and fished out a box, while suppressing a yawn.

"Working long hours?"

"It's just this case." She shook her head, a burning ache budding behind her eyes. "I'm sure you've been following the news. There's understandably a lot of pressure."

"That sounds rough. But that's what I've read about small towns. That everything and everyone are connected."

Mackenzie handed her the tube. "Especially if you're in law enforcement. I wish I could just solve a murder without having to worry about media and politics. Go to some idyllic English village and become a sleuth."

"Like Miss Marple?" Irene rubbed the ointment on her wrist.

"Exactly like Miss Marple."

"That does sound delightful."

Mackenzie relaxed, and then her eyes caught something. There was an impression in the rug that didn't align with the leg of one of the chairs. The armchair had been moved slightly—just a few inches. She never would have noticed if it weren't for the groove.

A cold chill travelled down her spine. Was someone in the house?

"Thank you for this," Irene said, standing up. "I really appreciate it. I should head back home now."

Mackenzie held her face in forced composure. "Anytime. I was wondering, did anyone come by my house today?"

"Hmm." Irene twisted her lips, thinking hard. "There was a delivery guy outside your door around the afternoon, I think. But that's it. I didn't see him drop anything off though."

"Right."

Closing the door behind Irene, Mackenzie inched closer to the armchair. Cold sweat matted her back, making her blouse stick closer to her skin. She gulped for air. Maybe she was overthinking it. It was possible that she had moved the armchair inadvertently during cleaning and only noticed now. Though she hadn't ordered anything, so there was no reason for a delivery man to show up. He might simply have been looking for the correct address—hence there was nothing left for her.

That must be it.

How would anyone enter her house anyway? No one had the key, and there were no signs of a break-in.

She took a strained breath and went upstairs to draw herself a bath. But as she sank into the hot water, her muscles knotted even tighter. Charles's death had already left her paranoid. And now it seemed more likely that his death wasn't a result of some robbery gone wrong, she felt like a ghost was haunting her.

CHAPTER TWENTY-TWO

March 7

Lucas's body had been released to his family more than twenty-four hours ago. Today was the day they were burying him. It was a beautiful day. Poppies sprang to life around the church. The black spire of the church pierced a stark blue clear sky. A twisty, cobbled path led to the entrance. Next to the wooden double doors was a framed picture of Lucas, a growing pile of flowers placed in front of it.

Mackenzie leaned against the door of the car in her sunglasses, sipping on iced tea. Nick sat on the hood drinking coffee. They faced the church. She couldn't tear her eyes away from Lucas's face, grinning at the camera with dimples on either side. Mrs. Williams had told them that, on the day of the field trip, Lucas had woken up before the alarm even went off. For a moment Mackenzie closed her eyes and imagined what it would be like to be Lucas's mother that morning, to wake up with bleary confusion as Lucas ran into the room. She'd want to berate him at first, but seeing him beaming with joy, she would wrap her arms around him and tickle him. Then she'd slip out of bed and remind him to start getting ready, while she packed his lunch. She'd watch him sprint back to his room, hearing his small feet slapping against the wood. Now, Lucas was gone, and she'd never hear that sound again.

"Mack?"

Mackenzie jumped, coming out of her daze. "What?"

"Were you listening to anything I said?"

Her eyes were damp. She sighed a breath of relief that they were hidden behind shades as she wiped them discreetly. "I zoned out. Sorry."

"I said it's a big turnout despite it being a Thursday. The church is full. The mayor came too."

Right on cue, an old couple walked past them carrying a bouquet. They couldn't even stand straight and the man used a walking stick. But they left flowers for Lucas in front of his picture.

"I don't have the courage to face Lucas's parents. You know me, I'm too awkward with things like that," Mackenzie said, uncomfortable, wanting to go to the office and talk to Rivera about giving her access to the other case file. But Nick had suggested meeting at the church on the way to work.

"I… I went to every kid's funeral," Nick confessed, tightening his grip around the cup.

"Oh?"

"Out of respect and to keep an eye out. Especially when we realized it was the work of a serial killer, I thought maybe he attended his victims' funerals to get his rocks off."

"I don't see anyone suspicious right now. But I did call the Sheriff's Office this morning to get an update on the search," Mackenzie informed him, her resolve hardening to bring back Theo and Noah alive before it was too late. "They're almost done and have inspected all the cabins and sheds in the surrounding area. Considering the nature of the case, the judge signed a blanket search warrant. Unfortunately, they haven't found anything yet. But they're going to continue to keep looking."

"Another week I'm assuming? To cover the other half of the woods?"

"Yes. The other half is a bit tricky because of the terrain, but a record number of people have volunteered." If it were up to

Mackenzie she would have joined them, inspecting every inch of Lakemore if she could. But as a detective she didn't do that kind of grunt work anymore.

Nick's smile didn't reach his eyes. "Wonder if those kids know that the entire town is rallying behind them. They have a big army."

"Was it like this before?"

"Yeah. He'd take someone, and they'd be found dead a week later. That one week would be hell."

"It's a beautiful day, and I hate it," Mackenzie confessed. The kiss of sunshine on her skin felt repulsive under the circumstances.

"Are you okay?" His dark eyes bore into hers. She knew the concern behind them was genuine, but she could also see how weary he was.

"Yeah," she lied. "You?"

"Yeah," he lied too.

She looked around, when her eyes caught something. A figure stood next to the church by the flowerbed, wearing a bright yellow jacket that was too conspicuous. "Who's that?"

Nick angled his head, squinting. "I don't know."

"Looks like a woman based on height and frame. Plus that bag." Mackenzie began to cross the street to get closer. Nick hopped off the hood of the car and chucked the cup straight into a trashcan.

The woman's side profile was visible, but she wore a hood, concealing her hair. Her yellow tote bag with ladybugs on it almost blended with the vines crawling up the walls next to her.

It was an odd place to stand—not in front of the church but on the side. Did she not want to be seen? Why was she just hovering there? Was she waiting for someone?

Mackenzie and Nick were closing the distance when the doors to the church opened and sad faces spilled out. Mackenzie stood on her toes to look over the top of the heads. But the woman was gone.

"Who was she?" Mackenzie asked, scanning the surroundings for her.

Nick shrugged. "This case is all anyone is talking about these days. A lot of people are just curious and come to watch."

They left the church in silence, wondering about the woman.

CHAPTER TWENTY-THREE

Back at the station, Rivera motioned Mackenzie and Nick into her office. This case was testing the entire police force. Even the imposing lieutenant looked like she hadn't slept a wink.

Rivera was an active participant in all their cases. She exercised a balanced amount of control—demanding efficiency without micromanaging. Mackenzie often felt her demeanor reflected her own—steely, a little standoffish—and liked her for it. She was the wall between them and the political powers. While Mackenzie and Nick dealt with reluctant witnesses and contradicting evidence, Rivera had to appease nervous politicians and give answers to people who didn't understand the nuances involved in an investigation.

She stood behind her chair, cracking her neck and rubbing her shoulders. "Sully updated me on your last meeting with him, but I wanted to check again. Have you made any progress? Please, sit down."

Mackenzie took a seat. "The woods are still being searched—"

"Right. The sheriff called this morning. Their office along with the patrol and volunteers are on top of it." She pinched the bridge of her nose, pacing back and forth. "There's a bigger possibility that they aren't being held anywhere in the woods. I doubt our killer would be that stupid. Do you have any new leads?"

"We found a link to Ian Rowe, a convicted sex offender," Mackenzie said. "The handkerchief found next to Lucas belonged to him. He has a sound explanation and an alibi."

"What's his alibi?"

"We have accounted for the time between when he left the festival and met his parole officer. He swung by the furniture store, as reported by several eyewitnesses. Jenna confirmed it."

"Okay, what else you got?" Her eyes hopped between them, hungry for answers.

"Patricia. Jeremiah's sister would do *anything* for him," Mackenzie assured her. "She's on our radar. She even refused to cooperate with us without a lawyer."

"What does she do for a living?"

"She works from home for some travel agency," Nick answered. "Managing their website and stuff."

"What was her alibi for the abduction?"

"Working from home. And she lives alone," Mackenzie said.

Rivera pinched her bottom lip. "She could just log in and then go wherever she has to. It's not really a strong alibi. Send uniform guys to ask neighbors if they remember seeing Patricia leave that morning." She dragged her hands down her face. Her phone trilled with a notification. She looked at it and slammed it on the table with force. "I have to meet with the mayor in an hour." Mackenzie and Nick exchanged a tense look as Rivera fell on the chair, looking uncharacteristically flustered. "The mayor is worried about re-election."

"Of course, he is." Mackenzie snorted. "During the Erica Perez murder case, his only concern was how his campaign funds would get affected and now this."

"Lakemore has always had high crime rates, but now his opponent has a new platform. *Children aren't safe in Lakemore.* The mayor's approval rating has gone down. If the election were to happen anytime soon, he would lose by a landslide."

"Then maybe he deserves to lose," Nick said in a clipped tone.

"I'm not a fan of the guy. Trust me." Rivera sighed, exasperated. "I don't like adding pressure because I trust my detectives to know the gravity of the situation. But this time we're dealing with something else altogether. Anyway, let me know what happens with Patricia."

"Can we talk, Lieutenant?" Mackenzie asked in a small voice.

"Nick, could you give us a moment?" Rivera gave him a strained smile.

From the corner of her eye, Mackenzie saw Nick slowly stand up. His eyes were trained on her, but she needed to check this alone first—to see if there was anything in it. Nick was too close to this for her to start sharing her unconfirmed hunches.

The door closed behind her, and she relaxed. "Lieutenant, there was a robbery around where Patricia lives the day Johnny disappeared. I wanted access to the evidence."

"Why do you think that's related?" Rivera frowned.

"The trailer in question is the one across from Patricia's. Frankly, I'm just following a hunch."

She lifted a corner of her mouth. "That's good enough, Detective Price. Who was the lead detective on that case?"

"It falls under Special Investigations Unit, so I don't have access to it. That's why I came to you."

"I see. You know the drill. I'll sign off on it."

Outside, Mackenzie saw Clint, their IT person, at Nick's desk. He typed on Nick's computer with lightning speed. "What's up?" she asked.

Nick pressed a fist to his mouth and stood behind Clint, looking at the screen. "I've asked Clint to see if Patricia has any properties other than her current address."

"Why?"

"If Jeremiah is orchestrating this, then Patricia is the first person who comes to mind who'd do anything for him," Nick said flatly. "It will take uniform some time to collect statements confirming her alibi for the time of the abductions. I thought we could get a head start this way."

"If Patricia did abduct those kids, then where is she keeping them?"

"Likely in some other property she owns. That trailer is too small and not private enough."

Mackenzie agreed with the course of action. Since they had confirmed that Ian Rowe couldn't have abducted the boys, they had hit a wall.

"She owns a place other than that trailer park she lives in." Clint swiveled his long neck and gestured Mackenzie and Nick to look at the monitor. "I have an address. I'll look it up right now."

Street view showed a small house situated in sparse woods.

"I didn't know this." Nick leaned forward. "Since when?"

"Five years," Clint replied.

Nick's eyebrows knotted, and his lips pursed.

"What is it?" Mackenzie asked.

"That's where Jeremiah used to live, in the area where Johnny was last seen," Nick replied.

"Well, Jeremiah's in prison, and Patricia lives in her trailer. So who lives there?"

"She must have put it up on rent. Otherwise it's just sitting empty."

"An empty cabin in the woods is an ideal location to hold someone captive," Mackenzie noted.

CHAPTER TWENTY-FOUR

The minute Mackenzie's feet hit the ground, a chill penetrated her bones. It wasn't cold; it had been a pleasant day. However, Mackenzie couldn't help but feel the ice forming right under her skin.

In front of her were sparse woods where a few run-down houses were situated, right next to a busy road with moving vehicles. It was the last place where Johnny had been seen alive. The isolated and dangerous path he took because he wanted to be alone.

"Have you come here since the investigation ended?" she asked Nick.

He loosened his tie. "No. You always find your way back to unfinished business." He shoved his hands in his pockets, eyes scanning the woods. "I read that somewhere."

Together they entered the woods, following the path that Johnny once took. The trees surrounding them were thin but leafy, distributed far apart. Their footsteps crunched twigs and leaves. The soil was hard. There weren't many shrubs or thickets. This was one of the few woody areas in Lakemore that didn't look dense enough to hide a secret.

Except it did. It was here that Johnny was last seen, before his body had turned up in a quarry miles away.

One of the houses directly in view was wooden with a wide porch, less shabby than the others.

"That's Jeremiah's. Or Patricia's now." Nick pointed at it. "It didn't look like this before."

"Looks kind of fancy." She studied the gleaming wood and clean windows. There was a symmetry to the house that indicated that money and care had been spent on it.

The front door opened, and an old man stepped out dressed in black robes.

"Pastor Giles?"

Giles's mouth fell open. He walked toward them with a slouch. "Detectives. What are you doing here?"

"What are *you* doing here?" Mackenzie asked.

"Oh, I maintain this house."

"Maintain it?"

"Patricia lets the church use it." Giles's chest swelled. "It's a home for disturbed youth. College youth who can't afford professional help and would like a more spiritual approach to recovery. We don't judge here. They feel safe without any *authorities* involved."

"Like rehab?" Nick guessed.

"Exactly." Giles looked pleased. "This is where they live."

"Interesting idea."

"Thank you!" Giles chuckled. "It took me years to get the approval of the board. But we want the church to come up with some innovative ideas to increase community engagement. We really want to make a difference. And Lakemore is plagued with troubled youth, unfortunately."

"And Patricia agreed to it?" Mackenzie couldn't hide her doubt.

"She's a good person, Detective," he said gently, with pity in his eyes. "She might carry a lot of anger and bitterness. But that's only human. How come you're here?"

"Just running down some leads," Nick answered vaguely. "I remember coming here many years ago, and it looked very different. These renovations must have been expensive."

"The church funded it. We would have been up and running nine years ago, but a significant amount of money was stolen from the church." He frowned. "It was recovered a few days later. But the board took it as a sign not to green-light the project until two years ago."

"How many people are living there right now?"

"Six."

Mackenzie and Nick exchanged a disappointed look. Theo and Noah weren't being held here.

"Is this about Jeremiah?" Giles asked. When they nodded, he clutched the cross hanging around his chest and kissed it. "I hope whatever this is that it's cleared up soon. He has repented for his sins."

"You actually believe that?" Mackenzie retorted. "Eight years in prison is enough for the crimes of killing children?"

A defiant look crossed his face. "The purpose of prison is rehabilitation, not punishment. Jeremiah is a changed man. He has realized his mistakes and has pledged never to repeat them again. He's no longer a threat to the community."

"And why should you be the judge of that?"

"Because I've known him since he was a child," he cried. "I *know* him."

With a joyless smile, Mackenzie slid her gaze over his reddening face. "He knows you too. He knows exactly what to say to convince you. Because the man we met a few days ago is exactly where he should be for the rest of his life."

"Pastor," Nick tried to defuse the tension. "Maybe you can help us. You have known him for years. Is there anyone else Jeremiah is close with other than you and Patricia? A friend?"

Mackenzie knew what Nick was thinking—perhaps Jeremiah had a strong ally other than his sister, someone who was loyal to him and would be easily manipulated.

"He was antisocial and unintentionally rubbed people up the wrong way sometimes." Giles trailed off. "The truth was that no one ever really noticed Jeremiah. He was part of the shadows and stayed to himself. No one knew what he was doing, how his demons were eating away at him."

"Pastor!" A young woman with a long nose and silky brown hair joined them. "You're needed inside. It's the plumbing again."

He rolled his eyes. "Sorry, detectives, but I have to go."

She gave them a small smile and turned around when Mackenzie asked, "You live in this house?"

"Yeah, I'm Summer." Her skin glowed, even though she was woefully skinny.

"How long have you been living here for?"

"Around two months now," Summer replied. "I decided to move here for my winter semester at community college."

"And nothing suspicious has happened? Have you seen anyone act strange or say something odd?"

Summer shook her head. "Sorry. Nothing like that. I have to go. It was nice meeting you."

As she went back to the house, Mackenzie felt a pit in her stomach, fearing that Theo and Noah were slipping away.

CHAPTER TWENTY-FIVE

As soon as they got back to work, Nick disappeared, muttering some vague excuse about making a phone call. Mackenzie reckoned he had gone out to get some fresh air. She would have offered to give him company, but at the speed at which he hightailed out, she decided it was best to give him some space.

There was a sluggishness to the air in the office. Finn and Austin were at their desks, straining to concentrate, but fatigue was sinking in. Mackenzie decided to utilize the time Nick was out to look through the evidence in the robbery in the trailer across from Patricia's.

She was immersed in accessing everything when Jenna waltzed into the office wearing knee-high boots. "Where's Nick?"

Mackenzie rubbed her eyes. "On a call." Jenna huffed and spun on her heel. "You can tell me, Jenna. I'm also on the case."

The two had an icy relationship. There had never been a confrontation, but their personalities hadn't gelled from the beginning. Mackenzie found Jenna to have an attitude problem, while Jenna clearly thought Mackenzie was stuck-up.

"Nobody other than his sister, pastor, his lawyer, and the documentary crew have visited Jeremiah. I just wanted to let Nick know that I'm still looking into Jeremiah's prison correspondences," Jenna said. "There are *a lot*. And most are anonymous."

"Nothing out of the ordinary?"

"Not yet." Jenna sighed, exaggerated, and made a show of checking her watch.

Mackenzie tapped a pen against her temple. "Clint has a program. You can scan all the letters and then just search for keywords. It would be faster than reading them one by one."

"Oh?" She looked mildly flustered before gathering herself. "I was thinking of that too."

"Sure, you were," Mackenzie muttered inaudibly as Jenna exited.

She skimmed over the incident reports and witness statements for the trailer robbery. There was a security video submitted in evidence. The owner of the trailer had one at the entrance. It was used to show how the culprit—a disgruntled ex—had picked the lock in the front door. Mackenzie found the video on their digital archive and hit play.

The camera was perched on top of the front door, also giving a view of Patricia's trailer.

Mackenzie opened the map on her computer. The distance between Jeremiah's place and the trailer park was ten minutes by walking, as one could just cut through the woods. By car, it would take a lot longer, due to all the one-way streets.

People moved in and out of view of the trailer park as the sun rose. Some heading to work and some just stepping outside to soak up the crisp fall morning. Mackenzie paid closer attention.

Johnny never reached school and was last seen alive at twenty minutes to eight. If Jeremiah were indeed visiting his sister, then he must appear in the video.

At seven forty-five, the man who was later arrested came into the frame and tried picking the front door lock. Apparently, he had wrongly assumed that his ex-girlfriend had left for work. Within ten minutes, he had gained entry, and there must have been some screaming and shouting because people began gathering around the trailer.

Mackenzie's eyes scanned the crowd. Some people had even entered the trailer to break up the fight before the cops arrived.

At ten minutes to eight, someone walked into the frame.

Jeremiah.

"Shit," she hissed. She paused and zoomed in. It was undoubtedly him. That rough appearance. Long, greasy hair, hawkish nose, dark eyebrows and a savage sneer. He was dressed in a white wifebeater and black jeans. The same clothes he was wearing when he spoke with Johnny.

Mackenzie played the video again. Jeremiah was behind the crowd. He peeked curiously, curling his hand into a fist and knocking the door. Patricia opened the door and let him in. Less than five minutes later, the cops showed up. The commotion died down an hour later. Jeremiah left Patricia's place at noon.

The killer had been right. Jeremiah was telling the truth. He didn't kill Johnny.

Then who did?

CHAPTER TWENTY-SIX

Mackenzie waited for Nick to return, ready to break the news that she knew would unravel him. She wanted to warn him before, but he was nowhere to be seen, and it was getting late. Sully would leave soon. And she needed to bring this information to light for everyone as soon as possible.

There was no time to waste.

Sighing, she entered Sully's office. It was littered with archery equipment, from chest guards and finger tabs to quivers and bowstrings. They were all miniature—toy-sized. The sergeant was focused on assembling them, while reading instructions from a manual.

"Dammit." Sully sighed. "This glue won't hold." He proceeded to sift through the material covering his desk and gestured Mackenzie come in.

Before she closed the door, Nick came up behind her with a glazed look in his eyes. The sight of him filled her chest with ice. He had no idea what she had just discovered.

"Didn't know you'd called a meeting, Sully," Nick said.

"I didn't. Mack wanted to talk."

"What's up with all this?" Nick rocked on his heels.

Sully put everything away. "My daughter told me to watch *The Hunger Games*. That Catpiss woman inspired me. I'm thinking of enrolling in archery classes."

"It's Katniss," Nick corrected.

"You've watched it?" Mackenzie raised her eyebrows.

"Yeah some of us watch movies like normal people."

Mackenzie shook her head, used to being teased for her lack of pop culture knowledge. "This is important, Sully."

Sully's giddiness dissolved, and he nodded gruffly. "What do you have?"

Mackenzie glanced at Nick, who was watching her expectantly. "Rivera asked me to look over Johnny's case file, just in case. Since I wasn't here, she believed I'd be more objective."

"Okay." Sully seemed to accept the logic. "Did you find something?"

"I did."

Blood drained from Nick's face. "What?"

"It's not your fault. You did nothing wrong. Everything was in order," she pacified him, knowing that he was going to take it hard. "But I was able to confirm Jeremiah's alibi. He was telling the truth about being with Patricia."

Mackenzie relayed what she had discovered. She played the video on her laptop for Nick and Sully. As they looked at the screen, blood pounded in her veins. There were going to be grave consequences, especially for Nick. He had been so adamant that Jeremiah had been playing his twisted game. But when the video stopped, Nick hung his head low and pressed the heels of his hands into his eyes.

"Jeremiah couldn't have... killed Johnny and then gone to Patricia's?" Sully asked.

"The fastest time to reach Patricia's from Jeremiah's place is ten minutes, and he got there twelve minutes after being last seen with Johnny." Mackenzie shook her head. "That's not enough time to follow Johnny, kill him, and deal with a dead body."

"And Johnny never reached school."

"Nope. And Jeremiah left his sister's place at noon."

"Uniform interrogated the neighbors! Why didn't anyone see him?"

"Because when he arrived, there was already that commotion." Mackenzie pointed out. "As you can see in the video, everyone was preoccupied by that. No one paid attention to Jeremiah."

Nick stayed eerily quiet. He hadn't moved, still hiding his face. But his broad shoulders moved like he was breathing hard.

"I should have checked this." His voice was a whisper.

"Why would you check the evidence of another case in another department?"

"You did!" He finally looked at her. His stormy eyes searched hers.

"Because I was looking for a mistake. I went in with the motive to check everything. It's a different perspective."

Nick shook his head, not convinced. He blew out a breath and sat back, blinking against the piercing bright light overhead.

Mackenzie felt helpless. She had been his partner for eight years. She knew in her bones that Nick was a responsible officer, and he had done everything right. Johnny's murder fit the M.O. of Jeremiah's other victims, of course Nick and the team had been convinced it was him. While she had pursued the evidence looking for something that had been overlooked, they did so from the position of thinking they already had their killer.

"It's not just your fault, Nick." Sully's voice punctured the deafening silence. "You came to me with a hunch, remember? And I told you it was just the trial jitters."

"What? What hunch?" Mackenzie asked.

"I had this voice in my head that *maybe* Jeremiah didn't kill Johnny," Nick recalled, his voice almost breaking. "I never got Jeremiah's letter about Johnny. And he was the only one we didn't find… fresh."

"Johnny matched the victim profile, and the M.O. was exactly the same," Sully argued. "I told Nick that he was overthinking because this was his first case and trial was starting. He was getting paranoid."

"I rationalized it too, Sully. This is not on you. This is on me. I ignored my instinct and believed the easier explanation."

"We have to focus on moving forward," Mackenzie said. "Jeremiah didn't kill Johnny, but whoever did used the same M.O. How is that possible?"

"The M.O. was hidden from the public when Johnny went missing. But there could have been some leaks. You know what some of the junior officers can be like," Sully said, visibly agitated, squirming in his seat. His eyes kept straying to Nick. "Nick?"

"I'm going to head out for a while." His face was flushed as he stood up. Quickly, he left Sully's office.

Without thinking, Mackenzie followed him, eager to placate him. She had never seen him this affected. It wasn't just stress and fear that he had to battle now, but guilt too. And Mackenzie knew how heavy a burden that was.

"Nick! Stop!" She caught his elbow at the top of the stairs.

He turned around, and Mackenzie's heart sank. His face was haunted. Like after all these years of being in this job, something had finally cut into his soul. "Because of me Johnny's killer has been walking free all these years. And now one kid is dead and two more are in danger."

CHAPTER TWENTY-SEVEN

Mackenzie lay in bed, bone-tired after the day she'd had. Her mind spun in all directions, firing randomly, but she was getting nowhere. Worrying about Nick, dreading the fate of Theo and Noah, and wondering who killed Johnny—a little boy who had only his older brother looking out for him.

It made Tim look even more of a suspect. But they still needed concrete evidence to get hold of his phone and bank details. At least uniform was keeping an eye on him. They'd alert them of any suspicious behavior.

Mackenzie watched the shadow of the tree outside on her ceiling. It danced and writhed in the wind. She tracked its movements, hoping the mundane activity would lull her into sleep. But her brain was lit up like a bulb.

Johnny had been dealt more than his fair share of bad cards. He never had a mother, his father died in an accident, and he was forced into the care of a stepmother who clearly didn't give a crap. And then he was murdered, and he joined the many victims of Lakemore.

Just like Robert Price and Charles. Both were killed in this town.

Even Melody was dead. Mackenzie was the sole survivor of that disastrous night—but for how long? Was it her turn to die?

She didn't believe in karma, but she couldn't entirely dismiss the thought that they were all paying for their terrible sins of that night.

Suddenly, something flew into the bedroom, cracking the window glass and piercing the silence sharply.

Mackenzie shot up, her spine straight as an arrow.

Utter silence. Her scream never came out—stuck in her throat like an itch. Sweat coated her hairline.

What the hell was that?

Gathering her wits, she scrambled out of bed and inched closer to the broken window. She looked out to the street, her mouth dry. There was no one there. She crossed the room to see what was thrown into her room. It was a rock.

Mackenzie picked it up guardedly, her heart still racing. For a moment she considered calling 911. But that would lead to more questions.

It enraged her to think that someone had the audacity to throw a rock into her bedroom and damage her window in the process. She decided to equip the outside of her home with some security cameras. After all, she was a woman living alone. It was only wise to take some precautions.

That night Mackenzie couldn't sleep a wink. After cleaning up the broken glass and going through a list of what to do next, it dawned on her. The anger slowly receded, paving way for fear. It held her heart in a death grip.

This was a message. She was next.

CHAPTER TWENTY-EIGHT

March 8

"*It has been seven days since three nine-year-old boys were abducted from their field trip to the annual spring festival,*" Debbie announced, having perfected her persona of being a reporter to be taken seriously. "*Tragedy struck when Lucas Williams was found dead. While the race is still on to bring back home Theo Reynolds and Noah Kinsey, our sources have told us that the disappearances are linked to the infamous serial killer, Jeremiah Wozniak.*" The screen divided, showing Elliot Garcia on the right side. "*Elliot Garcia joins us today. Mr. Garcia, you prosecuted Jeremiah Wozniak. Are these rumors true?*"

Elliot cleared his throat and raised his eyebrow. "*Due to the sensitive nature of the case, we're not at liberty to reveal much, Debbie.*"

"*There are talks of a wrongful prosecution?*" Debbie pushed regardless.

"*There was no wrongful prosecution,*" Elliot clarified with an edge to his voice. "*Jeremiah was convicted based on irrefutable forensic evidence.*"

"Do you have reporters following you now? Like paparazzi?" Troy leaned back on his chair and swayed. "It's kind of flattering."

"Shut it, Troy."

As Nick and Troy engaged in mild banter, Mackenzie chewed on her nails. Their bickering drowned into silence. A high-pitched sound keened in her ears. She had spent the previous night pacing around her house, visiting every room and inspecting every corner. As if Charles's murderer would be hiding in her home.

"Mack?" Nick poked her shoulder.

She jolted out of her reverie and looked around the conference room with bleary confusion. "What? Wait, where's Troy?"

He raised his eyebrows. "He left. Around two minutes ago. What happened to you?"

"Nothing," she snapped.

"You sure?"

Mackenzie gritted her teeth and seethed in silence. She didn't know where the flash of annoyance came from. But she felt irritated, like she was wearing an itchy sweater.

When she looked at him, guilt flooded her. Nick also clearly hadn't slept. There were bags under his eyes. Speckles of hair dotted his jaw. His tie was askew. But more so than anything, his eyes were dim. She chided herself for being selfish.

"How are you?" she asked softly.

He looked away. "Fine."

"Nick… you can talk to me."

He flipped closed a file harder than necessary. "There's nothing to talk about, Mack. I screwed up, and now I have to figure out how to live with it."

"You didn't." She maintained and grabbed his arm in an unforgiving grip. "*You* caught Jeremiah. That filthy serial killer who killed almost a dozen kids. And, frankly, the evidence I found proving his innocence in the case of Johnny was a lucky break. Even I wouldn't have checked that if I were you."

"I should have checked."

"That case was under Special Investigations' jurisdiction, not ours. We don't even have access to that video! I had to go through Rivera to get it. And it's not just you, Nick. The detectives who actually watched it could have picked up on Jeremiah, but they didn't. This was your first case. Please cut yourself some slack."

He picked up pictures of Theo and Noah and waved them at her, challenging her. "How?"

She let it go. He just needed more time to process everything. It wasn't an easy revelation to digest by any means. She just hoped he would come out of it soon.

There was a knock. "Am I interrupting?" Spencer stood by the door, his thick hair gelled into an arch and teeth gleaming white.

"Not at all." Nick put distance between him and Mackenzie. "What are you doing here?"

"Your bosses called me in for a meeting. They told us about that video you found. Elliot was supposed to be in too, but I'm sure you saw the interview. He was busy."

"What happens now that you know that one of the charges against him doesn't hold?" Nick folded his arms.

"We'll have to inform Jeremiah's lawyer for starters, which risks her using this to declare the whole thing a mistrial—"

"*What?!*" Mackenzie was alarmed.

"But it won't happen," Spencer pacified. "If one charge was false, then others could be too. She could use this to get him a new trial altogether. But before we talk to her about any of this, we have to conduct our own assessment. For example, authenticate that tape, try to get a clearer image of him, and make sure our other charges are airtight. Which they are. And all these things can take a lot of time."

"So you're stalling." She picked up on his insinuations. Thanks to Sterling, she knew more intimately how lawyers functioned.

Spencer nodded with a coy smile. "Exactly. Everyone's decided to wrap up this case first before we delve into the past. The outcome is critical."

"How so?" Nick asked.

"It's just we don't know who's behind this," Spencer said. "It could be Jeremiah, like you'd proposed. And if that's true, then both the cases will influence each other heavily. The situation is a tangled web. Best not be rash and deal with one thing at a time."

"I see." Mackenzie chewed the pad of her thumb in thought.

If Jeremiah somehow got out of prison thanks to Holly's clever maneuvering and then Lakemore PD brought new charges against him, he would play the victim card. How Lakemore PD were harassing him. How they were wrong once and were again.

"Also," Spencer warned, "Noah's father has decided to sue the school."

Nick ran his hand through his hair. "Why? That's not going to bring his kid back."

"He's angry. There's nothing he can do but wait, so he's punishing whoever he can."

"I see," Nick said, then glanced towards his phone as it started ringing. "I have to take this. It's Theo's father. Again."

Mackenzie crossed her arms while Nick engaged in an animated conversation over the phone. She saw him through the glass, clearly begging and pleading and trying to keep his cool. Mackenzie's heart lurched in sympathy; for Nick, for the boys, for their parents, for everyone affected by this horrifying crime. She felt guilty for snapping at him, especially when she could see the hell he was going through—how he clenched his hand in his pocket, how his eyes pinched shut, how his shoulders stiffened.

"I had brunch with Sterling today."

Mackenzie's head snapped to Spencer, who looked at her with a soft smile. "Oh?"

"I'm sorry, I didn't know you separated."

"Divorced," she said firmly. All it had taken was a stroke of a pen to end what had once been the most meaningful relationship in her life.

His head tilted as he regarded her curiously. She caught the tattoo snaking up his neck from underneath his shirt. Now that she was standing closer, she realized they were vines, but the flowers and leaves were replaced by letters.

"Nice tattoo."

"Thanks. I would have made it bigger, but people don't take you seriously in court if you've got tats." He winked.

"Does it mean anything?"

"The name of my foster sister," he said fondly.

"Oh, I didn't know you grew up in foster homes."

Spencer swallowed hard. "It was one of the reasons I became a lawyer. I saw a lot of injustice growing up. Somewhere down the line, it became my passion to fix that."

"Yeah," Mackenzie whispered, memories of her childhood taking over. "Trying to right all the wrongs. Never feels you're doing enough."

Nick returned to the room, wrung out from his talk, and Mackenzie collected herself. "Sorry about that. Mr. Reynolds is aggressive. Can't blame him. I'd lose my mind if I were in his place."

"By the way, since Sully and Rivera informed us about the latest development, I started thinking back to the trial," Spencer said. "I was hoping maybe there's something there that you could look into again now that we know the killer's not mistaken."

"Yeah?" Mackenzie picked up her notebook, ready to jot down anything.

"I suggest looking into Ruth Norman?"

"The teacher?" she remembered. "We talked to her already."

"About Johnny?"

"Not this time. But I did when Johnny went missing," Nick said. "Why?"

"Her behavior stood out."

"Yes. She's very attached to her students."

"She took a few weeks' leave after Johnny's remains were discovered. She couldn't handle it, which I found a little strange," Spencer said. "I don't mean to be insensitive. I understand being upset as his teacher. But taking such a significant amount of time off for a student seems a little… excessive?"

Mackenzie nodded and scribbled down Ruth's name in her notebook. "Okay, we'll go speak to her today. Thank you."

"Good luck," Spencer said before taking leave.

"Ruth Norman. Maybe she knows something about Johnny that no one else has been able to tell us. They were close," she said, feeling hopeful. "It could lead us to who killed Johnny and bring back Theo and Noah."

CHAPTER TWENTY-NINE

Mackenzie remembered herself as a nine-year-old kid. She was the quiet one. The one who hid behind a book. The one who never raised her hand to ask a question. The one who never made the effort to talk first. The one who never fought back when the mean kids teased her for her blazing red hair. She watched from afar as girls in her class whispered secrets into each other's ears and giggled. She wondered what secrets they had; she wondered if she could ever share her secret that her father used to get drunk and beat up her mother. She watched the boys cause a ruckus, run around, jostling and screaming. She envied their freedom, their disregard for rules and consequences. Because there were days she wanted to do just that: scream until her lungs tore ruthlessly.

But her mother told her every single day. *Don't tell anyone what happens at home. This is a family secret, Mackenzie. And you never betray your family.*

Mackenzie knew it was wrong; it felt wrong. But she never questioned her mother. Her mother always knew better. She yearned to share her burden with someone, to cry on someone's shoulders. There were moments when a teacher would be kind to her and she'd consider letting it slip. But her mother's words would blare loudly like a siren in her head.

Her father was a growling madman stomping around the house. The last thing she wanted was for her mother to get angry with her.

Now, as Mackenzie stood in front of the school, surrounded by children running around her, their laughter ringing in the air, she couldn't help but search for a meek girl, standing in the shadows and watching her classmates with a mix of pain and envy. Would things have been different if she'd confided in a teacher?

"I called the school," Nick said, as they entered the building. "They should be expecting us."

A lanky, old man dressed in a loose suit that swallowed his frame approached them. "I'm the principal. Hugh Devon."

"Thanks for doing this, Mr. Devon." Nick shook his hand.

Devon's forehead creased. "We're obviously horrified about what's happened. It's a nightmare, really." He led them through a strip of hallway with a glass case of trophies and certificates covering one wall. Since it was recess time, almost all the children were outside by the swings or in the cafeteria. They walked alone, their footsteps echoing. "We have increased security at our school. All field trips have been cancelled. But a lot of parents are still very apprehensive."

"We heard that Mr. Kinsey is considering filing a lawsuit," Mackenzie treaded carefully, trying not to offend him. Devon looked like a proud man.

"Yes." He looked angry. "We weren't expecting a large gathering at the festival otherwise we wouldn't have scheduled the field trip. Though Ruth should have come back after seeing the crowd instead of letting the children off the bus."

"You're blaming her?" She remembered how Ruth had broken down when they first spoke with her.

The image of Ruth standing behind her students holding up signs was haunting and embedded in the memory of every resident of Lakemore. It had achieved a somewhat iconic status. Years from now when the town would remember this tragic event, that image would be evoked and replayed.

"She's a good teacher. One of the best ones. She's very devoted. But she made a mistake. And it's not right for the school to pay for it. She's in there." Devon gestured to a room with a blue door and left to "deal with lawyers".

When Mackenzie entered the room, she was greeted by an earthy smell of clay with a hint of fruity perfume. The bright room had a window overlooking a fenced yard. Paint buckets, brushes, and canvases sat in one corner of the room. The other walls were covered in paintings made by children; lacking finesse but bursting with sincerity.

Ruth sat on a stool in the middle, working with a pottery wheel. Her hands were smeared with clay. Around her, some tools lay—sponge, trimming tool, wooden ribs, and a piece of leather. She wiped her hands with a towel and stood up. "Principal Devon told me to expect you."

"Aren't these tools dangerous for the kids?" Nick pointed at them.

"They're under lock and key when the students are in. They only play with clay. This is for me." Ruth looked at the bowl she was making. "I find it very therapeutic." Ruth's hands clasped in front of her shook. She blinked rapidly, her eyes glazed with tears. "I'm so sorry. The school wants to throw me under the bus to save themselves from a lawsuit. Most of the parents hate me too. They said that they wouldn't send their kids to school anymore if I was still their teacher. So I'm coming to work, except I'm not assigned a class anymore. The only thing getting me through is that the children love me." She sniffed. "I wouldn't have survived this without them."

Mackenzie and Nick shared a glance. Ruth had a manic, unpredictable look in the eyes, like she could either break down into tears or kill someone. But Mackenzie supposed her fragile state of mind was just a consequence of her three students vanishing from right under her nose, and the persecution she now faced.

"We're not here to talk about Lucas, Theo and Noah," Nick said softly. "We want to talk about Johnny Cooper."

Ruth gasped. "Oh dear God."

"Eight years ago, I questioned you. He was your student."

"Y-yes. P-poor boy."

"You were close to him."

Ruth exhaled and sat on the bench again, smoothing the rim of the half-shaped bowl. She moved her hands in clay, like the touch was calming her jangled nerves. "Yes. He was almost like a son to me."

Nick kneeled in front of her and dropped his voice. "Can you tell us anything about him, Ruth? We're looking into his death again?"

"W-what? Why?"

"We're not at liberty to discuss," Mackenzie said in a firm voice that made Ruth recoil. "We're just ticking off some boxes."

Nick shot Mackenzie an indignant look. He tended to be kinder in his approach, encouraging witnesses to cooperate. Mackenzie's more blunt approach could be helpful with slippery suspects, but she knew it came off as insensitive in certain situations.

"Ruth, unfortunately we can't share that," Nick said. "But I know how much you loved Johnny. After he was found dead, you took some time off, didn't you?"

Her lower lip trembled and tears unleashed onto her freckled face. "I did. I-I needed to get away. It was too painful."

"Is there anything you remember now about him, or the days leading up to his disappearance? Please think hard. Something you forgot back then? Did he tell you anything?"

She pushed away the wheel. "I'm so sorry."

"I know that. But please think."

She suddenly shot up and marched to one of the cupboards, rummaging through it. She took out a folded piece of paper and stared at it, horrified. "I'm sorry. But I… I was so ashamed."

Mackenzie stepped forward, wanting to rip the letter from her hands. But she refrained, as Ruth broke down into quaking sobs that rattled her body.

"I should have given this to you before," Ruth continued. "B-but when you found him d-dead… I'll never forgive myself. I'm sorry! That's why I l-left. I couldn't believe I d-didn't think."

Nick took the paper from her and unfolded it. Mackenzie peeked to get a look. It was a letter written by Johnny.

"Why didn't you give this to me before?" Nick's eyes widened.

"Because Johnny had a wild imagination!" she cried. "He was a good boy, but he made up stories. He was only nine. When I saw this, I asked his brother, Tim, about it. He denied the contents of it. But when I found out he'd died… I realized I made a horrible mistake. Do you think it's related to this?"

Mackenzie took the letter from Nick to read it carefully, while Ruth sank to the floor, weeping and blubbering apologies.

Dear Miss Tanner,

My name is Johnny Cooper. I'm a fourth-grader at Lakemore Elementary. My stepmother, Heather, doesn't care about my big brother, Tim, and me. She doesn't pay attention to us. Whenever I get sick, she doesn't want to take me to the hospital. One time, Tim fell down and was bleeding, and she didn't take him to the doctor. She doesn't give us food at home or lunch money. She has scary friends over all the time. Sometimes she even hits us. It's just Tim and me with her. We have nobody else. Please help us. I don't want to live with her anymore. I don't feel safe.

Thank you
Johnny

CHAPTER THIRTY

Mackenzie sat in the passenger seat as Nick stared down at the letter. He mulled over it for the umpteenth time, but his expression remained unchanged. The corners of his eyes crinkled, his lips parted. Like reading it would change the words.

The weather had dulled abruptly. Rain began to fall softly, more like mist.

Nick clenched his jaw, his fingers tightening at the edge of the letter. "Ruth found it on his desk and when she confronted him, he got scared and closed up. Why?"

"He probably thought Ruth wouldn't believe him." Mackenzie blurted and looked away. A nine-year-old boy's cry for help had been ignored and buried. She understood his fears. It was the same one she had carried for years as a child. That no one would believe her. And if she told anyone, it would only make things worse. "She kept the letter after Tim told her that it was a lie."

Nick rested his head back and closed his eyes. "So Johnny made it up? Why would he do that?"

"Or Tim is lying."

"Why would Tim lie?" Nick challenged.

"Because he was scared it would make things worse. I can believe that Johnny had a wild imagination, but to write a letter accusing his stepmother of abuse? That's a bit much."

Nick folded the letter and placed it in his pocket. His knee bobbed up and down, and then he smacked the wheel hard.

Mackenzie glared at him, startled. "Nick!"

"He wrote a letter, begging for help! And what did Ruth do? She was his teacher."

"I know."

"How does it not piss you off?" His burning eyes searched hers. "Can you believe this happened?"

Johnny's words had left her limp on the inside. "I've been disappointed by the adults who were supposed to take care of me."

It was a rare moment of vulnerability. Nick was the person she was closest to, but she rarely confessed anything meaningful. Somewhere over the years of hiding, first Charles's abuse, then burying a body with her mother, Mackenzie got used to keeping everything hidden. It became her nature. She became too comfortable behind the fortress she had built for herself.

"We have to find Tanner. Who is she?" Nick turned the key in the ignition, and the car went over a pothole.

"She's not anyone at the school otherwise Ruth would have known." Mackenzie took out her phone and began searching.

"Won't be a friend of Heather's. I'd say a social worker."

"Cheryl Tanner." She found her information. "She's a CPS caseworker."

"Child protective services. Johnny never got a chance to post the letter, but we should still talk to her."

"Also Tim. He should be able to shed light on this."

Back at the station, Mackenzie opened Johnny's autopsy reports again. She had absorbed all the information relating to his death and ante-mortem injuries. But if Johnny had been abused, then there must have been physical evidence to corroborate his claims in the letter. While Nick called CPS, arranging a meeting with Cheryl, she flipped through the pages with a sense of urgency.

Please help us.

I don't feel safe.

His words were trapped inside her head like a buzzing fly. She closed her eyes and imagined him, wearing the clothes he had on when he was captured on the camera. His ghost drifted in and out of the pages of evidence; his truth somewhere lost. It's like he was still waiting after all this time.

She glanced at Nick. If Johnny was embedded in her mind, he was embedded in Nick's soul.

"Detective Price?" Austin appeared at her side. "Do you have a minute?"

"Sure." She forced a cooperative smile. "What's up?"

Austin placed an elbow on the wall of her cubicle, making himself comfortable. "I tracked down an old friend of Charles's in Dallas from his time in rehab. He said that Charles told him about a falling out he had with your mother, Melody, some night twenty years ago. Something involving you."

Mackenzie's face grew hot. She placed her hand on the desk to stay rooted to her reality. Austin looked casual, nothing in his conduct suggesting he suspected anything. It was the night Melody had coerced her into burying the unrecognizable body of Robert Price in the woods. Charles had hid behind the curtains and later fought with Melody for getting Mackenzie involved.

"Charles used to hit my mother when he got drunk." Mackenzie started with the truth, then improvised. "But twenty years ago, he hit *me*. He had never touched me before. My parents got into a huge fight. He must be referring to that."

"And that's the night he walked out?"

"Yes. I never saw him after that until a few months ago."

Austin rubbed his fingertips together and frowned.

Mackenzie's blood ran cold. What did he know? Had Charles's friend said something else that contradicted Mackenzie's statement? Was this a trap? Was he testing her?

"Okay," Austin said. "I'm sorry about what happened."

"Ancient history." She shrugged, hiding her relief.

"What's that?" He tipped his chin.

"Autopsy reports on Johnny Cooper. He died nine years ago."

"Oh, right. *Find his killer or they all die.* What are you looking for?" He crossed his arms, almost crowding her space.

Her heart still beat an erratic drum in her chest. Why was Austin trying to help? She couldn't help but wonder if this was all a ploy. "I'm looking for signs of abuse and neglect."

"May I?"

"Sure."

He skimmed through the pages, face pinched in concentration. "His weight should be around sixty-three pounds based on his age and sex. But he's underweight."

"Yeah, though not to the point of being malnourished. Earlier I thought he was probably just a scrawny kid, but now we suspect he wasn't fed properly. So it could be a sign of neglect."

"Was he an active kid? Play a lot of sports?"

"No. He liked to stay indoors and play with action figures. A quiet kid."

"These injuries." His finger traced the words on the report. "Remodeling of the metatarsophalangeal joint on the right thumb. Bone chip at the radial portion of the left wrist. A spiral fracture on the humerus. Either this kid was active, falling around a lot or these are signs of abuse. I've seen worse, to be honest."

She took out her notebook and looked at the notes she'd made during Heather's interview. Heather had claimed that he was active and liked to run around. But everyone else—his friends, Tim, and Ruth—stated that Johnny wasn't into sports or outdoors activity at all.

"The stepmother said that Johnny played a lot of football and was sporty, which contradicts the statements given by everyone else."

"Sounds like she was covering her tracks."

"Why didn't anyone realize this before?"

"Like I said, these could *easily* be explained as injuries commonly found in someone athletic. And they aren't extreme enough to raise suspicion if you think the victim was physically very active."

She slammed the notebook on the desk. "Can't say I'm surprised. I thought she was a monster before I even knew about the abuse."

"I'll leave you to it."

"Yeah. Thanks."

Regardless of how busy she was, she felt Austin's presence like a pebble in her shoe. Slowly the events in Charles's life were unfolding, and Austin was creeping closer to the truth Mackenzie was desperate to keep hidden.

CHAPTER THIRTY-ONE

It was a starless night in Lakemore, clouds coating the sky like wisps of smoke. Mackenzie stared out the window, into the myriad eyes of the night, feeling a sense of calm before the storm.

"Did you get in touch with Cheryl Tanner?" she asked Nick.

"She's in Rochester. She'll be back tomorrow evening. That's when we'll meet her."

Their floor had emptied out. Nighttime had put a pause on the search through the Fresco woods. The conference room table was littered with three used coffee cups, courtesy of Nick, who was typing away on his laptop.

"Anthony just emailed us." Nick pressed his lips together, referring to the crime lab in Seattle. "They ran tests on Lucas's clothes. There were traces of soil and vegetation matching the woods."

"That's it?"

"They tested for any samples from cargo trays and trunk liners, which would indicate he was put in the back of a car at one point, but found nothing."

"That means he never left those woods," Mackenzie said.

"Remember there were no signs of him being held captive either. No ligature marks. Sounds like he was either drugged or killed almost immediately after being abducted."

An officer escorted Tim to the conference room. Tim dragged his steel boot covered feet, disinterested, with a hard hat tucked under his arm. His hair was disheveled and face smudged with dirt. He had come directly from work. The officer led him inside the room and left.

"What is this about?" Tim placed his hard hat on the table.

"Have a seat please," Nick said.

Tim looked puzzled and sat on a chair. "What's going on?"

Mackenzie showed him the letter Johnny had written. "Do you recognize this?"

He rolled his eyes and picked up the letter. A second later, his face fell. "Where did you get this from?"

"Ruth Norman. His teacher," Nick said. "She said she asked you about it and you said Johnny made it up."

Tim's face was ashen. "H-he didn't."

"He didn't lie?"

"No."

"Then why did you tell Ruth he did?"

"Because it wouldn't have made a difference!" he argued hotly, tears welling in his eyes. "I knew nothing was going to change. Instead it could make things worse. And it did."

Mackenzie froze. "What are you talking about? Heather found out that Johnny wrote a letter?"

"After Ruth confiscated that letter, Johnny wrote another one. Same words, but he posted that one. And guess what? Nothing happened." Tim let out a dry laugh. "Well, Heather found out and locked Johnny in his room for twenty-four hours. Didn't give him anything to eat. Slapped me when I tried to unlock the door. I was right to lie to Ruth, but Johnny had to go ahead with it behind my back. I used to tell him to be patient. As soon as I turned eighteen, I would take him away with me. But he couldn't take it anymore."

Silence descended in the room. It was confirmed. Heather had abused Johnny and Tim, and Johnny had tried to save them. The sight of the messy strokes of his pen on the paper weighed heavy in the pit of Mackenzie's stomach.

"Did… um… did Heather say how she found out about the letter?" Mackenzie asked.

"Not exactly. She just said she had friends in high places. Whatever that means."

"Why didn't you say anything when I talked to you all those years ago?" Nick begged. "I would have helped. I would have—"

"Johnny asked for help, didn't he? And look what happened. I was a kid myself. When Heather told me she had powerful friends, I believed her."

"I have to ask," Mackenzie said. "Do you think Heather could have hurt Johnny?"

"I don't know." He shook his head, exhausted. "I did for a while, but then you arrested Jeremiah."

"And have you had any contact with Heather?"

Tim's face contorted in a sneer. "I haven't spoken to that bitch since the day I turned eighteen and cut her out of my life. She can die in a ditch for all I care. She deserves to."

"Thanks, Tim." Nick extended his hand. "If you remember anything else about Johnny then please let us know."

Tim eyed Nick's hand as he stood up. He turned around and left.

Nick curled his fingers in a fist and pulled his hand away. "The statute of limitations has expired so we can't bring child abuse charges, but she obviously knows a lot more than she let on."

"Johnny's tongue was removed. If Heather did hurt Johnny, then how did she know to remove the tongue?"

"We should look for a link between Heather and Jeremiah. To see if they crossed paths at any point."

Mackenzie looked at the letter, feeling sick. "This is what the killer wanted us to find out. The message left inside Lucas's throat. It was written on an envelope with a postage stamp. We didn't know what that meant until now." Her stomach turned at the thought of a brutal killer being their ally. "I think he was trying to tell us about Johnny's letter to Cheryl Tanner."

"I'll start working on a warrant to get Heather and Cheryl's bank statements. I doubt Heather is going to talk, and she knew about the letter. So something must have happened between them," Nick said with renewed energy.

CHAPTER THIRTY-TWO

March 9

The engine roared, the exhaust forming a blackish cloud. It had been a bumpy ride from the main road to the house, which sat atop a little hill. The path was rutted with pothole after pothole. Now Mackenzie sat looking at the old house as she waded painfully through her fading memories of Robert Price—her legal father. She didn't want to forget him. It was the least she could do after burying him, ignorant of the true identity of the body.

The house arrested her gaze. Her family lived there. Robert's brother and her uncle, Damien Price.

It had taken her just under three hours to drive from Lakemore to Salem in Oregon. She had woken up early and left before sunrise, deciding not to procrastinate anymore. Heather wasn't available to meet them before lunchtime, since she worked day shifts as security at city hall, so Mackenzie figured she'd make the drive to Salem and be back right on time. With the rest of the team chasing leads and Heather being busy, Mackenzie finally found a few hours to squeeze in a visit.

She felt guilty dropping in at Damien's early in the morning, but with the case taking up all her time she rarely had a few hours to herself.

During the drive, questions had clattered in her brain. Would he recognize her? She was a reflection of her mother, after all. Did

Robert confide in him about his efforts to search for her after Melody ran away? Did Damien know about Charles?

Maybe this is a bad idea.

Mackenzie's head drooped and she put the car in reverse, ready to head back to Lakemore. But her conscience wouldn't let her leave.

Damien had been living all these years without knowing what happened to his brother because of her. The least she could do was not balk at the thought of meeting him. She had to start somewhere as she tried to repair her mistakes.

She braced herself and turned off the car. Climbing out, a light wind blew gusts of dirt across her path and into her eyes.

She rang the bell and waited. Time seemed to stretch for hours. And then too suddenly, the door swung open and a man was in front of her.

"Yes?"

Mackenzie had seen his picture on the internet. His face had a gentle quality to it that she remembered Robert having from her vague memories.

"Detective Mackenzie Price with the Lakemore PD. Sorry to drop in unannounced at nine on a Saturday, but I was hoping to talk." She flashed her badge. "Can I come inside?"

Damien blinked at her name and let her in. Usually Mackenzie registered the quirks and décor of every house she visited, trying to capture some insights into the person. But the only thing she could pay attention to was the old man with gray hair.

"A detective came from Lakemore PD a few days ago." He walked with a limp and collapsed on one of the chairs. "Detective Kennedy, I think. Is this regarding that?"

It dawned on Mackenzie that she had been so nervous about seeing him that she hadn't thought about what to say. She tucked a stray hair behind her ear and swallowed to soothe her dry throat. "Yes. He told you that Charles Laurent was murdered?"

"He did. And I told him that I had never even met the man."

"How did you hurt yourself?" She gestured to him rubbing his knee.

"I fell down the stairs."

She kept looking around the house and pacing, but not observing anything. Her eyes glided over the antique furniture and blue walls. "Did you know who Charles was?"

Damien frowned. "Why are you here and not the other detective?"

The seconds ticked loudly on the grandfather clock, every muscle in her body tensed. Then, she decided to just be honest. "My mother was Melody Price."

"Oh dear God." Damien sounded breathless. His jaw hung open and eyes scanned her face. "You do look so much like her. You're Robert's little girl."

The words twisted the knife further into her heart. Burying him in the woods. Even though it was unintentional, even though she had assumed it was an abusive Charles she was burying, the end result had been the same.

She looked at her fingers, holding back her tears. After a very long time, she felt like a little girl again and not the steely woman she had become. "I… I don't remember him much. I was hoping you could tell me what happened between him and my mother?"

"What happened to Melody?"

"She died in a car accident many years ago."

"I see… Melody was a cunning woman." Damien went into the little kitchen and offered her water, which she accepted. "She and Robert were having problems, but he never thought she'd take you away so suddenly."

"Did you know about Charles?"

He nodded. "When Robert spent all those years searching for you, he discovered that Melody had been having an affair with a man named Charles."

"Did he suspect that Charles was my... biological father?"

Damien paused. "He did. But he told me it didn't matter to him. He was there the day you were born. He was there every day, bathing you, changing you, teaching you how to walk, talk, playing with you. To him, you were always his daughter. He always said that raising you for those four years was the most beautiful time of his life."

Mackenzie grasped the glass tightly, controlling the sobs that rose up her throat. She blinked away her tears. Growing up, she had resented Charles and envied people with good fathers. She never imagined that she'd had a great one.

"Did he find us?"

She already knew the answer. He had, the same night Melody had killed him. But she had to tread carefully.

"He told me he might have." Damien shrugged. "Truth was that, after a while, I told him to move on. He was going crazy looking for you. He went all the way to the east coast, trying to look for Melody's estranged mother but he couldn't even track her." Mackenzie knew that her grandmother and Melody were estranged for years and had reconnected only a few years before Mackenzie was sent to live with her.

Damien continued, "I wasn't as informed about his progress. But one day he called me up and told me he had a strong lead. I didn't take him seriously. There were several strong leads over the years. All he said was that he was going to Washington. No mention of which city. That was the last time I heard from him."

"So you filed a police report?"

"Yes. But they never found him." He placed his hands on the counter and dropped his head. "He was my big brother. Our parents died when we were young. He took care of me. He was a good man, Mackenzie. A very good man." He wiped away his tears.

Mackenzie didn't know what to do. The bond between them was wafer-thin, but they both shared something deeper—both had been loved by Robert. "I'm sorry. You must miss him a lot."

"Every single day." His voice was thick. "It's been twenty years. I know he's gone. I feel it. I just want to know what happened to him. That's the worst thing in the world. Not knowing. Life went on. I got married, had a son, and got divorced. Just last year, I became a grandfather. But he's always there."

The guilt was suffocating; it smothered her. Damien wanted answers, and she had them. But the last shred of self-preservation kept her from saying the words. She imagined what would happen if she told him. He'd loathe her. Maybe even go to the police. The statute of limitations had long past—she wouldn't go to prison—but her reputation and credibility would be destroyed. Even if some people understood her actions, they would always look at her as the woman who buried a body when she was twelve. They would always whisper behind her back. They would maintain a distance.

Life as she knew it would be over.

It was selfish but self-preservation.

She raked her mind for possible scenarios where she could ease Damien's pain without drastically altering her life.

"You used to visit this house when you lived in Minnesota." Damien broke the silence.

"What?"

"Yeah, this is our parents' home. Robert and Melody used to visit often and stay weeks at a time. In fact, they moved here for a few months toward the end of Melody's pregnancy so that my parents could help out. After that, you'd come here during the summer. When my parents died over a decade ago, I sold my house in Nashville and moved here."

Mackenzie looked around, this time absorbing her surroundings. But none of it rang a bell. "I don't remember."

"Well, you haven't been here since you were four years old. Do you want to see the room you stayed in whenever you visited?"

"Yes." Her heart raced. "Please."

He led her to a narrow, wooden staircase. "Actually, I can't go up because of my knee. Luckily my room is on the first floor."

"It's okay. Where's the room?"

"Second floor. Third door on your right."

"Thank you."

She looked up the dark staircase and took a shaking breath. The floorboards squeaked in protest under her hesitant steps. Specks of dust floated in the air. Radiators lined the walls. She trailed her hand along the wooden bannister, trying to remember its touch.

A vision appeared in front of her. A strong man climbing up the stairs, carrying a small girl tucked under his arm.

"*Daddy!*" she yelped, her red pigtails swinging.

"*Time to sleep, Mack.*" He ruffled her hair.

"*Take me up! Take me up!*"

He flung her up and sat her on his shoulders. Placing a hand on her back to make sure she didn't fall, he raced up the stairs. The girl spread her arms like wings, her giggles echoing.

"*Daddy! Faster!*"

Mackenzie hastened to catch up with them, but they vanished into thin air at the top of the stairs. Suddenly, she was alone. Instinctively, she extended her hand. As if she would be able to feel their love and laughter, like it was still a part of the air. She pushed open the door to her room and breath squeezed out of her lungs. The walls were yellow—her favorite color growing up. There was barely any furniture—a minimal bed and a dresser. The curtains looked old, with stars and galaxies on them.

She waited for memories to invade her. But nothing came. Still something tangible chained her to this room. It's like she found another part of her she didn't even know was missing. Except she didn't know how to fit that piece.

After spending several minutes in her old room, she came back downstairs to find Damien on the phone. He saw her and hung up. "Everything okay?"

"Yes."

He smiled awkwardly. "You were a kid when I last saw you. I never thought I'd see you again."

"I didn't know about anything until recently," she admitted. "I'm glad to have met you."

"Same. You're always welcome to visit."

They said their goodbyes, and when Mackenzie strutted back to her car, she resolved to find a way to let Damien know the truth.

Mackenzie was on her way back when her phone rang. She turned on the Bluetooth and Nick's voice boomed in the car. "Mack?"

"Shit. Hold on." She reduced his volume. "Yeah?"

"Where are you?"

Her grip on the wheel tightened. "I'm on my way. Will reach the station in an hour. I told you I had to go somewhere."

"Is everything okay?"

Mackenzie bit her tongue. It's not like the visit was a secret. She was certain that Austin would find out about it if he met with Damien again. But something held her back from sharing the truth with Nick. He already had a lot on his mind. The last thing he needed was to listen to her drama. "Yeah, thanks. I'll be back in time to meet with Heather."

"I already met with her."

"I thought she wasn't available until later."

"Her shift got postponed so she contacted me. I texted you about it, but you didn't reply."

"Oh." She frowned. "I'm driving. I haven't checked my phone. Why didn't you wait for me?"

"Because her shift starts now. If I hadn't met with her then, we would have to wait until tomorrow, and we can't waste time with this case," he explained. "Anyway, Heather clamped up and denied everything when I confronted her about the letter."

"Did you find any connection between her and Jeremiah?"

"Nope."

"In that case, I don't see how Heather would have known to remove the tongue. Maybe there were leaks? We should check if Heather knows anyone from the police, though I don't feel she'd run in those circles."

"The warrant came through. We're pulling the financials on Heather and Cheryl soon."

Mackenzie was annoyed that she had missed the interview with Heather. She changed lanes and noticed something in the rearview mirror, and all thoughts of Heather disappeared. A black SUV was following her. She had spotted the car multiple times in the last hour at least.

It's a common car. It doesn't mean anything.

"Mack? You still there."

"I'll call you later." She squirmed in her seat, as her heart rate began picking up.

"What's going on?"

"I don't know. I think someone's following me." The words just came out.

"*What?*"

She disconnected the call before she blurted more. Adrenaline swarmed through her veins, overloading her senses. She switched lanes abruptly in an effort to reach the upcoming exit. The surrounding cars honked and swerved as she disrupted the flow of traffic. Easing into the ramp, her eyes kept checking the black car.

The car following her also cut across the lanes and made the exit right in the nick of time.

"Shit."

The back of her neck prickled, and her chest felt hollow. Her hands on the wheel got jittery as she strived to be in control.

Who are you? What do you want?

Mackenzie turned into another street and raced ahead, just teasing the speed limit, wondering how to get him off her tail. Possibilities browsed through her mind. The best option was to stop the car and get out of it. She was armed and trained to face this kind of danger. She just needed to stay away from a residential area.

It was then she realized the car was getting too close. She didn't want to go over the speed limit, but the car showed no sign of stopping. There was no other car on their stretch. She wrestled with various options, her adrenaline reaching fever pitch.

The car suddenly got too close. She let out a shriek and swerved the car to the left. Tires hissed on the hot tarmac, and she floored the brake as she crashed into a tree.

"Shit!" She jerked against the seat belt. The airbag inflated, hitting her in the face. Her head banged against the window.

The SUV zipped past her, ignoring the accident it had caused.

Mackenzie nursed her head, realizing it was bleeding. As the adrenaline receded, the pain amplified. But all she could think about was that someone had just tried to run her off the road.

CHAPTER THIRTY-THREE

Hours later, Mackenzie was dropped at the Lakemore PD headquarters. She smelled like the hospital—of iodine and disinfectants—and ignored the curious glances thrown her way at her disheveled appearance. Her forehead had stitches, her makeup was smudged, her hair scruffy. She saw Nick and Clint in the conference room. Clint was on his laptop, while Nick leaned behind him with a brooding look on his face.

"What are you guys doing?" Mackenzie asked as she walked in.

They looked up at her, a little lost.

Clint was the first one to recover. "Looking for you actually."

"Huh?"

"You hung up after saying someone's after you and then disappeared for hours!" Nick said with a wild frenzy in his eyes.

Mackenzie sighed and fell on a chair. Her body ached everywhere. "I got into an accident, and my phone died."

"What accident!?" Nick almost shouted.

Immediately, Clint picked up his laptop and left the room.

"Why are you freaking out so much?"

"Because you said that someone was following you." He glared at her like she was the one losing it. His tie was askew and sleeves rolled up, his pale cheeks tinged red. "Charles was murdered, Mack. I know Austin doesn't think it was a robbery, and we don't know who killed him. And then you have someone *following* you, and you get into a car accident? Do you not realize why this is a bad situation?"

Mackenzie's knee bounced under the table. She had spent the last few hours trying to wrap her head around what had happened. First the rock through the window and now this. Whoever it was, was escalating. But seeing Nick's blatant concern, as much she appreciated it, wasn't doing anything for her anxiety levels.

Nick was now the person she was closest to in the world. Maybe he always had been. But she wasn't used to people interfering in her personal business. Even with Nick, there were some aspects of her life that were unchartered. And she intended to keep it that way, no matter how much the investigation into Charles's murder threatened to bring to light her darkest secrets.

"I was mistaken. I thought someone was following me," she spoke calmly. "And then I crashed into a tree because the tire gave out. The airbags got released, so I had to call 911 and give a statement and go to the hospital. That's all that happened."

"Are you sure?"

"Yes."

"I need to take a walk." He rubbed his eyes, suddenly deflated. "Mack, I'm tired. With everything. I just need a break."

Before Mackenzie could respond, Nick dragged his feet out the door.

She reprimanded herself. She had an out. A friend had given her a window to reach out, and in that moment, she wished she were a person who didn't struggle to open up.

An hour later, Nick returned looked refreshed, smacking gum and escorting a woman dressed in trousers and stilettos. Her ropey hair was dark and devoid of shine sitting atop a double-chinned face.

"Miss Tanner, this is my partner Detective Price," Nick made the introductions.

"How're ya?" Tanner shook her hand vigorously.

Mackenzie noticed the expensive peacock brooch glittering on her beige polyester trousers. Her handbag was a knockoff, and her nails were fake with dirt under them.

"Sorry I was making visits all day." She beamed. "It's a very important job."

"How long have you been a social worker for?" Nick sat across from her.

"Over fifteen years now." She pressed a hand to her chest and sighed. "A very fulfilling job. Stressful, mind ya. They keep talking about doctors and nurses, but no one gives credit to us. We're doing the real work. Ensuring the safety of children—the *future* of this country."

Mackenzie instantly didn't like Cheryl Tanner, who continued boasting about the nobility of her work.

"I've been following the news. Are you any closer to finding those two boys?"

"We're getting there." Nick tightened his tie. "We wanted to speak to you regarding Johnny Cooper. Does that name ring a bell?"

Tanner's smile remained unchanged but the corners of her eyes wrinkled. "Sorry, who?"

Nick showed her the letter. "He had posted you a similar letter to this?"

She picked up the letter and gulped. "Oh y-yes. I remember now."

"And what happened?"

"I investigated." She scratched her ear and rubbed her hands together like a sudden case of nerves had taken hold of her. "I talked to his stepmother, and my conclusion was that the boy was making it up."

"Do you find that's common?" Mackenzie couldn't keep the scorn out of her voice. "Children sending letters in which they lie about being abused and neglected?"

"It's rare, but it happens."

"Somehow I find that hard to believe."

"You're not in my profession." Tanner raised an eyebrow. "You haven't seen what I have."

Mackenzie straightened and leaned forward, glaring at her with a fierce expression. "And you're not in *my* profession. You haven't seen the liars I come across."

Tanner pressed her lips together and inhaled. "I do *not* appreciate what you're implying."

Cheryl Tanner had walked in with an air of confidence, but now her behavior had become restless. Her hands twitched on the table. She kept touching her brooch, the sole valuable possession she wore; she seemed ready to dash out the door anytime.

"How do you explain this?" Nick pulled out the smoking gun. It was Tanner and Heather's bank statements from nine years ago. "Heather withdrew five thousand dollars on the same date you deposited that exact amount. The account numbers match."

Tanner blanched. "I-I don't…"

Nick flipped the page, showing rows of highlighted entries. "In fact, you deposit five grand in your account pretty often. They're sporadic and from different accounts, so it's not a salary or rent money or anything."

Mackenzie's blood fizzed with anger. "You have been taking bribes from families. You ignored Johnny's claims because Heather paid you off."

Tanner was cornered. She looked like she was on the cusp of having a breakdown. Sweat broke across her hairline, and her breathing became shallow. "I'm not saying anything without a lawyer present."

"That's your right." Nick gestured at the detective from Special Investigations Unit standing outside the conference room—the unit in charge of looking into fraud and corruption. "You should probably make that call."

CHAPTER THIRTY-FOUR

"Heather is also going to be under arrest," Nick informed Mack after Tanner was taken away to be processed.

"They might have nothing to do with the murder, but they wronged Johnny."

"Like me?" His smirk was sarcastic.

She sighed. "Nick, it was the same M.O. And it was fair to assume that the DNA got lost."

Nick's face was distant as he stared out the window into the night. Mackenzie felt the distance between them stretch. If only she could get through to him like he so often did with her.

Jenna knocked on the door. "Got a minute?"

Everyone had been working after hours on this case.

"You got anything?" Nick asked.

"I think so." Jenna beamed and brought her laptop inside the conference room. "Clint helped me go through Jeremiah's correspondences as there's been so much in the last eight years." The laptop screen was flooded with scanned pictures of the letters and red circles around some words.

Mackenzie and Nick stood close, leaning in.

"Most of the letters were hate mail. People wrote to him telling him to go to hell, but there were a few fan letters. There was one sender in particular that stands out though. It's the most elaborate and disturbing. Unlike some people merely expressing their admiration, she's the only one who actually engages with him." She pulled up a letter. "She always signs off as Martha and calls him Raymond in her letters."

"Raymond and Martha?" Mackenzie frowned. "Why those names?"

"Raymond Fernandez and Martha Beck were a serial killer couple," Jenna replied. "Back in the forties, they admitted to killing over twenty women."

Nick's eyes widened. "What do they talk about?"

She scratched the back of her neck. "That's the weird part. They make up stories. It's all fiction. Like they're living a fantasy life through the letters. They often talk about how they want to go on road trips and buy dolls and take care of them. But I think they're using code words. Like doll refers to victims, buying necklaces means strangling them, combing hair means grooming, bathing them means drowning them, et cetera. That's what I got based on context at least."

Mackenzie's mind reeled. "But Jeremiah's victims were young boys…"

"They don't specify how old the dolls need to be. And every single letter they exchange is just some version of this fantasy. It's the woman who sent him the first story, he replied with another version of his, and it's been like that ever since."

"How long have they been communicating for?" Nick asked.

"Almost three years. She sends him a letter at least every month. But she didn't *this* time." Jenna twirled a strand of her hair around her finger.

"Jeremiah hasn't told her to do anything?"

"They just talk through stories. They have character names. Now if there's more code hidden in them, then I don't know. It's tough to crack."

"What's the return address on the letters?" Mackenzie asked.

Jenna emailed them the information. "She uses the name Martha Beck, and the address is a PO box number."

"Good work, Jenna," Nick praised.

Jenna smiled haughtily. "I think I've earned a bubble bath tonight. I'll see you tomorrow."

Nick absentmindedly tapped his pockets before crossing his arms. "So, Jeremiah found someone who thinks like him. The question is, could he have manipulated her or did she just take matters into her own hands?"

Mackenzie leaned against the edge of the desk; her face melting into a frown as the information Jenna had dumped on him simmered inside her. "This is someone who approached *him*. She took the initiative. I think if Jeremiah left any instructions in the letters, then it would have been more obvious? But if they're talking in some deeper code within the code through the stories, then it's hard to crack it."

He paced the room. "We can't put anything past Jeremiah. He's capable of anything. But what if she just got bored of making up stories and decided to try the real thing? Do all this to feel closer to Jeremiah and try to exonerate him in the process?"

"I guess we'll find out." She checked her watch. "I'm going to head home. I have dinner plans."

"Oh?" He raised an eyebrow.

"It's just with my neighbor. Irene." She swallowed the words that she could use the company. It was usually Nick she'd hang out with.

"Yeah, it's a good idea to socialize after the day you've had."

Goosebumps sprouted on Mackenzie's arms, recalling the accident. She wanted to avoid spending time alone in her house after everything. The accident hadn't been that bad, but she still felt like she'd barely escaped death.

Or, rather, she'd barely escaped *someone*.

CHAPTER THIRTY-FIVE

March 10

Downtown Lakemore was only three blocks long. Devoid of any glass high-rises and shining billboards, it was a stark contrast to what Mackenzie had become used to when she lived in New York. The streets were cobbled and narrow, the restaurants and businesses housed in lines of box-like brick structures. The apartment buildings were never taller than seven-story; there was no financial district or cultural hub. When Mackenzie had arrived, the lack of stimulation had troubled her, but she soon began to see the beauty in an ordinary town like this. The woods and lakes provided a sense of tranquility and isolation. The silence meant she could hear her thoughts. People weren't always dismissive or in haste—they smiled, chatted, and invested in each other's lives.

But the smaller the town, the bigger the lies it buried.

"Mack?" Nick clicked his fingers. "You okay?"

"Yeah," she said half-heartedly and rubbed her chest.

"You not feeling well?"

"Just have a bad feeling." She had woken up with an odd feeling dancing on her skin.

She followed him inside a small building with "Fort Point Post Office" branded on the front door.

They headed toward one of the counters with a stout, middle-aged man working diligently behind it.

Nick tapped on the counter and showed his badge. "Mind if we ask a few questions?"

The man called Russell—according to his name tag—looked up with bright green eyes speckled with gold. "Yes?"

"We're looking for information on the owner of this PO box number." Nick slid a piece of paper to him. "She gave her name as Martha Beck."

Russell didn't even look at it. "That's confidential information, sir. I'm sorry."

"Have you been watching the news?" Mackenzie perked up, trying a different technique.

"Yeah…" Russell's face grew dim. "Is it about those missing kids?"

"Yes. So if you could give us the billing information it would really help."

He licked his lips and looked around, conflicted. "It's a personal box. You'll have to get a court order. And then I'll gladly help you."

Mackenzie exhaled and dropped her head. She turned to Nick, who was already on his phone, probably thumbing instructions to Jenna to get started on a warrant. It was a long shot, but they had hoped that someone would do them a solid.

"Do you remember anything about this person?" Nick asked, desperate. "You're not allowed to hand out confidential information, but you can tell us if you've seen anything."

Russell sighed, defeated, and asked to see the paper again. He frowned and tilted his head. "Oh, this one."

Mackenzie straightened. "What about it?"

"The only reason I remember this is because she keeps ordering these big packages that don't fit in the PO box so we have to set them aside for her."

"Can you tell us what she looks like?"

He shrugged. "Middle-aged, Caucasian, with long brown hair. Nothing special. Oh, wait. She always wears the same thing. Yellow jacket, funny bag with insects on it. Ladybugs. I asked her about it once, and she said they were her favorite growing up."

Mackenzie whirled her head to look at Nick, his dawning realization reflecting her own. It was the woman at Lucas's funeral, standing outside the church.

After thanking Russell, they walked out of the post office.

"So it wasn't just some curious bystander at the church," Mackenzie said.

"The court order won't take long with this case, but I'll get a uniform to keep an eye on this place. If she shows up, we can follow her."

They got inside the car, and Nick pulled out of the parking lot when Mackenzie's phone rang. It was Sully.

"We have a good lead, Sully. We're going to—"

"Mack." He just said her name, and she felt the gloom in the pit of her stomach. "A jogger called 911." And with each word, Mackenzie's chest caved in inch by inch. "We found Theo Reynolds."

CHAPTER THIRTY-SIX

There was one lighthouse in Lakemore. Looking over the calm waters of Budd Inlet, it was like the town's own personal guard, standing gallantly since the late 1800s when it was founded. Nobody came here anymore. A hundred years ago, a boat washed ashore carrying the slaughtered bodies of five women. No one ever found out what happened to them. Since then, the lighthouse had become a favorite subject for local storytellers, who told legends and poems about the ghosts of the five women still haunting it. There were accounts of locals and some daring tourists having paranormal experiences in the area, but nothing was ever confirmed, as was the norm with most cases of this nature.

Many in the town believed this space was a waste—a lot could be done with it. But Mackenzie liked the area being left alone. There were so few parts that were untouched. The lighthouse's beauty lay in its remoteness and lack of human presence.

Even the air tasted different here—cleaner and fresh.

Mackenzie got out of the car. A crowd of uniformed cops and men and women in forensic suits gathered around the large rocks at the base of the lighthouse where Theo Reynolds's body had been found.

After a century of being associated with death, the lighthouse's ghosts weren't going anywhere soon.

Mackenzie and Nick navigated their way across the sand toward the others.

Atlee Rivera was there as well. She stood away from the scene, facing the still water that somehow seemed more threatening than crashing waves.

Yellow and black tape was erected around the crime scene, with wooden sticks driven into the sand. The uniformed cops were huddled together, shaking their heads and looking over at Rivera. There were four techs, including Becky—one taking pictures, one making an inventory, and the last one scraping off evidence from the rocks.

Mackenzie stood behind the crime scene tape, finally getting a view of the body. Theo was splayed against the rocks in a sitting position, looking even smaller than he had in photos. His hands were positioned across his chest in an X-sign. Purple and brown marks blemished his neck. His eyelids were open, staring ahead at the vastness of the still water.

"Oh no," Mackenzie croaked. She didn't dare look at Nick. She could feel his anger.

Becky kneeled across Theo. She parted his lips and pointed a flashlight at his mouth. She looked over at Mackenzie and Nick. "His tongue has been cut out."

Nick growled, turning around and kicking the sand.

"Any other signs of assault?" Mackenzie inquired, keeping her wits.

Becky studied the body. "Clothes are intact, and they match the description of what he was wearing when he went missing." She pointed at his wrists. "There are ligature marks around his wrists. He was tied up. But his arms don't have any bruises."

Mackenzie followed Becky's finger, pointing at Theo's arms. They were so tiny. Grief threatened to burst out of her, but she swallowed it down. Now wasn't the time. Especially when Nick was pacing behind her like a caged animal.

"It's just him? Nothing else?" Mackenzie looked around the beach.

"No, ma'am," Peterson, a uniform, answered. His thumbs hooked into his belt. "We had people walk up and down the beach. There was nothing."

"What about footprints?" Nick asked.

"There were plenty by the time we got here," Peterson admitted.

"You took the jogger's statement?"

"Yes, sir. He saw no one else hanging out at the beach."

"And why was he jogging *here*?" Mackenzie pressed. "It's not a good terrain to go for a run."

"He says he lives close by."

"We'll need his information."

"Yes, ma'am."

Mackenzie glanced at Nick—a muscle in his neck throbbed and his jaw vibrated. "Becky, does he have anything in his throat?"

Becky peered into Theo's mouth with a flashlight. "Nothing's visible in the back of his throat. He does have large tonsils though." She pressed his throat lightly. "Hang on, I feel something. There's definitely something there. But I can only extract it during the autopsy. He does have an injury to the side of his head, a blow to the mastoid process like Lucas." She circled a patch of his hair.

Mackenzie squinted and saw the blackish dried blood mixed with his dark hair. Same brutality, another victim. "What can you tell us about time of death?"

"I'll know more after, but looks like he's been dead for over twelve hours at least."

Rivera joined them. "They left another clue in there for us?"

"Going by the first victim, I'd say so," Nick replied.

Rivera let out a juddering breath. "I might be new to Lakemore, but I know enough about this town to know that people don't just come here jogging."

Mackenzie addressed Peterson and the cops. "Do we have any surveillance in this area?"

"There's a camera monitoring the base." Peterson looked past Mackenzie to the lighthouse. "I don't know how much coverage it has."

"Get that footage," she instructed when her phone rang. It was John Newman, a deputy with the Sheriff's Office, who often helped them on cases. "Hey, John."

"Detective Price," his gravelly voice warbled slightly. "I thought to give you an update on the search. Is this a good time?"

Mackenzie ambled away from the commotion. "It's not public yet but will be soon enough. We just found another boy. Theo Reynolds."

"Oh shit."

"Yeah…" She noticed Nick and Rivera engaged in a heated discussion. Nick was fidgeting while Rivera kept pushing him. "What do you have?"

"We've covered sixty percent of the ground. Might feel slow, but we're being very thorough. And we recovered something."

"What?" She went alert.

"A backpack pin. It has Spiderman on it. Based on the descriptions provided to us, this belongs to Theo. I'll email you a map of the woods, marking where we found it."

"Great. Thanks, John."

After hanging up, Mackenzie stared at Theo's lifeless body slumped against the rocks. Her mouth went dry, her tongue sticking to the roof of her mouth. They had found something of his in the woods, something left behind in the moments he was taken. It was only a backpack pin, but it was still a piece of him.

The edges of her vision began blurring, the sight of Theo brightening until he was all she could see.

Two down. One more to go.

CHAPTER THIRTY-SEVEN

The screen was cluttered with animation and headlines, which all disappeared when music played and the words "Breaking News" flashed across the screen.

There was a podium with blue curtains in the background and the seal of the Lakemore PD. Rivera looked sharp as she walked up to the podium and put on her glasses to read a statement. Cameras clicked and flashed. A low drum of whispers around the room came to a halt when she started talking.

"*Lakemore PD is deeply regretful to inform that the body of Theo Reynolds was discovered by the lighthouse this afternoon. We have had the difficult conversation with the parents and extend our deepest condolences to them.*"

Mackenzie growled under her breath and turned off her phone.

Nick kick-started the engine again, turning into Marine street—the closest residential area to the lighthouse. Box-like houses lined both sides with cracks in white paint and loose hinges. The lush green trees in front of the houses formed a thick canopy over the street with sunlight leaking through the branches. The front yards were barren and yellow. Not a single one with healthy grass.

Mackenzie checked the address and directed him to the house on their left. A middle-aged man dressed in a tracksuit and baseball hat held a hose in his hand and watered the soil by the fence. When he saw them pull up next to his house, he removed his hat, revealing a receding hairline and forehead with permanent lines.

The temperature was cool, but the air was humid. The moment Mackenzie escaped the cool bubble of the car, a layer of sweat coated her skin and her hair began expanding.

"Toby Adler?" Nick asked.

"Yeah." He dropped the hose and shook his hand from across the fence. "Is this about that body I found?"

"It is. Mind if we ask a few questions?"

He shrugged. "No problem. Shoot."

"Do you usually go out for runs on that beach?" Mackenzie asked. "People usually avoid that place."

Toby snickered and puffed his chest. "I don't believe in that nonsense. Ghosts don't scare me. I'm a real man."

Mackenzie contained a chuckle in her throat and took notes in her notepad. Toby was instantly unlikeable—a quality he shared with Heather. The anger of being snubbed and overlooked manifested itself in a false sense of pride.

"What time did you find the body?" Nick inquired.

"After midday."

"And is that your usual time to go for a run? The hottest time of the day?" Mackenzie raised an eyebrow.

"Yes." He enunciated like he was talking to a child. "I like to sweat."

"Did you see anyone else there?" Nick interrupted in a tight voice, clearly not liking the man's standoffish attitude. "A car maybe? Anything?"

"No, it was deserted, like it always is."

"And what do you do for a living?"

"Why are you questioning *me*?" He crossed his bulging arms. "I was just a Good Samaritan, calling 911 immediately after I saw that boy. This is why people hesitate to do a good deed."

"You did the right thing, and we're grateful." Nick stroked the man's ego, which seemed to placate him. "These are just routine questions we ask."

"I work for a landscaping company," he replied gruffly. "In fact, I'm supposed to leave for a job any minute now. I didn't even get a chance to change. Have been doing chores since I got back. I bet I reek of death."

Mackenzie trailed her eyes over his white tracksuit, crinkled at the right places. His shoes were still caked in sand. She frowned. Something was wrong.

"You didn't get close to the body right? We just have to confirm that the crime scene was untouched," Nick continued.

"I didn't touch anything." He raised his hands. "I didn't get too close. I felt sick just looking at it."

"Are there any other regular runners in that area except for you, Mr. Adler?" Mackenzie asked. "Someone else you often see?"

Toby replied in a heartbeat. "It's always just me. Like I said, every single person here is scared of that beach and that lighthouse. I'm the only one with the brains and balls to realize it's bullshit."

After exchanging more routine questions and insisting Toby contact them if he remembered any information, they headed back to the car. Mackenzie watched Toby retreat back into his house, with a slight limp, to get ready for work.

"He's kind of an ass," Nick said.

"He's lying."

Nick paused at the door of the car. He looked at Mackenzie from over the car wryly. "Why do you say that?"

She tipped her chin in his direction. "He's not walking straight."

Nick followed her gaze and saw Toby's unbalanced gait disappear into the house. "Doesn't look bad enough for him to not go for a jog. Plus he's built. He's probably used to working through mild injuries."

"He wasn't wearing running shoes." She smiled conspiratorially. "He was wearing Toms, which were covered in sand."

"No way. He lied about his reason for being there."

"He'll probably come up with some excuse if we confront him," she said, climbing into the car.

"I'll run a background check on him when we get to the station." Nick got inside, looking thoughtful, and turned on the air conditioning. Both breathed a sigh of relief at the cool air. "Why is it this hot all of a sudden?"

Mackenzie tried to relax her muscles, still wound up from the discovery of Theo. The more she thought about it, the more her nerves sizzled. "I miss the sound of rain."

"You're in luck. There's a thunderstorm tonight. Why would he lie about his reason for being at the beach?"

"I don't know," Mackenzie said. "But the killer left us another message. Becky is starting the autopsy this evening." Her stomach swooped at the thought of what message their killer had left behind this time. Another clue left inside his victim meant to aid their investigation. They had failed Theo Reynolds. The mere possibility of failing Noah Kinsey was out of the question.

"Jenna texted me. She has prepared the affidavit for the post office. We should get a judge sign it this evening, and we can go tomorrow." Nick blinked rapidly. "Maybe we can finally end this when we find that *Martha* woman."

CHAPTER THIRTY-EIGHT

Mackenzie had lost count of how many times she had told someone that their missing loved one had been found dead. She tried keeping count at the start of her career. She didn't want her victims to blur into one over the years—and assigning each of them a number seemed a good way to account for their distinctness. But after her first year, she couldn't take it anymore.

It was always the same: they looked at her with wide, teary eyes, their bodies restless and a desperate prayer on their lips. Their brains whispered that the worst had happened. That's what logic dictated; that a missing person wasn't often found alive. Especially when they had been missing for more than a few days. But hope was the hardest emotion to kill. No matter how dire circumstances were, the flicker of hope always remained, refusing to be extinguished.

And then Mackenzie would crush that hope. She would say the words that they would always remember; words that they would replay over and over in their minds years later. Some would cry immediately, grief slamming into them in full force. They'd collapse, physically unable to grasp the meaning of her words. While others would dissociate from reality, like their souls had partially detached from them. They looked like ghosts; lost, confused, and not belonging to this world anymore.

Mackenzie held Theo's backpack pin in her palm. The mere feel of it was almost scorching, as though it was branding her skin.

She was in the lounge and looked up at Theo's parents with Sully and Rivera in the conference room.

This time she hadn't been the one to break the news to them. She had missed the moment that ruined them forever, but she was here to see the aftermath. Mr. Reynolds tearfully engaging in a shouting match with Sully and Rivera, his face red, tears flowing unchecked. He kept pacing back and forth, breathing hard, unable to find an outlet for his rage, confusion and misery.

He never would.

Behind him, Mrs. Reynolds sat on a chair, staring into empty space, completely removed from her husband's meltdown. A ghost, like Mackenzie had seen many times before. But no matter how many times she'd encountered mourning families, she wouldn't grow numb to it. It was an ache that manifested in a different form in a different place, impossible to train oneself to expect it.

Finally, Mackenzie mustered the strength to enter the conference room. Nobody noticed her. The loud voices of her bosses and Mr. Reynolds didn't register in her brain. She made her way to Mrs. Reynolds with woolly legs. Her heart galloped inside her chest. Blood roared in her ears. Gingerly, she sat next to Mrs. Reynolds, struggling to find her voice.

"Mrs. Reynolds?" she whispered.

Mrs. Reynolds didn't reply; her face had fallen, like she had permanently lost control of the muscles.

Tears pricked Mackenzie's eyes. She took Mrs. Reynolds's hand; the latter didn't flinch at the touch. Mackenzie opened her palm for her and placed the backpack pin in it. "Mrs. Reynolds, we found this in the woods. Looks like it snagged off Theo at some point."

Mrs. Reynolds jerked at that. She looked at her hand like she was looking at it for the first time. Her fingertips kept grazing the pin, like she was memorizing its texture. Like she was trying to find Theo's touch on it. And that's all she did. Obsessed with the pin, staring at it with a longing wonder, as if it was her talisman. The only thing in the world she cared about anymore.

Mackenzie couldn't handle it. She dashed out of the room and straight to the washroom. She locked herself shut and went over to the sink. Her breaths came in short spurts. The first sob came. And then the second. And the third.

Next thing Mackenzie knew she was crying in full force. Little whimpers escaped her throat, snot dripped down from her nose, and her eyes ached from the tears bursting out of them.

She turned on the faucet and washed her face again and again and again. By the time she turned off the water, her fingers were pruned and her face almost rough from the repeated scrubbing.

Pulling herself together, she came out of the washroom. Her eyes were red, face swollen. Anyone would look at her and know that she cried. Mackenzie didn't cry. Usually she prided herself on her ability to stay composed. But she didn't care today. The sadness of the situation was deeper than her fear of exposing her vulnerability.

Nick wasn't in the office, but his computer was running and jacket hanging behind his chair. Even his phone was sitting on the desk. When he didn't return after five minutes, she decided to look for him.

An instinct told her to look outside. Maybe he wanted fresh air. Outside, the sky was a midnight blue with clouds rolling in. Thunder grumbled low, beckoning a thunderstorm. Walking around the building, she saw Nick. He stood with his back facing her, one hand in his pocket. And then she noticed smoke slithering away from his face.

"I knew it!" she cried, stomping toward him.

Nick turned around and dropped the cigarette under his boot. "Mack."

"That explains it." She got in his face, irrational anger taking over. "That's why sometimes you show up eerily calm, why you're wearing a lot of body spray, why you disappear so often to get *fresh air!*"

He sighed and rubbed his eyes. "I relapsed, but it's not a big deal."

"If it wasn't, you wouldn't have been hiding it."

"I'm an adult. I don't need this." He snapped and walked past her, but she grabbed his elbow.

"Just because you're stressed out that doesn't mean you should pick up habits that will kill you, Nick. You're stronger than this."

"Not everyone is perfect like you, Mack. Some of us have vices."

The sky tore open then. It grew darker, their faces submerged in shadows, Mackenzie's eyes blinking against the sudden rain. Her clothes clung to her skin, and her teeth chattered. "Your mother died of lung cancer. Don't do this."

He pushed his hair out of his eyes and interlaced his fingers behind his head. "Don't you get it? I'm the reason they're dead."

"No!" she shouted over the noise of rain hitting asphalt. "Whatever mission this killer is on is *not* your fault. Just because Johnny's killer is still at large that doesn't justify this person abducting and killing more boys."

"But they wouldn't have if I had made more of an effort to confirm Jeremiah's alibi. If I had caught Johnny's killer, those three boys would be at home with their families," he said, his face tortured.

"You don't know that."

"What?"

"I said you don't know that!" she shouted. "Whoever this is, they're unhinged. They're just looking for an excuse to hurt people. How do you know they wouldn't have hurt someone else?"

Nick shook his head, unwilling to listen to reason. He back-tracked and loosened his tie. "You can't convince me otherwise, Mack. No matter what reasons I might have had in the past for making that call, *I* was responsible for Johnny. And I failed him.

And now others are paying the price. The truth is that sometimes intent doesn't matter. Only the end result does. But I don't expect you to understand."

He left her standing in the rain alone. Not knowing just how much Mackenzie understood that sentiment.

You have to help me bury him.

They both were stuck in their past, punishing themselves for mistakes that were beyond their control. But neither of them could help each other.

CHAPTER THIRTY-NINE

Mackenzie was dripping wet when she went back inside the building. The thunderstorm was visceral and growing. There were moments when she felt that the building itself was shaking. When she reached the office, she saw Nick, Troy, Austin, and Finn sitting around, talking and drinking.

"What are you guys doing?" Mackenzie frowned.

"Not hanging outside in a thunderstorm for starters." Troy smiled and handed her a beer.

"I'm not really in the mood to drink." She shook her head and went to her desk, to pack up.

"Then you definitely should." He nudged her. "These aren't celebratory drinks, trust me."

She looked around at her coworkers, all fatigued and dim, slumped on chairs.

"Becky won't be done with the autopsy until tomorrow evening," Nick said. "What are you going to do when you get home? Be upset on your own?"

Mackenzie sat on a chair and took the bottle from Troy. They raised the bottles together, a ripple of unenthusiastic grunts. Finn played jazz music, to which Troy raised an eyebrow.

"I swear we're more fun than this, Austin," Troy said.

"Nah, I get it, man. We've all had bad days like these."

"Where did you transfer from?" Mackenzie asked, curious about the man investigating Charles's murder.

"Port Angeles."

"That's a big city. Why did you move to Lakemore?"

He shrugged. "I was looking for a change. This was one of the departments that happened to be looking for a detective."

"You showed up at the wrong time." Finn shook his head. "No football, FBI investigation winding down, recession, constant scrutiny, and now these kids. Am I missing something?"

"Rain," Troy said and, just like that, thunder boomed, rattling the windows. "Bang on. Though I'm sure you were used to worse in Port Angeles."

Austin shrugged.

"When's the wedding, Troy?" Nick slapped his back.

"June."

"You have a date?" he exclaimed. Troy and his fiancé, Ella, had been going back and forth for over a year.

"We're going to elope," he replied proudly.

"What about you, Austin? Anyone in your life?" Mackenzie asked.

"No." He took a hesitant swig.

"We usually go around and talk about the moment we decided to get into law enforcement when there's a new addition to the team," Troy intervened. "It's tradition. Let's just get on with it. I'll go first. I was eleven years old, and I was mugged. He ran away with my bag, which also contained the last story my father had written before he died. I never got it back." Troy gave them an easy smile. But he always wore one. It was how he covered everything up, wrapping a joke around all problems. But Mackenzie saw the hint of regret in his eyes. The pain of losing this last token of his father, his last words gone forever.

"I thought being a cop would be cool." Finn snorted. "Chasing around bad guys with guns. I didn't know all this would be involved." He jutted his thumb toward the piles of paperwork on his desk.

"I grew up around politicians," Nick admitted reluctantly. "Naturally, I didn't want to become one." Everyone chuckled. "I believe in public service. And this is how I do it."

When they looked at Mackenzie expectedly, she said, "I've lived in New York." It was the white lie she conjured up when she was ambushed with the tradition. Truth was, she was desperately trying to atone for her sins, to do enough good until she could erase the bad. But it never seemed enough. Her coworkers seemed to buy it. "What about you?" she asked Austin.

"Uh, I guess I just like justice. Righting wrongs." His body tensed as he gave Mackenzie a fleeting glance.

The conversation flowed freely after that, though Mackenzie and Nick mostly stayed quiet. But the distraction was a soothing balm to the horrors of the day. Every time Mackenzie and Nick caught each other's eyes, they exchanged something. A helpless feeling fraught with an overpowering sense of determination. They knew that they had to get back to work, because neither of them could live through another day like this—have another boy murdered on their watch.

CHAPTER FORTY

March 11

Mackenzie pushed the cart in the crowded aisle, feeling overwhelmed by the variety of spices and sauces on the racks. Everyone around her expertly plucked off their trusted brands, while she stood there feeling sixteen years old, when she had started cooking for her sick grandmother on a daily basis.

Her ex-husband had spoiled her for the last six years.

"Take this one." Irene handed her pasta sauce. "It's tangier."

"Thanks. Trust me, I'm not a lost cause. I'm just out of practice."

"No judgment here." She raised her hands in surrender. "You have a lot on your plate. Chasing bad guys and busting your head open."

Mackenzie's hand flew up to her forehead. It wasn't too deep of a cut, and she didn't have a concussion. The stitches would dissolve soon enough. But the memory of the fear and the frantic pounding of her heart was still fresh. Someone *was* after her. She had been followed and then left alone once she swerved off the road and right into a tree.

"Yeah." Mackenzie sighed, as they walked around the store, collecting various items.

"I'm thinking of going hiking next weekend," Irene said. "But I reckon I've explored all the trails in Lakemore now. Do you have any suggestions further afield?"

"Well, you have to go to Mount Rainier. It's basically tradition. It's a bit of a drive though."

Irene waved her hand. "I'll rent a car. Which reminds me, when will you get your car back?"

"End of the week." She loaded up on bleach, to which Irene smirked. "Clean freak."

"I've noticed. Aren't you going to have trouble getting around?"

"I'll just take a bus or a cab. I'll manage." They joined a long checkout queue as all the self-checkout machines were out of service.

"You said you have a partner, right? Nick, was it?"

Mackenzie swallowed. "Yeah."

"What?" She noticed her stiffen.

"It's just he's going through some stuff right now, and I'm not getting through to him no matter how hard I try. So maybe I should give up and let him be?"

Mackenzie hated it. Months ago, miscommunication and misunderstanding had driven them apart. She had been furious with him in the past, feeling betrayed. But he hadn't given up on her. No matter how hard she pushed him away, he had never stopped trying to fix their friendship. It was something he'd always done. But this time, the roles were reversed, and Mackenzie found herself at a loss. She was the one who was usually so closed up—how was she supposed to help him open up?

"Maybe you shouldn't," Irene suggested as they moved forward in the queue.

"Why?"

"I think sometimes the other person needs you to force your way in even if they don't realize that's what they need. And even if you're not good at it, it's more the gesture that counts. My dad was a proud man," she smiled fondly. "He'd never say it, but me interfering helped him."

Mackenzie had ended up spending a lot of time with her new neighbor. She'd come to value her advice and her company. "I'll try."

"It involves putting your ego aside. I'll tell you that." She chuckled.

"I can't afford to have an ego when I already have so few people in my life." Mackenzie bit her tongue. "Sorry. I didn't mean to sound that sad. I swear."

Irene smiled, a dimple appearing on one side of her face.

The car wobbled, going over potholes and soft mud before Mackenzie finally killed the engine, putting an end to the awkwardness of the car ride. She had spent the drive testing words in her mind, following Irene's suggestion. But her tongue was too heavy to articulate anything. Worse was that she felt like Nick hadn't even noticed the jarring silence between them.

"We here?" His tone was curt.

He didn't wait for Mackenzie to reply and exited the car.

She followed suit and cringed at the tires of Nick's car caked in soil. Ahead of them, a run-down house sat on a marsh along the edge of a small lake. The air was infused with smells of saltwater, fertilizers, and rotten eggs. "That's her house."

The warrant had been approved early in the morning. Jenna had received the billing information of Martha Becks—real name Agatha Bellini—and traced her address to an isolated house in the middle of nowhere.

They trudged light-footed through the soft land with long grass brushing the hems of their pants.

"Around a decade ago, she was charged with assault," Mackenzie said, ignoring the urge to hurl, seeing her soiled boots. "Attacked her boyfriend after he broke up with her. Smashed a bottle on his head."

Nick didn't respond, merely nodding while scoping the area. "She shares her fantasies with a child killer and obviously lives a very isolated life."

When they reached the house, the hum of the traffic dissolved. Wind caused blades of grass to brush against each other. Mackenzie didn't know whether to appreciate the seclusion or be terrified by it.

The house was ramshackle, with peeling paint and rusty frames. Despite the sun being out, it looked like it was under constant shadow, somehow shirking the light. Plants reached out from the earth, covering the bottom as if trying to pull the structure down.

"Lakemore PD!" Nick knocked on the door.

It swung open with a creak.

Mackenzie's hand went to her gun out of reflex. But what greeted them was a musty smell, cold air, and bottomless darkness.

"Ms. Bellini?" she called out, and her voice bounced back.

"Looks like no one's home. We're not allowed to enter."

She took out her phone and turned on the flashlight, casting it ahead. "What the hell?"

The living room was stuffed—packed—with dollhouses of all sizes. Some looked elaborate and expensive with toy furniture and others handcrafted and sloppy. Dolls were in the houses. Some were positioned on the miniature beds tied up, others nailed to the wall, and a few submerged faces down in tiny bathtubs filled with water like floating bodies.

It was so cramped that the room had nothing else—no couch or table or television or shelves. There was just enough space to maneuver for one person. It reminded Mackenzie of a hoarder's place. An unusual if generally harmless sickness, except in this case there were undertones of violence.

"Holy shit," Nick whispered. "Point the light at the walls."

Mackenzie did. The walls were covered with newspaper clippings of Jeremiah and presumably the letters they'd exchanged.

Nick's phone rang and he stepped away, while Mackenzie continued her limited exploration of Agatha's sick mind. There was nobody inside and nothing in this area. Where was Agatha? She spotted a plate on the floor with a moldy loaf of bread on it.

"I asked Jenna to visit Agatha's workplace. Agatha hasn't been there in three days," Nick said. "They said they have no idea where she is. She never informed them of any leave."

"I think she might have left in a hurry. There's moldy food on the floor." She pointed it out to him.

His eyes glinted. "I'll get an emergency warrant to search her place and her phone location."

"And track her credit cards. Provided we don't find any of those things in there."

While Nick got on the phone, firing orders, Mackenzie swept her eyes over the house one last time. If her obsession with Jeremiah as they bonded over their twisted desires wasn't enough, the fact that Agatha had apparently fled in a hurry cast a major doubt on her innocence.

Something visceral flared inside Mackenzie's gut. Agatha was clearly a deranged and potentially dangerous woman, and she was missing. But was she alone? Or did she have Noah with her?

CHAPTER FORTY-ONE

Back at the station, Nick immediately went to his computer. "Clint has started monitoring Agatha's phone. It's turned off, and the last location it was active was her house. Three days ago."

"Peterson's with the team at her house." Mackenzie read Peterson's text. "He says they couldn't find her phone or wallet. Her cupboards and drawers were open. Looks like she left in a hurry."

"Any sign that the boys were there?" Nick fiddled with his lighter. "Rope? Theo was bound."

"Nothing obvious as of yet. But she could have gotten rid of it or taken it with her."

He sighed, disappointed, and turned back to his computer. "Toby Adler has quite a rap sheet," he told her, looking at the information obtained from WASIS. "He's been busted a few times when he was young for drug possession and intent to sell."

Mackenzie shimmied her jacket off and hung it on the back of the chair. "What kind of drugs?"

"Just cocaine."

"Just?" She scoffed. "Anything else?"

"That's it. I can't find any connection with any of the victims or Jeremiah."

"When will Becky be done with the autopsy?"

"Tonight," he assured her. "And Theo's clothes have been sent to the crime lab."

"Lucas was killed in the woods almost immediately, but Theo had been held captive for almost a week." She nodded, her thoughts spinning. "There must be some evidence on his clothes that can give some indication on where he was held."

"Let's hope so."

The map of Washington was pinned to a wall in the office and next to it a map of Lakemore with its deep woods and many lakes. There were several hiding places. Cabins tucked in the safety of forests or a basement in an inconspicuous house. Her imagination ran amok.

Justin arrived, his mustache bushy enough to cover his entire upper lip. "I was able to get the security tapes from the lighthouse. There is only one camera, and it's an old system."

"Tell me they don't delete recordings every day or something?" Nick asked.

"They do, sir," Justin said. "But Clint was able to recover the deleted CCTV footage from the hard drive. He's working on it right now."

"Let's go," Mackenzie suggested, springing up and leading them to the lower floor where Clint worked with other forensic IT professionals. "This killer doesn't do anything without a reason. Why did he choose the lighthouse?"

"No one goes there," Justin remarked.

"Exactly! He wants us to find them," she said. "Why would he leave Theo there knowing that it could take days for us to find him?"

"Maybe he disposed of the body there because he didn't want to risk being seen by anyone else?"

Mackenzie agreed—but her gut feeling told her that there was a reason beyond his desire not to be discovered.

Clint was in a fortress behind four giant monitors. His office was almost as big as Sully's, with a series of open windows running along the walls.

"Do you have something?" Nick asked.

Clint didn't look up. His giraffe-long neck meant the top part of his face was visible behind the screens. "I'm just sharpening the footage. The camera they use is super old, clearly barely any money goes into maintaining the lighthouse since it's decommissioned, and on sale apparently. Not that anyone wants to buy it. If I could just enhance the edge contrasts, you'd be able to actually make out shapes."

"Can you get the footage for a week before yesterday?" Mackenzie said. Nick shot her a puzzled look. "I just want to be thorough. I think the killer could be trying to tell us something."

"Sure." Clint nodded.

After almost half an hour of watching Clint work efficiently, he sighed.

"This is the best I can do. Don't ask for zoom and enhance because the cameras are really bad."

They crowded around one of the monitors. The camera gave a partial view of the beach on the side and the direct view of the road ahead.

"It doesn't cover where the body was found." Mackenzie clicked her tongue.

"The camera is there to only monitor the entrance of the lighthouse," Justin said.

"I guess this was expected. They're not stupid enough to get recorded."

The video played for the day Theo's body was found. The timestamp indicated hours going by with no person coming into the view of the camera. At just before two in the afternoon, Toby Adler appeared to walk toward the lighthouse from the road.

"It doesn't look like he was jogging," Nick said.

Toby stood in front of the lighthouse, then froze. He tilted his head and disappeared out of the frame. Minutes later, the beach was crawling with police and squad cars.

"That's when he must have noticed the body and called 911," Justin concluded.

Clint played the footage of the night before—and there was nothing to notice. They went back further, checking both day and night, unfortunately coming up empty-handed. Mackenzie's shoulders began to slump in disappointment. She had hoped to catch someone scoping the area. Surely the killer must have visited the lighthouse at some point before dumping the body.

"Didn't Toby say he goes for a run every day at the beach?" Mackenzie's eyes narrowed in suspicion.

"Maybe he does. The beach is barely in the frame. We won't see him," Nick said, absorbed by the mundane reiteration of events on screen. It was like watching paint dry.

When they checked the recording for four days ago, Adler appeared again. Just as before, he walked up to the entrance of the lighthouse and stood there.

"What is he doing?" Mackenzie murmured.

Exactly eleven minutes later, a woman appeared in the frame. She was large, with black hair falling over to her shoulders. But her features were too vague to make out.

"Can you improve the resolution on her face?"

"Sure, Mack. I'll just do pixel interpolation," Clint quipped, always showing off his skills. He began muttering as he worked on improving the quality.

Mackenzie looked at Nick, whose lips were parted and forehead bunched.

"Here you go," Clint announced.

The image cleared, confirming Mackenzie's suspicion.

It was Patricia Wozniak—Jeremiah's sister.

CHAPTER FORTY-TWO

"What's Patricia doing talking to him?" Justin voiced the question on everyone's mind.

"Nick, you said that Toby had no connection to Jeremiah?" Mackenzie asked.

"There's no record of anything. Their jobs don't overlap. Didn't go to the same school. But clearly they know each other."

The video kept playing. Toby and Patricia talked for five minutes, at the end of which Toby handed her a parcel.

"Pause!" Mackenzie said. "Can we get a better look at that?"

Clint hissed through his teeth. "Sorry, but there isn't enough light on the parcel. This is the most adjustment I can make."

The video was in black and white, obscuring the color, but the parcel was average-sized. Patricia took out a wad of cash from her pocket and handed it to Toby. She tucked the parcel under her arm and left the scene, with Toby walking in the opposite direction.

They went over the tapes for the other days, but it seemed Patricia and Toby had met only once that week.

"He gives her a parcel and then she pays him," Nick repeated. "Toby lied. He was standing at the entrance of the lighthouse. Probably waiting for Patricia until he saw the body and cancelled their meetup."

"We need to talk to Patricia," Mackenzie noted.

"You better take the lead. She hates me."

Mackenzie scoffed. "Look at that. There's a witness who'd rather talk to me than with you."

*

The thunderstorm had subsided in the early hours of the morning. But Lakemore didn't look like itself anymore, not since murder and corruption had ruined their chances of winning the Olympic Championship one year ago.

Today, as Nick drove through the streets, Mackenzie saw the town as a reflection of herself. Lakemore had put its faith in the wrong people, much like she had done with her mother that night, and later with Charles when he came back into her life. Now, something unknown was haunting Lakemore, a resurrected danger that made the residents skittish and fearful, just like Mackenzie felt. Someone was toying with her, and she felt sure it was to do with her past.

"When are you getting your car back again?" Nick asked.

She jolted out of her thoughts. "Later today. The shop called and said the repairs were faster than anticipated. Do you mind taking me around?"

"No. I was just making conversation… Austin talked to me about you."

"What?"

"Yeah, before you came in today."

Irritation prickled her. "What did he ask?"

"Your whole story. How long you were in New York for? Why were you in New York at all?"

She held the armrest in a tight grasp. "Why is he asking these questions?"

"It has to do with Charles, right?"

"He can ask me these questions himself."

Nick gave her a dry look. "He's just following protocol, Mack. You're a person of interest. He's gathering intel on you from others. Don't worry. I didn't say anything that could get you in trouble. Not that there is anything."

A rock turned over in Mackenzie's stomach. Austin was asking questions, inching slowly towards a gruesome truth that no one would ever guess.

The trailer park came into sight, pulling her out of her fears.

Their boots landed in moist soil as they walked over to Patricia's mobile home. Nick stood behind, and Mackenzie knocked.

Patricia opened the door with a scowl. "Oh, it's you again."

"We have some questions," Mackenzie said.

"What if I don't want to answer them?"

"What if I tell you we have you on tape visiting a place where a boy's body turned up? Same M.O. as your brother."

Patricia kept the door ajar and leaned against the frame, not inviting them inside. "Ask your questions."

"Do you know Toby Adler?"

She waited a beat before answering, looking at Nick warily. "Yes."

"When was the last time you met him?"

"Sometime last week. I don't remember." She put an arm across the doorway, blocking the entrance. "Why?"

"How do you know him?"

"We're dating."

Mackenzie turned to exchange a look with Nick but found him ogling the mobile home. "And how long have you been dating him for, Patricia?"

"A few months." There was nothing in her expression that indicated that she was talking about someone she was intimate with. No hint of fondness or desire for a man she claimed to be dating for a few months.

"We have your meeting on tape. There was nothing romantic about it. What was in that parcel he gave you?"

"He bought something for me, and I paid him. I'm a modern woman. I pay for myself."

"And what was in that parcel?"

"Nobody's business," she replied cagily. "Look I'm busy. I don't know what happened to that kid who was found at the lighthouse."

"Just one more question!" Mackenzie piped up. "Do you know anyone by the name Agatha Bellini? Has Jeremiah ever mentioned her?"

Patricia narrowed her eyes. "No. Stop wasting my time."

Before Mackenzie could react, Patricia shut the door in her face with enough force for the hinges to squeak out a protest.

"Well, she wasn't cooperative with me either," Mackenzie sighed.

"She's lying," Nick bit out, heading back to the car. "That exchange was purely transactional. They barely talked. No way they're in a relationship. Do you think she was getting something for Jeremiah?"

That piqued Mackenzie's interest even further. "Like what?"

Nick ran a hand through his hair. "I'm just throwing ideas around. Patricia is actively involved in Jeremiah's defense, and she's been regularly visiting him at least once a week since he was locked up. She might be trying to help him somehow, or doing him some favors?"

"I'll ask Justin to keep an eye on Patricia." Mackenzie was already on her phone. "It's no coincidence that the body was left there. She could have been lying about not knowing about Agatha too. Maybe they're all in it together somehow. Doing all this shit for Jeremiah."

"She's loyal to a fault when it comes to her brother," Nick agreed as they drove out of the trailer park and headed to Olympia to pay Becky a visit.

Mackenzie got a notification on her phone confirming that a picture of Agatha had been circulated to everyone in Lakemore PD and the media. The public was urged to help look for her, as she was a person of interest. It wasn't typical for Lakemore PD to aggressively hunt down persons of interest, spending money on posters and getting authorization requests from the merchant to track credit card activity. But this case had injected a sense of urgency into everyone higher up in the food chain.

"Was it like this the last time?" Mackenzie asked after the silence in the car became too overbearing.

Nick knew what she meant. "Yeah."

Suddenly, she wished she hadn't asked. His face clouded with darkness, and he tapped his pockets.

"Looking for cigarettes?" She cocked an eyebrow.

"Yes," he said exasperated. "I'm stopping, okay? No need to bust my balls again."

She recalled Irene telling her not to give up, but she didn't know how to get through to him. A plan was forming, but with the case trampling in full speed and the clock ticking, she hoped she'd be able to execute it.

CHAPTER FORTY-THREE

They reached the building that housed the morgue. It was situated in a drafty basement with yellow tiles and undertones of a stench of death. Whenever Mackenzie walked through the hallway, she was reminded of the time her grandmother had appeared at the end of a similar hallway in a hospital all those years ago to inform her that Melody had bled into her brain and wasn't going to make it.

Becky opened a door and gestured them into her office. Her messy hair was tied up with stray strands falling to her chin. She rubbed her eyes and suppressed a yawn as Mackenzie and Nick entered her cramped office with her research articles framed on the wall. "I thought it'd be easier for us to go over the findings here. Unless you want to look at Theo…"

"No," Nick replied immediately, his lip quivering. "What do you have?"

Becky showed them pictures of Theo on the table with a Y-incision running down his abdomen. His eyes were closed, his neck covered his bruises. His skin was so pale that his lips had turned blue. His eyelids looked thicker. His feet and back were hues of purple and blue. Mackenzie looked at his fingers and remembered the backpack pin. A piece of him left behind for his parents to hold on to.

"Piophilidae eggs put time of death within the last two days," Becky said. "Based on the rate of decomposition and ambient temperature, I'd say he died around twenty-four hours before he was found."

"And the cause of death?" Mackenzie asked.

"Same as Lucas." She directed them to a close-up picture of the wound on Theo's head. The dried blood had been cleaned up, revealing a bumpy scar running along his scalp. "It was a single blow to the mastoid process. A quick and painless death. Unlike with Lucas, Theo was killed in a single strike, which means they're getting better with human anatomy."

"And he was also strangled after dying?" Mackenzie asked.

"That's correct. His tongue was cut post-mortem too. There were no signs of any physical or sexual assault. He had ligature marks, but that's about it." Becky inhaled with a shiver. "I've collected samples of bile from his gall bladder, eye fluid, urine, and liver to check for poisons and hair and blood samples to test for any drugs. But the main discovery of the autopsy was the item left inside Theo's throat."

"What is it?" Nick demanded.

Becky withdrew an evidence bag. "See for yourself."

Mackenzie picked up the bag and turned it in her hands. It contained a little wooden disk with symbols running along the rim. "What's this? Some kind of toy?"

Nick took it from her. A deep frown marred his face. "It sort of looks like a cipher wheel."

"But those have letters in concentric circles. This is just one row of strange symbols."

"I haven't seen anything like this. Hopefully it's not a common item. Maybe we can track it down and find out who bought it." He took pictures of it on his phone.

Mackenzie studied the symbols—some were repetitive, and all consisted of straight lines at different angles and dots. What was the killer trying to tell them now?

*

At night, when Mackenzie parked her car in the driveway, her phone rang. Her pulse picked up, but when she saw the name, she relaxed.

"Hi, Damien," she answered the call, turned off the engine and got out of the car.

"Mackenzie, I hope I'm not disturbing you?" he asked politely, and for an aching moment she wondered if his voice resembled his brother's. Her memory of Robert's voice was faint; she heard it, but she had to strain her mind, and if she did too much, then it would go further away from her. It's like the memory stayed at a distance to punish her.

"Not at all. Is everything okay?"

"Yes, yes. I just called because I have something of Robert's that I think you should have."

She froze in her tracks. "What is it?"

"It's a watch. Our father gave it to him. He used to wear it all the time." Damien's voice grew soft and longing. "We used to joke that it was his lucky charm. He forgot to wear it the day he…"

Mackenzie's chest grew tight, and the tremor rendered her temporarily unable to speak. "Damien, are you s-sure?"

"Yes. He's your father. He'd want you to have it."

This was so utterly twisted that Mackenzie had to scramble to wrap her head around it. She couldn't share with Damien why she had no right to have that watch, not after what she did with Robert's body.

"Okay. T-thanks."

"Send me your address, and I can just drop it off?"

"I will." She disconnected the call and pressed her hand into her chest. If only Damien knew…

The loud music from Irene's house distracted her from her thoughts. Through the window, she saw shadows of moving people and remembered Irene was having a party for some coworkers. Mackenzie was invited but had declined.

She unlocked the door to her house and stood at the precipice of the darkness that had swallowed her house. Something made her pause briefly and peer into the darkness, sniff the air.

Chalking it up to not liking coming back to an empty home, she turned on the light.

She saw it immediately. Her body wilted out of fear. Her ears burned.

On the kitchen island, there was a knife. She remembered clearly that she hadn't left it there.

Adrenaline came roaring back in, and she dropped her bag and pulled out her service weapon, pointing it directly ahead.

"Who's here?" she shouted in a menacing voice.

No response.

She bolted the door shut behind her and propped a chair against it, making it a little more inconvenient for anyone to escape. This was her home. There was no doubt that someone had been inside, not only trespassed on her property but also violated her space and privacy. A strong sense of protectiveness surged through her as her training kicked in and she began surveying every room and corner one by one, like she was on a mission.

She strained her ears, listening out for the faintest of sounds. It was deadly silent. She checked the study, the powder room, all the bedrooms, and even the attic. There was no one else in the house. When she came back downstairs, the chair was balanced against the door, just like she'd left it.

Whoever it was, they had left.

Reaching the bottom of the stairs, she felt lonelier than ever. What was their endgame? Trying to run her off the road suggested someone wanted her dead. But moving her furniture, leaving knives out, and throwing a rock through her window? What did they hope to accomplish?

Mackenzie went to the kitchen to put the knife away when a scream got stuck in her throat.

There was blood on the knife.

"Shit!" She growled and thought of her options. She could call 911. But what can of worms would that open? Austin was already sniffing around.

But whose blood was on the knife? She frowned and picked up it, carefully inspecting the tip of the blade dipped in red. It wasn't blood. It was ketchup. The ketchup bottle on the counter was lying horizontal.

This was a message, but what did they want from her?

CHAPTER FORTY-FOUR

March 12

Mackenzie parked the car and turned to the passenger seat. "I really hope this works."

"You worry too much, Aunty Mack." Luna's legs dangled off the booster seat. She tipped her chin up to be able to look above the dashboard. Her small, chubby face was pinched in fierce concentration.

"What are you looking for?" Mackenzie followed her suspicious gaze.

"Daddy says always keep an eye on your surroundings."

"Okay, kid." She helped her climb off. "You're at the police station. It's pretty safe here."

She caught herself, remembering how only a few months ago a squad car was set on fire in this very parking lot. Lakemore had revolted due to the sudden turn of events following the outcome of the Perez case. It was a painful adjustment period to live with dwindling jobs and no football to distract them from their woes.

Luna's blonde hair was tied in two pigtails like always, which swung in a steady rhythm when she walked.

Mackenzie held her hand, guiding her across the parking lot under the pouring rain. "It was generous of your Mom to allow you to skip school today."

"She knows Daddy is having a rough time, and half of my class is sick with the flu."

Mackenzie had driven to Olympia, asking Shelly to let her borrow Luna for brunch. Luckily, Shelly wasn't planning on sending Luna to school anyway and needed someone to watch her for a few hours while she was at work. It had all worked out.

At the station, Luna waved and greeted everyone. Like a breath of fresh air. Before opening the doors, Mackenzie took a breath in anticipation, hoping her plan worked. If there was anyone who could cheer Nick up, it was Luna. They'd had dinner recently, but she reckoned they should spend more time together if possible.

"Look who's here," Mackenzie announced.

Nick was perched on his chair, his fingers crunching his hair as he stared at the computer screen. He looked at them distracted. Then his eyes lit up. "Luna?" He shot up from his chair, just in time for Luna to wrap her hands around his waist.

Troy took off his headphones and beamed. "Hey, Luna!"

She gave him a high five.

"Mack, what's going on?" Nick looked worried. "Luna, are you okay?" He inspected her from head to toe.

"Yes, Daddy. We're going for brunch." Luna rolled her eyes.

"I hadn't seen her in a while. I thought we should catch up," Mackenzie explained slowly.

"Now's not the time." He pressed her with a warning look.

"We have to eat, don't we? Why not just eat with her?"

Nick didn't look convinced. He handed Luna his phone to keep her distracted and pulled Mackenzie aside. "Mack, she's supposed to be at school."

"Shelly wasn't planning on sending her today anyway. She looked relieved that I showed up since she was scrambling for a babysitter last minute."

Nick clenched his jaw. "I… I'm not in the right headspace."

Her eyes raked over his unruly appearance. His hair was messy and his beard was growing out way past his usual stubble.

"How can anytime not be the right time to have a meal with her?" Mackenzie turned him to face Luna. "Look at that face."

Luna stared at Nick's phone with furrowed eyebrows and razor-sharp focus.

Nick sighed. "Yeah okay. Well played, Price."

She shrugged innocently. "What were you doing?"

Nick showed her his computer screen. "I uploaded the picture of that toy found in Theo's throat to reverse search it. It is a cipher disk, but it can be bought online from a couple of places. So we won't be able to track the buyer."

"What cipher is that?"

"Pigpen cipher."

"Also known as Napoleon cipher," Luna added from behind them with a grin.

Mackenzie looked at Nick, surprised, who shook his head, defeated. "I've honestly stopped asking at this point."

"We can't find the buyer, but we can crack the code," Mackenzie suggested in a whisper.

"Daddy, I'm hungry!" Luna whined behind them.

"Wait, Luna. Remember last year Sully got into decoding ciphers?"

Mackenzie felt hope surge through her.

"Troy, can you just watch her? We have to talk to Sully for a minute." Nick grabbed the picture of the cipher, Mackenzie on his heels as they rushed toward Sully's office.

"Maybe Luna can help me with my case!" Troy called out.

Nick flipped him the bird.

They found Sully inside his office, grumbling, his hair and clothes sopping wet from the rain. His umbrella was broken from the strong winds that slammed the windows into the hinges repeatedly.

"We need a quick word, Sully," Nick said.

"Let me get settled please." Sully raised a hand and moved around the office, fixing little things and taking out two slices of cucumber from the mini fridge.

Mackenzie crossed her arms and tapped her foot.

Sully sank down on his chair and placed the two slices over his closed lids. He sighed, sitting with his head inclined back and cucumbers on his eyes. After exactly a minute, he ate the slices and straightened up. "Don't judge. It's my routine. You should try it. Wakes you up immediately after you've had a long night."

"Why did you have a long night?"

"Just because I'm not the investigating officer on your case doesn't mean I'm not just as busy," he said sharply. "Who do you think is supervising resource shuffling while you two focus on your case?"

"I wasn't accusing you of anything, Sergeant. I was merely asking."

Sully frowned. "Sorry. Cucumbers fix lethargy not attitude. What did you want to talk about?"

Nick showed Sully a picture of the cipher disk. "It was found inside Theo's throat. Can you crack this for us?"

Sully held out his hand and waggled his fingers. Nick placed it in his hand, and he analyzed it with a pout. "Aha! I knew one day one of my hobbies would come in handy." He wheeled toward his shelf and pulled out a book. "It's Pigpen cipher. Very easy to crack. A simple substitution code."

Mackenzie and Nick waited as Sully took a piece of paper and scribbled on it intently, while referring to the book. The tip of his tongue poked out from in between his lips. After a minute or so, he slid the paper toward them.

The words "ICFSFPC 2010" were written on the page.

"What is this?" Mackenzie asked.

Sully raised a finger and typed it on the computer. "International Conference on Forensic Sciences, Forensic Pathology and Criminology."

"A conference." Her mind raced. "In 2010."

"It's a big conference, lot of speakers and presentations."

Nick was already ahead of them. "We need to look into everyone who attended and find a link with Jeremiah, Johnny, Lucas, Theo or Noah. Thanks, Sully."

They didn't wait for his reply, blasting out of the office while formulating a plan of action.

"We should also look into the organizers of the event," Mackenzie suggested.

They almost bumped into Luna standing with her hands on her waist. "I'm hungry."

"I'll tell Justin to get started on it. He's been tailing Patricia, but he can multitask." Mackenzie pressed her phone to her ear.

As Justin's phone trilled, she watched Nick lean down and hold Luna by the shoulders, peace returning to his eyes. He already seemed calmer. "What do you want to eat, Luna?"

"Chinese."

"For brunch?" Mackenzie said.

"Is there a law?" Luna replied, as haughtily as an eight-year-old could.

"It's always Chinese for this one." Nick ruffled her hair. "Never pancakes or waffles."

Mackenzie smiled, her heart warming. She wondered briefly if Robert had talked to her with the same affection. Then Justin answered his phone, pulling her back, and she left him instructions to look into everyone associated with the conference.

The Asian Market was crawling with people. Couples walked hand in hand and children ran around excitedly, stimulated by the colors and scents. The streets were barricaded, not allowing any cars in. The city had to build a special parking lot just for this. All restaurants had kitchens visible through the windows and red awnings. Toddlers and preschoolers pressed their noses against the glass, staring at the cooks at work. There were some shops dispersed throughout. They had an authentic vibe to them. Small, rustic, and unique.

The restaurant had red walls with pendant lights. Waiters wheeled dim sum in carts, and the sound of clacking chopsticks and conversations was like white noise.

Mackenzie watched Nick and Luna joking with each other while they waited for their order to arrive. Luna had decided to order for everyone. Mackenzie was pleased to see Nick relax for the first time in days. Guilt wasn't easy to shake, but it pleased her to see that it was set aside for the moment.

Luna's cheeriness was infectious as she talked about how much she was looking forward to Halloween.

"You already have plans for Halloween?" Mackenzie exclaimed. "It's *months* away."

She bounced on her chair. "I wanted to dress up as Alexa Grady, but there's no one to be Alexie Grady."

"What?" Mackenzie looked at Nick for clarification.

He raised his eyebrows and shook his head. "Oh, dear God."

"I don't have a twin, Aunty Mack," Luna went on. "The Grady twins from *The Shining*."

"You've watched *The Shining*?" She gaped.

"Luna, you're a bit young to watch such things," Nick explained half-heartedly, knowing his advice was falling on deaf ears. "Does your mom know?"

"She played *Frozen* for me and left the room, but I got bored. So I changed the channel." Luna shrugged like it was no big deal.

Mackenzie swallowed her laughter as Nick glared at her from across the table. Their food arrived, and her stomach growled in anticipation. Since the case had started, she had been surviving on snacks. Her body was ready for some real fuel.

Luna tucked her chopsticks under her upper lip, like a walrus. She told Nick to do the same, and he didn't have it in him to ever deny her anything.

"I'll take a picture." Mackenzie waggled her eyebrows. "This moment needs to be captured for blackmail purposes."

Nick scoffed but didn't protest. Mackenzie took a picture of him and Luna posing together, when their waitress stopped by their table.

"Oh, I can take a family picture!"

"Oh no, no." Mackenzie waved her hand. "I'm not—"

"Yes, do the walrus!" Luna urged.

Nick sat back with his arms crossed and a smirk on his lips. "Yes, Mad Mack. Do the walrus."

She handed her phone to the eager waitress, knowing Nick had called her Mad Mack on purpose. It wasn't like her to do anything silly especially in public. She had an image to maintain. But she couldn't disappoint Luna.

Biting her tongue and feeling her cheeks heat, she stuck the chopsticks between her teeth and upper lip. Luna pulled her closer and together they smiled as the waitress snapped a picture.

CHAPTER FORTY-FIVE

After dropping Luna back at home, Mackenzie and Nick returned to the station. She could already feel the difference in him. He squeezed her shoulder and gave her a grateful smile. The two hours with Luna had been a breath of fresh air, but it was time to get back to work.

"Anything on Agatha?" Mackenzie asked after a while, turning on her chair.

"Still hasn't used any of her credit cards." Nick tossed a stress ball between his hands. "And her phone is still switched off. She's gone off the grid."

"Sending codes and playing games sounds like something she would do." Mackenzie recalled the house stuffed with dollhouses and snippets of Jeremiah's pictures from the internet. "She's clearly a nutjob."

"I haven't found anything strange in her finances and phone records," Nick added. "But she could be smart enough not to leave a paper trail."

"Whoever is behind this has been very strategic until now."

When Justin walked into the office with purposeful strides, Mackenzie knew he had something. She had worked with the junior detective for the last two years and recognized his habits.

"Ma'am, I'm still looking into the conference," Justin informed them, with his hands behind his back. "I was able to narrow it down to twenty-five people who are connected to Washington State.

Rest are either from other parts of the country or international. As you know, I've been tailing Patricia..."

Nick wheeled closer to drop in the conversation. "Did you find anything?"

"This morning I followed Patricia to a coffee shop. She spent a long time speaking to one of the girls working there. At first, I figured they were just being friendly to a regular visitor, except the girl actually sat with Patricia and spoke with her. And they looked close."

"As in they're romantic with each other?" Mackenzie asked.

"No, it was more like a friendship," Justin clarified. "Patricia looked almost motherly toward her. She also gave her a box."

"A box?"

"I was too far away to see anything clearly."

"Could it be the parcel that Toby Adler handed to Patricia?" Nick mulled.

"The box and the parcel looked approximately the same size to me," Justin confirmed.

"Did you find out anything about the girl?" she asked Justin.

"Yes, ma'am. Her name is Summer Jaffe. She's nineteen years old and an English major at the community college."

"Summer!" Mackenzie turned to Nick.

"You know her?" Justin asked them.

"Nick and I met her briefly when we went to Jeremiah's house. She's staying there, part of the church's troubled youth program. She probably struggles with drugs or something."

Nick leaned back on his chair and clasped his hands behind his head. "It explains how they know each other. And since Patricia owns that house, maybe she was just giving her something related to that?"

"No." She shook her head determined. "The killer *chose* the lighthouse for a reason. It's certainly not a coincidence that he dumped the body at an isolated place where Patricia happened to go too."

"Only one way to find out." Nick picked up his keys. "Let's pay Summer a visit."

Mackenzie and Nick entered the coffee place where Summer Jaffe worked. It was a café situated close to the community college, and at least a ten-minute drive away from Patricia's house.

They stood in line, mostly crowded with students in sweatshirts with haphazard hair and unpleasant body odor, owing to the all-nighters they were pulling during midterm season. The café had bright colors everywhere, from pink tables and yellow stools to blue counters and green shapes on floor tiles. It was like a child had designed the décor.

When Mackenzie and Nick reached the front of the line, Summer's mouth curved into a smile. "What will you have?"

Mackenzie showed her badge. "Remember us?"

"Oh!" Her jaw went slack. "Right. Sorry." She turned to her coworker. "Can you cover for me?"

Summer led them to a table in the corner, ignoring the curious glances of her coworkers and patrons. She sat down and tightened her fingers into a tight clasp on the table.

"Is everything okay?" she asked.

Her skin had patches of discoloration and her voice sounded scratchy. She was a frail woman but looked worse than the last time Mackenzie had seen her.

"Are you feeling okay?"

"Yeah." Summer grimaced, clutching her stomach. "I just have these muscle cramps today."

"Is this part of your recovery?"

"It is." She licked her dry lips. "Withdrawal symptoms. The price of getting your life back."

"We just wanted to ask you a few questions about Patricia," Nick said.

Summer smiled fondly. "Of course."

"We assume you know her because of the church's program?"

"Yes. The church rents her house. She's not officially involved in the program, but she's very nice. Drops in once in a while to spend time with us."

Mackenzie had seen only one side of Patricia—the blindly loyal sister mistrustful of the system. She hadn't seen the kindness that Summer obviously had. "Has she given you anything recently?"

Summer sensed some suspicion. "Yes… why? Is she in trouble?"

"Not exactly," Mackenzie said. "What did she give you?"

"A box of cookies. They're from Germany and hard to find here. She has a friend who travels there often, so once a month she gets them for us."

A box of cookies from Germany? Is that what her "boyfriend" Toby had given her? Patricia had said that she ordered something and paid Toby for it. Perhaps Toby knew someone who made frequent trips to Europe.

"Well, thank you for your—" Mackenzie started, when Nick interrupted.

"Summer, do you still have the box of cookies?"

"No, I took it home and shared them with everyone."

"You don't have any left?" Nick pressed, and Mackenzie bit her lip, wondering what he was getting at.

"I have two cookies left in my backpack…"

"Can we take a look?"

Summer stood up with a wobble and disappeared around the back.

"What's that about?" Mackenzie asked him.

Nick dusted his cuffs. "Something's not right. Like you said, there didn't seem to be anything romantic between Patricia and Toby. And if they're just cookies, then why did she meet him at the lighthouse?"

"In an isolated place where no one would see them," she agreed.

Summer returned with two cookies inside a Ziploc bag. She passed it to them, looking unsure. "What's going on?"

"We're going to take them to run some tests," Nick added smoothly. "If that's okay?"

"Why? What do you suspect?"

"We can't say anything, but you're not in any trouble and neither is Patricia. We just need to confirm some things."

Summer's eyes moved between them like a pinball. It was clear that she was reluctant, but gave in. "Okay, sure."

"Thanks, Summer." Mackenzie made a show of sounding cheery to put her at ease.

When they left the café, dusty winds swept the streets, sending litter dancing in the air. Mackenzie blinked, the dirt stinging her eyes.

They sprinted to the car and once inside, she turned to her partner. "You suspect drugs?"

Nick unzipped the bag and sniffed it. "Doesn't smell like anything but chocolate. They're in the program for drug addiction, right?"

"So you think Patricia is sneaking them drugs behind the church's back and making a quick buck?"

"It's worth checking out."

"Can we make a stop along the way? I'm changing the locks in my house."

"I thought Sterling had returned the keys?"

"Yes. Um. I just think it's time for an upgrade. I live alone, so I want a better system," she replied, straining to sound casual. Earlier in the day, she had gotten a glimpse of what normalcy would be like when she had brunch with Luna and Nick. And momentarily she had forgotten how the danger from her work had spilled over into her personal life as well.

CHAPTER FORTY-SIX

Mackenzie's nails were jagged at the edges. She had been biting them, before catching herself, only to do it again. It would irk her greatly if it developed into a habit. She took out a nail polish from her drawer and began painting the edges of her nails to hide them.

"You keep makeup at work?" Nick smirked.

"Yes." She knew what she came off as. Vain. But it didn't matter to her. It was better than the alternative—letting anyone realize she was a ball of anxiety, even after getting new locks for her home. The stronger her armor was, the clearer she could think. Otherwise her brain would just get fuzzy. "John Newman just messaged. They've finished searching the woods and found nothing."

"The killer must have parked their car around the edge somewhere and drove off."

"Too bad there's no surveillance." She put away the nail polish and blew on her nails, satisfied. "They planned this precisely. Made sure they lured them during the commotion of the spring festival and took them through those woods."

Nick stroked his jaw. "Yeah, Ruth Norman posted on the school website about the field trip. That's how they must have known."

Rivera came into the office and gestured Mackenzie and Nick to follow her. She walked wordlessly ahead of them, entering her office, where Elliot Garcia was already seated, typing furiously on his phone. He nodded curtly at them.

Rivera sighed and went behind her desk, placing her hands on it. "Any progress?"

"Becky found a puzzle piece lodged inside Theo's throat," Mackenzie said. "Justin is tracking down anyone with a link to any of the victims or to Jeremiah. He said he'll have something by tomorrow."

Elliot put the phone in his breast pocket. "A puzzle piece?"

"It's sick." Mackenzie gritted her teeth. "Like they're testing us to see if we're smart enough; like it's some sort of game."

"What about Agatha?" Rivera demanded. "Has she used her phone or her credit cards?"

"No. We have forwarded her information to neighboring cities, in case she left town."

She exhaled sharply, her bow-shaped lips pinching. "Our prime suspect is missing."

"Did any of the autopsies hint if the killer is a man or a woman?" Elliot asked.

"We can't say," Nick admitted. "There was no physical assault on Lucas and Theo—other than the fatal blow to the head. But that doesn't give us a clue."

"Patricia was at the lighthouse days before the body was found. She was buying a parcel from Toby Adler, the man who reported the body. We just came from Seattle, dropping off what we suspect to be in the parcel at the crime lab with Anthony to run some tests," Mackenzie said.

Rivera looked exhausted. She turned the monitor to them and played the news.

"*Thank you for joining us, Mr. Lambert,*" Debbie said, sitting across from a lanky man with salt-and-pepper hair and fake tan. "*You're blaming Mayor Rathbone for this.*"

"*Absolutely I am!*" Lambert's voice reverberated with passion. "*The people of Lakemore placed their trust in him. He is the leader of our community. If he's not held accountable then who will be?*"

"*Mayor Rathbone has made it clear that all the best resources are on top of this—*"

"*What best resources?*" he challenged. "*It's not a secret that the chief of police is incompetent. It's fair for us to question the people hired in that department. It's fair because the Lakemore PD was under FBI investigation for months. Not to mention that the Perez case showed us how the mayor was protecting his friends. His whole office reeks of unethical practice.*"

"*And you think you'll do a better job as mayor?*"

Lambert looked directly at the camera. His feverish appeal aimed at the audience. The rich baritone of his deep voice, correct tonal inflictions, pleading eyes, and energy made him magnetic. "*I will be a better mayor. Because I care about the working-class families more than my rich friends. Because I will put people in charge based on merit and not personal relationships. Because I will value justice over politics. And, most importantly, because I will keep our children safe.*"

Rivera stopped the video. "Now you see why nerves are frayed."

"Murphy has turned against all of you," Elliot stated in a dull tone. "Lieutenant Rivera is the wall between the brass and you."

Mackenzie felt uneasy. "What's Murphy going to do?"

"I'm here to assure you that your department has the full support of the DA office. But if Noah isn't found alive, then there will be consequences, like cuts and transfers. Murphy is going to throw you under the bus and not take responsibility for anything."

"We're on our own," Rivera said gravely. "I despise the fact that this case has turned into a political agenda and people are more worried about their asses than about a child's life. You should know what's happening, but don't let it interfere with your process. Find him alive."

Night rolled in too soon. Mackenzie had spent the entire day going over the forensic reports for Lucas and Theo. She had called Anthony to get an update on the particulate analysis from the clothes Theo was wearing to get some clue as to where he was being held.

"*Can you tell me how long it will take?*"

"*Mack, there's a lot on our plate. But I will definitely have something by day after tomorrow around the afternoon.*"

"*I get you're busy, but we have a missing kid!*"

"*Yeah, you aren't the only ones with a missing kid.*"

Mackenzie had hung up, dejected. Going by the pattern, they didn't have very long before Noah could end up dead. Her heart pounded as she stared at the clock. For some reason, it felt like each second was ticking by faster than usual.

It was almost midnight and dead quiet. Everyone had gone home.

She sat back and thought about who could have killed Johnny, and who had Noah. Her two suspects were Tim Cooper and Agatha Bellini. The former had motive to avenge the injustice done to Johnny, but in the last few days the deputies keeping a close eye on him had reported nothing out of the ordinary. Tim went to work and came home and occasionally hung out with friends at local bars. The officers had been tailing him 24/7 and had confirmed that Tim at no point had gone anywhere near the lighthouse.

Unless he had an accomplice.

The prime suspect was Agatha Bellini. A deranged sociopath, enamored by a child killer, who harbored dangerous fantasies. But where was she?

Mackenzie was getting nowhere. Various theories circling inside her head like wisps of smoke. Nothing was concrete. She decided to call it a night. On her way out, she noticed that the light on the stairway going down to the basement was turned on. It was motion-dependent. Who else was working this late in the basement?

A blast of cool air slammed into her when she descended the stairs to the coarsely built basement. It was a dingy hallway with swinging bulbs overhead. She wasn't the kind to scare easy, but ever since someone had started messing with her, she was wound up, ready to jump out of her skin anytime.

For a fleeting moment, she felt like a victim and not a trained police officer.

She heard a sound and froze. Not footsteps or a voice. But like something dropped on the floor. All her muscles ceased to move. It was then she noted that one of the doors was slightly ajar. She hadn't noticed it before. Someone was inside that room. It was the room where they stored physical copies of all the case files. By the end of summer, they were discarding all the physical copies and moving everything to a digital database. The transition had been taking longer with budget cuts.

Mackenzie crept closer to the room. Her hand hovered over her gun tucked in her waistband. She peered through the little space of the open door. Someone was inside, rifling through the files and taking out boxes and setting them on the floor. She couldn't see a face, only a blurry frame. It looked like a man based on height and build. He moved with a sense of urgency. Then he sat on the floor and angled the flashlight from his phone that made his face visible.

It was Austin.

He leafed through page after page with piercing concentration. It was bordering on desperation.

What was he doing here? Mackenzie had come to the same room months ago because she didn't want a record of her accessing case files. Which was the only reason Austin would be in this room.

Before he could come out and catch her, she quickly padded back upstairs, all the while musing.

What was Austin looking for? And why was he keeping it hidden?

CHAPTER FORTY-SEVEN

March 13

Mackenzie's feet pounded against the concrete as she pushed herself forward to run the last mile. Shreds of clouds chased each other in the gloomy sky; the town was on the verge of a storm. A cold sheet of sweat coated her skin, and a spasm threatened to hinder her all together. She tried working through it but came to a halt, unable to continue.

"Dammit!" she growled and removed her earbuds. The thumping music was replaced by the little sounds of Lakemore. Birds chirped, morning joggers puffed and panted. Leaves rustled. She heard a burst of giggles. A group of young girls played in a pond, splashing water at each other, without a care in the world. They were yet to learn about the evils of the world. At least, Mackenzie hoped they were. You could never tell what went on behind closed doors.

She spotted their parents sitting on a bench nearby and heaved a sigh of relief. This is what Lakemore had come to, when seeing a child alone made her question their safety. And it wasn't just her—the fact that the football-coaching center had temporarily closed was a sign that parents were scared too. Because who was to say that this killer would stop after Noah? What if their vigilante killer took more children if they didn't catch Johnny's killer?

*

Mackenzie reached work to find a ripple of commotion around her; her coworkers turning off their computers and closing files in unison. She gazed around in confusion, when Nick appeared in front of her.

"Are you ready?" He changed his tie to a black one.

"For what?"

He gave her a flat look. "Mack, we have to go the town square. Town's honoring Lucas and Theo, remember?"

"Of course." She sighed.

"We'll ride with Rivera and Sully."

"I thought they'd postpone it?" She glanced at the window behind Nick. Beads of water traced random paths down the glass. Every now and then, a flashing sheet of rain would smash into the window, making it clatter.

"Apparently not."

She edged her way past the moving bodies to Sully's office. Catching Austin going through old case files in the storage room had ignited suspicion.

Sully was wearing his raincoat, when she approached him with hesitance. "Sergeant, can I ask you something?"

"Yeah."

"Why is Austin on Charles's case?"

"He asked to be on it." He sounded distracted, looking for his keys.

"But *why*?"

"He's new and hungry to prove himself. Where is this coming from?"

She twisted her fingers, tracking his quick movements as he sifted through the clutter on his desk. "We don't know anything about him. Do we even trust him?"

Sully froze and stared at her like she had grown two heads. "What are you accusing him of?"

"Nothing." She realized she wasn't really prepared for this conversation. What did she have to go on really? "I'm invested in the case. Obviously."

"And Austin will solve it. He's good. We're lucky he was desperate enough to leave Port Angeles and move here." He found the keys and gestured her to follow him.

The ride in Nick's car was filled with thick silence, only punctuated by the howling winds and the game Sully played on his phone. From the rearview mirror, Mackenzie saw Sully's absorbed expression, his eyebrows dipped low. Rivera stared outside into the storm, picking at her thumbnail. Nick sucked on an unlit cigarette. Since Mackenzie had caught him smoking, he seemed to have returned to just playing with his cigarettes.

When they reached the town square, there was a bigger crowd than Mackenzie had expected. She had thought that the weather would turn some people away. But a large throng of people had assembled around the center, where the statue of a local Lakemore man who had served valiantly in the Second World War stood. The entire street had been blocked by cars. All the shops and restaurants were closed. It was only late afternoon, but the storm had blotted out the sun. The entire scenery was a pallet of gray and black. Puddles pooled in clusters in every dip in the road. The rain pelted on umbrellas and asphalt. It cascaded around her like a shield, and when she reached the crowd, they edged their way closer to the front.

Mayor Rathbone was giving a speech on a raised platform. Next to him was a gleaming black bench with a scripture whittled into it in gold.

"This town will never forget the young lives that were tragically lost," Rathbone addressed the glum residents of Lakemore, united in their grief.

It was hard to make out the faces in the rain, but Mackenzie recognized Ruth Norman sniffing into her handkerchief, Lucas's mother, Elliot Garcia, and Spencer Irving in the crowd. News anchor Debbie Arnold was also among the attendees, her camera-man filming the event from a respectful distance.

Mackenzie approached Spencer, who had been standing closest to her. "They're giving the boys a bench?"

"Yes," Spencer informed. "And making a sculpture in their honor, to be installed at the art center."

"Oh wow. That's thoughtful."

"Yeah. They've already engraved Lucas and Theo's names on the bench."

"What if we need to add another name to that bench?"

Spencer paled, and his voice dropped. "Are you saying that Noah—?"

"No!"

He let out a breath. "You scared me there."

"I meant not yet." Saliva thickened in her throat.

Rathbone continued to drone about how Lakemore would never forget the boys. He was a short, meek man, with a strong sense of pride but lacking the charisma of his opponent.

Mackenzie looked over to where Elliot was standing. He had a detached look on this face and was covertly typing on his phone.

"I've never worked with him closely before." Mackenzie tipped her chin towards him. "But I thought he'd be different in person. In court, he's a…"

"Vision." Spencer smiled. "It's a performance. Right now, he's trying to get a wrongful conviction overturned. An innocent man has been in prison for over twenty years. The truth is that he doesn't believe in honoring the dead, only the living."

Mackenzie made quick work of Elliot. He was a man of few words and even fewer expressions. He looked at people like he had X-ray vision, like he could see under their skin.

"You really admire him, don't you?"

A smile tugged on Spencer's lips. "He was my idol when I was in law school. It was my dream to work with Elliot. His quest for justice and fairness is so pure; it's almost utopic. He might appear to be insensitive, but he would take a bullet for a stranger in a heartbeat."

The mayor offered his hand to Ruth Norman, who stepped up. She grazed the bench with a trembling hand and cried into her handkerchief. She took the microphone and spoke over the battering rain.

"I haven't been paying attention, but why did the mayor invite Ruth to speak?" Mackenzie asked Spencer.

"Dedicating the bench was her idea. And she'll be sculpting that art piece. I think she's also an artist? She felt so guilty for what happened to the boys under her watch that she pitched the idea to the mayor's office at a very opportune moment for Rathbone."

"Ma'am." Justin diverted her attention from behind. The rain bounced off his umbrella and flew into her eyes. He stepped back, muttering an apology.

"Don't worry about it. I didn't know you were going to be here."

"Most of the force is here." He looked uncomfortable. "I have good news."

Mackenzie excused herself from Spencer and pulled Justin aside. "What do you have?"

"I found one person with a connection," Justin said. "Bonnie Yang. She was a presenter at the conference. Eight years ago, she worked at the Washington State Patrol Crime Lab as a forensic technician and was listed as one of the personnel who worked on the Johnny Cooper homicide."

"That's great work, Justin!" She clapped his back with a grunt of excitement.

"One more thing." He frowned. "It might not mean anything, but Bonnie quit her job a month after being on the case."

CHAPTER FORTY-EIGHT

Everyone returned from the dedication ceremony drained and muted. The rainstorm had lulled into a softer pour, but the sky was gray, casting a bleak shadow over Lakemore. Mackenzie sat at her desk conducting a background check on Bonnie Yang.

"Anything?" Nick asked, sipping his coffee.

"No arrests. Clean record," she replied, browsing. "I'll just pull up her address from DMV records. Did you hear that Murphy and Rivera got into a spat?"

"Mad Mack *gossiping*? What has the world come to?"

She shook her head. "It's not gossip. I'm conveying information."

"That is gossip."

"Murphy is furious. He's talking about firing people if necessary."

"I heard that too," Finn interjected. "He's putting a list together."

"No!" Nick protested. "I'm sure he's mad, but these are all just conspiracy theories. He can't just put together a list of people to fire because he's in a bad mood."

"Easy for you to say," Finn mumbled. "No one's going to fire a senator's son."

The topic ended on a tense note when Peterson walked in.

"Detective Blackwood, Detective Price, there's someone here to meet you," he said with a solemn face.

Mackenzie and Nick weren't expecting anyone. They followed a hesitant Peterson to the lounge. A middle-aged man wearing a suit with gray sideburns stood staring outside the window.

"Mr. Kinsey?" Peterson grasped the attention of Noah's father and made the introductions before leaving.

"Mr. Kinsey, what can we do for you?" Nick asked.

He twiddled his thumbs, and his nostrils flickered. "You went to the dedication?"

"Yes." Mackenzie sounded breathless.

"Hmm." He looked around, his thin veneer of poise barely holding up. "Had Theo been dead for a long time or murdered just before he was found?"

"I'm sorry, Mr. Kinsey," Mackenzie shook her head, "but we really can't reveal case details to anyone."

He pursed his lips and placed his trembling hand in his pocket. Mr. Kinsey was a dignified man, but Mackenzie could see the anger simmering beneath the surface. The storm inside him was visible through the cracks. She feared it would eat away at him, until there was nothing left but a shell of a man.

"Let me ask again, Detective. My son has been abducted by some serial killer. All his other victims have been killed, and now my son is the only one left. I need to know if my son could be alive at this moment." His voice broke, but he held his composure. "Or if he's… gone."

"Mr. Kinsey, I can't even imagine—"

"He's alive," Nick answered across her. Mackenzie shot him an incredulous look, which he ignored. "Your son is alive right now."

"And he's all alone and terrified."

"We're doing everything we can to make sure he stays alive," Nick swore.

"Keep your reassurances to yourself," Mr. Kinsey murmured, tears misting his eyes. "Two out of three boys are dead. It's impossible for me to have any confidence in your abilities. Do either of you have children?"

Nick's Adam's apple bounced multiple times before he replied. "I do."

"So you should be able to imagine how I feel right now."

"Mr. Kinsey—" Mackenzie said, but he cut her off.

"You aren't a parent," he stated firmly. "If you were, you wouldn't try to reassure me. You would stay quiet like your partner. Because he understands that at this point words aren't just pointless, they're insulting. As if you think you can say anything that will even remotely make me feel better."

Mackenzie dropped her gaze. Mr. Kinsey's words cut through her like a knife.

"I'm a single parent," he continued. "My wife... she left us a long time ago. Motherhood wasn't her cup of tea, and she never looked back or even checked in. I have dedicated my life to my son. It's not just his life at stake. It's mine too. You have to save the both of us."

Mr. Kinsey didn't wait for a reply. He walked away, holding his head high.

Mackenzie didn't pretend to understand his pain. Instead, she was reminded of what her grandmother, Eleanor, always used to say: the weight of a heart dead from grief in your chest is the heaviest.

"I might not understand what a parent must feel like in a situation like this," Mackenzie said. "But there is no way in hell I'm letting another boy die. Let's go and see Bonnie."

After retrieving Bonnie's address, Mackenzie, Nick and Justin immediately left for Seattle. Lakemore was on edge. Everyone sat on the brink of bad news. There was only one boy left.

"You've never met Bonnie Yang?" Mackenzie asked.

"No." Nick scratched his jaw. "I was just in contact with Thomas—the man Anthony replaced after he retired."

"Bonnie was just a technician, and she doesn't have personal connection with Jeremiah or any of the victims," Justin confirmed.

"Maybe she knows something," Nick said.

"Take the lead on this one, Justin," she said. "You found her."

He flushed. "Yes, ma'am."

Mackenzie threaded through the gridlock of downtown Seattle, passing by the vibrant streets and cafés and people who walked with bouncy strides. The pulsating energy of the city was a stark contrast to the sluggish life in Lakemore. Even the colors shone brighter, like light reflected better on surfaces here. She often used to drive to Seattle when she first moved to Lakemore. It was the closest place that reminded her of her life in New York. She'd visit the museums and then have oysters at restaurants facing the bay. Until life in Lakemore snuck up on her, until that dullness morphed into simplicity and predictability into stability.

She found expensive parking, and they headed to a condo building that looked like a tall glass tower.

They took the elevator to the highest floor and found Bonnie's apartment, knocking on the door. A middle-aged woman with thin, dark hair appeared, wearing a baggy blue sweater that engulfed her bony frame.

Her eyebrows drew together. "Yes?"

"Ms. Yang? Lakemore PD." Mackenzie showed her their credentials.

Bonnie actually spent a few seconds checking everyone's identity, something rarely any of the people they spoke with did. "Come inside."

Mackenzie made a casual assessment of the condo—all windows overlooking the bustling downtown street. Dark Ikea furniture artfully arranged with the only splash of color a bright red armchair.

"What is this about?" Bonnie sat on the red chair and wrapped her arms around her chest.

"Eight years ago you worked as a technician in the crime lab, reporting to Thomas?" Justin asked.

Bonnie stuttered, blinking rapidly. "Y-yes. Why?"

"Were you part of the team that analyzed the forensic evidence obtained in Johnny Cooper's murder case?"

Blood drained from her face. She looked at the three of them like they were ghosts from a treacherous past. "I did."

"Is there something you'd like to share with us?"

"Excuse me." She went to the kitchen and poured a glass of water. "I knew this day would come."

"What do you mean?" Nick stepped forward.

"It was only a matter of time, wasn't it?" She spoke to herself, not even looking at them. "I thought it was in the past. That I could move on. But the damn thing about truth is that it always comes out." She guzzled the water and took deep breaths. "I was just a technician. I didn't want to do it, I swear."

"Didn't want to do what?"

"But Thomas pressured me after everything that happened!" She broke into frantic ramblings. "I was so disturbed, so *consumed* by guilt, that I quit. But there are times now I still feel terrible. Especially with the young boys disappearing in Lakemore. I see it on the news here. It's starting again, isn't it?"

"Ms. Yang," Justin said. "Why do you feel guilty?"

"Because I buried evidence," she cried and then gasped at her outburst.

CHAPTER FORTY-NINE

Mackenzie immediately looked at Nick. Puzzlement and denial were written all over his face.

"What evidence?" Justin's question fractured the silence that had followed.

Bonnie sighed and fell on a chair. "Johnny's remains were fairly decomposed. He had been dead for almost over a year. There were some fiber samples found on him. Most of them were blue denim—they take one to five years to degrade. But there was also silk fiber on him."

"Silk?" Justin repeated. "Could that have been from Johnny?"

"No. He was wearing a yellow T-shirt made of pure cotton. It had decomposed completely. And the silk strands obtained were red and blue in color. Inconsistent with everything the victim was wearing based on the information that was given to us."

"What was Jeremiah wearing that day?" Justin whispered to Mackenzie and Nick.

"A white wifebeater and black jeans," Nick answered, recalling every vivid detail of that video.

"It wasn't Jeremiah." Mackenzie bit into the pad of her thumb, the wheels in her brain turning. "But the silk was on Johnny. So it came from the killer."

"You were the one to make the discovery?" Justin turned to Bonnie.

"Yes. As soon as I analyzed the samples under the microscope, I made a report of it with Thomas's authorization. We submitted it to the DA's office. But then I found out that the report had been altered. The page where this finding was recorded was removed. And I was called into a secret meeting with Thomas where he informed me that the samples I analyzed weren't from Johnny, but some other victim."

"And you didn't think that was possible?"

"First of all, those samples were mixed with the blue denim fibers lifted from Johnny. It's very hard to mix up *microscopic* evidence," Bonnie pressed. "Secondly, if a mistake was made, then who was the alleged original victim the silk fiber was found on? How were the samples mixed up in the first place? When I asked Thomas all these questions, he didn't have an answer. He brushed it aside saying it would all be looked into, but nothing happened. There was no inquiry, *no* investigation. A month later, I couldn't handle it anymore. It was obvious that I was part of a cover-up. I *quit*."

Mackenzie kept nibbling on her thumb, still processing the information Bonnie had given them. There had been a conspiracy to bury and amend critical forensic information in Johnny's case. If a genuine mistake had been made, then the nature of that error would have been thoroughly explored—traced back to the point it happened. The chain of custody would have been checked. Slip-ups weren't just dismissed as "innocent mistakes" in crime labs. After all, they were part of the legal system, handling evidence that was key to determining someone's innocence or guilt. Mackenzie had gone through all the forensic work. She remembered coming across the denim samples found on Johnny from his jeans. But no mention of red and blue silk samples.

Even Nick hadn't heard of it before. He looked like he had been transported to another world, where he was still wrapping his head around everything. Powerful forces had to be involved to bury evidence like this. Unfortunately, Thomas had died two years ago following a cardiac arrest.

"Did you tell anyone about this?" Justin asked. "A coworker? A friend?"

"Thomas warned me to keep it between us. Another red flag. I didn't tell anyone. Frankly, I was terrified that I had unwittingly become part of something completely corrupt." Bonnie's dubious eyes searched theirs. "Am I in trouble?"

"No," Mackenzie assured. "But do you know who pressured Thomas? Did he ever say anything?"

"He didn't have to. He had a meeting in his office, after which he told me to forget what I had found, citing that chain of custody had been compromised. I saw who he met with."

"Who?"

"Elliot Garcia."

CHAPTER FIFTY

"Ladies and gentlemen of the jury, this woman is a coward." Elliot's voice echoed in the courtroom. "Her husband collected incriminating information against the fraudulent practices of his company. He was a whistleblower. He took a risk because he didn't want his clients to be swindled out of their hard-earned money. They all sit in this courtroom today. They sit here so that the man who stood up for them gets justice, because in death he deserves honor. But he was betrayed by his own wife. An ambitious, greedy woman who looked the man she was married to for twenty years in the eye, and stabbed him *fifteen* times." He placed his hands on the railing marking the jury area—unafraid to get close to them. Looking directly into their eyes. "No one should be punished for doing the right thing. In a world of lies and manipulation, sacrifice and courage are the pillars that hold up our society, that define a man's character. We can pity her for her tragic past, but that doesn't distort the truth. The truth must come out, and it is our duty to uphold it. And the truth is that she murdered her husband for money. Now it's on you, the chosen members of the jury, to decide if this truth *matters* or not."

Mackenzie and Nick stood in the back of the courtroom as Elliot Garcia weaved a tale, spellbinding the room. He shone—all that charisma, sincerity, and passion reserved for the courtroom. Outside of it, he was introspective and deceivably dull.

"The white knight of Thurston County." Nick scowled at her side.

After around ten minutes, the judge adjourned, and Elliot, along with Spencer and another associate, stood in a circle around their table in serious discussions. The jury was sent to deliberations, and everyone filtered out of the room, whispering about the possible outcomes of the case.

"Nice speech." Mackenzie's smile was caustic.

Elliot frowned at them and dismissed the associate. "Do you have updates?"

"We need to talk." It almost sounded like a warning coming out of Nick's mouth.

Elliot had grasped that something was amiss. Their anger was barely concealed. "Let's go to my office. Spencer, you come too."

As Mackenzie followed him toward his office, her eyes found Sterling standing at the end of the hallway, talking on the phone. Her feet slowed to a halt. The bustle of the courtroom blurred, and all sound got sucked into a vacuum. She hadn't seen her ex-husband since they signed the papers. It had been less than three months, but it felt like yesterday.

He continued to chat on the phone, grinning, looking just like that handsome lawyer who had wooed her and captured her heart. Before he had cheated on her and torn their life into pieces until there was nothing left to salvage.

Like Sterling sensed something, his head snapped in her direction. One second. Just for one second, their eyes collided.

"Detective Price?" Elliot's voice punctured the bubble.

Mackenzie tried to still her hammering heart and stepped into the smaller room next to the DA's office.

The walls were wood-paneled, his expensive desk clear of clutter, and all files neatly stacked in shelves in one corner. It was a quaint office for a man of his stature—who was more famous and revered than his boss.

He went straight to the minibar and poured himself a whiskey. "Do you want some?"

"No," Mackenzie said. She and Nick sat on the two chairs across from Elliot, while Spencer stood next to Elliot.

"We know you buried evidence, Elliot," Nick stated.

Elliot's hand holding the sculpted glass froze midway to his mouth. Spencer made a sound in the back of his throat and glanced at Elliot.

"I see." Elliot took a hesitant sip and took a seat.

When he didn't defend himself, Mackenzie pitched in. "In the case of Johnny Cooper, you manipulated a forensic report from the crime lab."

"How did you know?"

"The clue left inside Theo's throat led us to the technician who discovered the evidence you chose to bury."

Elliot and Spencer glanced at each other, clearly shocked.

"You knew too?" Mackenzie hitched her breath.

"It's not Spencer's fault." Elliot jumped to his defense, while Spencer turned red and looked down. "I was in charge. It was my decision."

"But we're still a team, Elliot," Spencer argued. "We're in this together. I told you I understood why you did that."

"Why?" Nick demanded in a loud voice. "You'll get disbarred!"

"Let's keep this quiet, please," Elliot suggested in a calm voice. "This is a sensitive matter."

Mackenzie's nerves were raw with rage. The squeaky-clean image of Elliot Garcia was in tatters. "*Why?*"

Elliot finished the whiskey in one go. "It was important for Jeremiah to be found guilty of Johnny's murder."

"Jeremiah was charged with multiple counts," Nick argued. "He had many victims! You didn't need Johnny."

"We did. Going after Jeremiah was an aggressive prosecution. You remember, Nick. The case had gotten so big that even your father had been asked about it on many occasions. When we finally had him, it was made clear to us: go after him with *everything*.

Don't waste a single piece of evidence. The public needed that—a spectacle to watch the man who terrorized children be brought to justice. Johnny was the *only* victim who was seen being approached by Jeremiah."

"So?"

"So it established a stronger link!" The passion reserved for the courtroom slowly trickled back in. "His DNA found on *three* of the boys was deemed inadmissible by the judge due to Jeremiah's savvy lawyer. They argued that the chain of custody was broken for one, and the sample was contaminated for the other two. We couldn't tell the jury that his DNA was found in them."

Spencer pulled up a spare chair and infused some composure into the charged atmosphere with his gentle voice. "If the jury saw that there were fibers found on Johnny that couldn't have come from Jeremiah, meaning someone else had killed him, the defense could have cast reasonable doubt on his guilt altogether."

"But you found his DNA on the other victims. That's irrefutable," Mackenzie said.

"Not if the other side argued that the real killer wasn't Jeremiah, but someone with access to him. They would have said that someone had framed him," Spencer said.

"It would have been enough to plant doubt in the jury's mind," Elliot said gravely. "That's why Johnny was an important victim during the trial. With that video evidence, we were successfully able to argue that it doesn't matter if his DNA wasn't on him; Jeremiah was undeniably linked to him. Hence others could be too."

"It was important for us to make sure Jeremiah went to prison for life." Spencer licked his lips and fidgeted. "We all *knew* he was guilty of killing those boys."

"But not of killing Johnny," Mackenzie snapped. "Did it ever occur to you who might have killed him if not Jeremiah? Or were you too *blinded* by making sure your trial strategy had no loopholes for the other side to exploit?"

"It was necessary," Elliot said with his chin up. "It wasn't easy. And definitely not our first choice. But we couldn't afford to leave any breadcrumbs for his lawyers to sniff out. Catching and convicting Jeremiah was the most important case in Lakemore, until your Perez case, of course. You weren't here, Detective Price. But your partner remembers the pressures, the madness, the rage..."

Nick didn't deny any of it. He clasped the handles of the chair with whitening knuckles and looked away, breathing hard.

"So it doesn't matter who killed Johnny?" Mackenzie asked.

"It does. But Jeremiah murdered *ten* children in your small town. Ensuring justice for ten people trumps justice for one." Elliot's nostrils flickered. He stood up abruptly and poured more whiskey, chugging it. "It wasn't a decision we made easily. But that's the hard truth. Ten lives are more important than one."

"You can't place value on people's lives like this!" she cried. Her heart pounded in her chest. "Johnny was also a little boy. First his stepmother failed him, then his teacher, then the social worker, and then *you*."

"This world places values on people's lives every day." Elliot placed his hands on the table and leaned forward. His voice had dropped to a whisper, but his harsh words blared in the room. "It decides whose life is more important based on ethnicity, gender, religion, socio-economic status, nationality... you name it, and this world divides and ranks us on every issue. What you say is a fantasy. It *should* be true, but it isn't." He took a breath. "Johnny deserves justice. But not at the cost of denying it to ten kids. I still stand by that. You saw what Lucas and Theo's deaths did to their parents. Imagine *ten* families like that. How do I live with myself knowing that I let the killer of their kids walk free because there was another unknown killer out there who murdered one boy? How would I explain that to them? That I had the opportunity to put away Jeremiah for good, but I let it slip away for some anonymous killer?"

Spencer squeezed his eyes shut and took off his glasses. "Detective Price, we couldn't risk Jeremiah being acquitted. That fiber evidence was too damning for us."

"All your talk about truth in there." Mackenzie shook her head. "It was all a sham. *You* are a sham."

Elliot was unfazed by her disappointment. "I meant what I said in that courtroom, Detective. But truth is utopic; perspective is reality. The jury likes to see everything in black and white, because they are entrusted with a very important decision. They hold someone's fate in their hands. It's easier for them not to understand all the nuances."

"We have codes for a reason. Morals. Ethics. Doing the right thing. It's our duty as law enforcement officials to—"

"Live in the real world, for God's sake!" Elliot slammed the glass on his table. Drops of alcohol flew out of it, landing on the walnut wood. "You've been a police officer for eight years. You've seen firsthand the complicated nature of people. Are you really that naïve? Do you not realize that sometimes the truth needs to stay buried for the greater good?"

You have to help me bury him. Melody's plea sharply echoed in Mackenzie's ears. The irony wasn't lost on her—how she fought tooth and nail for transparency and honesty when she was hiding a devastating truth.

She sealed her lips shut and raked a hand through her hair, coming undone.

"Why wasn't I told?" Nick asked in a calm but menacing tone. "Johnny was my case. I deserved to know that his killer was still out there."

"We couldn't tell anyone." Spencer sighed. "Even your superiors don't know anything about it. This was kept from the Lakemore PD. It was an arrangement strictly between the DA's office and the crime lab—and only Thomas there."

"Who is conveniently dead." Mackenzie rolled her eyes. "What you didn't know was that Thomas had instructed a technician, Bonnie Yang, to ignore that evidence. She knows what you did."

"Yeah well, if she hasn't gone public by now, I doubt she ever will," Spencer said with a nervous tick in his jaw.

"We will have to inform our bosses about this." Nick nodded at Mackenzie. "And with this buried evidence out in the open, we might finally be able to track down Johnny's killer and bring Noah home."

As Mackenzie stood up, she knew this was far from over. She understood the logic behind Elliot's reasoning, but that didn't make it right. Everyone else had failed Johnny Cooper. And she had no intention of joining that list.

CHAPTER FIFTY-ONE

Two hours later, Mackenzie and Nick were finally called into the conference room. After returning to the station, they had provided Sully and Rivera with the details of the cover-up. For the past two hours, Sully and Rivera had been in constant meetings with Captain Murphy, the DA, and the mayor himself.

Mackenzie couldn't guess which direction the discussions were going. All she could tell was that there were some heated arguments going on, and some resigned conversations.

When they joined their bosses in the conference room, Mackenzie noted the distress in Sully as he rubbed his temples. Rivera paced the room, her hands gripping her waist.

"The FBI investigated *us* for corruption when they should have been looking at another office," Sully muttered.

"What's going to happen?" Nick asked.

"You are going to continue with your case," Rivera said with a straight face. "And not ask any questions or be concerned about this alleged cover-up."

"*Alleged?*" His eyes widened. "What the hell happened?"

"Bonnie Yang's official statement hasn't been taken. All her doubts that there was a cover-up are pure conjecture. And the only other person who could have confirmed anything is dead."

"I don't understand. So there won't be any consequences?" Mackenzie asked.

"The DA and mayor are throwing their support behind Elliot." Sully's mouth was pinched in disapproval. "We tried convincing them, but they have their reasons."

"Like what? We are now part of *another* cover-up." Mackenzie couldn't believe what she was hearing.

"If this evidence becomes public knowledge, then *every* case that Elliot has prosecuted would come under review," Rivera explained. "Every single one of them. He has jailed the highest number of murderers and rapists in the history of the county. Reviewing all his cases means spending a lot of money, resources, and time. It will be expensive. And, more than that, the matter becomes political. District attorney's elections get impacted. So does the mayoral. This will have a domino effect. And the dominos will fall for a very long time. This cover-up is not about protecting Elliot's career, but about protecting multiple offices and not disrupting the process of justice."

"Justice wasn't done," Nick said tightly. "The process was disrupted when he buried the evidence."

"I know," she replied in a hard voice. "I don't like it, but he has his reasons."

"And that's good enough?" Mackenzie scoffed sarcastically.

"No. But you two have to realize that sometimes there is no winning in a situation. This is one of those. No matter what we do or what Elliot did, there will be fallout. And we have to minimize that fallout. At least those are the words that were thrown at me by the mayor." Rivera rolled her eyes, quoting him. "*There's a time to be right, and then there's a time to be smart.*"

"You engage in one cover-up and then you engage in another," Mackenzie said.

"Mayor Rathbone is very clear about not wanting to investigate this infraction."

"Lieutenant." Nick shook his head. "This is murky."

"Coming clean would lead to large collateral damage. Other than the reasons I mentioned, it *will* end the career of one of the most celebrated prosecutors in Washington," River said. "I don't like this either. But there's nothing we can do if the Mayor and the DA don't want to pursue this."

Mackenzie growled, clasping her hands behind her head. "There must be a way to find a suitable compromise."

"We need Elliot Garcia, Mack. This town and county need him. He has the highest conviction rate. And one day that man will run for office."

"But this sets a precedent!" Nick snapped. "We allow this once, and we'll have to allow it again."

"We are not allowing anything, because there is no proof. It's all hearsay." Sully finally broke his introspective silence and walked around the table.

"You too, Sully?" Nick raised an eyebrow.

"Investigating Elliot Garcia is not our jurisdiction. We informed our superiors about it, and if they don't want an inquiry, it's out of our hands." He rolled out his stern tone. "Johnny's murderer walks free. As does the person who abducted three boys and killed two of them. You need to go after *them*. And not after Elliot, who did a slimy thing to put a monster away for good."

"You support all this," Mackenzie observed quietly.

"I live in the real world, Mack. We all want to do the right thing. But people forget that doing the right thing also has consequences. There is collateral damage. You saw it with the Perez case—"

"Yes, but we arrested them. We knew what it would mean for Lakemore, but that didn't stop us!"

"Because they were raping and murdering girls!" Sully threw back at her. "Are you really going to compare that to what Elliot did?"

Mackenzie looked away, feeling torn. She had spent her life playing by the rules, always obeying every single one of them with the utmost dedication. She never even once jaywalked when there was no car in sight. Being a part of this made her question just who she was. Burying bodies in the woods, lying to surviving family members, and now covering up unethical and illegal practices.

But Mackenzie composed herself, steeling herself. "It's not right."

"I know. But doing the right thing has a cost. And in this case, no one deserves to pay the price." Sully clapped his hands. "Let us handle this. Go and find Noah alive."

CHAPTER FIFTY-TWO

Mackenzie dragged her feet back to the office, still fuming over the mayor's decision not to pursue Elliot's violation. Nick's face was red. He collapsed on his chair, unrolled his sleeves and loosened his tie, his nostrils flaring.

She almost gasped when Austin's head popped up above the cubicle wall across from her. "You're here."

"Huh?" She shook her head, still frazzled.

He walked around, approaching her slowly. Like a predator stalking his prey. "I'd like to ask you some questions, Detective Price. Will you come with me to the interrogation room?"

Silence descended on the office at Austin's words. Nick's constant clicking of the pen lid paused. The paperclip Troy was trying to balance on his puckered upper lip dropped.

Mackenzie stiffened. What had he discovered?

Austin stood with a file in his hands, patiently waiting for Mackenzie. He had a neutral expression, but she couldn't help but notice a calculating gleam in his eye. He was taking her to an interrogation room. He had found something.

Mackenzie stood tall and walked behind him out of the office, not showing a hint of emotion, even though fear held her insides captive. Even though she knew that her coworkers might speculate and gossip about her.

Austin led her into one of the better interrogation rooms—spacious and not intimidating. He sat across from her, luminous against the backdrop of the inky sky visible through the window behind him. "Comfortable?"

"Very." The temperature of the room had shot up. Underneath her pantsuit, she sweated. "So what's this about?"

"As you are aware, we never found Charles's mobile phone. We assumed that the killer must have taken it. But his phone turned on two days ago."

Adrenaline flooded Mackenzie's body, sending her heart into overdrive, hammering in her ribcage. What was on Charles's phone?

"We found a spy app covertly installed on his phone."

Mackenzie had installed the app when she bought Charles the phone. It was to keep an eye on him, see who he was meeting and talking to. He was supposed to have been dead; of course Mackenzie hadn't trusted him.

But she maintained her composure, waiting for Austin to elaborate further. When she didn't budge, he continued.

"We traced that app to you. You had been keeping tabs on Charles. And then he was killed, and his phone went missing."

"Are you accusing me of killing him?"

He smirked. "Charles was a drunk, based on the reports from the time he disappeared years ago. I can imagine you probably didn't have the most pleasant memories of him."

Mackenzie blinked. The image of Melody curled up in a ball in the washroom with fresh bruises marring her skin flashed before her eyes. When she opened her eyes, the image dissolved, along with the confusion and rage she had felt as a child.

"You are insinuating that I killed him, when I have an alibi. I was working a case."

"You might not have pulled the trigger, but that doesn't mean you aren't involved."

Mackenzie was almost offended at the accusation. Did everyone else think that she had something to do with the murder? "Charles showed up after a very long time. It's understandable that I didn't trust him. I'm a police officer. Just like you, I'm trained to be more cynical. So I installed an app to keep an eye on him."

"What do you mean you didn't *trust* him?"

"He had gambling debts from Vegas. I was concerned that he might have been after my money. And I had no interest in getting involved in that kind of mess," she replied with confidence. Every ounce of her motivation for her actions was accounted for. She reminded herself that she was still in control of the situation. All she had to do was project an air of calm.

"Even for your father?"

"Even for my father."

"And why didn't you tell anyone about this spy app before? Charles was murdered months ago."

"Because I forgot about it." At least that part was honest. "The truth is that the spy app hadn't revealed any suspicious activity. He wasn't in touch with anyone criminal. I stopped checking the app pretty quickly after he returned."

"You kicked him out of your life after finding out his real identity from Senator Blackwood. Did you monitor his activities after that?"

"No."

"Really?" He raised an eyebrow.

"Really." She ignored his jab.

"Would you please elaborate on that?"

The room was charged with tension as they regarded each other in silence for a few seconds. As if to Austin this was a game of cat and mouse. He relished the fact that he had her cornered. But he didn't know she had sharp teeth.

"I wanted to move on. I tried making it work with my estranged father, but that lie was too big for me to accept. I wanted to erase him from my life and simply stopped caring."

"Clint is in the process of getting into Charles's phone."

"Where did you find it?"

"On a homeless man. Looks like the killer threw it away."

Why did the killer take Charles's phone at all?

"Lucky break," she muttered.

"Oh, definitely." He smiled. "I for one can't wait to get to know more about Charles. There's some damage, but Clint will repair that easily. We did see that he called you the day before he was killed."

"Yes, but I didn't pick up." A pang of regret.

"Did he leave a voicemail?"

"Yes."

"What did it say?"

"I deleted it without listening to it."

"Now, why would you do that?"

"Like I said, I decided not to care." Defiance burned in her eyes. Charles had taken away too much from her. From her childhood to participating in the lies forged by Melody.

"We're going to need to take your phone."

"*What?*" She blanched at his words.

"Your phone has all the information on Charles's GPS and online activity from the spy app. We have to go through the contents."

"But there's nothing there."

"I thought you had stopped checking." Austin feigned an innocent face like he'd caught her in a lie.

"This feels like an invasion."

"You're on the other side for the first time, Detective Price. This is what it's like. Your phone will be returned to you as soon as we extract relevant information from it."

"I'm on an important case." She grasped at straws. "There's proprietary information on it."

"You can get a temporary phone. And don't worry. We're not accessing your email. That's a serious breach. Now, will you submit your phone to us? I don't want to go through the trouble of writing up a warrant, but if you don't cooperate I won't have a choice."

Was he enjoying this? Had Sully let slip to Austin about Mackenzie not trusting him? Had he realized that Mackenzie had seen him snooping around?

Realizing there was no way out of this, she handed him her phone. "When will I get it back?"

"Tomorrow afternoon. I'll make it a priority."

"Thanks."

Austin leaned forward and asked deliberately, "Detective Price, are you sure that you've told us absolutely everything there is to know about Charles? If there's anything more, even from way back in the past, please tell us. It will help."

"I've told you everything."

"Alright then." His gaze held hers. "Thank you for your cooperation. I'll keep you updated."

He left her alone in the room and a chill went through her. Austin was clearly determined to get to the truth. She wanted him to find Charles's killer, but not at the cost of what transpired that night twenty years ago becoming public knowledge.

When Mackenzie came out of the room, she found Nick leaning against the wall, his knee bobbing to a random rhythm. "Mack? What was that about?"

"He took my phone."

"What? Why?"

She rehashed her interview with Austin.

"I have a spare on me. You can use it," he offered.

"Thanks. Why are you still here?"

"I was worried about you. Thought I'd wait for you, but two minutes ago we got an email from the toxicology lab about Patricia's cookies."

Nervous energy bubbled inside her, her own problems vanishing for the moment. "And?"

"They screened for all the common drugs from marijuana to cocaine. It tested negative for all. But they found dextroamphetamine."

"That's Dexradine right? To treat ADHD?"

"Dose is very high too—100 mg."

"That's a lot."

"Not only that. They were laced with fentanyl." He looked grave.

She paused, thinking. "Fentanyl increases addictiveness."

"Summer said Patricia sends them a batch almost every month."

Mackenzie was dumbfounded. "She's drugging them."

CHAPTER FIFTY-THREE

Mackenzie checked the time with a sigh. Her uncle, Damien, was supposed to drop by to give her Robert's watch. She had baked a cake and planned to invite him inside, even though it pained her to face him, the obvious grief he still felt about his brother a sharp reminder of what she'd taken away from him.

Faint laughter filtered inside her home from outside. Mackenzie went to the window. Usually, she kept the curtains open, liking the view of the garden she tended meticulously. But since recent events, she had kept them closed, feeling more secure knowing no one could look inside her house.

Nudging the curtain aside, she saw Damien and Irene engaged in animated conversation. Irene beamed and chuckled, while Damien blushed and stared at her eagerly.

Did they know each other?

Mackenzie clicked the door open. "Hey!"

Irene looked at her and smiled. "Hey, Mack!"

She approached the pair, her eyes flitting between them. "Hi, Damien."

He jolted. "Mackenzie, sorry I ran into your lovely neighbor and got talking."

"Yes, well. I should go back inside, otherwise my dinner will burn," Irene said good-naturedly. "It was nice meeting you, Damien. See you tomorrow, Mack!"

"You two seem like good friends," Damien said, gazing after Irene as she disappeared inside her house.

"Yeah." It made her a smile; the thought that she'd made a friend. An ability that didn't come easy to her. "Would you like to come inside?"

Damien's eyes travelled to Mackenzie's house. He swallowed and gave her a begrudging smile. "I'm in a rush. Some other time."

She was mildly disappointed but didn't show it. "Of course."

He took out a watch from his pocket. The band was toffee brown leather, with stainless-steel buckles.

Mackenzie's fingers shook as she took it from him and held it in her hands. It had a weathered look to it, but the centerpiece was dazzling and elegant. Perfectly circular with roman numerals. The dial moved smoothly without actually ticking. She didn't tend to place much value on material things, but sometimes they became important. She knew she would cherish this. It was the only tangible piece she had of Robert—the father she deserved.

"Thank you." Her voice broke.

Damien appraised her. "I can see it means a lot to you."

"What was he like?" she blurted.

"He was never afraid to express himself. He was kind and loyal and generous." Damien's eyes drifted into a fond memory. "He always used to say that time fixes everything, only if you let it." Damien's eyes searched hers. Mackenzie wondered if he saw right through her, her inability to move on. "He was never one for regrets," he went on. "Even when we were children, he'd say that to me and tap at that watch. I keep that in mind. Seems like a good way to honor him."

Mackenzie tried swallowing down the lump in her throat and failed. "You're right."

CHAPTER FIFTY-FOUR

March 14

Mackenzie clamped her hands tightly over the wheel of her car and turned on the engine. The rumble set her nerves on edge. She picked up Nick from his place, to go and see Patricia directly.

Nick looked sharp, freshly shaven and wearing a crisp suit. Mackenzie sniffed the air, no sign of cigarettes or overwhelming deodorant.

"Summer is a college student and so are the others living in that makeshift rehab house. A lot of them get prescription stimulants like Ritalin to study," Nick explained.

"Disappointing." She bit her lip. "They enrolled in the program to treat their addiction, but now they're on amphetamines."

He wound down the window, letting air into the car. "Trust Patricia to sell drugs."

"And the killer clearly knew about it. That's why they left Theo at the meeting point."

"Did you inform Special Investigations about this?"

"I told them to be on standby." She pulled up in front of the trailer park. "But how will this help us get closer to what happened to Johnny? How will it help us find Noah?"

Nick flattened his mouth. "Maybe it won't. We're still looking for Agatha. But the DA office is going to send us the forensic evidence they buried."

She dreaded the thought of Noah's body turning up somewhere. "This entire time Elliot and Spencer were hanging on to key forensic evidence knowing we have a vigilante killer at large."

"That's self-preservation."

The words stung Mackenzie; she couldn't entirely ignore her hypocrisy. All these years, it had been a comforting thought that she was the only victim of her selfishness. Until Charles was murdered.

It was a warm day, the temperature reaching seventy degrees, and the residents of Lakemore had flocked outdoors to enjoy the sunshine. People sat on cheap plastic furniture drinking beers from a cooler and reading newspapers. They glanced casually at Mackenzie and Nick as they approached Patricia's trailer.

Patricia opened the door after a few minutes. "What now?"

"We need to talk." Mackenzie didn't hide the scorn in her voice. She had never liked Patricia, blinded as she was by her loyalty to her brother.

"Then wait while I call my lawyer." She made a show of taking out her phone.

"We know about your special gifts for Summer and others at the shelter," Nick said.

Patricia staggered backward.

A voice came from inside her house.

Pastor Giles appeared at the doorstep. "Is everything alright? Patricia?"

Mackenzie and Nick pushed their way inside. Patricia's face had turned crimson. She cowered like a cornered animal, sinking into the couch. Her breaths came short and quick, like she was trapped.

"What are you doing here?" Nick asked Giles.

"Patricia called me for spiritual guidance. We meet at this time every other day."

"Maybe you should stay for this," Mackenzie suggested. "It concerns you too."

Giles looked at them quizzically.

"Patricia gives 'special' cookies to the college kids staying at the shelter every month. We obtained samples from Summer, one of the teenagers there. There are high levels of Dexradine, an amphetamine."

"*What?*" Giles fell on a chair, trembling. "Surely there must be a mistake?"

"The man she bought the cookies from has been arrested and is being interrogated as we speak," Nick informed him.

"So you're selling drugs to college kids. Ironically when they're in rehabilitation for drug addiction," Mackenzie snapped.

Patricia wiped her face with the edge of her sleeve, glaring at the other three, looking for an escape. "I... I need the money!"

"Explain," Nick ordered.

"It wasn't a big deal. You don't know these kids. Half of them are on Ritalin. They don't even think of it as a real drug. I've become friendly with them, and a few of them expressed an interest in getting some stimulants," she sniffled. "I thought I could make some extra cash on the side."

"It was present at very high doses, Patricia." Mackenzie felt anger course through her veins. "Higher than recommended. And they were laced with fentanyl. A very dangerous opioid."

Patricia looked at Giles with beseeching eyes. "I swear I didn't know that!"

Giles looked away, disgusted.

She turned to Mackenzie and Nick. "I didn't know about the high doses or the fentanyl! I just found Toby and told him I wanted to buy ADHD stimulants. He never mentioned anything about fentanyl—"

"Of course, he didn't." Mackenzie seethed. "How else do you think these dealers make sure their clients come back for more? They lace the product with other substances to make them more addictive."

"Is that why they're sick?" Giles whimpered, horrified.

"A lot of the symptoms Summer exhibited could pass as withdrawal," Nick nodded.

"Oh my God. I thought that the program was just slow."

"I'm so sorry." Patricia was frantic as she grabbed Giles's hands. "I didn't know they were laced and the doses were so high. I just trusted whatever Toby gave me. I don't want to hurt anyone."

"So Summer and the others knew that the cookies contained stimulants?" Nick asked, trying to extract information from Patricia before she became hysterical.

She closed her eyes. "Yes. The church keeps checking their belongings for drugs to make sure none of them have relapsed. That's why I had to supply it to them in a way it's not suspicious. Please. I didn't know Toby was giving me the bad stuff. I really needed the money. You don't know how much I struggle. The church rents the house from me on a month-by-month basis. The income from that and my job isn't enough to keep me afloat—"

"So it's extra pocket money for you to sell drugs to those college kids, which will conveniently extend their rehabilitation program, giving you more rent," Nick said.

"What did you do, Patricia?" Giles shouted. Tears swam in his eyes. "You are *poisoning* them! That's a sin."

"Pastor, please." She fell to her knees in front of him, making for a peculiar sight. "I'm not killing anyone! I just meant to extend their recovery period and make extra money. I was going to stop, I swear."

"How did you meet Toby Adler?" Mackenzie asked.

"Someone at work buys from him."

"You blindly trusted a drug dealer without a thought to the damage it could cause?" Mackenzie spat out.

But Pastor Giles jumped in before Patricia could respond. "This is going to ruin everything," he snapped, spit spraying out of his mouth, face like thunder. "The church will scrap this program altogether. Not to mention the police involvement. I spent *years* getting this program to take off. It was my dream project."

"I know. I know," she hiccupped, tremors raking her body. "I didn't mean to hurt the program. I'm sorry! Please forgive me." She clasped his hands.

Blood crept up Giles's neck as he tried to control his anger. He tugged his hands free and covered his face. "The damage you've done, child. It was wrong of them to want the prescription drugs in the first place, but you facilitated their addiction. How will you ever atone for this?"

Nick stepped forward and cuffed Patricia, reciting her Miranda rights. But she only had eyes for Giles, clearly devastated by how much she had disappointed him.

Nick took her out, leaving Giles and Mackenzie alone in the mobile home. She considered leaving, but Giles was visibly agitated. He rubbed his hands together and squeezed his eyes shut. The cross dangled from his neck, swinging like a pendulum with every jerky breath he took.

"Will you be alright?" Mackenzie asked. It struck her suddenly that he was quite elderly, and he'd had a shock.

"Maybe you were right, Detective. Maybe some people are beyond redemption. I can't believe Patricia would resort to selling drugs."

"You're God's man. I thought you'd be firmer in your belief that people can be saved?" She didn't say it as a challenge; she was genuinely intrigued.

Giles clenched his cross and pressed his lips to it. "I'm still human. There are days even I can't see the hope, when I'm too weighed down by the evil in the world."

Mackenzie nodded. She knew the feeling.

"Take care, Pastor," she said, as she and Nick turned to leave.

*

They handed Patricia over to the Special Investigations Unit, where she was placed in a holding cell while she contacted her lawyer. Toby Adler had been arrested too. The Lakemore PD had contacted the church and arranged for all the young adults who were part of the "rehabilitation" program to be taken to the hospital to be treated. The church had immediately hired a PR firm for damage control and counsel was on standby. The scandal was kept under wraps for now, especially with Lakemore utterly transfixed by the last missing child. But it was only a matter of time before Patricia's operation would see the light of day. Luckily, they had caught it at a relatively early stage, before anyone had accidentally died of an overdose.

Mackenzie updated the detectives from the Special Investigations Unit on what she knew, using the opportunity to steal some of their coffee for Nick, which was far superior to the coffee from their machine apparently.

She placed the cup on Nick's desk. He wrapped his hands around it and took a large gulp. "Bless you."

"The DA's office sent us the file?"

"Not yet. But we'll get it today." He relished the coffee. "They removed that page from the official filings so they're going to retrieve it from backups."

Sully emerged from his office, visibly agitated. "I just got a call from Holly Martin."

"Jeremiah's lawyer?" Nick asked. "What did she say?"

"Jeremiah wants to meet with the two of you. He said he might have useful information on Johnny."

CHAPTER FIFTY-FIVE

"Are you kidding me?" Nick growled and kicked the tire of Mackenzie's car. She had rarely seen him blow a fuse. "What the hell does this asshole want to remember eight years later?"

"I don't know, Nick," she said, exasperated. "But before we go in, you need to calm down. Don't give him that satisfaction."

He pulled at his hair. "Do you know how much time I spent with him back then? It's all just a game to him."

"Yeah, and he's a psychopath, what do you expect?"

He nodded, licking his lips and loosening his tie. "Alright. Let's find out his *useful* information."

Inside the correctional facility, Holly Martin greeted them. Behind her thick glasses, her eyes were ringed with eyeliner. She toyed with her shawl and shook their hands. "Nice to see you again, detectives."

"Your client has new information that could help us?" Nick asked.

"He certainly does."

"Eight years later?"

She tilted her head. "Memory is a funny thing. Jeremiah has had such a rough time in prison. He has gotten in touch with his faith again. It's clearing up his memory."

"Let's drop the pretenses and cut to the chase. Why now?" Mackenzie demanded.

Holly sighed. "That upcoming true crime documentary is garnering a lot of interest. Especially since Lakemore is in the news due to these recent abductions. The director may have encouraged Jeremiah to dig deeper into his psyche and unearth more information for the documentary."

"So Jeremiah has decided to come forward *now* so that he can get more clout? So that there's another angle to the documentary?" Mackenzie spat out each accusation.

Holly raised a hand. "That would be an unintended perk, Detective Price. Jeremiah merely listened to the advice he was given and remembered a detail he had suppressed. You know about the trauma he went through as a child himself..."

"I also know the trauma he inflicted on others."

"I think it's best if we go in, instead of wasting our time." Holly flashed them a sour smile and led them to the same room as before.

This time when Mackenzie met Jeremiah, she was fuming. The fear, confusion, and morbid curiosity replaced with a burning desire to rip his throat out. Everyone knew the damage he had done, but she had seen it firsthand in the past few days: what a missing and a dead child did to a family, what chasing a monster had done to Nick.

The room was washed in dim, yellow light. A clear steel table was at the center, and a stern guard stood at the door across from them.

Jeremiah's long, gray hair was tied in a bun. His dark skin was marred with lines, his mouth contorted in a twisted smile. "You don't look any wiser, my old friend. Who is troubling you now?"

"We're not here to make small talk. What do you have for us?" Nick pulled the chair back, the leg scraping against the tiles.

"That's rude. Where are your manners? You hate depending on me, don't you? You have always loathed the power imbalance in our relationship."

"Need I remind you that you're in prison?"

"Physically, yes. You put the bad guy in jail. Congratulations," he mocked them. Mackenzie noticed a shift in him. Last time, he had taunted them more coyly. This time, he was brazen. Probably the attention making his head bigger. "But I'm still always on your mind. I never left. How much time do you spend regretting that you didn't solve my poems fast enough? How often do you think about Johnny? It doesn't look to me that I lost entirely. We both lost. Maybe you more than me. Because you have a conscience. I don't."

Mackenzie dared to look at Nick. As much as she was sure he was unraveling inside, he kept his cool in front of Jeremiah.

"Okay, we're done here. Clearly your intention is to just waste our time. Let's go, Mack."

"Your new killer holds you captive." Jeremiah's words stopped them in their tracks. "They're worse than me. They *feel*. They *plan*. They see more than you did."

"How do you know so much?" Mackenzie questioned.

"I have been keeping tabs through people and the news."

"Do you know who this killer is? Your pen pal Martha Becks AKA Agatha Bellini for example?"

He scoffed. "She's harmless, just an overactive imagination and an immature fantasy. I'm bored in here."

"You're engaging with someone who is clearly unstable. Maybe you don't know what she's capable of, or what effect your words have had on her."

"Do you think I care? But back to your killer. I like how they remind your partner of me." He turned to Nick, his eyes twinkled under yellow light, growing darker as his pupils dilated. "You are experiencing the same fear of being trapped. He has you in a cage, and he forces you to watch as he kills one by one. And he tells you that the key is in your gilded cage for you to escape and stop him. But you just can't find it."

"Can your information help us get to the key faster?" Mackenzie snapped.

"Perhaps."

"What is it?"

"I was remembering the time I met Johnny and spoke with him."

"You said it was small talk," Nick said. "And that you'd forgotten most of it."

"It was, and I had. But it wasn't all that." He gave them a roguish grin. "Johnny was pretty talkative. I asked him what a boy like him was doing in the woods. And he said that he had recently discovered this route and enjoyed walking in nature."

"You said all this before."

Mackenzie nudged Nick to remind him to be patient, while Jeremiah continued. "He was very interested to see that I lived in the woods. Asked me all sorts of questions about if I see any wild animals or if I get television. I told him he was a curious boy, asked if he'd like to be my friend. Since it gets lonely in the woods."

Mackenzie felt bile bubble in her throat. Even Holly looked away, masking her discomfort with annoyance.

"He asked me what it would mean being my friend… and I said it meant that we could meet the next day and hang out. I'd show him a new video game."

Mackenzie wanted to leave. His words stung her ears and made the air all the more stifling.

"But he said he couldn't be my friend because he wouldn't be around the next day."

"What?" Nick frowned.

Jeremiah snickered, the sound of it grating. "Johnny said that he was leaving home, running away."

"Why didn't you say this before?"

"Because my client has poor memory," Holly interjected. "As I've conveyed to you already."

"What else did he say?" Mackenzie pressed. "Did he say why?"

Jeremiah didn't acknowledge her, watching Nick. "He said something about not being happy."

Mackenzie's heart dropped sharply. It was because of Heather.

"But you two don't look very surprised at that," Holly commented, making a face similar to a vulture circling the carcass, close to descending. "Did you already know that Johnny planned to run away from home?"

"No, we didn't." Mackenzie rooted her jaw. "Did Johnny mention anything else? Had he told anyone? Where did he plan to go?"

"I told the boy that running away was a big decision. Asked him if he'd thought it through and had enough funds to survive out there alone. He said he had thought of everything and said he was late for school. Unfortunately, I was supposed to meet with Patricia or…"

"Or else you would have followed him and murdered him?"

"Or else he could have perhaps convinced the boy not to run away," Holly pitched in with a strained smile. "Or talked to him long enough so that whoever it was who did kill him—"

"Oh, cut the crap." Nick scowled. "Seriously? We all know what he is. There's no jury here."

Holly raised an eyebrow and leaned back, giving up.

Nick's dark eyes were bottomless pits of fury, illuminated by the bulb above them. "Jeremiah, is there any further detail you think you might remember after your *memory* clears up more?"

"I guess you'll just have to wait and see." He cackled again.

The officer came forward to escort him out of the room. As Jeremiah was dragged back to confinement, the sound of his ringing laughter echoed, making Mackenzie want to cover her ears.

CHAPTER FIFTY-SIX

"*With two young boys dead and one still missing, the pressure on Lakemore PD is building. With the FBI investigation looking into police corruption still wrapping up, their recent record of negligence and dishonesty isn't giving hope to a lot of people. Can they be trusted? Can—*"

Mackenzie closed the tab before Debbie continued on her rant. Ever since the Perez case, she had relentlessly attacked the police to boost her ratings. Suddenly, the obnoxious reporter no one took seriously had figured out the magic formula. She titillated the audience by giving them a villain to blame all of Lakemore's problems on.

Mackenzie used to find it offensive, but after uncovering so many bad seeds in her line of work, she wasn't sure she completely disagreed.

"I heard she had a very generous offer from a large network to work out of the Seattle office," Troy gossiped. "But she rejected it. Better being a big fish in a small pond."

"It's a smart decision. She's riding high and establishing a good network. If only she were more professional in her reporting."

Troy looked around. "Where's Nick?"

"He's in a meeting," she said casually.

Troy didn't think much of it and went back to work. Only Nick and Justin knew of Elliot's actions and the subsequent decision of brass to overlook it for the "greater good". She wondered if she was the only one who felt shackled by this information. Now the DA had called Nick to meet with him personally.

Mackenzie wiggled, shaking off her thoughts and focusing on the evidence. Noah Kinsey's face was inked in her mind. His father had been in constant touch with Sully, spending his own money on a private investigator, rumor had it, but nothing had come of it.

As she had expected, the sight of Ruth Newman with her students holding signs of "Bring our friends home" had become iconic. It had flooded social media. Her project of creating sculptures of Lucas and Theo was also gaining a lot of support online.

Mackenzie got a notification on her phone. A graffiti artist had painted a mural on the wall of an abandoned building. The mural was dedicated to Lucas Williams and Theo Reynolds—their grinning faces looking at the onlookers and a pair of angel wings extending from behind. She tossed her phone away, tears pooling in her eyes. She was unable to push away the dead look in Mrs. Reynolds's eyes, unable to silence Mr. Kinsey's pleas constantly ringing in her ear.

When she saw Austin in his cubicle immersed in work, she decided to work elsewhere. Her phone had been returned to her, and she bet he was going over the details of her messages right now—her private messages with Sterling, the carcass of a dead relationship. She might as well be naked in public.

Mackenzie picked up her things and left the office, hunting for a quiet spot. The conference room had been booked. Instead, she took one of the fire exits and decided to settle on the stairs in the back entrance of the station.

No one ever came here.

Despite the chillier air, she felt herself relax away from prying eyes.

Mackenzie went over Johnny's forensic reports again and played the video of his last sighting on her laptop. Silk fabric—red and blue—was found on him. It could easily have been a complete stranger who killed him. But how would he know to cut out the tongue?

As she watched Johnny and Jeremiah's exchange play out once again, she wondered if Jeremiah had an accomplice. But a partner didn't match his profile. He was a lone wolf on the hunt.

Johnny had wanted to run away, according to Jeremiah. Not that Jeremiah's word was reliable at all. Mackenzie watched Johnny closely. He kept touching his red fanny pack while he spoke to Jeremiah, shifting and fixing it. Like it was about to fall off? Or he was worried about it?

Mackenzie played the video again and observed the special attention he paid to the fanny pack.

She checked the report again. His backpack and fanny pack had been retrieved the day after he went missing in the same woods, not too far from where he had spoken with Jeremiah.

Then she remembered something. Something she hadn't paid much attention to before. It took her a few minutes to confirm her suspicions.

It all came together so seamlessly. Little pieces of information that she had collected over the past few days stitched together into a theory. All that was left to do was check a website.

Her breath hitched in her throat. Fingers froze on the keyboard. Scalp prickled.

She rang Nick. "Sorry, are you busy?"

"No, I just got out of the meeting. What's up?"

"Nick, I think I know what happened to Johnny."

Silence. As if she had said something taboo. They had wanted answers for so long, but were they prepared to receive them?

"What happened?" he asked.

"You found Johnny's belongings the day after he went missing. And you assumed that they fell on the ground either while he was running away from someone or during a struggle when he was abducted, right?"

"That's correct."

"His backpack contained his books and pencil case, but his fanny pack was empty."

"Yes, sometimes Johnny would carry an empty fanny pack to school to bring food home. The lunch lady pitied him and his brother so she would sneak them some extra snacks. At least that's what Tim told us."

"Except I don't think that his fanny pack was empty," she whispered. "I watched the video several times, and it seemed like it kept slipping down his pants. He had to keep it up. I checked its pictures, but the clasp wasn't broken or anything—"

"Maybe he didn't tie it properly."

"That's what I thought at first, but why wouldn't he just fix it if he didn't wear it correctly at first? It's annoying to keep lifting it every time it threatened to slip. But more so, when he met Jeremiah, he paid extra attention to it. He had a protective hand over it. I didn't think much of it before, but, assuming Jeremiah was telling the truth, now that we know that Johnny was running away…"

"He could have been guarding something important. Like how you hide something valuable when you meet a stranger," Nick added.

"*Exactly*. Jeremiah told us that Johnny claimed to have thought of everything, including funds. Nick, I think he had money in there. But that money was never found. Because the killer must have taken it."

"But Heather didn't report any money going missing."

"I just checked, and someone else did exactly around that time. And then also said that the money was later recovered."

Nick took a beat to answer. "Pastor Giles."

CHAPTER FIFTY-SEVEN

The clergy house where Pastor Giles resided was a block away from the church on an elegant street. It was a little pocket of history with traditional-looking houses with bow windows and cobbled streets. The estate surrounding them glistened a rich green, as if light trapped every blade of grass. A thick spread of trees circled the area—those woods weren't wild. One on side it led to a lake and the other to the main street.

Dressed in black robes, Giles watered the flowerpots outside his home. He was old but sturdy, walked with a hunched back but with strength. His jaw was dotted with white hair. His square-shaped face was serene, enjoying the crisp air and bright sunshine.

"Pastor Giles?" Nick called out as they approached him.

He waved back and put away the watering can. "What brings you here? Did something happen with Patricia? Did she get bail?"

Mackenzie fidgeted. "We need to talk."

"About what?"

"Nine years ago, you reported that three thousand dollars were stolen from a church fund," Nick spoke deliberately. "Three days later, you withdrew the complaint saying the money was recovered."

Giles's face twitched. "Yes. I… I was mistaken. It wasn't stolen. It was just misplaced."

"Where did you find it?" Mackenzie asked.

It was a beautiful day. And Giles's wilting expression was a stark contrast.

"It was somewhere else in the church." He shook his head.

Mackenzie tilted her head. "We found evidence on Johnny Cooper."

Giles let out a shaky breath. His hands trembled as he scrambled to sit on a stone bench.

"We found red and blue silk fibers on him," she continued and displayed a picture of the church's website. Giles stood wearing a clergy stole of red and blue strips. "You were wearing this the first time we met. It's made of silk, I'm assuming?"

Giles's hands gripped the edge of the bench and rocked back and forth, swallowing incessantly. "I'm so sorry."

Mackenzie looked at Nick, not expecting Giles to break down so quickly. But as the old man started to weep, it was obvious his guilt had been on the verge of bursting out anyway. Nick was the sensitive one—the "good cop" who would usually spur the suspects into a confession. But this time his face spelled fury. He crossed his arms and watched Giles without an ounce of pity.

Mackenzie kneeled in front of him. "What happened?"

"I had been trying to start the rehabilitation program for *years!*" Giles's eyes were bloodshot. "I didn't want to just read sermons and listen to confessions. I had concrete plans for the church to expand and actually contribute, to be more than just a symbol. The churches in other towns do so much more. And we did nothing. People were old, lazy, and lacking any vision. I wanted to help people. But it took me too long to convince people above me to lend their support. They finally agreed, if I could raise the money. So I did. I established a fund and collected donations."

"Three thousand dollars?"

"It was a start. Things were finally heading in the right direction. I was over the moon. It was God's blessing." He held the cross around his neck as a fierce expression took over his face. "Johnny and Tim used to come to the Sunday mass sometimes. They used to regularly attend with their father, and after he died, they would attend sporadically. One day, the money went missing. I was devastated and filed a police report. But the police in Lakemore had much bigger fish to fry so they didn't seem too keen to investigate immediately. I asked around, and someone at the church had seen Johnny around my office. I decided to confront him and give him a chance. I knew which school he went to and met him on the way."

Mackenzie saw it play out. Johnny skipping to school—his last day before he intended to run away—unaware of how complicated the world was. A nine-year-old even with money wouldn't have been able to survive. He probably didn't even fathom how much money he had taken, just blindly grabbing the thick stash he found. A desperate and childish attempt to escape his horrid stepmother. But Giles had caught him.

"I had expected him to give me back the money. He made a mistake; he was a kid! I told him he wouldn't get into any trouble. And that we could pray to God to forgive him for stealing. But he... he refused." He paused, wincing at the memory. Like it was a scab he was picking at. "I tried reasoning with him, but he grew antagonistic. He wouldn't listen. He was so stubborn!"

He was just a kid—and they could be stubborn. Especially if Johnny had made up his mind about running away. He'd already had bad experiences with the adults in his life. Only Ruth Norman had shown him any kindness, but her inadvertent negligence had hurt him too.

"I thought I'd just take it from him. But he was stronger than I'd anticipated. That money belonged to the church! It came from the people! It was supposed to be used for *good*. Things got out of hand. He started shouting, and the next thing I knew..." A cry spluttered out of his lips, saliva pooling in the corners of his mouth. "I was choking him. I just wanted him to stop. The rage came over me out of nowhere. The Devil had possessed me. When the rage subsided, he was dead."

"And you didn't call 911?" Nick growled. "You disposed of his body and lied? Those aren't sins to you?"

"I fell weak!" he cried. "I have been atoning for my sins for a very long time." He lifted the hem of his robe to reveal his skin covered in bruises and grooves—some old and some fresh, from what looked like a cilice. "God knows how much I repent. I did everything so that my program took off."

"How did you know to cut out his tongue?" Mackenzie asked.

"Because I took Jeremiah's confession."

Nick was ready to lunge at him. "You knew what he had been doing!" Mackenzie stood up and held him back. "You knew the entire time?"

Giles averted his gaze. "It's the sacred seal of confession! I couldn't defy my God and religion. I tried my best every time to steer him in the right direction, but it was of no help."

"Who the hell cares?" Nick's voice boomed. "You could have saved all those kids' lives! How is anything more important than that?"

"Nick, please," Mackenzie hissed and turned to Giles. "So you knew what Jeremiah's M.O. was. When you killed Johnny, you cut out his tongue so that whenever his body was found, suspicion would fall on Jeremiah?"

He nodded, breaking down. "I'm extremely sorry. I can't go to hell. I just can't go to hell."

Nick wrenched free from Mackenzie and paced, heaving and panting. A muscle in his jaw ticked incessantly.

Mackenzie took out cuffs. "Pastor Giles, you're under arrest for the murder of Johnny Cooper." She recited him his rights.

Giles didn't resist, willingly submitting to his fate. He didn't pay attention to anything she said. Instead his eyes were closed and his lips mouthed a prayer. Like anything could absolve him for what he did.

While Nick teemed with crushing disbelief next to her, Mackenzie focused on the wispy silver lining. They had caught Johnny's killer. Did that mean Noah would be released alive?

CHAPTER FIFTY-EIGHT

The Lakemore PD had Giles's signed confession. He had been transported to lockup, where he would await arraignment. He was resigned, calling it "God's will"—he had no intention to fight the charges.

Elliot and Spencer were coordinating with Jeremiah's lawyer, Holly, on getting the charge of Johnny's murder dismissed. A shrewd Holly fully intended to exploit this opportunity to file appeals for post-conviction relief. Mackenzie reckoned that she was clever enough to know that the evidence against Jeremiah was overwhelming enough for him not to walk free—even if she were able to knock off a few more charges.

"Then why is she doing all this?" Mackenzie asked.

"This is what lawyers do. Whatever is best for their client," Nick replied, resting his head on the heels of his palms. His coffee was untouched, his pack of cigarettes splayed in front of him.

Mackenzie looked out of the window of the conference room onto the empty street. There was a special kind of blackness to the sky, the stars hidden behind clouds. The scenery caused a roiling sensation in her stomach. Like the darkness and solitude might suffocate her. "What happens now? The forensic evidence led us to Giles so it will see the light of day, right?"

"I don't know." Nick sighed. "Based on my meeting with the DA, I think they're going to try weaseling their way out of this one."

"*How?*"

"He didn't say anything directly, but they might try to explain it away by saying that a mix-up at the crime lab is the reason this evidence was *missed*." He made air quotes.

"So nothing was done intentionally. Basically come up with lies so that they can protect Elliot?"

"They'll try their best. I don't know if it will work. It also depends on what Holly plans to do, like challenging the other charges, suing for wrongful prosecution, et cetera, which was what I think Elliot and Spencer are convincing her not to do."

"Even with this one charge dropped, Jeremiah's other charges would keep him in prison. That's something." She kept twisting Robert's watch on her wrist, the feel of it foreign but welcome.

"That new?" Nick looked pointedly at her watch.

"Family heirloom." She gave him a genuine smile. Her phone rang, and she picked it up immediately. "Detective Price."

"Mack, I got results on Theo's clothing," Anthony said in his monotonous tone. "I have emailed you the report."

"Okay, did you find anything?" She put it on speaker.

"Yes, we were able to pick up macroscopic samples."

"Macroscopic?"

"Yes, and they weren't substances found at that beach." He coughed. "In a nutshell, there were significant amounts of silica, magnesia, alumina, lime, bauxite, sand, sulfur trioxide, among other things."

Mackenzie nodded, absorbing the rapid stream of words. "Okay…"

"That's cement and mortar. A construction site, I'd say."

"A construction site." She stilled and hung up, thanking Anthony. "Nick…"

Nick was already ahead of her. He stood up and grabbed his jacket. All his reluctance to consider Tim as a suspect had withered away over the course of the case. "Let's go and talk to Tim."

*

Tim Cooper's house was a single-story log house, nothing grand but cozy-looking and well maintained. Lush green grass surrounded it, a stark contrast to the brown unpaved land the property was situated on. Mackenzie and Nick had had to wind their way through small country lanes, veering off onto a dirt track. He lived in a secluded area that seemed devoid even of wildlife. Tall trees loomed behind the house, sprouting fresh leaves on skeleton-like branches.

They reached the door. A few potted plants sat next to the entrance. Knocking on the door, there was no response. He hadn't answered his phone when Nick had called, so they didn't know if he'd be home.

"Should we wait?" Mackenzie asked.

"We had uniform keeping an eye on Tim, right? He didn't go anywhere near the lighthouse."

"He could have an accomplice," Mackenzie said, as they circled the property. "Maybe now we'll have enough to get access to his phone and bank statements. He's the only one with motivation and now this potential physical link."

They noticed nothing strange about the property. But it sat at the edge of the woods with no close neighbors, providing tactical advantage if Tim were to engage in any illegal activity.

"Who would help him do something like this though?" Nick asked. "Someone for hire? A girlfriend?"

Mackenzie looked inside through the windows out of curiosity. "Nick! Look at this."

Nick came up beside her, cupping the sides of his eyes and peering in. The room looked like a brightly illuminated office. Disorderly and ordinary. There was a wall covered in pictures of Johnny—a collage from Johnny as a baby in the arms of his late mother, sitting in a shopping cart, eating hummus with his fist dunked in the dip, with his father teaching him how to ride a bike, wrestling with Tim, his first day at school, and every little moment captured over the years. There was a shelf with coloring and children's books with yellowing pages and threadbare spines. An open cupboard revealed a child's clothes hanging there—old, but washed and ironed.

Mackenzie's skin crawled.

It was like Johnny was still here—still alive in the crinkles of his clothes and pages of his books. Like he was part of the air here, still amongst his things, living the life he should have been. Like he never quite left, waiting patiently for someone to finally realize that his story had been told wrong.

"What the hell is going on?" Tim's voice boomed from behind them. He came out of the woods, carrying logs under his arms. His chest heaved. "Why are you looking into my house?"

"We were actually waiting for you," Mackenzie said, sizing him up. "Mind if we talk inside?"

Tim's face glowed red with embarrassment as his eyes kept flitting to the window behind. "Why do you want to talk?" he said.

"Just have a few questions. Can we come inside?"

Tim was clearly temperamental and always seemed on the brink of exploding. Mackenzie believed that a pointed conversation with him might cause him to crack and inadvertently reveal something. He was not good at hiding his emotions; his anger was clearly painted on his face.

"No."

"Then we can talk here." Mackenzie crossed her arms. "You don't have an alibi for the abduction of Lucas, Theo, and Noah. Can anyone confirm you were at home? Anyone you're close to?"

The deputies following him had confirmed that Tim was at a job on the morning of March tenth, when Theo's body was left at the lighthouse. He could have had an accomplice, but they hadn't found any evidence of that yet.

"This is harassment. I know my rights. Next time you want to talk to me, get a warrant." He gritted his teeth and walked past them.

"Tim, we've arrested Johnny's killer," Nick said.

Tim froze. The logs from under his arm slipped and rolled on the ground. A gust of wind blew in their faces, roaring in their ears. He turned around slowly, his eyes wide and lips parted. "What?"

Nick licked his lips. "It wasn't Jeremiah. It was Pastor Giles. Johnny was planning on running away and had stolen money from the church. Giles confronted him and… things escalated."

"*Pastor Giles?*" he repeated.

"Thought you should know."

With that, Nick and Mackenzie walked to the car, leaving Tim standing frozen on the spot.

Mackenzie had an uneasy feeling jabbing at her like a woodpecker. She didn't want to condemn the man for grieving his younger brother, but his lack of alibi for the morning of the abduction still troubled her. And there were the traces on Theo's clothing.

"That shrine he has in there. It's not healthy."

"His record is squeaky clean, and he doesn't have any other property registered to him," Nick revised their discovery. "I'll go back to the station and start preparing an affidavit. If he has an accomplice, we'll find it in his records."

"It's getting late." She looked up at the darkness slowly bleeding into the sky. "You won't get anyone to sign it tonight."

Their phones chimed. It was a text message.

"Agatha used her credit card at a motel in Riverview twenty minutes ago," Mackenzie blurted in a rush.

Nick was already swerving sharply, his back pressed into the seat and his arm on the wheel straight. "Where?"

"Uniform is picking her up right now and bringing her directly to the station," Mackenzie replied, her skin tingling with anticipation.

CHAPTER FIFTY-NINE

Agatha Bellini sat in the interrogation room, her chest rising and falling irregularly. She was tall and broad, but incredibly frail. She sat with her shoulders drawn together, her skin a thin film over her pointy bones. She scratched her wrists and tapped her foot. Her gaze flitted about jerkily, like she was trying to trace the path of a fly. Under the bright white lights, the lines and pores on her face were visible.

"She was alone?" Mackenzie asked from the other side of the one-way mirror wall.

"Yes," Peterson replied, who had escorted Agatha from Riverview. "We checked her motel room, and there was nobody there."

"What did the motel manager say?"

"Just that she checked in minutes before we showed up. She was alone, and he's never seen her before."

"Is she on something?" Nick tilted his head, scrutinizing her.

Agatha swiveled on her chair, still looking around and getting impatient.

Sully came in wearing a grumpy face. "She got a thing for Jeremiah?"

"Justin reported that he found a lot of letters and journals where she described her fantasies," Mackenzie updated him. "Nothing more."

Sully peered through the glass. "That's the devil, right there. She came voluntarily, Peterson? She's not under arrest."

"I explained to her that we need to ask her a few questions and she should come with us, Sergeant," Peterson answered. "She was too spooked to resist."

"Do you think Jeremiah would have told her about him not killing Johnny?"

Nick continued staring at Agatha icily. "Seems like it. Their letters contain very elaborate stories. Some have been inspired by real life. It's difficult to crack it all, but they could have easily communicated information through that."

Mackenzie put on her jacket and buttoned it, priming for a grueling interrogation. "Nick? Ready?"

He looked even more determined than her as they entered the room.

Agatha shot up, her back straight as a rod. "Why am I here?"

"Why did you run?" Mackenzie volleyed back. "You left your place in quite a rush. Dirty dishes in the sink. Drawers open."

The space between her forehead wrinkled. "And my dolls. I left my dolls. But I took my favorite ones."

"You're friends with Jeremiah?" Nick asked.

"Not friends. We're a part of each other," she explained with a sincere smile, like she was giving a job interview.

"We've read some of your letters," Mackenzie said.

"That's private!" Agatha snapped in a sharp voice. "You had no right."

"It's a murder and abduction investigation. Nothing's off limits."

Nick shifted in his seat. "You and Jeremiah share a special bond."

"Yes." She nodded encouragingly.

"With a child killer?" Mackenzie retorted.

There was a flash of anger in Agatha's hazel eyes. She placed her palms on the table and dug her nails into it, the tendons of her hands carved out. But then her face changed. It was pitiful and patient. "Detective, haven't you ever had any forbidden desires? Even for a split second, when your mind wanders to that dark place where it's you all alone and you can't tell anyone about it because you feel ashamed? Imagine sharing that part of you with someone. Imagine the trust you'd have to place in someone to reveal your darkest self. That level of intimacy is rare and exceptional. It liberates you. I feel bad that you haven't found someone you trust like that…" Her face tilted and mischief danced in her eyes. "Because you look like someone who has a lot of secrets."

Mackenzie almost swallowed her tongue. Agatha was messing with her, surely, but the longer she watched her with that knowing look, the more Mackenzie felt undone. Like her armor was being dismantled by the woman in front of her.

"Why did you run, Agatha?" Nick brought her back to the point.

"I watched the news. Debbie mentioned that the cases have something to do with Jeremiah. I knew it was only a matter of time before you found out about me. I knew you wouldn't understand." She pouted like a child.

"Where were you on the morning of March first?"

"I don't remember."

"On the morning of March tenth?"

"I don't remember."

Mackenzie snuck a look over her shoulder, knowing Sully was watching. Agatha wasn't cooperative. She didn't think for a second before responding; she was shutting them out.

"It would be in your best interest to cooperate," Nick said. "We'll find out some other way, and that won't bode well for you."

Agatha took a fluttering breath and held back a giddy smile. "He talked about you, you know."

"What?"

"Jeremiah. In one of our stories, he had a character just like you." She bit her lip. "Someone who challenged him. Someone Jeremiah had fun toying with. I never thought I'd meet you. It's so satisfying."

Mackenzie looked at Nick, whose eyes were narrowed. Her sudden switches in attitude kept Mackenzie on her toes. She knew her direct and to-the-point approach wouldn't work with a mind that was far too deranged.

Nick stroked his chin. "You know, Agatha, we're looking for the person who killed Lucas and Theo and abducted Noah. What do you think about it?"

"Me?"

"Yeah." He shrugged. "What do you think?"

"Hurting children is one thing Jeremiah and I differ on. It's something I respect but don't completely understand."

Mackenzie's palm itched, wanting to inflict some damage.

"Did Jeremiah ever have a character based on any of his victims?"

"Yes, of course."

"Someone like Johnny Cooper?" he proposed casually.

She replied with a shrewd gleam in her eyes. "He calls this one character John. He says he has a recurring nightmare that he's chasing John, but he always gets away."

Mackenzie's eyes drilled into Agatha's. "Would you do anything for Jeremiah?"

She actually considered this for a while. "No."

Then Nick spoke up, unable to hide the scorn in his voice. "Would Martha do anything for Raymond?"

A string of chipped, yellowing teeth. A beam that lit up her face. A delirious enthusiasm. "Anything."

CHAPTER SIXTY

"She's either genuinely mentally ill or very good at acting," Mackenzie groaned, rubbing her eyes. They had spent hours trying to wrench information out of Agatha but to no avail. The woman was erratic, incoherent, and downright chilling at times.

"What about the bag she packed?" Rivera asked with sleep in her eyes. "Anything in there?"

"Just clothes and some of her favorite dolls and letters from Jeremiah." Nick sighed, making patterns with cigarettes on the table in the conference room.

Mackenzie paced the room. "Her phone was off for the last three days so we can't trace her location. And she won't answer where she was. She essentially has no alibi."

"We have to let her go," Rivera said with an edge to her voice.

"What? But she's insane!"

"I can see that." Her eyebrows shot up. "But we have no reason to hold her. Her letters with Jeremiah aren't enough."

Mackenzie's mouth was left open. "But she's potentially dangerous."

"We can't punish someone for something they *might* do," Nick said, swiping his hand over his creation in frustration.

Mackenzie knew that. But, still, the inability to keep Agatha away from society made her restless.

"I'll get people to keep an eye on her." Rivera clicked her tongue. "That's the best we can do unless we find something concrete. Try to get some sleep tonight, the two of you. It's been a long day."

When the lieutenant left, Mackenzie slammed the file she was holding on the table. "I'm not comfortable letting someone like her roam free."

"She might have a split personality disorder?" Nick mused. "Our background search on her didn't reveal her seeking any treatment so could be undiagnosed."

"Because of her distinction between Agatha and Martha?"

"They aren't very different. But it all boils down to how far she would go for Jeremiah. Like she told us, Martha would do anything. So did she?"

Sleep usually eluded Mackenzie. No matter how hard she tried to catch it, it was always just another inch away. Sleeping in her warm bed at home was a luxury Theo and Lucas would never have again. Not that she hadn't dealt with several abduction cases over her last eight years with the force, but when children were taken it always hit that weak spot in her heart. It left a permanent bruise.

When she got home, she went to wash her face, yawning at herself in the mirror. When she looked at her reflection, she saw how much she had taken after her mother. A memory clawed its way out and transpired behind her eyes.

"*Honey, stay still,*" Melody chided gently as she combed Mackenzie's hair. Mackenzie sucked her thumb. "*You shouldn't do that.*"

"*Why not?*"

"*It's a bad habit, sweetheart.*"

"*What's that?*"

Melody's face became crestfallen. "*Anything or anyone that brings you down. It's very difficult to get rid of a bad habit, sometimes even impossible.*"

"*Can it be a person?*"

"*Yes,*" she whispered, teary. She turned her around, grabbing her shoulders in an unforgiving grip. Her eyes were ablaze. "*But you'll be stronger than me, Mackenzie. Promise me.*"

Mackenzie jerked out of the memory like she had been pinched. She had no idea what her mother had been talking about back then. She must have been only three years old. But now she wondered if Melody was referring to Charles—the bad habit she couldn't shake off for years, the toxic relationship she was too weak to end.

Mackenzie sighed and focused on the work that needed to be done around the house. The light in the pantry had to be changed. She hadn't cleaned the attic in a long time. It was meant to be a family house, one that required regular upkeep. With her stressful job and erratic hours, she couldn't find the time. Now, as she caught up on some household chores, she considered moving to a smaller place. It was just her now after all.

After changing the light, oiling the squeaky hinge to the room that used to be Sterling's office, and cleaning the attic, she decided to check her mail. It had been a few days.

The sky was dotted with stars, and the street was empty, all lights turned off. It was chilly, but Mackenzie was almost sweaty from her exertions. She opened the mailbox and took out a stack of envelopes and went back inside, appreciating the new locks she'd had installed.

No incidents had occurred. It didn't mean that danger had been removed; it merely lurked at a distance now. She had been so preoccupied by the case that she hadn't even thought of how to tackle the problem. She'd have to hope Austin would catch Charles's killer without discovering any more secrets from her past. But were they even the same person? What did they want from her?

Most of the letters were coupons and advertisements, but there was one piece of paper—without an envelope.

As soon as Mackenzie saw what was written on it, she dropped it. She stumbled back, her hand flying to her throat. Wheezing and grasping, her heart went into overdrive. Fear crept up her spine. Sweat pooled in her hairline.

There was one word spelled out in letters cut out of a newspaper.

M.U.R.D.E.R.E.R.

Someone knew. Someone knew what she and Melody had done that night.

CHAPTER SIXTY-ONE

March 15

Mackenzie ran wildly, like a boulder rolling down a cliff. Even if she had wanted to stop, she wouldn't know how to. She had to reach her target. Noah Kinsey—a missing boy who was supposed to be safe right about now. But she imagined him curled in a ball in a blindfold. Frightened, hungry, and woozy from drugs.

Her steps smacked the concrete as if she was trying to punch holes in the ground. The morning air was soupy with humidity, but she tore through it. As if running blindly and angrily would lead her to him.

"Mack! Stop!" Irene's faint voice trickled into her ears from behind.

Mackenzie slowed down, coming to a reluctant halt, her body still buzzing. Unfortunately, she wasn't alone. She turned around and saw Irene panting and sweating in her tracksuit.

"I got a stitch," she moaned, clutching the side of her waist, catching up to her. "If I knew that you ran like a maniac, I wouldn't have joined you."

"Sorry. I'll slow down."

"Can we walk for a bit? Take a break?"

"Sure." Mackenzie caved out of politeness. It was obvious her neighbor wasn't a runner. She was well over forty and did yoga. Mackenzie believed that there were two kinds of people: those who ran and those who did yoga.

"Were you chasing that runner's high?"

Mackenzie smirked. "I've been trying to."

"You look stressed out." She eyed her. "Is it about those kids?"

"Yeah. We still don't know who took them. But we're making progress."

"I've been glued to the news." Irene offered Mackenzie water, which she refused. "Debbie has offered a reward for information on the case. She put up her own money. Can you believe that?"

Mackenzie rolled her eyes. "Even though it stems from a disingenuous place in my opinion, I'll take it. Anything that can help."

"It's weird. I don't like her, but I can't stop watching. She's so popular!"

"Yeah, the fallout from the Perez case last fall was a turning point for her. People wanted a villain, and she gave them one." She cast her gaze over the expanse of the lake they were running along. The still waters were comforting, reflecting the sunlight, which was brighter than ever. Not even a trace of wind.

"I keep hearing about that case. I'm still learning a lot about Lakemore." She tightened her ponytail. "A lot of bad stuff happens here."

"And affects everyone. The curse of a small town."

"Why did you do it?" Irene cupped her hand over her eyes against the sun. "Become a police officer? Doesn't all this take a toll on you?"

"It does, but I… I've just always wanted to do the right thing." She cringed. "I know that sounded cheesy, but I don't know."

"That's a noble reason."

Mackenzie looked around again. It was late morning so most of the runners were gone. But people hovered, walking, stretching, going places. A slew of mundane activity.

"You keep looking around. Is everything okay?" Irene clicked her fingers in Mackenzie's face.

She jolted. "Yes. Sorry. I've been distracted."

"How's your partner? Nick?"

"Yeah… he's doing better, I think," she answered honestly. "Not quite there yet, but your advice helped. I planned a little something a few days ago and looks like he needed it."

"Glad to help. I'm ready to get back into it. Ready?"

"Yep."

They started running again, slowly picking up pace. And Mackenzie sneakily surveyed her surroundings. It was becoming second nature to her. Someone was after her, possibly watching her at that very moment. She felt it in her bones—that uninvited attention. She was both: hunting and hiding at the same time.

Mackenzie removed her earbuds when she reached the station, too distracted to acknowledge anyone. She encountered Justin on her way up to the office. His facial hair looked unkempt, and he had dark circles surrounding his eyes.

"Didn't sleep last night?"

"No, ma'am. I was out with patrol doing rounds all night, checking out the construction sites." He looked disappointed. "But we didn't find the boy."

She bit the insides of her cheek and saw Mr. Kinsey in the conference room with Nick.

"I'll go over the new routes with patrol. Today we're expanding our search to Riverview and Tacoma." Justin excused himself, uncomfortable at the sight of Mr. Kinsey.

Like almost everyone else, Mackenzie cowered at the thought of showing him her face. The team shared a collective shame at their failure for two deaths and a missing child. She had done daring things in her life and found herself in the most blood-curdling of situations. But nothing made her insides twist like facing the parent of a missing child.

Mr. Kinsey was visibly losing it, glaring at Nick and shaking. Through the window, Mackenzie watched them engage in a battle.

Mr. Kinsey wasn't aggressive; he didn't shout or tremble like Theo's father had. But his eyes spoke volumes. He didn't need to raise his voice to project his anguish. Soon enough, he marched out of the conference room, holding back his tears.

"Justin will be assisting patrol with checking out construction sites outside of Lakemore," Mackenzie informed Nick, ignoring the throbbing in the back of her eyes from stress and sleep deprivation.

"The warrant went through early in the morning. We have Tim's phone and bank records."

"Alright, let's go through them."

Mackenzie was hard at work at her desk, though her eyes ached from reading line after line. Nick was chugging coffee like a man who'd found an oasis in a desert. He was looking over Tim's bank statements to see if he had purchased anything out of the blue—like rope and duct tape. But the deeper Mackenzie analyzed his call logs and GPS location provided by the phone company, the more she wondered if Tim fit the profile. He had the motive, and the physical evidence on Theo pointed a big finger at him. But their killer was an acute planner—was Tim strategic enough to pull this off?

Suddenly, their phones chimed in unison. It was a message from Sully.

They had found Noah.

CHAPTER SIXTY-TWO

Mackenzie and Nick barged into the hospital, the door whooshing open. The white clinic surroundings hit her all at once. Tired doctors and nurses in scrubs shuffled around. A row of plastic seats was occupied with frail-looking patients sniffling or coughing or ready to throw up. There was a cluster of cops by the reception. Mackenzie spotted Justin and Sully in the crowd.

"What happened?" Nick asked, joining them.

"Noah was left at the back of the hospital," Sully informed, stuffing his face with a donut. "A couple of nurses found him when they went out for a smoke break. He was unconscious, and the doctors are in with him right now." He pointed at a closed door on the side. "Mr. Kinsey has been informed and is on his way."

"He's alive."

"Yes. I haven't seen him, but the doctors told me that he didn't present with any major external injuries. They're going to bag his clothes and give them to us."

"I'll arrange for the crime lab to receive them." Nick moved away.

For the first time in days, Mackenzie's stomach unclenched a little. Noah was safe and alive. He was about to be reunited with his father.

Sully plopped on a chair, gobbling an entire donut. His bushy mustache was caked with chocolate dip. "This case made me lose my appetite. Now that Noah's been found alive, I can finally eat again. Seems like you were right, Mack." He appraised her. "He did return the boy. Usually Nick is the profiler."

"This one was personal for him, you know that." She turned to Justin and Peterson. "Let me guess, there's no surveillance at the back of the building?"

"There is," Justin corrected her. "The hospital security is getting us the tapes."

"There is? Why would the killer risk that?"

No one had an answer. They just shrugged.

They stayed outside, shifty and queasy, but Mackenzie repeated that Noah was safe. That was the most important thing. Except she didn't know what his condition was behind the closed door. He had been held captive for multiple days, and two of his classmates had been murdered. He was only nine years old, but that was old enough for the trauma to stick to him forever.

Mackenzie took a seat and crossed her arms. The smell of hospital was a medley of iodine, disinfectant, rubbing alcohol, and death. White strips of light overhead lit the hallway. She closed her eyes, and her imagination carried her away.

A much younger Mackenzie being comforted by her very alive grandmother.

"*Will she be okay?*"

"*Yes, dear. The surgery was a success. Melody is going to live.*"

"*I want to talk to her.*"

Melody was on the hospital bed with a bandage wrapped around her head and a few cuts and scrapes covering her face. It wasn't jarring. Mackenzie was used to seeing her mother bruised. Suddenly, Mackenzie wasn't younger. She was exactly like her present self. "*Mom, I deserve to know.*"

"*What are you talking about, Mackenzie?*"

"*What did you do with Robert's body? Did anyone else find out what we did that night? No more lies.*"

Mackenzie shook away her thoughts. The door to the room opened, and an old doctor emerged with thick white hair and tanned, leathery skin. "Has his guardian been informed?"

"Yes, he's on his way." Mackenzie stood up. Nick also returned. The five of them almost cornered the doctor, forming a huddle around him. But the doctor didn't seem to mind. Every breathing person in Lakemore knew who Noah was and how sensitive the case was.

"Noah has no life-threatening injuries." The doctor spoke with a blank face. "He has a few bruises and cuts. A lot of them were old, but they weren't infected and are healing. It looks like they were treated with ointments. We do suspect he has been drugged. We're flushing it out of his system and, as per protocol, we'll do complete urine and blood analysis. We'll have those results in a few hours. He is a bit dehydrated and has lost a significant amount of weight. Common conditions associated with abduction cases. They don't eat properly. But he's physically fine."

"No life-threatening injuries or conditions?" Sully confirmed.

"Not as of now. He is complaining of severe abdominal pain and has constipation. I've scheduled an ultrasound just to confirm, but I believe the symptoms are manifesting due to improper diet during his captivity. His blood work will give us some answers; I'm suspecting some deficiencies. Nothing that can't be fixed. His psychological trauma on the other hand… I've called for a psych consult. But first we'll wait for his guardian."

Mackenzie looked down. They all nodded, understanding.

"How is he doing? Is he responsive?" Nick asked, worry etched all over his face. Mackenzie knew this was a question from a father not a detective.

"He's extremely fatigued and quiet." The doctor pursed his lips. "His responses were just a yes or no. He's visibly traumatized. I believe when his father arrives, he will feel better."

The doctor excused himself.

"After you collect the footage from the security, send it to Clint." Mackenzie started firing orders at Justin and Peterson. "We're looking for anything. Even a shadow would do. But something. And then get a manifest of the staff in the hospital working today, from nurses to administrative to cleaning crew. Interview each and every one of them. Employees take breaks outside all the time."

"Yes, ma'am," Justin responded in his typical military fashion.

"Also figure out what rooms have a view of the back of the hospital," Nick added. "Maybe a patient or someone saw something through the window."

"On it."

They scurried off like their lives depended on it.

"Where is he?!" Mr. Kinsey arrived, red-faced and panting. He barreled toward them, the underarms of his shirt soaked in sweat. "Where's Noah?"

"He's inside. We'll let you have a moment and after that we'll have some questions for him," Sully said, but Mr. Kinsey didn't pay attention.

He shouldered past him, inside the room where Noah was. They heard Mr. Kinsey's gasp and wail of relief.

"I'll let the doctor know that Noah's father is here, and then I'm going back to the station to update Rivera and Murphy," Sully said.

"I can't believe we have him." Nick leaned against the wall.

But the knot in Mackenzie's chest hadn't fully loosened yet.

The doctor hastened back into the room. After a few more minutes, he came out and allowed Mackenzie and Nick inside.

When Mackenzie entered, the first thing she registered was how tiny Noah was. He looked like a pile of bones and incredibly small on the large bed. Mr. Kinsey was on the bed, tucking his son under his arm. Noah clung to his father, his blinks were languishing in fatigue, but his arms were wrapped tightly around Mr. Kinsey's torso, his fingers interlaced. Needles went into his skin attached to drips. His eyes were sunken. She had seen several pictures of Noah—and like the doctor had said, it looked like he had lost half his body weight.

Mackenzie looked at Nick, hating to interrupt this delicate moment. But it was necessary.

"Hey, Noah. Think you're up for answering some questions?" Nick asked, exuding a friendly charm.

"Buddy, you don't have to. They can come back later," Mr. Kinsey said.

"It's okay, Dad." Noah's voice was breathy. He sounded even younger than he looked.

"We won't take long." Nick sat on the bed.

Mackenzie stood behind, adopting a softer expression than usual.

"Do you remember what happened at the festival?"

The corners of Noah's mouth turned down. "Theo, Lucas, and I were at a hotdog stand. After Lucas got a hotdog, we decided to check out another stall, but the line was too long. There were a lot of people. We stepped away from the market and started playing with the football Theo had. But then Lucas heard something in the woods… he went in but didn't come out. Then Theo and I went to look for him. I don't remember the rest. I'm sorry."

"You don't have to be sorry," Nick assured. The boys must have been drugged very soon after being lured into the woods for them not to remember the events. The killer must have known the field trip was scheduled to happen. He'd lurked at the edge, waiting to lure kids out. Rohypnol caused memory loss. If Noah had been kept on drugs throughout his ordeal, there was only a slim chance of his brain retaining much about where he'd been the past few days. "Where were you held? Do you remember anything about the place?" Nick asked.

"It was a dark room," Noah said. "Our voices echoed. It was only Theo and me."

"You never saw whoever took you?"

"No. My wrists and ankles were tied. There was tape on my mouth. I had a blindfold on for the entire time." He squinted at the bright lights of the hospital. "I'm not used to it."

Mr. Kinsey shielded his eyes. "It's okay, Noah. I'll ask the nurse to dim the lights."

"You were given food and water?"

He nodded and pressed his tummy, moaning lightly. "Twice a day. Noodles. My wrists would be freed. But my feet were still tied so I couldn't run. What happened to Theo? He was with me, but then he was taken away."

Mr. Kinsey shot them a warning look. It was wise not to divulge the sad news to him just yet. He had a long road of recovery ahead of him.

Nick's smile was pained. "You never heard their voice or felt their touch? Could you tell if it was a man or a woman?"

"Sorry. All I heard was the door opening and closing and footsteps."

"I'll leave you to be with your dad, but, Noah, if you remember anything at all, no matter how small, let us know?"

Noah nodded. Nick offered his fist, and Noah bumped it with his. Just as Nick turned to leave with Mackenzie, Noah started convulsing in Mr. Kinsey's arms. His eyes rolled back in his sockets. His body writhed in jerky motions.

"Noah!" Mr. Kinsey cried.

"He's having a seizure!" Mackenzie was quick on her feet and pressed the button to alert the nurses. Within seconds, medical professionals filtered into the room, and the three of them were ushered outside.

"He's never had a seizure before!" Mr. Kinsey sobbed, pacing and clutching his head. "*Never.*"

Was it a reaction to the drugs? Or something else? Mackenzie felt helpless as the doctors and nurses worked behind closed doors.

Mr. Kinsey marched over to them, shaking. His eyes were wild with fury. "Someone did this to my son! He's nine! He'll have to live with this trauma! I won't back down until that person is behind bars. And I speak for the other parents too, who lost far more than I did. Just because Noah is safe doesn't mean you can sit back now. This is *far* from over."

CHAPTER SIXTY-THREE

"Detective Price, are you busy?" Austin appeared on her side, tall and imposing, with a casual elbow resting on top of the cubicle wall.

Mackenzie stirred out of her thoughts. They had just returned from the hospital, feeling a mix of both relief and anger. Noah was alive, but the person responsible for it all was still at large.

"Yes." She sighed. "Is this urgent?"

Austin was that niggling thought at the back of her mind, an annoyance worming its way under her skin. "It won't take long. Do you know anyone by the name Harold Lewis?"

"You went through my phone. I'm sure you could answer that question." She continued working.

He smirked. "I meant if your mother or Charles ever mentioned that name to you."

That made her freeze. "My parents?"

"Yeah. Do you remember anything from your childhood?"

She stretched her brain, trying to remember the name. But nothing came to her. "I'm sorry; I don't remember. Who is he?"

Austin tilted his head and narrowed his eyes, silent for a second. "Never mind. Sorry to disturb you. Carry on. I know you're on a tough case."

He walked away, handing Finn a file as he went.

"He's working a case with Finn?" Mackenzie asked Troy.

"Nah. He's just very helpful."

"Yeah."

Harold Lewis. Who was he? Someone from Charles's past, or Melody's? Or Robert's? Her mind started spinning. She took out a toothpick and began scraping off the dirt lodged in the keys of her keyboard. This Harold Lewis could be nobody—someone insignificant or a dead end. It happened in investigations all the time.

Or maybe he wasn't.

Austin was making progress, gaining momentum. How much longer before the truth came out? Was this Harold Lewis a friend of Charles? What if Charles told someone what happened? He had been an alcoholic for years. He could have divulged the secret under the influence. After all, someone had sent that letter calling her a murderer.

Someone out there knew what she and her mother had done to Robert.

"Mack?" Nick's hand came on her shoulder.

She jumped, her hand flying to her chest.

Nick stared at her. "Are you okay? You're pale."

"Yes." She blinked and dusted the keyboard of the dirt she had managed to dig out.

"We were just about to watch the footage from the hospital." He jutted his thumb over his shoulder at Justin, who was standing behind.

"Right." She took a few deep breaths to gather her jumbled thoughts and put her work face back on. "What do we have?"

While Nick plugged in the USB stick, Justin updated her. "Peterson and I are still asking around at the hospital, but no one saw anything."

"How's that possible? What about any patients?"

"The curtains are closed after sundown, and Noah was dropped there very early in the morning."

"And the staff didn't notice him until hours later?" Mackenzie was appalled.

How long was Noah unconscious at the back of the building before he was spotted?

"Probably this explains it," Nick said, drawing their attention to the screen. "This is the camera that covers the part of the back area where the staff take smoke breaks."

Mackenzie leaned over Nick's shoulder as he played the video on his monitor. It was a small section at the back of the building, with barbed wire marking the border, beyond which there were woods. Between the barbed wire and woods, there was a strip of unpaved road. On the other end of the barbed wire were wild bush plants.

Several people slipped out the back smoking, chatting with each other or on the phone, for no more than ten minutes. Later in the morning, a pair of nurses was taking a smoke break, when one of them noticed something in the bush plants. What followed was commotion. Noah had been lying there, concealed.

"When did he drop him there?" Mackenzie asked, her brain hurting. "Nick, can you go back?"

"Clint said this video didn't need cleaning up," Justin said. "Maybe we should reduce the speed."

Nick slowed it down and played it again. Three pairs of eyes were glued to the screen. At 6:57 a.m. there was movement in the bushes, like a rabbit or squirrel was scurrying around in there.

"That's when they dropped off Noah." Nick folded his lips over his teeth.

Mackenzie blew a breath. "They are familiar with the surveillance. Just like they were when they left Theo at the lighthouse."

"The planning is very precise," Nick agreed. "It hints at someone highly intelligent."

"Or someone who watches a lot of *CSI*. They've scoped out all the places."

"I'll head back with Peterson and finish taking witness statements at the hospital." Justin left them.

Mackenzie twirled on her chair, her mind racing. "You're right, Nick. They have thought this through from every angle."

The brutality of what happened to Lucas and Theo had been a new addition to the tarnished legacy of Lakemore. Forever residents would talk about the last two weeks—and the boys who had died. The idea that the culprit could slip through the cracks and disappear was abhorrent to Mackenzie. She was determined not to let it happen.

Nick's phone pinged. "Noah's blood and urine analysis came back."

"The same drugs as Lucas and Theo?"

"Yeah, but wait." He frowned. "There's more."

"Like what?" She leaned forward and read the email with him. The hospital had highlighted a particular entry. "*Lead?*"

"That's a lot of lead. It must be at toxic levels," Nick muttered and dialed the doctor for a consult. They went outside the office in the empty hallway, as Nick transferred the call to the speaker.

The doctor answered; his monotonous mannerisms from earlier had turned slightly confused and anxious.

"Dr. Brown, we just received Noah's blood work, and there is something that concerns us," Nick said.

"Yes, yes. I'm glad you called. I was just about to if you hadn't," Brown replied. "We expected some drugs in his system, but the levels of lead found are concerning and not normal."

"Could this have anything to do with the seizure he had?" Mackenzie asked.

"Yes, it also explains his abdominal pain, vomiting, and constipation. They're all symptoms of lead poisoning. I have obviously informed Mr. Kinsey. Since the levels are around 50 mcg/dL, we're going to start with chelating therapy immediately. I can't share his medical records, but I can confirm that this lead exposure is recent."

Mackenzie and Nick caught his meaning.

"What do you think the source of this lead could be?"

"It's hard to say. Paint used to be a source back in the day. Though lead-based paints were discontinued in the seventies. But even so, it's hard to achieve high levels when the exposure was short term."

"Could it be water?" Nick asked, a look of understanding crossing his face. Like something had clicked in his brain.

Brown paused. "Yes, it could be. Though I'm not sure where you'd find water with high lead levels…"

"Thank you, Dr. Brown." Nick quickly wrapped up the conversation and hung up.

Mackenzie was standing slack-jawed, waiting for him to spill. "*Well?* What is it?"

"Come with me."

Nick turned on his heel and marched with long strides, Mackenzie having to sprint to catch up. With a fresh burst of energy, he went into Clint's office. Clint was immersed in his multiple screens and didn't even flinch at the intrusion.

"Clint, where do you keep city plans?" Nick asked.

He pointed at a drawer without looking away from his work.

Nick rummaged through the drawer and pulled out a large rolled-up piece of paper. He crouched and unrolled it on the floor. It was a map of the water distribution system in Lakemore.

"What are you thinking?"

Nick raised a finger as his eyes scanned the map. He marked an area with a pen. "Years ago, the city decided to put a condo building there. That's when they found out that drinking water in the area would be contaminated because the pipes used for water supply there are corroded. And as per EPA regulations, drinking water should have zero lead."

"Why didn't they just change the plumbing?"

"It would cost them a lot of money," he said testily. "It's better to just build the condo elsewhere."

"So there's nothing there now?"

"There is an abandoned building," he emphasized. "Only half constructed. But—"

"It would have the cement and mortar found on Theo's clothes. That's where they were held captive."

CHAPTER SIXTY-FOUR

Mackenzie fidgeted with her fingers on her lap on the drive to the abandoned building. The radio filled the silence in the car. Nick kept pushing the speed limit.

Mackenzie switched the radio channel absentmindedly.

"Do you feel better?" she asked over the pop song that was playing.

"About what?"

She hesitated, testing the words in her mind first. "After finally catching who killed Johnny?"

Nick swallowed hard. "No."

His answer didn't surprise her. "Why not?"

He struggled to reply, while she searched his face. Strangely enough, Mackenzie wondered if something he'd say would be the key to the lock in her brain. That the answer lay in the layers and crevices of his mind. "It doesn't change anything. There's a difference between getting closure and moving on."

"Time fixes everything, only if you let it," she blurted, her hand going to her watch.

Nick veered off into a dirt road with bumps and holes and trees on both sides. It was a bumpy ride with Mackenzie having to grab the dashboard. They reached a clearing with woods surrounding them. A derelict unfinished building stood in the middle—no more than three stories tall. An amateur stack of construction blocks, discolored and unpolished. Stained steel frames supported the structure in some parts. Large metal rods stuck atop.

"I didn't even know about this place." Mackenzie exited the car. "How did you know?"

"My cousin's in urban planning, so I remembered something about lead in water supply halting construction."

Crows cried, their tuneless screeches filling the air. They flocked across the blue sky like one organism constantly changing shape.

"Doesn't look like anyone's here," Nick observed. "Too late to pick up tire tracks. It's rained too often."

Tentatively, they entered the building. The first floor at least had rooms with no doors or windows. There were construction braces, spools of electrical wiring, and stacks of ceramic tiles, beams, and rods. Material scattered around.

"Noah said he was in a room with a door," Mackenzie said. "Upstairs?"

There were makeshift stairs with no railing on either side. "Place is isolated. Chosen after careful consideration."

"Like everything else they've done."

The staircase ended at a narrow hallway—dark and claustrophobic. Like just enough space was carved into a large block of concrete. The only source of light was a cluster of little holes in one section of the wall. It shone light on the dancing dust particles. There was a waft of pungent smell in the air—sweat and human waste.

"Ugh. Someone's definitely been here. I reckon they were held on this floor." Mackenzie proceeded with caution. There was one door on their right. A piece of an old garage door—rusty but strong. "It's the only room with a door."

Nick wore latex gloves and tried opening it. "It's locked."

She analyzed the shiny lock. "This is new."

"But the door isn't." Nick picked up a log lying behind them and pushed it into the door until it dented and disconnected from the hinges. The room was pitch black. The only source of light would have been through the sliver under the door.

Mackenzie turned on the flashlight of her phone and angled it across the room.

Even though she wasn't alone, a cold sensation seeped into her chest. Her lungs tingled. The air stank. She was half-expecting something to jump out of the darkness and grab her. "There!"

There were ropes on the floor without their prisoners. A pile of utensils was in another corner with rotting food and buzzing flies.

"It's disgusting," Nick said, crunching his nose.

"I'll call the CSI. We have to verify the boys were here, but we'll lift their DNA and prints." Her eyes swept over the stench-filled dark room, still echoing the crushing trauma Theo and Noah had to endure. "Let's hope we can say the same for our killer."

CHAPTER SIXTY-FIVE

Mackenzie pushed a glass of red wine toward Nick on the kitchen island. He looked around her house with a watchful eye. "You haven't made any changes?"

"Haven't had the time." She shrugged and took a sip. Her place still looked exactly like it had when Sterling lived with her. The little things they bought together, the things he'd liked and touched still exactly where they always were.

"Well that's new." He pointed at the wind chime by the window, overlooking the front yard.

"Yeah, Irene has one, and I liked it, so she bought me this."

"That's nice of her," he commented. "I'm sorry I haven't been very... *present* lately."

"It's fine." She leaned forward on her elbows.

Goosebumps sprang up on her arms at the thought of how lonely her life had become in the space of a year. Last year, she had felt like she had everything. But life had a funny way of turning everything upside down. Happiness was just an illusion.

"You should get a pool table," Nick suggested. "And put it right here. There's enough space."

"It would look weird to have a pool table in the middle of the living room."

"Who the hell cares? You live alone now. Enjoy the perks. Or a pinball machine."

She pressed her lips in a thin line. The confession that living alone had no perks if there was someone after her sat on the tip of her tongue. But what good would it do to burden Nick with that? There were more important matters at hand. Yet increasingly she felt like she was carrying around a heavy weight on her chest, one she was desperate to offload.

Nick kept checking his phone. "I told them to send us whatever they got as soon as possible."

The CSI were at the scene combing for evidence. Mackenzie could feel their culprit on her fingertips like a faint caress. Anticipation burned inside her. She was so close to wrapping her fingers around them, finally catching them.

"We wouldn't have known about Heather and Tanner's bribery, Patricia's drug business, Elliot and Spencer's corruption, and Giles if…" She resorted to picking the skin around her nails, thoughtful.

"If this vigilante hadn't decided to abduct and kill kids?" Nick lifted an eyebrow.

"Ends don't always justify the means." She poured him another glass.

"You don't keep anything stronger, do you?"

"What do you think?"

He shook his head and took a big sip. "I have a bad feeling they won't have left prints or DNA anywhere."

"Then we'll find another way." Her resolve steeled, seeing Nick's haunted eyes. "You caught Jeremiah when that was your first case. We'll catch this one too."

Nick made a sound in the back of his throat and looked away, taking off his tie and dropping it on the counter. Since Giles's arrest and Noah returning alive, it looked like the noose around Nick's neck had loosened. But it was still there.

"Mr. Kinsey told Rivera that Noah is responding well to treatment and will be discharged tomorrow," Mackenzie said. He nodded, his face tight. "Nick—"

"Don't."

"Don't what?"

"Don't try to tell me it wasn't my fault. I can't take it anymore." His eyes were pleading.

She cleared her throat and fidgeted. "Actually, I was going to ask you if you've ever heard of anyone by the name Harold Lewis?"

"Harold Lewis?"

"Yeah, Austin was asking me about him. Something to do with the investigation into Charles. I figured since your father briefly knew my parents, maybe Harold was in their social circle. Do you remember anyone by that name?"

"No. Have you googled him?" He was already taking out his phone.

Mackenzie hadn't. She had been too immersed in the case. She watched Nick with bated breath.

"It's a very common name, Mack. People in the government, professors, a dead businessman—"

"Dead businessman?"

"Yeah someone in Boston committed suicide and left behind a wife and kid more than thirty years ago. Why don't you just talk to Austin?"

She didn't trust Austin. What was a detective from a big city like Port Angeles doing in a town like Lakemore? And why volunteer to reopen a case that had already been ruled a robbery gone wrong? The team saw him as a keen detective wanting to prove himself and fortify his position in the squad. But Mackenzie had seen him in that basement, flipping through pages like a madman in the dead of night. She had seen his eyes linger too long on the computer screens and files of other people. There was a reason he was here.

"I'm not sure if I like him," she muttered.

"He's investigating a case you're close to and has treated you as a suspect. It's not the best start to a working relationship." Nick clearly didn't think much of it. "I should probably head out."

"No. Stay!"

He was bewildered at her reaction. "You okay?"

Mackenzie didn't want to be alone in the house. She had installed cameras outside, changed the locks and even the back door. It was a fortress. But it couldn't keep away the black cloud of danger always looming above her head. "Let's finish the bottle."

"Ah, sure."

After a few minutes, their phones pinged with notifications. It was the crime scene pictures. "Anthony's working late."

Together they skimmed over the pictures. Ropes, zip ties, duct tape, garbage full of snack wrappers, some gauze tape with dried blood, ointments. All indicative of multiple people being held captive.

"Remember Dr. Brown said how some of Noah's external injuries were treated with antibiotic cream?" Nick showed her a picture of the over-the-counter antibiotic tube kept in a corner of the room.

There was a picture of a faucet covered in rust. The team was going to test the water samples for lead concentrations to confirm. "We'll lift Theo and Noah's DNA from these duct tapes." She caught her reflection in the mirror. Her lips were stained purple from the wine. Dismayed, she rushed to scrub them clean.

Nick chuckled behind her back.

"Wait. What's this?" He showed her an image of the wall next to the door with a reddish-brown smudge.

"I don't remember seeing this when we were there."

"This is from inside the room. It was dark, so we didn't see it."

Mackenzie studied the arbitrary splatter. "It's an old, dirty building. It could be just part of it."

"Yeah, but the CSI marked it. It looks a lot like blood." He thumbed his phone. "I'm going to call Anthony."

Anthony's grumpy voice filtered through the speakers. "I'm busy."

"Got a question about one of the pictures you sent us," Nick said.

"That quick? You're good."

Nick directed him to the picture they were referring to.

"Yeah, yeah. It looked like dried blood so we labeled it. That was the room the boys were held in, so we were being even more thorough. And it wasn't present anywhere else in the building so it stood out even more."

"Do you know what it is?" Mackenzie asked.

"Well, I can tell you that it's not blood. We're running analysis to confirm, but based on physical characteristics, we're certain that it's clay."

"Clay?"

"Yeah, for sculpting and pottery," he continued. "Based on the placement by the door, distance from the ground and direction of the stain, it looks like it got rubbed off on the wall while someone was walking out the door."

When he hung up, Mackenzie's mind reeled. "A lot of people do pottery."

Nick cursed under his breath. "There's only one person connected to this case who does. She's making sculptures of Lucas and Theo for the art center."

"Ruth Norman."

CHAPTER SIXTY-SIX

March 16

It was a rainy morning. Thick, gray clouds swirled in the sky, obscuring sunshine. Beads of water rolled down the windows, offering a grainy view of the parking lot of Lakemore PD. Everyone worked quietly against the gentle tapping of the rain. There was no idle conversation and no idle hands—everyone was in their cocoon, absorbed by their tasks.

Dear Mr. Damien Price,

I have it on good authority that your brother, Robert Price, is no longer with us. He has been dead for a long time now. You'll never find out who I am. But I thought you deserved to know. I'm sorry. Take care.

Mackenzie groaned, deleting the words, feeling incredibly stupid. But how else was she supposed to let Damien know without implicating herself? She had to tread carefully. Charles's murder had caused a little tear in the life she had fashioned for herself. She had to stitch it back up before the truth gushed out for all to see and judge.

She drummed her fingers on the keyboard, contemplating. She typed another message with more sensitivity.

Dear Mr. Damien Price,

I know you've wanted nothing more than finally knowing the fate of your brother. I'm deeply saddened to inform you that your brother is no longer with us. He passed away a very long time ago. I understand you will have more questions surrounding his unfortunate demise, but this is all I can share. Please believe me—if I could tell you more, I would. I hope just knowing he is gone, even without the how or why, will be enough to give you some kind of closure.

Your well-wisher.

Mackenzie bit her lip, reading the words over and over again. She had positioned the monitor in such a way that no one could spy on her. But still the back of her head burned. The plan was to print it out—so that no one could match her handwriting—and leave it at his doorstep late at night.

It was absolutely ridiculous. But was there any other way?

Damien's sad eyes taunted her. Twenty years later, the bond between brothers was as strong as ever.

But what if Damien went to the police with the note? She could make sure not to leave her fingerprints on it. There was no surveillance around his house that she noticed. Should she check again? But Damien would make the connection—for an anonymous note to show up around the time he and Mackenzie got acquainted was too big a coincidence for him to overlook. And if he confronted her directly, would she be able to look him in the eye and lie?

Rivera's booming voice cut through Mackenzie's bubble. "What's the status of the CSI?"

She quickly closed the tab and swiveled in her chair to face the lieutenant. "It's going to take them some time to run tests for prints and DNA. It's a big building. But we're calling Ruth Norman."

She crossed her arms. "Why are you questioning Ruth?"

"There was some clay on the wall, like someone brushed against it while walking," Nick said.

Rivera made a face. "Ruth Norman has been busy making the sculptures for the art center. The school has forced her to take leave, so all her efforts are focused on that."

"Oh, how do you know that?"

Rivera spread her arms. "Who do you think? Debbie. She knows everyone's business in this town."

"Ruth had an alibi for the abduction of the kids," Mackenzie pointed out.

"She could have an accomplice, if she's involved. Or that smudge on the wall was planted by the killer. Can't put anything past this one." Rivera pressed her lips in a tight line.

"Her husband is a dentist. Gives her access to the drugs used to knock out the kids?" Mackenzie proposed.

"Think her husband would help her with this?" Nick looked skeptical.

"I don't know. Maybe she convinced him? It's not uncommon for people to coerce their spouses or families into doing something illegal." The words almost died on her lips, as she realized what she'd just said.

You have to help me bury him.

"Yeah, but this is killing kids, not a casual bit of money laundering. He'd need to be as sick as her," Nick said.

"Keep me in the loop," Rivera ordered before leaving.

Mackenzie twirled a pen between her fingers, looking over at Nick's screen. He was checking Ruth's background. It made her wonder about Ruth's trajectory and how the unassuming, plain woman had been catapulted into fame.

Ruth Norman was on the frontlines of the 24/7 news cycle. The local schoolteacher was at risk of losing her job after her colossal failure of losing sight of three students in the chaos of the festival. Though she hadn't lost her job—yet—somehow she had fashioned herself into a martyr in the midst of the tragedy. The unlikely hero who had emerged from the ashes. When Mackenzie and Nick had met with Ruth, she had been emotional and erratic. It was an understandable response to the situation—coupled with her guilt of letting Johnny down.

Mackenzie had assumed that the media had engineered Ruth's resurgence into the public sphere. They saw a guilt-ridden and caring teacher, but maybe Ruth had reinvented herself on purpose.

"She has a career in politics now," Mackenzie commented. "People went from hating her to loving her."

"The public has a short-term memory." Nick guzzled in coffee.

"It's disrespectful of her really."

"What do you mean?"

"This drama. It's all a bit attention-seeking. No one's hurt more than Lucas and Theo's parents. And yet it's Ruth playing the injured party to the public."

"Maybe that's how some people mourn?" He hitched a shoulder.

"Genuine mourning happens privately." She played with the clasp of her watch. "It's a solitary process."

Nick glanced at his phone. "She's here."

When Ruth reached the second floor, she blended in with her surroundings. There was nothing striking about her face, but her dyed dark red hair grabbed attention. At first she clung on to her tote bag with rigid shoulders, like she was afraid. But slowly people started recognizing her. It had a ripple effect. Soon people shook her hand and congratulated her on her gestures. Her eyes brightened. Giddiness spread on her face.

Mackenzie threaded through the crowd, unable to bear the strange adoration. "Ms. Norman? Come with me."

They led her into the conference room.

"I heard Noah's safe now." Ruth took a seat across from them. All her nervousness from before had evaporated. "I've been meaning to visit him, but no one's letting me."

"He's been through a lot. It's polite to give him some privacy for a while, don't you think?" Mackenzie snapped, unable to control herself.

Her lips parted. "Oh, of course! I... I didn't mean it... Anyway, you're right."

"How's your project coming along for the art center?" Nick asked politely.

"Wonderful." She smiled. "I'm up to my elbows in clay and paint. It's my passion, but it's for a good cause. I'm happy to be able to contribute in some way."

Mackenzie showed her a picture of the building. "Have you ever been to this place before?"

She took a peek and shrugged. "No."

"Your husband is a dentist?"

"Yes." She frowned. "What is this about? Why am I here?"

"Please answer the question." Mackenzie remained standing and crossed her arms.

Ruth looked at them, panic rising. "He is."

"Does that give you access to some medication? Like ketamine, which is used as an anesthetic drug?" Nick asked.

She squirmed and grabbed the handles of the chair tightly. "I don't know what kinds of medication my husband uses."

"Ms. Norman, this is the building where Theo and Noah were held captive. We found clay there."

Just like that, Ruth wilted. "That doesn't mean anything. A lot of people do pottery."

"That is true. But you have a personal connection to the case. Lucas and Theo were murdered out of revenge. For Johnny, to whom you were very attached."

She closed her eyes and pinched the bridge of her nose. "I wouldn't hurt the children, detectives. Please believe me. I have nothing to do with this."

Mackenzie was unmoved by the beseeching look in Ruth's eyes. Regardless of whether she was innocent or not, she had benefited from this crime. A woman under whose nose three of her students were abducted was now a town hero with potential political footing. "Where were you on the mornings of March tenth and fifteenth?"

Ruth exhaled. "At the art center. I'm there every day. The mayor has allowed me to use the studio. You could confirm?"

Despite her personal feelings toward Ruth, Mackenzie couldn't dismiss the possibility that the clay lightly smudged on the wall didn't come from her. Leaving faint but not too faint evidence on the wall might have been a deliberate move as Rivera suggested.

"This is what was left." Nick showed her a close-up picture of the clay stain.

Panic rose like a tide in Ruth's eyes. "I… I don't know how else to convince you. This didn't come from me." She took the picture from them and glanced at it carefully like she was desperately searching for something that would exonerate her. Then her eyes lit up. "What kind of clay is this? Do they know?"

"Why?" Mackenzie raised an eyebrow.

"I might be wrong, but the texture doesn't look like pottery clay."

Nick checked the file. "It's polymer clay."

Ruth looked relieved. "I don't use this clay. I *can't*. I only work with pottery clay—earthenware specifically."

"What do you mean by you *can't* use polymer clay?" Mackenzie prodded, curious now.

"There's something in it that I'm allergic to. Probably the artificial coloring or the plasticizers? I'm not sure. But I get rashes if I touch it too much. And I refuse to wear gloves when using clay. I need to feel the texture."

Mackenzie narrowed her eyes. Was Ruth telling the truth? Or was this a ploy?

Ruth looked hysterical. "I swear it! I'll prove it to you if I have to! I had nothing to do with the murders. I would never—*could* never—hurt a child."

And, whatever Mackenzie's feelings about the woman, she believed Ruth was telling them the truth. Mackenzie felt her blood boil as she stared at the picture of the stain on the wall, thinking about the killer who always seemed to be one step ahead.

CHAPTER SIXTY-SEVEN

Mackenzie sat on one of the benches outside the station, under an arch, safely tucked away from the drizzling rain. She tightened her arms around her torso, her eyes traveling across the slick concrete sidewalk and glistening tops of cars. Water pooled around crevices and tumbled into road drains.

Nick plopped next to her, handing her a copy of the file. "Anthony confirmed the boys were held there. Theo and Noah's DNA was on the duct tape."

Mackenzie flipped open the report from the CSI. "They're still processing everything?"

"Rivera gave them a courtesy call to speed it up, but yeah." His eyes were focused like a hawk as he went through the pages. "There must be something more."

She jumped back into work mode. "The killer bought all these supplies, like zip ties and padlocks. Can we track them?"

"They're all standard and could have been purchased from anywhere. Maybe even ordered online."

She found a page detailing the two faucets in the building. The water sampled from them contained extremely high lead concentrations, in line with the lead poisoning Noah had suffered. "They bought a new faucet aerator too. To fix the flow."

"They're incredibly resourceful."

"Do you think that clay stain came from the killer accidentally or did they plant it?"

Nick's eyes didn't leave the pages of the report, but he flicked his lighter on and off. "Can't say. I think it's more likely it was planted. The CSI didn't find any DNA or prints or hair from anyone other than the boys, so they have obviously been very careful. Having said that, even perfectionists make mistakes."

"Ruth loved Johnny. But if the killer tried framing her…"

"Because she didn't believe him when she found out about Heather. Heather and Tanner are facing bribery charges. Elliot and Spencer's actions are known, even if for now the mayor is pulling strings to protect them. Everyone who wronged Johnny."

"The final revenge."

The heavy words sat between them. Revenge was falling down a bottomless pit; it consumed the soul like smog. There was no coming back from it. Finally, there was justice for Johnny—but what about Lucas, Theo, and Noah? Who would avenge them?

There was a picture of a barrel stuffed with garbage outside the room where the boys had been held. The page listed an inventory of the items disposed. Mackenzie wrinkled her nose at the pictures of the rotten food. There were some bandages and white plastic bags, but mostly leftover noodles. "Noah said they were fed noodles, right?"

"Yeah." He raised his eyebrows.

"And threw away the leftovers. I guess the boys didn't have a big appetite. Being in a stressful situation does that." She flipped the page to find tire tracks. Most of them had been washed away by the rain, but a stretch was still protected, being under an overhead covering. "Look, they found impressions left by tires."

"Did they put it through SICAR?" Nick asked, referring to the Shoeprint Image Capture and Retrieval Database, which also included tire tread patterns.

"Yeah. It's a 1969 Mustang." But another thing had caught her attention. There were green and black shavings a few feet behind the tire treads, right next to a wall. They looked like chipped paint based on observation, but the crime lab was running tests to confirm. Apparently, the car had accidentally hit the wall at some point. "It's green and black. Who has that?"

Nick sighed. "We'll have to check. Though I would have remembered seeing that."

An idea came suddenly to Mackenzie. She spoke quickly, tripping over her words. "We know what time Noah was dropped off at the hospital from the CCTV. We know what car they were driving and where Noah was being held. There's a turnpike, it would *have* to have driven through it to get to the hospital. We can extrapolate the approximate time frame and get a visual. If not a face, then at least a license plate."

An hour later, Mackenzie was chewing on her lower lip and ignoring the voice inside her head telling her to fix her hair and face. She was flushed and tense. But she didn't care. They were so close to ending this.

Their strategy had worked. Clint had gathered the traffic camera's footage from the department of transportation, and there was a green 1969 Mustang with a black strip that had entered a lane within the right time frame. Despite Clint's many attempts, they couldn't get a clear image of the driver. But they had gotten a license plate number.

"That's our guy." Nick turned the monitor for Mackenzie to look at. The DMV records showed the picture of a young boy with a long face and thin nose and acne on his forehead and cheeks. "Bob Ford."

She frowned. "He's a twenty-year-old kid. Who the hell is he?"

"He works at a hardware store. Let's go talk to him."

CHAPTER SIXTY-EIGHT

The bell jingled when Mackenzie and Nick opened the door to enter the shop. There were multiple aisles lined with shelves that were stuffed with everything from clamps, fastening tools, power drills, and compressors to brackets, hasps, hinges, and hole saws. A distinctive smell saturated the air: wood, metal, and oil, masking the cloying smell from the restaurant next door. There were a few customers—well-built men, and women who seemed totally at ease with the equipment. Unlike Mackenzie; she was hopeless at DIY.

There was a television mounted on the wall. A familiar voice drew their attention to the screen.

"Jeremiah Wozniak is perhaps one of the most vicious serial killers in the history of America. But you've probably never heard of him," a rich and silky voice said in a dramatic voiceover, as various pictures of Jeremiah flashed on screen. He was the only one in color, while his surroundings were white and black. *"Michael Trelawney delves into the darkest of minds that snatched little boys and stole their screams."* A reel of yearbook pictures of Jeremiah's victims played—tiny, bright, and unaware of how brutally their lives were cut short. *"Jeremiah might be behind bars, but his story is far from over."* A series of short clips followed. Snippets of interviews from Patricia, Pastor Giles, and Holly Martin. The last clip was of Jeremiah speaking in an ominous tone in an old interview of him in handcuffs. *"I'm not the only evil that haunts Lakemore."* His words ended with static on screen, signifying the end of the teaser. The trailer was supposed to drop in two weeks.

"Not the only evil that haunts Lakemore?" Mackenzie repeated his words, appalled.

"Trelawney's keeping tabs through Holly. I bet they're going to find a way to fit our case into the narrative somehow."

Mackenzie felt the distaste on her tongue. "It's disrespectful. Has anyone from Lakemore PD agreed to participate?"

"Just a retired cop who worked the case. Must have been paid handsomely."

The boy they recognized as Bob emerged from one of the aisles carrying a clipboard. He was lanky and looked even younger in person. "Can I help you?"

They showed him their badges, making him stutter.

"I-I… Yes?"

"Do you own a 1969 Mustang? Green with a black strip?" Mackenzie asked.

"Oh, man!" Bob dropped his arms and looked over his shoulder. "My boss can't see you. He'll fire me."

"The sooner you answer our questions, the faster we'll leave."

He licked his lips, almost sweating. "Can we talk later? I promise. My boss is kind of a jerk. He doesn't like a *scene*. And I'm new."

Nick picked up a pack of strip hooks with adhesive. "I'll take this. We can talk at checkout."

Bob took the strip and mouthed a thank you, going behind the counter.

Mackenzie noticed a burly man with a cranky face, glancing over.

"Your car was used in a crime," she said.

Bob scanned the barcode of the strip with panic rising in his eyes. His face turned redder, the acne becoming more pronounced, spreading across his face like branches. "I knew it! It was so shady, but I was desperate for cash."

"What do you mean?"

He kept looking over at his boss. "Weeks ago, I had no job and no savings. I just had a car, so I thought I should lease it out or something. I put an ad out and this one person responded, saying that they only needed it for four weeks. But they were willing to pay the most. I figured it was a good deal. I wouldn't be without a car for long, and I'd make a lot of money."

"Who were they? What was their name?" Nick asked.

Bob proceeded to make random gestures at the spools of cables and ropes hanging on the wall, pretending to give out casual information. "Their username was John Smith. I knew it probably wasn't real, but I didn't care. I was supposed to leave the car in front of an apartment building. He told me that he'd leave the cash inside a light sconce outside his apartment. That was weird."

"So you never saw him?"

"No. I offered to drop the car and collect my money when he was home, but he didn't budge. I had a bad feeling, but I was desperate." He implored with big eyes. "I swear I don't know who this John Smith is or what he used the car for. Please believe me."

"Where were you on the morning of March fifteenth?" Mackenzie asked.

"What day was that?"

"Friday."

"I was here. I work until five. You can ask my boss if you have to."

Mackenzie saw no reason not to believe him. "Okay. Give us the address where you left the car and picked up your cash," she instructed.

"Time to catch this asshole," Nick mumbled at her side.

CHAPTER SIXTY-NINE

The address led them to an old modest apartment building close to downtown Lakemore. There was a flutter of activity around the entrance; a hotdog stand with a queue of customers and a homeless man begging for change. A small group of teenagers stood in a huddle wearing hoodies and dismissive expressions.

Nick rolled into a spot and headed to the parking meter, being petulant about the rates.

Mackenzie's phone vibrated with a text message from Austin.

Detective Price, please let me know when you'll be back. Have a couple of questions.

She shoved the phone in her back pocket, clenching her teeth. Austin was just doing his job; she knew that. But his persistence irked her. She had no idea who had killed Charles. She didn't know who was after her either. Nothing had happened in the last few days, but that didn't stop her from jumping out of her skin at home at the slightest sound. It didn't stop her from waking up every hour to glance around her room, expecting to find a dark figure standing by her bed, watching her sleep.

Nick waved his hand in her face. "Earth to Mack."

"Sorry." She blinked.

"What happened?"

"The apartment is on the fourth floor." She dodged the question, entering the six-floor walk-up building.

The building smelled like cat piss. Mail and newspapers were piled up in a corner, patches of carpet were soaked and torn out. Dust collected on the bannister. Mackenzie was convinced that this was the type of building with a bedbug problem. They landed on the fourth floor—a dingy, poorly lit hallway with yellowing walls and fruit flies buzzing around.

"Rent must be cheap," Nick said, stopping in front of the apartment in question. "This is it."

"That's where he left the cash to pay Cliff." Mackenzie pointed at the light sconce.

Nick was ready to knock, when Mackenzie stopped him. She heard something. Shuffling. Footsteps and chair scraping. She pressed a finger to her lips and strained her ears. The noise was coming from inside the apartment. It sounded like someone was moving around—in a hurry, not at leisure.

"Lakemore PD! Open up!" Mackenzie pounded on the door, as Nick stood a few steps back, ready to break the door down if necessary.

Chairs toppled. Tables shifted.

Nick ran straight into the door. It crashed on the floor with a loud thud. A figure in black sprinted across the apartment, tearing through the furniture, mounted out of the window into the fire escape.

"They're getting away! Go around the back!" Nick ordered, running toward the fire escape.

Mackenzie turned and barreled down the stairs in full speed. Her heart beat like a drum, adrenaline coursing through her veins. She had only caught a flash of someone in a black hoodie. A tall and muscular figure. Most likely a man.

She pushed her way out of the building, quickly assessing which way to the back of the building would be closer. A second later, she was jamming her way past the group of teenagers, who shouted profanities at her.

"What the hell?!"

"Watch where you're going!"

"Screw you, bitch!"

But Mackenzie didn't listen. She only felt the hot air against her face as she ran so fast she almost felt like she was flying. Her sole focus was on cutting down the man's path before he disappeared into a crowd on the main street. All they had to do was corner him at the back of the building.

Her breaths came in bursts, but her lungs were healthy, used to the stretch and burn that came with her regular jogs. She sped up—he was within reach; the man who had orchestrated one of the worst events in Lakemore. Anger boiled inside her. She growled, seeing through a space in the building on her left that the man in the black hoodie was coming her way.

With full force, she ran into him, intersecting him at the right angle. The force of the impact sent them both crashing down on the ground. Mackenzie rolled away from him, clutching her arm. A searing pain shot through her chest. Her head bounced off the asphalt—missing the curb by an inch, which could have spelled her death. She rolled on the ground, for a moment only able to focus on the pain. The sudden halt in momentum had disorientated her. It hurt to breathe—and she knew she had cracked a rib. There was a dull ache in the back of her head. Her arm was heavy, and it made her chest hurt more if she moved it.

When the shock ebbed, she tethered herself to the present and turned her head to find the man in the black hoodie also on the ground. He wasn't as hurt as she was, owing to his larger frame. His face was still concealed. He got on all fours, attempting to stand up, when Nick caught up behind him.

"Don't move." Nick pointed his gun at the man's head. "Hands in the air. Now!"

The man followed Nick's orders. Slowly raising his hands. Still on his knees.

"Mack, are you okay?" Nick asked even though his eyes never left the suspect.

"Yeah," she croaked and raised herself. The side of her chest throbbed with every breath she took.

Nick kept the gun aimed at the man's head with one hand and extended the other one to pull back the hoodie.

And Mackenzie almost collapsed on the ground again.

It was Spencer.

CHAPTER SEVENTY

Mackenzie never thought that any coffee could be too hot for Nick. She was convinced that he had burned his tongue and esophagus off a very long time ago. But he blew on the coffee in the cup he held. Again and again. The coffee rippled to the edges of the cup. Again and again.

Spencer sat in the interrogation room on the other side of the glass wall. In a black hoodie and sprawled on the uncomfortable steel chair. Mackenzie tried to erase him out of that room. She traced back to the memory of Nick unmasking the killer that had been eluding them, and she tried changing the memory. It wasn't Spencer; it was someone else. A stranger even. Because that would make it easier to absorb the sight in front of her. Unseemly and unnatural.

She took quick, short breaths to avoid moving her chest too much. Nick noticed.

"Mack, you should go to the hospital. You have definitely cracked a rib."

"I can't right now."

"I know you want to be here but—"

"I *need* to be here." She gave him a pressing look, which made him cave. It must have been visible in her eyes—the desperation to understand what had happened.

Sully walked in the room, his face pale. "He didn't ask for a lawyer?"

"*He* is a lawyer," Mackenzie muttered. "I'm sure he'll defend himself."

"Did he say anything?"

Nick shook his head.

"I can't believe this," Sully muttered and looked around the room, dazed, as if searching for something to distract him. He picked up a Rubik's Cube and started fiddling with it mindlessly.

"Why are we waiting?" Mackenzie asked.

"Rivera is going to be here any minute now." Nick looked like he had aged ten years in the last hour. Lines on his forehead had deepened, and he looked totally spent. "Should I get you some ice for your head?"

"No, my head is fine." She winced. "It's just my ribs. As long as I don't move my right arm much, it's not too bad." She kept her right arm pressed into her chest. The throbbing still hadn't subsided. But Mackenzie couldn't leave now. She had to know *why.* What made a successful, clean-cut lawyer like Spencer kidnap and *murder* children?

"I want to talk to him!" Elliot filed inside the room.

Rivera shadowed him. "I think it's best if Nick and Mack do it. You can watch."

Elliot licked his lips and dropped his briefcase on the floor carelessly. Mackenzie had never seen him slip. He had mastered hiding his emotions, or at least keeping them at bay, which is what he'd done when he'd confessed to hiding evidence. But now he was unraveling. "No. You don't understand. There *must* be a mistake!"

"Look at him, Elliot," Nick said. "Is he acting like someone who's been falsely accused of something this terrible?"

Elliot was panting when he glared at Spencer. "He owes me. This… this can't be it."

Spencer stared at the glass with a martyred expression. Like he was bravely trying to walk on hot coals.

Nick emptied the coffee in the trashcan. "Alright. Let's do this."

Mackenzie clutched her arm to her side, loathing any weakness being on show.

As soon as they entered the interrogation room, Spencer's eyes found her arm. "You should be in the hospital, Detective Price."

"Thanks for your concern," she replied icily as she took a seat across from him.

The air in the room was cold. It wasn't soupy or suffocating. Instead it felt sharp against Mackenzie's skin. She winced every time she breathed. But she was distracted by the gentle expression on Spencer's face, so at odds with the brutality of his crimes.

"The crime scene investigators are at the apartment you rented under an alias," Nick started. "They're still taking it apart, but they found a lot of files and some gasoline. Looks like you were burning evidence when we showed up."

Spencer didn't reply. He held his head high. His face was a blank canvas.

"You planned everything to a T but missed one tiny detail," Nick said, passing over a picture. "The car. The rain didn't wash out all the tracks, and at some point you accidentally hit a wall, which left shavings on the ground."

Spencer glanced at the picture and nodded.

"You tried to direct us to Ruth," Mackenzie accused. "That's why you left that clay stain on the wall. Except you used the wrong kind of clay. It's the kind she's allergic to."

"I see," Spencer said mildly surprised, but accepting of the situation.

Mackenzie and Nick looked at each other. It was the first time Spencer had spoken since being discovered. But he was holding back. He wasn't mocking them or challenging them. He wasn't playing any games. Not spewing any riddles or taunts.

"Why did you want to lead us to Ruth?" Nick asked.

"Because she deserved to be punished for what she did to Johnny."

"And why do you care so much about Johnny? How are you related to him?"

"I'm not." There was a void in Spencer, a numbness that no one could penetrate. "I wanted balance—to right a wrong."

"So that's what your motivation was?" Mackenzie snapped. "Justice?"

Spencer looked beyond them at the mirror. "I know you're there, Elliot. This is all because of you."

"What are you talking about?"

He cracked. Tears pooled in the corners of his eyes. "When I was sixteen years old, a girl and I were in a foster home. Our foster *dad*," he spat the word. "He used to go to her room and... molest her at night. She told everyone about it, but nobody listened. They said she was making up stories." His fingers on the table clasped and unclasped repeatedly. "One day she asked me to sleep in her room to protect her. He came in again that night. But this time, I saw red. I got into it with him. Naturally, the child services got involved. He wanted to press charges too and called his lawyer. His lawyer came with an intern—Elliot."

Mackenzie looked over her shoulder, knowing very well that Elliot was listening intently.

Spencer spoke directly to the mirror, as if he could see Elliot's betrayed eyes. "I was going to get in trouble. Who was going to believe a punk who grew up in foster care? Of course the world would believe that man who had been kind enough to take foster kids for years. His lawyer was going to pin it all on me, but it was Elliot who sensed something was wrong. He talked to me, to my foster sister. He was still in law school—inexperienced and righteous. He proved that my foster sister was telling the truth. No charges were pressed against me, and that filth of a man was imprisoned. Elliot did that." Spencer's eyes shone with veneration. He looked down and shook his head. "I was so angry growing up, angry at being born to a crack whore who left me, angry at the rich kids who had it easy, angry at my damn luck. The world was a very dark place. Unfair. Uncouth. Hypocritical. But then I met Elliot." He spaced out, cherishing the feelings that arose in him. "He was the first person in my life who did the right thing simply because it was the right thing to do. For a teenager who loathed every inch of this world and every face he saw, it was the most unusual thing. It changed me. For the first time in my life, I had purpose."

"Elliot was your idol. You wanted to be like him." Mackenzie remembered how Spencer had spoken of him with such admiration.

"I worshipped him. I turned my life around after that incident. I went from someone who was going to end up selling drugs on the street to getting into the best law school in the country on a full scholarship."

"I don't understand." Nick shrugged. "What does your relationship with Elliot have to do with what you did?"

Spencer's upper lip curled in a sneer as he looked up at the two-way mirror. "Elliot, you shouldn't have buried that evidence."

Suddenly, Elliot burst inside the room, panting with rage. "What the hell are you talking about? We both agreed to do that!"

"You did!" Spencer retorted with a madness in his eyes. "What choice did I have?"

"Why didn't you say anything?"

"Everything I believed in… Every single thing I believed in crumbled into dust before my eyes the day you made that call. Everything I knew fell apart. You and I were the good guys. We were bringing justice and fairness and honesty into this fucked-up world. But you were corrupt. You were just like the rest of them!"

Elliot's mouth was left hanging open. Disbelief suspended in the air.

"The man who went out of his way and saved a young kid." Spencer beat his own chest. "That same man *sacrificed* Johnny! You couldn't have saved him. But you could have saved his memory. His legacy. Instead you chose to disrespect it."

"You understood," Elliot whispered, defeated. "When I said, it was necessary to ensure that Jeremiah went to prison—"

"I understood that I had been disillusioned. That whatever we call doing the *right thing* is all a fantasy. I thought we did it right. But it was a lie. You have to get your hands dirty. You can't avoid it. That's what you made me realize, Elliot."

"You certainly got your hands dirty," Mackenzie said. "Murdering Lucas and Theo."

Spencer frowned, clearly having forgotten momentarily that she and Nick were also in the room. "It was for Johnny."

"You didn't have to kidnap and kill those kids!" Nick shouted, slamming his fist on the table. "You could have just told us to look into Johnny again. Hell, send some anonymous message."

"Like that would have made a difference! How can you two of all people say that? You solved the Perez case. You uncovered massive corruption in this town. Do you think if I had just sent some letter to you the brass would have allowed you to investigate?" Spencer challenged. "The higher powers protected Elliot *again*. Even after I set the trap to implicate him, he got away. That's how deep cover-ups run in politics."

Mackenzie pressed her nails into her palm. "You murdered two boys! All so that Johnny could get justice? Because you thought you owed him something?"

"Justice for ten victims trumps justice for one," he echoed Elliot's words to him.

Elliot was horrified. He swayed, bracing himself against the wall. Like the force of Spencer's words and betrayal had knocked the wind out of him. "We've worked together for over a decade."

"And this is what you taught me."

"And how did justice for Johnny trump the *lives* of Lucas and Theo? And the trauma that Noah has to live with?" Nick demanded.

"You saved a lot more lives," Spencer said, wiping a stray tear. "Cheryl Tanner had been taking bribes from abusive parents, like

Heather and my foster dad. Those kids aren't in danger now. They won't be beaten up or neglected or starved or assaulted anymore. And Patricia had been selling drugs to recovering addicts. Not to mention her associate, Toby Adler, who was running a bigger operation. At least I made sure that Lucas and Theo didn't feel any pain when they died. There are fates worse than theirs."

"Sounds like you thought of everything," Mackenzie said, her stomach flipping in disgust. "And what about Ruth?"

"She's a teacher! And she made a bad call by not believing Johnny." He grimaced. "I had decided to abduct them when they were supposed to be under her supervision. And the spring festival presented the perfect opportunity. Plenty of people and thick woods close by. I thought of letting her live with her guilt, but then she became a local hero. Like a phoenix she rose from the ashes of her disastrous mistakes. People forgot about her negligence. That wasn't right. It was disgusting of her to achieve fame using *this*. So I left a clue pointing the finger at her."

Mackenzie hadn't dealt with a criminal like Spencer before. He was a puzzle. All the pieces had fit together perfectly, but the picture was jarring, lacking cohesion. She had seen unveiled cruelty before; criminals who were drunk on power and entitlement, criminals who just wanted to cause pain in exchange for pleasure, criminals who weren't really criminals but victims of a desperate situation.

And there was Spencer, who couldn't be boxed into any of those categories. He was an educated man, but with a troubled childhood. And then a switch had flipped. The world around him rearranged in a way he didn't understand anymore. And he went on a mad quest to try to make it right again. As if it were his responsibility; his right to dispense justice and change the world.

"How long have you been planning this for?" Mackenzie found her voice.

"A year. After we buried the evidence, I was different," Spencer said calmly. "Something physically changed inside me. It took me years to understand and accept it. I continued to live my life, but I was numb inside. Then, about a year ago, that director, Michael Trelawney, started making phone calls. He was showing interest in Jeremiah, and it hit me all at once. The past staring at me. My role in the injustice for Johnny mocked me. And it destroyed me that Jeremiah was going to get all that attention when he deserves to be forgotten."

"I know what I did was wrong," Elliot said, trembling and baring his teeth. "I know I'm the reason that boy didn't get justice for a very long time. But you *killed* two children."

"My stakes were higher. I had to clean the system, so I had to take drastic measures."

Nick was furious. He kicked back his chair and paced the room to dissipate his bubbling energy. "There are other things we can do to clean the system. Things that don't involve *murder.*"

Spencer's chuckle was mirthless. "Yeah, yeah. You two went about it the right way. Conveyed the knowledge of evidence tampering to your superiors. And what did they do? Told you to forget about it because God forbid the office loses the white knight of the county. Don't give me this shit."

"It's not your place." The vein in Nick's head throbbed. "No one anointed you to fix the system or save anybody."

"So a year ago, you decided to be a vigilante," Mackenzie said, bringing everyone back to the point. "Did you know who killed Johnny before we did?"

"No. I started doing research. Tim had confessed to some friends after a lot of drinks that Heather had been an abusive stepmother. When I started following Heather around, I wasn't surprised at that accusation. I found out that child services had been alerted in this case, through the letter that was sent by Johnny. I tracked Cheryl who had paid the family a visit. But clearly nothing came of it."

"You didn't know about the bribe?"

He shook his head. "I didn't know what happened between Heather and Cheryl, but it was odd that no action was taken, since I didn't think Tim would lie about something like this. I knew about the former technician at the crime lab who knew what we did, even though I'd never met her. When you weren't able to find his killer, I realized that maybe you'd need the forensic evidence. Even though I always planned on exposing Elliot somehow, I was a little reluctant, knowing it would also implicate me. But then I remembered the big picture and left you that clue."

"What about Patricia? You led us to her."

"She was one of the people I was trailing. That's how I knew about the lighthouse and her dealing with that Adler guy."

"And then you let Noah go, planting that clay stain as the final piece in this elaborate plan."

Spencer swallowed and nodded. "My work is done. I kept my word. I didn't want to hurt them. I was relieved that I wouldn't have to kill Noah as you'd arrested Giles. And now you've caught me. You should be happy, detectives. I heard you weren't comfortable with the mayor's decision to ignore Elliot's infraction. But now everything will be forced out in the open. All these selfish politicians, like the mayor and the DA, who only care about their elections, who want to suppress the truth. But now they can't. Johnny is avenged, and everyone who wronged him will suffer punishment."

"If you're such a martyr then why did you run from us?" Mackenzie asked.

He sniffled, a smile tugging on his lips. "I still have some sense of self-preservation, I suppose."

"You are the one who betrayed me," Elliot said with gritted teeth. His eyes were bloodshot. "After years of friendship between us, you went ahead and did something like this."

Spencer looked up at him slowly with the expression of a man who had walked towards death with pride. "Blood must be spilled for justice."

CHAPTER SEVENTY-ONE

"You have a fractured rib. It should heal in around six weeks." The doctor showed Mackenzie an X-ray of her chest and then began detailing the treatment course.

She had been shipped to the hospital to get her injuries checked. After Spencer had signed his confession and was taken into custody, silence had fallen in the interview room. Elliot had slumped against the wall, still processing what had happened. Rivera had plunged straight into work, informing Murphy, Mayor Rathbone, and Mr. Kinsey. And Sully had solved the Rubik's Cube.

"I call it doing the PIM. Painkillers, ice, and minimal movement," the doctor said, baring his gleaming teeth.

Mackenzie gave a polite smile. Once the doctor left, permitting her to leave, she took a moment for herself. Just beyond the curtain, there was activity, wheels squeaking on the floor and the hum of whispers and hushed conversations. She waited. What for? Even she didn't know. But she wanted to spend time inside a bubble—or on an island—far away from everyone.

Nick ripped open the curtain, pulling Mackenzie back into the world. "Ready to go?"

"You didn't have to come," she mumbled, hopping off the bed and securing her right arm close to her chest. The movement sent a sharp pain through the side of her chest. "Ouch."

"Have you never broken your ribs before?"

"Luckily enough, no." She walked stiffly to the parking lot. "I'm thinking of taking a holiday."

He threw his head back and laughed. "Yeah. Good one."

"I'm serious!" she griped. "I'm exhausted."

"You can't leave." Nick's face changed. "Charles's case is still open, and Austin watches you like you're hiding something."

"You've noticed it too."

They stopped in front of Nick's SUV. He sighed and leaned against the car. "He's looking into your background. Your time in New York. Your record at the academy. Any friends you had, et cetera."

She tried to hide the shock on her face, but she couldn't control the hair on the back of her neck from rising. Why was Austin after her? She had nothing to do with what happened to Charles. He must have uncovered some information that made him suspect Mackenzie of something illegal. And he wouldn't be wrong. She had buried an innocent man. But how did he know?

"Don't worry about it," Nick said, noting her expression. "He's just chasing a pointless lead."

"He wanted to talk to me, but then we caught Spencer and got busy."

He nodded. "I'll head back to the station after dropping you off to wrap up some paperwork. I'll let him know you were injured and went home. No big deal."

Wasn't it? Wouldn't Austin think she was avoiding him? In a way, she was.

She climbed inside the car, and Nick peeled out of the parking lot, turning onto the main street.

Mackenzie looked out the window at the lights from shops and restaurants popping up against a darkening sky. After the Lakemore PD had made an announcement that they had apprehended their killer, the town began to heal again. At a red light, she saw a family on the crossing with a skip in their steps and smiles lighting up their faces, carrying takeout boxes. On the surface, there was an innocence to Lakemore. A small town filled with locals who had an unembellished desire to do honest work and provide enough for their children. But just as the car swerved to drive alongside the thick woods, Mackenzie was reminded that there was nothing innocent about Lakemore. The thick woods and deep waters hid the darkest of secrets. Corruption and violence were sewn into the fabric of the town.

"I can't stop thinking about Spencer," she admitted.

"He was delusional." Nick took a sharp breath.

"Was he?"

"Seriously?" His head whirled to pin her with a glare.

"No, I didn't mean it like that. Obviously I could never condone what he did regardless of his reasons. But I don't think it was delusion. It was blind passion. Elliot, Giles, and Spencer—all were so hell-bent on wanting to do good that they ended up doing bad things."

The rest of the ride was mostly silent. She knew Nick was still struggling with the aftermath of the events. Guilt had sticky and sharp tendrils that once hooked into the soul were difficult to extract. As he pulled up in front of her house, she patted his shoulder. He looked at her, puzzled. She opened her mouth to offer words of comfort but couldn't find any.

Mackenzie watched him drive away and savored the perfumed spring air. She spotted Irene in the hammock in her front yard, reading her Kindle while listening to something. They waved at each other.

When Mackenzie turned, she saw a package on her doorstep. It was the new juicer she had ordered, and it was heavy.

"Irene?" she called out.

She took off her earbuds. "Yeah?"

"Don't suppose you could give me a hand? I can't lift things at the moment."

Irene craned her neck to see what Mackenzie was talking about. "Sure. Give me a minute." She went inside and returned sans Kindle. "What happened to you?"

"I cracked a rib."

Her eyebrows shot up, as she lifted the box with strong arms. "I saw on the news you caught your guy."

"Yep." She didn't offer any more details, and Irene didn't press. Mackenzie let Irene inside and asked her to put the box on the kitchen island. Her eyes made quick work of her house as she placed her service weapon in a drawer in the foyer table. Everything was in place just as she remembered. "Do you want tea?"

"I'll make it. You're banged up pretty bad."

Mackenzie flopped on the couch, exhaustion seeping into her bones and turning her muscles tender. She could feel herself numbing to the chaos surrounding her, like her skin was hardening into steel.

Irene handed her a cup. "You should take some time off. Looks like you could use it."

"I want to. But I don't know if it will help."

Irene sat down and curled her legs on the couch. "Why not?"

"Because it never ends." Mackenzie took a sip. "It's amazing how you can spend years in this work, and people still surprise you. They're like Russian dolls, but you never reach the core."

"I never thought of it that way."

"Sorry, I'm feeling philosophical after the day I've had." She pressed her lips in a thin line.

Irene shrugged. She started telling her about work, updating Mackenzie on her quirky coworkers. It was a fruitful distraction. Plus the painkiller the doctor had given her at the hospital was beginning to take effect, diminishing her pain—but not enough. From the corner of her eye, she caught a glimpse of someone standing.

It was Charles.

She blinked, and he was gone.

"But I don't know how you feel about that." Irene finished her tea.

Mackenzie hadn't listened to a word. "About what?"

"About your uncle, Damien, kind of showing interest in me."

"*What?*"

Irene giggled. "Maybe I should catch you another time."

"No. Sit. Sorry, I zoned out. Tell me everything." She stood up. "I'll make you more tea."

"You should rest!"

"It's alright." She regretted being nonchalant because the throbbing had returned. But she muscled through and poured fresh water into the kettle. "So what happened again?"

"Nothing. I just got a vibe from him when I met him outside your place."

Mackenzie took out a bag of peas from the freezer and tucked it under her arm against her ribs. Her phone rang. "Excuse me. It's my partner."

"Hello?"

"Mack? Where are you?" Nick sounded urgent.

"At home. Where you left me like thirty minutes ago." She scoffed. "What's up?"

The engine thundered. "Don't go anywhere. Austin and I are on our way right now."

"Okay, you're scaring me. What happened?" She chuckled nervously.

"Remember Austin asked you about Harold Lewis?"

"Yes…"

"He was referring to the businessman who committed suicide." The car honked in the background. "He is survived by his only child. A daughter. Irene."

The kettle whistled. A sharp keening that pierced the air. It dissolved the sound of blood roaring into Mackenzie's ears. She felt gutted, like someone had stabbed and twisted a knife inside her. Slowly, she lifted her gaze to find Irene sitting on the couch leisurely, admiring the twilight. Her silhouette was almost iridescent. She looked at Mackenzie and smiled.

"Mack? Mack?" Nick's voice tunneled back. "Are you there?"

Mackenzie turned around, hiding her face. She spoke in a measured voice with her heart in her mouth. "Y-yes. It's actually not a good time right now, Nick. I'm with my neighbor, Irene. She's come over for tea."

"Got it. Act normal. We'll be there soon."

"Perfect." Mackenzie hung up and took a deep breath that hurt her chest.

She counted to ten in her head, but her hand on the counter was vibrating like it was being electrocuted. Since the kettle had stopped whistling, it was eerily silent in the house. So silent that her eardrums could rupture. Her head swam with a million questions. But right now, she had to pretend. Striving to put on an act, she turned around.

Irene wasn't on the couch anymore. She was standing close to her. Around six feet away. Her smile had slipped. There was nothing on her face. No anger, no threat, and no frustration. "You know."

Mackenzie's tongue was too heavy for her to reply.

"You weren't supposed to find out, Mackenzie," Irene said, pointing a gun at her.

CHAPTER SEVENTY-TWO

Mackenzie experienced a nerve-splintering terror.

"You keep a gun on you." Mackenzie noted the safety was on.

Irene's nostrils flared. "I like to be careful."

"It was you." Her voice cracked, the sting of the betrayal echoing in her words.

"Yes," she said, ice-cold.

Suddenly, Irene had transformed. Mackenzie could no longer see the kind, level-headed woman who had become a friend. Because she had never existed.

Mackenzie's brain leapt into overdrive—how to get out of this situation? Her service weapon was in the drawer on the foyer table. But that was on the other side of the room. "Did you kill Charles?"

"Yes."

"Why?"

Irene didn't answer right away. Her grip on the gun was steadfast, but her lips quivered. Even as Mackenzie tried to hatch a plan, her heart thundered too wildly. Everything in her life—the ghastly event from twenty years ago, the guilt she carried, Charles's return and murder—it all boiled down to this moment.

And she might not survive. Nick and Austin might be too late.

"Your father was Harold Lewis," Mackenzie said. "How are you related to Charles?"

Her eyelid twitched. "The newspapers mentioned Harold's wife and child but gave no names. His wife was Melody. Your mother."

"No." It was a reflex.

"You wouldn't know. It was years before you were even born."

Mackenzie leaned against the counter, the edge digging into her skin. Her arm was glued to the bruised side of her body. She tried to grasp the meaning of Irene's words. But it was like throwing stones on a wall. "She was your mother too?"

"Oh, no." She cringed. "She was my stepmother. My mother died when I was only two years old. When I turned eleven, my father married your mother."

"What happened?"

Irene crinkled her nose and took sharp breaths. "Your mother was a real piece of work. The fakest bitch I've ever come across. She only married my father for his money. Of course, he didn't realize because he was so enamored by her. She was beautiful and charming. Always partying with her friends."

Melody had been striking. With her saucer-shaped gray eyes and thick black curls, there was an ethereal quality to her. But Mackenzie had always seen her as afraid and abused. She had seen her milky skin covered in strange bruises, her pallid face stained with dried tears. She couldn't imagine her mother being vibrant and chatty, surrounded by friends, dolled up and laughing.

But she hadn't known her mother at all.

"She cheated on him," Irene continued, with disdain dripping off every word. "With Charles. I saw them a couple of times around the house when my father would travel for work. One time she caught me watching them and told me they were just friends. But I was twelve years old. Your mother obviously underestimated just how much a twelve-year-old understands and feels."

Mackenzie didn't argue with that. It was something they both shared. She was twelve when Melody had asked her to bury a body in the woods and then believed that sending her off to a new city would be the remedy to that trauma.

"She wouldn't leave my father, of course. Charles was poor. When I told my father about what I saw, he didn't believe me. He chalked it up to me being unable to accept Melody and making up lies. He was bewitched, until he saw them for himself. And that's when Melody truly sank to a whole new level. She divorced him and took all his money." A tear rolled down her face and fell on the floor. "My father had been betrayed. All his savings and hard-earned money swindled by your whore of a mother and her deadbeat boyfriend."

"That's why your father committed suicide."

"I was only thirteen years old." Her grip on the gun wobbled. "Melody destroyed my father. He was all I had. But I was a child. Who would believe me? What could I have done? I was just a helpless kid."

Mackenzie saw the kettle still had hot water and an idea sparked. If only she could move fast enough. But her right side was still weak—aching with every breath.

"But I didn't forget anything," Irene enunciated, stepping closer. "When I was old enough, I made it my mission to hunt them down. I found out that only a year after my father's death, Melody had married again. Her new mark. Robert Price. Except this time she got pregnant by Charles, so it kind of derailed her plans to steal his money and make a quick exit."

Mackenzie instinctively touched the watch on her wrist. It reassured her somehow. Like someone was watching over her, that today would not be the day she died.

"Almost ten years ago, I finally tracked down your mother."

All the plans that were materializing in Mackenzie's head shattered. She blanched at the insinuation, her jaw hanging slack. She could only whimper. "What?"

The corner of Irene's mouth lifted in a cruel smile. "I followed her and ran her off the road. Luckily it was the dead of winter, and the roads had black ice. So everyone just assumed that the car skidded and wrapped itself around a tree. Poor Melody."

"You killed my mother?"

"Of course I did!" Irene yelled, tears springing her eyes. "She was a greedy monster in cahoots with that sleazebag and got away with killing my father. Ruining my life! Taking away my only family! I became an orphan because of her and Charles."

"Oh my God." Mackenzie pressed a hand to her chest and tried to control her breathing. Over the years, her love for her mother had died. The lingering love was killed the day Charles had revealed how Melody had manipulated her. But to think that Melody had been murdered? That it wasn't just a car crash…

"It took me a long time to find Charles. He was always on the run. And when I did, I knocked on the door and aimed the gun at him." Her eyes narrowed at the memory she clearly relished. "He was terrified and confused and asked me who I was. And I contemplated telling him, but he didn't deserve closure or answers. I told him *you should die without knowing*. And that was that."

"Why me? You've been stalking and harassing me!"

"I didn't know about you until a few weeks after I killed Charles. I was keeping tabs on the investigation, and people were talking about how his daughter was a detective. And when I saw you from afar, I knew you were Melody's daughter. You look so alike. And I hated you." She closed her eyes and shook her head. "I hated the blood inside your veins. I hated that a part of Melody and Charles was alive and breathing and *thriving*." Spit flew out of her mouth. "I dedicated my life to finding them so that I could avenge my father. And after I succeeded, I waited for peace. But it didn't come," she whispered like a wounded child. "Why wouldn't it come? I did right by my father. I fulfilled my purpose. But it evaded me. And when I saw you, I realized it was because of *you*. Because you existed, my work wasn't done. My mission was incomplete. *That's* why I didn't find peace."

Mackenzie slowly inched closer to the kettle. "So you moved in next door. Why didn't you just kill me?"

"I couldn't have done that. I'm not stupid. You're a cop." Irene wiped her nose with her sleeve. "But I could make your life miserable. Make you feel unsafe in your own home. I tried to make you slowly unravel."

"You tried to run my car off the road like you did with my mother!"

"It was a moment of weakness. I didn't plan to. I had been following you, and you just look so much like your mother... for a moment, I actually saw Melody. I wanted to relive that moment of finally killing her. My father's biggest betrayer."

Mackenzie's voice was tight with anger. "What my parents did to your father wasn't my fault."

"But with time I realized that you were nothing like them," Irene ignored Mackenzie. "In fact, the strangest thing happened. Knowing you, and your friendship, it gave me peace. I wasn't angry anymore." Her eyes shone with tears. Snot collected on her pouty upper lip. She didn't look menacing anymore, but like a terrified child. "I stopped."

"That letter in my mailbox. Calling me a murderer?"

"I left that when I first moved in," she snapped. "You just hadn't checked your mailbox in a very long time. I truly started thinking of you as a friend, Mackenzie. And I thought that the past would stay in the past. But I know your partner must have told you that he discovered the truth. It was written all over your face."

Mackenzie moved closer, bracing herself and confirming that the safety was off. Those quick seconds it would take for Irene to turn it on were critical and all that Mackenzie could rely on. "Are you going to kill me now?"

"It was a mistake to think that you and I could be friends," she whispered. "Looks like I'm going to end up in prison anyway, now that they know. But at least I should finish what I started. This was how it was always supposed to end."

CHAPTER SEVENTY-THREE

It happened at almost superhuman speed. Mackenzie picked up the kettle and swung it against Irene's raised hand. The gun flew out of her grasp, falling on the other side of the kitchen with a clatter. She smothered the rising pain in her chest and the feel of her bruised rib cracking open even more. It was adrenaline and rage that fueled her.

Irene struck a blow into the side of Mackenzie's ribs. Mackenzie cried, tucking her right arm in. Picking up the kettle with her left hand, she smashed it into the side of Irene's face. She collapsed on the floor, moaning.

Mackenzie hopped over her to the foyer and retrieved her gun. It was loaded.

She turned the safety off and swung around.

The house was shrouded in darkness now. The sun had disappeared and sucked out all light from the sky. She squinted to see through the darkness, to catch a shadow of Irene. It was deathly quiet. Mackenzie could only hear her own labored breathing. Sweat trickled down her back in ropes.

Gunfire. A single shot. She ducked on instinct. The bullet struck the mirror behind her. It cracked. The large popping sound caused a perpetual ringing in her ears. She wormed her way to the base of the staircase and concealed herself behind the banister. She tried to see Irene from in between the balusters.

A quick movement in the kitchen. Irene was crouched behind the kitchen island. Mackenzie pressed the trigger. A shot right at the edge of the counter.

Irene responded with another gunshot. It missed Mackenzie, hitting the pillar next to the staircase instead. Irene knew how to use a gun, but she wasn't an expert marksman.

Mackenzie wasn't in an ideal position. She wasn't completely hidden, and the only thing preventing Irene from taking a clean shot was the darkness. She picked up a few pieces of the broken glass and threw them across the room. Just as she expected, Irene fired two more bullets.

That was four down. Two more to go.

Mackenzie paused a beat. She had the upper hand—five bullets left. The silence that followed each shot was deafening. Her blood pounding in her veins was cold. She shot blind, a vague idea of where Irene was based on movement of the shadows. But her return fire was too quick and precise. It struck Mackenzie in her right bicep.

"Ah!" The gun slipped from her grip, and she fell back. Fresh pain seeped into her bones, her arm sinking to the ground like it weighed a ton.

Right at that moment, the front door came crashing open as Nick and Austin ran inside.

"She's armed! Stay back!" Mackenzie warned before they reached the living room.

Nick slipped outside the house again. Mackenzie knew he was going to come in from the back door—except it was thick and locked. It wasn't easy to get in since she'd changed it.

"Irene!" Austin was crouched by the door only a few feet on Mackenzie's right. "You don't have to do this. Engaging in this confrontation with the police won't end well for you. I suggest you surrender before you make things worse."

Irene didn't reply.

Mackenzie curled in a ball at the bottom of the staircase and reached out for her gun. Blood soaked her sleeve, dripping all over the floor. Her hand blindly shuffled around in the dark, searching for the weapon.

Her messy hair clung to the sides of her face. Her breathing escalated as she saw a shadow creep across the room. Irene still had one bullet left. But Austin was armed.

Where was Nick?

A crash. A grunt. A gunshot. A cry.

Irene had smacked a lamp into Austin's head, managing to weave her way to him undetected in the dark. Austin's gun went off, and Irene cried. Mackenzie saw the outline of liquid spurting out of her shadow. She was hurt and bleeding.

Mackenzie froze. Austin was unmoving on the floor. Irene fell down and began crawling toward her. Mackenzie could hear the sound of her dragging herself along the floor, now wet with blood. Her outline grew larger as she closed the distance between her and Mackenzie.

"You're making a mistake. Stop *now*." Mackenzie breathed. Her strength collapsed as the energy drained from the right side of her body. She could barely hold herself up anymore.

Irene rose above Mackenzie. She could only see her outline. But in that moment, Irene wasn't just a vengeful woman; she was all of Mackenzie's demons personified. Everything that Mackenzie had carried in the last twenty years: the guilt, the scars, regret, and haunting memories—they all distilled into one person. And she felt like it wasn't just Irene who was going to kill her, but all the poison that Mackenzie had bottled up. The day had come to pay the toll.

"This was how it was always going to end, Mackenzie. I was a fool to believe otherwise." Irene climbed on top of her.

"Ah!" Mackenzie sobbed, getting crushed under her weight, her damaged ribs on the verge of breaking further.

There was a loud sound. A door broke. Nick had managed to break it down. But would he get to her on time? Was this how she was meant to die all along? She had always known her past would catch up with her.

Irene's hands came around Mackenzie's throat and squeezed hard.

Mackenzie could only see Irene's eyes. They looked possessed.

Breaths tore inside Mackenzie's throat. Her head swam. The pressure skyrocketed in her face as if it was about to burst. Her legs flailed fruitlessly. She had no strength to fight off Irene. Her lungs stretched and pinched for air. She started slipping away. The umbilical cord that tethered her to this world was being slowly slashed.

Where was she going? What would it be like?

Light suddenly flooded the room. Three loud pops of gunfire. Mackenzie opened her eyes to find that Irene had frozen with wide eyes. Her hands had gone slack. She fell on Mackenzie with a thud, blood gushing out of the three bullet wounds in her back.

Nick stood above Mackenzie, panting. His face contorted in fury as he pulled Irene's body off Mackenzie and offered his hand. "You changed your back door? It was like trying to open a bank vault."

"Yeah. I changed it after all the threats I started getting." She grabbed his hand and slowly stood up, leaning against him for support.

"*Threats?*"

"It's a long story." She sighed and looked at Austin on the floor, groaning and clutching his bleeding head. "Call 911."

Minutes later, the peaceful street Mackenzie lived on swarmed with ambulances, squad cars, and the crime scene unit van. The light from the sirens danced in the night sky. Curious neighbors filtered out of their homes dressed in robes and pajamas to witness the commotion. There were at least fifty people outside, from the paramedics and police officers to the CSI technicians.

The paramedics immediately surrounded Mackenzie, checking her vitals and asking her questions. She answered, but her eyes didn't leave Austin sitting in the back of an ambulance with a blanket around him and an ice pack to the side of his head. A paramedic tended to his injury—luckily, he didn't require any stitches.

"What do you mean you were getting threats?" Nick was animated.

"Sir, please. We need to take her to the hospital immediately."

Nick huffed and placed his hands on his waist, pacing. The adrenaline still hadn't drained away.

"Can you give me a minute?" Mackenzie asked the paramedic. "Just a minute."

"Ma'am, we need to—"

"Please. It's a flesh wound. It can wait a minute."

The paramedic nodded reluctantly.

Mackenzie dragged herself toward Austin, her body feeling like a pile of bricks, and ignored the death glare Nick was shooting her.

"Detective Price!" Austin exclaimed. "You should go to the hospital."

Mackenzie knew she looked like she had been hit by a truck. Blood covered her arm. One part of her body had been almost crushed, making it hard to even stand straight. There were red marks around her neck. And then there was her face and body language of someone who had been through an entire lifetime in less than an hour. "Are you okay?"

"I have to get a CT scan. I definitely have a concussion."

"You…" she choked out the words. "I thought you suspected me."

He licked his lips. "I did. For a while. But then when I mentioned Irene's name to Nick, he told me that you have a new neighbor by that name. It couldn't have been a coincidence."

"How did you find out about her?"

"I traced your mother's life. Her actions after she sent you to New York were curious."

"How so?"

"I asked around, and Melody was trying to get close to a local businessman. Odd for a woman whose partner had gone missing. Even if he was an alcoholic. And then she started visiting a grave. But I figured it belonged to her father."

Mackenzie shook her head. Melody had already been looking for her next target. This was her game—first Harold Lewis and then Robert Price. Except with Robert things had changed when she got pregnant with Charles's baby, which she had pretended was Robert's. But it sounded like she had decided to get back into the game after sending away her child—an obstacle.

Wait.

"Grave?" Mackenzie asked, her brain lighting up like a bulb.

"Yeah. At the cemetery. Melody spent a few years in Lakemore as a child, right? I think her father was from here."

"Y-yes. He was."

But Melody's father was buried in New York. Mackenzie knew because she and Eleanor went to place flowers on his grave every year on his birthday.

People moved around them. Justin brought out Irene's gun in an evidence bag and gave it to Nick. They whispered amongst each other.

"I know you're hiding something. I can see it in your eyes. And I caught you snooping around in the basement."

Austin's lips parted, and his cheeks tinged pink. He didn't bother holding his composure. "I came to Lakemore for a reason. My fiancée."

"What about her?"

His forehead crumpled. "She's been missing for over a year. I tracked her last movements to Lakemore."

"But why are you accessing files and forcing yourself into other cases?"

"Because I thought maybe her name might come up in a case. I was looking for some clue or connection, anything at all. I just didn't know who to trust. Everyone knows how corrupt this town is."

Mackenzie's heart sank. "I'm sorry. We'll look into her disappearance together."

"Thank you," he said meaningfully.

Nick interrupted, "Mack, you need to go to the hospital, for Christ's sake."

"Yeah, I'm going. What were you and Justin talking about?"

"Irene's gun is a 9mm beretta pistol."

"The one used to kill Charles," Mackenzie said as she was ushered into the ambulance.

"I'll come and see you when I'm done here," Nick promised.

Mackenzie caught a glimpse of her home before the doors to the ambulance shut. It was a crime scene now—strung up by the yellow tape and in a way damaged beyond repair. But the weeping willow standing in her garden still looked healthy and sturdy and unblemished.

EPILOGUE

March 25

"You brought us to a cemetery?" Nick was startled.

Luna clapped her hands in ecstasy and bounced on her seat. "Yes!"

Nick turned around and glared at her in the back seat. "Luna!"

"I like cemeteries, Daddy." She beamed, pressing up her small nose against the window and looking outside in wonderment.

Mackenzie chuckled but reined it in when Nick narrowed his eyes at her. "It's a beautiful day to go out."

"Then we could have had a picnic at the park like regular people."

"I think it's rude," Luna said from behind. Through the rearview mirror, Mackenzie saw Luna holding her head high, very much confident in her opinion. "What if they feel bad about people ignoring them?"

"Who?" Nick frowned.

"The people in the graves."

"Jesus." He pinched the bridge of his nose, exhaling. "Mack, why are we here?"

"I have to visit someone."

"Can we go? Can we go?" Luna writhed on the seat, flopping her legs.

While Nick instructed Luna to behave with sensitivity in the cemetery, Mackenzie looked out the window at rows of tombstones of different shapes and sizes extending up the green hill. It was the only cemetery in Lakemore and it was vast; the city taking up more and more space to find a home for their dead. After spending an entire week recuperating from her injuries, she had been well enough to move around. Her ribs were still achy and tender. And her arm was in a cast from the gunshot. But it was the kind of pain Mackenzie could power through.

It was mustering up the courage to come here that took time. She had feared the anxiety would overwhelm her; stomach in knots, arms dotted with goosebumps, heart pressed up against her ribcage. But, now that she was here, she felt none of those things. Instead when she climbed out of the car, she felt an air of calm. She felt like she was coming home.

Mackenzie took out a tulip bouquet and took a steadying breath.

It was a magical day. A gentle breeze blew across the sky, lifting the ends of Mackenzie's hair. The crisp air of the past few days had turned balmy. Blue skies and fresh sunshine beckoned the summer that was to come. The green grass stretched in an expanse, dispersed with gold dandelions. Bunches of flowers were placed around some tombstones. The colors—pink, purple, red, and yellow—bloomed and infused the air with a soft fragrance. It was like a painting. Every petal and blade of grass oozed radiance.

"They've done a good job of maintaining it," Nick commented, holding Luna's hand as they climbed uphill, following Mackenzie.

In the center, there was a small house under an apple tree. It was where the caretaker lived. An old man was outside, dressed in suspenders and a beret. He picked apples from the tree and placed them in a bucket.

"Stay here." Mackenzie told Nick and approached the caretaker. "Excuse me?"

He turned around. He had a gaunt face with sagging skin, but his gray eyes were sharp. "Yes?"

"This might be a strange question, but I was wondering if you could help me. You've worked here for a very long time, I heard."

"Thirty-seven years," he answered in a voice raspy from old age.

"Wow." She smiled and fished out her phone, to show him a picture of Melody. "I was hoping you could perhaps—"

"You look so much like someone I knew a very long time ago." Mackenzie paused. "Who?"

He smiled fondly. "Melody. Are you her daughter?"

"I am." She put her phone back in her pocket. "You remember her."

He put down the basket and offered his bony hand. "I'm an old man, but my mind is sharp as ever." He grinned, pointing at his temple.

"She used to come here often?"

"Every Saturday morning for nine years. It didn't matter what the weather was. On Saturdays, she was here. We started talking. She spoke about a daughter. I asked her why she didn't bring you with her, but she said you lived out of state with your grandmother."

"I did." She fiddled with the bouquet in her hands.

"And she always brought those flowers."

A few days ago, Mackenzie had spoken to Damien over the phone, and he had given her another detail about Robert—Tulips were his favorite flowers. They made plans to catch up next month when she was feeling better.

It only confirmed what Mackenzie had strongly suspected—that Melody had been visiting Robert's grave for years and leaving his favorite flowers. She had somehow managed to move his body to the cemetery, no doubt in the dead of night. If nothing else, she had been a determined and clever woman.

Another memory took shape behind Mackenzie's eyes. She remembered Robert feeding her and Melody watching them with a smile. "*Who do you love more, Mackenzie? Me or Mommy?*"

Mackenzie sucked on her thumb. "*You!*"

Robert grinned, his cheeks lifting and dimples forming.

Melody smiled too with a tinge of sadness in her eyes. *"You're a good father, Robert."*

"Could you tell me which grave she visited?" Mackenzie asked.

He pointed at a lot on the other end with a cluster of tombstones not as fancy as the other ones. "Over there. The first time she came here, she brought a tombstone and said that the body was never found but she wanted a specific spot. Unfortunately, she didn't have any paperwork or nothing, but she looked desperate. It was obviously for sentimental reasons, so I caved. Plus that area is reserved for unmarked graves anyway. No harm in adding just another piece of concrete."

"Thank you very much."

Mackenzie joined Nick and Luna. "Over there."

They walked across the cemetery, passing by tombstones of people who died old and too young. Parents and siblings. Spouses and children. When they reached the designated lot of unmarked graves, Luna pouted. "Daddy, please?"

"What?" Mackenzie asked.

Nick rolled his eyes. "She wants to go around placing flowers on the tombstones. Especially on the less fancy ones. Okay, Luna. Just don't wander too far, please."

She wrenched her hand free with a yelp of joy. Mackenzie watched her tiny body bend down and eagerly gather stray petals and fallen flowers on the ground she could use. Her innocent chubby face was immersed in work. She wore a headband she got from Disney World last year. Her pigtails swung with each movement. Her shoes had lights that flashed. And Mackenzie felt her heart expand at the sight of her innocence, and the simple kindness she wanted to show to the dead.

"Kid, here you go." Mackenzie plucked out a single tulip from the bouquet and gave the rest to Luna.

"Thank you, Aunty Mack." She grabbed the flowers and dashed on her mission, placing flowers and petals at the base of every tombstone she could find.

"Who are you visiting?" Nick shrugged.

She found Robert's grave. It was the only tombstone in this designated area with one word engraved on it.

Robert.

It seemed like she was still discovering pieces of Melody. She had been greedy and manipulative, but she had left flowers for Robert every Saturday until her death. Charles had been right in saying that Melody was a very complicated woman.

Tears sprang to Mackenzie's eyes. Happy tears. The tears that came from being reunited after a long time. She kneeled next to the tombstone and grazed her hand over it. Placing the single stem of tulip, she felt like something inside her had mended.

"My mother used to come here after I left for New York."

"This is her father?"

She looked up at him. "No, that's *my* father. Well, my legal father."

"Charles?" He frowned. "When did you bury him?"

"This is Robert Price."

"I don't understand."

She stood up and brushed her knees. "Can you promise me that this will stay between us? Only between us?"

Nick nodded. "Of course."

Mackenzie decided to utter the words aloud that she swore to her mother she never would. "Twenty years ago, I came home and found a body on the kitchen floor."

Nick's mouth fell open.

"My mother, Melody, told me she had killed my father in self-defense. She convinced me to help her bury the body in the woods. I was only twelve so I listened to her. But months ago, the man I had thought I had helped bury showed up at my door."

"Charles?" Nick said in disbelief.

"Yep. You see, Melody married Robert Price but continued to have an affair with Charles, her boyfriend of several years. They were kind of con artists. Melody would marry a man, take his money, and then leave. Robert was supposed to be a mark, but she became pregnant with me and that interfered with their plans. Melody ran away with me when I was four, because Robert wouldn't leave her and she never meant to stay with him that long. It was Charles she loved. She brought Charles and me to Lakemore, where Charles went by as Robert Price—to avoid questions, legal issues, and to ease my transition since I had already bonded with Robert. Even though Charles was my biological father, legally my father's name was listed as Robert Price. I was so young at the time… in the end the two men became one in my mind. But the real Robert Price kept looking for Melody and me. And that night, he finally tracked us down."

"So he was the one you found dead?" Nick connected the dots. "But you didn't recognize him?"

"The body was beaten beyond recognition. And Charles was an abusive alcoholic. When Melody claimed self-defense, I believed her. But she and Charles had killed Robert, after he ambushed them, showed up unexpectedly and demanded answers. Then I returned home before they could get rid of the body. So while Charles hid in the house, I buried Robert Price. I thought I was burying a monster. But I ended up burying a good man. In a way, Robert was more of a father to me than Charles ever was, even if our time together was very brief." She thought of her first memory of her father—Robert not Charles—him bending down and planting seeds in the soil. His whole face lighting up with a smile as she ran toward him.

The regret Mackenzie waited for never came. Instead, something left her. A piece that had essentially become an organ broke off. Her bones felt lighter—the dark secret that had been so much a part of her that it had begun to control her began to diminish. Now she was in control. She took charge.

"Charles told you all this?" Nick asked, still sounding dumbfounded.

"Yes, he confessed everything after I found out about his real name from your father. That's why I kicked him out of my life."

"You said Irene was someone from Charles's past…"

"Harold Lewis, her father, was Melody and Charles's mark before Robert. Irene wanted revenge. Melody's betrayal drove him to commit suicide."

"It took you only two decades to trust someone with this." Nick raised an eyebrow.

"I was a kid. I know everyone would have told me that it wasn't my fault, but they would all have looked at me differently. My career would have been severely impacted. Also, my shame is private."

Nick sighed, struggling for words. He watched Luna making her way down another row. "And why were you ready to share this today?"

"I always knew deep down that this wasn't over. There was an instinct telling me that there was more for me to discover. When Charles showed up, I figured I needed answers for closure. But that wasn't it. I needed to know Robert again." She raised her wrist with the watch. "The only person who was a good parent to me and one of the few honest relationships I ever had. I needed to know where he was, so that I could give his family some closure. He was waiting for me all this time. I needed *him* to move on, needed to apologize to him for what I did." She swallowed her tears. "I'm telling you this because I see you stuck in your mistakes just like I was."

"Mack, what happened wasn't your fault—"

"What happened with Johnny wasn't your fault either."

He rooted his jaw, his dark eyes stirring up a storm. After an eternity, he nodded. "Have you forgiven yourself?"

"I will." She was being honest.

"If you can, then I should try too, right?" He scoffed but the vulnerability on his face was palpable.

Mackenzie nodded encouragingly. "Inner peace isn't always a state. Sometimes it's a choice. Make it. Like I am."

"Well, if Mad Mack can talk like a self-help guru, then anything is possible, right?" He smiled and nudged her with his shoulder. "Alright. I'll do it your way." Luna's mission was nowhere near over. Mackenzie and Nick sat on the grass, lounging in just the right amount of coolness. "Are you going to tell Damien?"

"I've thought a lot about how to do that. I can't tell him what exactly happened; if this comes out, then I could lose way too much. So I'll tell him that my mother had always hinted to me that Robert was dead. I'll bring him here and be honest about how I know that this is his resting place." She ran her fingers through the grass and moist soil. Several feet underneath; where Robert had been all this time.

"That's the best you can do for him."

"I hope so."

"Luna is too happy to be at a cemetery." Nick rested his elbows on his knees and wore his sunglasses. "Should I be concerned?"

She chuckled. "She's a child. Let her enjoy this."

"Yeah, it only gets worse with time." He laughed, the wind playing his hair. His phone pinged. "Go figure. One body at Hidden Lake."

Mackenzie stood up with some help, wincing at the dull pain still pulsing on her right side. "Let's go."

Nick called Luna, who looked mildly disappointed that she couldn't leave flowers at all the tombstones. But she cheered up after he promised to bring her back later. Holding hands, they jogged downhill with Nick yelling, "Mack! Hurry!"

Mackenzie followed them with a fresh drive and purpose. She was thrilled to get back to work and make Lakemore a better place. She was still Mad Mack—driven, determined and unflappable, and finally free.

"Coming!"

A LETTER FROM RUHI

Dear Readers,

I want to say a huge thank you for choosing to read *Little Boy Lost*. If you enjoyed it, and want to keep up to date with all my latest releases, just sign up at the following link. Your email address will never be shared, and you can unsubscribe at any time.

www.bookouture.com/ruhi-choudhary

I've had the most fun writing this installment of the Detective Mack Price series, and I hope that you had fun reading it. I'm incredibly grateful to all readers—those who have continued with Mack on her journey and those who have just joined her. She will return, along with the rest of the team, to solve another case in the fictitious town of Lakemore, which I've come to love. So I hope you stick around for more!

If you liked this story, then please consider leaving a review and spread the word to your friends and family. Reviews make a huge difference and help my stories reach out to new readers.

You can connect with me on Twitter.

Many thanks,
Ruhi

 @RuhiSChoudhary

ACKNOWLEDGMENTS

Writing is a lonely job, but publishing is all about teamwork. I have so many people to thank.

My very talented editor, Lucy Dauman, for her brilliant insights, commitment, and support and for being a pleasure to work with.

Editors Alexandra Holmes, Jade Craddock, and Shirley Khan, my publicist and Noelle Holten, and the cover designer, Chris Shamwana, for their hard work and passion. The entire team at Bookouture is dedicated and excellent.

My parents for their unconditional love.

My sister, Dhriti, for always being in our hearts.

My best friend, Akanksha Nair, for always being in my corner.

All my friends especially Rachel Drisdelle, Dafni Giannari, Scott Proulx, Kaushik Raj, Danyal Rehman, and Sheida Stephens for their excitement.

Most of all, I am grateful to the readers. Thank you so much for taking the time! I appreciate each and every one of you, and would love to know your thoughts.

Made in the USA
Monee, IL
09 May 2021

68233019R00218